MW00774974

THE SENIOR

THE SENIOR

MONICA MURPHY

Cover design: Letitia Hasser
R.B.A. Designs

Editor: Rebecca, Fairest Reviews Editing Services
Proofreader: Sarah, All Encompassing Books

PLAYLIST

"New Person, Same Old Mistakes" -
Tame Impala
"the 1" - Taylor Swift
"Make Believe" - Juice WRLD
"good 4 u" - Olivia Rodrigo
"High Road" - Cults
"Window Seat (feat. Wafia)" - Thomston, Wafia
"Meet Me At Our Spot" - THE ANXIETY, WILLOW,
Tyler Cole
"Earfquake" - Tyler, The Creator
"Morning Sex" - Ralph Castelli
"Fangs" - Matt Champion

Find the rest of **The Senior** playlist on Spotify: https://spoti.
fi/3FgIwZc

PROLOGUE
AVA

The moment my bestie walks through my bedroom door, I fall apart. The tears are flowing, and I can't even speak. Ellie doesn't say a word either. She just comes toward me, her arms outstretched as I collapse into her embrace. We sit on the edge of my bed, an open suitcase next to me as she holds me close and lets me cry all over her shoulder.

Ugh. Men. They're the absolute worst.

"Does he know you're here?" she asks, once my crying has subsided some.

I pull out of her arms, so I can look at her, furiously shaking my head. "No. And please don't tell him."

"I won't," she says without hesitation, though I'm putting her in a tough spot. She's with Jackson and he's one of my boyfriend's...

Wait. Excuse me. My *ex*-boyfriend's best friends.

Either Ellie will not tell Jackson I'm home or she'll swear him to secrecy. I won't even bother dragging Hayden or Gracie into this. Gracie lives with Eli—she'll have a hard time keeping this a secret. Not because she can't keep secrets but because she sees Eli pretty much every single day.

Of course, I have no idea what Eli is doing right now. We blocked each other on everything, which is so petty and stupid, but guess what? Sometimes, we can act petty and stupid.

"I still can't believe he gave you an ultimatum," Ellie says. I glance up to see her watching me, her eyes blazing with anger. "It's like he doesn't even care about what an opportunity this is for you."

"All he cares about is himself," I say, wiping any remaining tears from my face. "He's an asshole."

He cares more about how I make *him* feel. He cares that he doesn't get to see me as much and that fucks with his head and his game—direct quote. After a while, carrying the responsibility of Eli's mental state becomes downright unbearable.

Even going to another college hundreds of miles away couldn't help me escape that. I love my boyfriend—ex-boyfriend. I do. But I'm starting to realize I was too wrapped up in his emotional state. To the point that I sometimes forgot my own.

Maybe it's good we broke up. That last screaming match on the phone showed me that he's nothing but a selfish prick.

My eyes sting with tears and that's it. The floodgates reopen.

Who knew a human could cry this much?

Ellie rubs my back and murmurs sounds of comfort while I just sit there like the pitiful girl I am and cry. I'm not even excited about going to Spain anymore. I'm just...sad.

So, so sad.

"Maybe I shouldn't go," I say with a little hiccup. "I could stay home for the summer and once he's calmed down, I could go talk to Eli—"

"No," Ellie interrupts, her voice sharp. "Uh uh. Don't you dare give up on your dreams for him, not when he's treated you so poorly. He doesn't deserve you giving him another chance."

Dang, she sounds so...hostile. "I'm starting to wonder if you hate him."

"I don't hate Eli," she says with a sigh. "But I hate what he's doing to you right now. He's crapped all over your good news and now you're not even looking forward to going to Europe, thanks to him. It sucks, Ava. You shouldn't give him that much control."

My best friend has really changed, in a positive way, since she's been with Jackson. She stands up for herself more and isn't afraid to voice her opinion.

"He's never been that controlling..." My voice drifts when I see the look on Ellie's face.

"Please. He's always controlled the narrative of your relationship. You're a strong person, Ava, but he's always held influence over you. Maybe it's time you stood on your own for a little while," Ellie says.

I don't hold back on how that statement makes me feel.

"But that's scary," I whisper. I've been with Eli since I was sixteen. That's almost four years. He's my first love. My *only* love. Just thinking about him right now makes my heart swell with overwhelming emotion.

But thinking about him also makes me sad. And mad.

Actually, thinking about Eli and the things he said to me when we fought makes me fucking *furious*.

Ellie grabs my hands, clutching them in her own. "I know it's scary. But you're strong. I've always admired that about you. You do what you want, and damn the consequences. You stand up for what you believe in, and right now, you need to believe in yourself."

"Oh, I believe in myself," I say, determination steeling my voice. I can't be scared. I'm about to embark on the adventure of a lifetime. Going to a foreign country alone for the summer. Learning new things. Meeting new people.

"Good." Ellie smiles. "You're going to have the time of your life."

"I hope so," I murmur, my thoughts returning—as always —to Eli. "Damn it, why couldn't he support me? I always support him. No matter what he does, I'm right there by his side. And he rarely asks my opinion on things. He just does them without considering me or how I might feel."

Not that I believe he does that on purpose. Eli is impulsive. He always has been. And he believes I'll support his every decision no matter what because I love him, which is true.

I felt the same way about him, and look where that got me.

Despite my moving to San Diego and going to college, making new friends and having different experiences from everyone else back home, I made time for Eli. Always. Always, always, *always.*

And this is my reward. I make one choice just for me, one very temporary decision that's going to last all of three months, and he demands I stay home. Tells me I don't care about him or our relationship. And then gives me the ultimatum—if I study abroad, it's over between us.

Who *does* that?

Eli motherfuckin' Bennett, that's who.

"You are still going to Spain, right?" Ellie asks, pulling me from my thoughts. "Don't let him control your decisions. Do something for you. Just you, Ava. When you come home and you realize you still want to be with him, then go to Eli and tell him that. I'm sure you two could work it out."

I hate the idea of crawling back to him, begging him to be my boyfriend again. Talk about humiliating. That is so not my style.

"Or maybe you'll come home and realize you don't miss him as much as you thought you would," Ellie continues, her voice hesitant. "And that's okay too. High school sweethearts don't always last forever."

"You and Jackson are pretty happy," I point out.

"We didn't get together in high school," Ellie says.

"College. Close enough," I say, rolling my eyes.

Ellie jabs me in the ribs with her elbow. "Getting sassy, I see. A good sign. Look, you're leaving soon. I don't want you all mopey before you fly off to Europe."

Too late. Eli totally ruined my mood.

"Thank you for coming here to see me," I murmur. "It means a lot, that you dropped everything to be my support."

"Aw, Ava. I would do anything for you. You're my best friend." She wraps me up in another big hug, and it takes us a long, long time to let each other go.

————

After Ellie leaves, I take a shower, then make my way downstairs to face the music—aka my parents. I find them in the kitchen along with Beck, who's sitting at the counter eating something.

When is he not eating? He's growing into this giant hulk of a human, broader than Jake was at his age. As tall as Jake and our dad, maybe even taller. He's huge.

"There you are," Mom says, her voice light when she spots me. She's trying to act like I'm not completely heartbroken, and I appreciate her need to keep things positive before I leave the country for the next few months, but she's wasting her time.

Nothing is going to change the fact that I'm most definitely heartbroken. Not even the excitement of going to Spain for the first time in my life can fix it. I'm just trying to cope as best as I can.

"Hey," I say, as I go to the kitchen counter and sit on the stool next to Beck's. I can feel Mom's gaze on me, searching, looking for signs. And the signs are all over me, despite the long shower. Swollen eyes from crying. Splotchy skin on my face. Giant zit on my chin, thanks to stress and being hormonal.

I look terrible. I feel worse.

"You want some dinner? Your father is barbecuing tonight." She gestures toward the double French doors that lead out to the back yard, where my father is currently standing in front of his giant, fancy barbecue.

"I'm not that hungry," I say.

I think of the times Eli would come over and he would help my dad. Or he would throw a football with Beck outside, sending me hot, suggestive looks every chance he could. He'd take his shirt off to drive me crazy and I'd quietly admire his flexing biceps and flat stomach. Knowing I could explore all that smooth, hard skin later as much as I wanted to. When it was just the two of us against the world.

Now I'll never get the chance to do it again.

Pushing all thoughts of Eli aside, I focus on my mother, who's watching me with her worried, knowing gaze. We've talked some about Eli and what he's done, but not enough for her satisfaction, I'm sure. She has such a soft spot for him. She would never admit it, but damaged boys appeal to her. I think it's because they remind her of my dad when they first met.

She's never told me that, but I've heard enough stories over the years to put a few things together. Dad wasn't in the best shape when he met Mom, and neither was she. They helped each other. Fixed each other. And found love in the process.

I thought that's what Eli and I were destined to have—enduring love, but I was wrong.

So wrong.

The tears come and I squeeze my eyes shut, tuning out Beck when he asks what's for dinner, all while he sits there shoveling cereal in his mouth. His words grow distant and all

I can see is Eli's face. All I can hear is Eli's voice when he told me we were done. Finished. Over.

That was the first conversation we had. The second one was even worse. I can barely stand to remember it.

I called him one more time in the hopes we could talk about me leaving like two rational adults, but he told me there was no point. He accused me of leaving him behind and never discussing my choice with him in the first place. My mind was already made up.

Well, now his was too.

My phone buzzes and I check it. It's a text from my big brother.

Jake: **I hope you're okay. And if you need me to kick a certain someone's ass, I'm down. Just let me know when and I'll take care of him.**

A smile teases the corner of my lips and I send him a response.

Me: **Don't bother. He's not worth the trouble.**

Jake: **Look at you, pretending you're already over Bennett. Give me a break, sis.**

He knows me too well.

Me: **I appreciate the support. I'm going to miss you.**

Jake: **I'll miss you too. Be safe over there. Love you.**

Me: **I love you too, Jakey.**

I send him a string of heart emojis.

He sends me a couple of eye roll emojis in return. He doesn't like it when I call him Jakey.

"We're here!" a voice suddenly yells from behind me.

My eyes fly open, and I swivel on the stool to find my big sister entering the kitchen from the garage, her gorgeous fiancé, Ash Davis, standing directly behind her with a wary expression on his face when he spots me.

Crying women have always freaked him out.

"Autumn!" I squeal as I lunge for her, delivering such a brutal tackle hug that she literally flies backward. I tighten my arms around her, so she doesn't fall, crying into her hair as I squeeze her tightly.

She pats me on the back, her voice muffled. "There, there, baby sister. Tell me where he's at so I can murder him in his sleep."

We used to fight a lot when we were younger. I just wanted her to like me and she wanted me to leave her alone. Our age difference was too great at the time, but now, Autumn is my right hand. My go-to. She will defend me to the bitter end, even if I'm wrong. Even if she doesn't agree with whatever I'm doing. She'll stand by me and take care of me, no matter what.

I would do the same for her, no questions asked.

"He's at his apartment," I tell her, my voice soft.

My sister pulls away from me, the look on her face nothing short of furious. "Let's go then."

"Autumn—" Mom starts.

"Mom, I'm serious. We need to go kick Eli's ass," Autumn says firmly.

Ash exits the kitchen as fast as humanly possible. So does Beck.

"But I don't want to kick his ass," I say, hating how whiny I sound.

Why do my siblings want to beat Eli up so much? I guess I should take it as a compliment. They're only watching out for me.

"Well, I do," Autumn says, not missing a beat. "Little prick. He can't just throw ultimatums at you like that and expect you to give up your life for him! Who the hell does he think he is?"

"Autumn—" Mom says again, but my sister gives her a death glare, which makes Mom go quiet.

"Please don't tell me you think Eli isn't in the wrong," she says, sounding hostile.

"Of course I think Eli is in the wrong," Mom retorts, "but

you can't just storm into his apartment and hold a knife to his throat."

"I wouldn't use a knife at first." Autumn stands up straighter, her expression turning downright haughty. "I'd knee him in the balls to disarm him. Then I'd pull out my knife."

She probably would. Our father gave both me and Autumn a pocket knife when we first moved out. Along with mace and a keychain whistle. All the things dads can give their daughters to protect themselves once they're on their own.

"You're not going to knife my ex-boyfriend," I say, my tongue tumbling over the word ex. "Showing up on his doorstep makes him think we care."

"Oh, I care," she says vehemently. "I care enough to want to do bodily harm to him for hurting you and breaking your heart."

I give her another hug because she deserves it. Her fierce loyalty makes me feel a tiny bit better. "We need to ignore him. Giving him a reaction is what he wants. He's probably dying right now to know what I'm feeling. What I'm doing. Well, forget him."

"Yeah, forget him," Autumn says in agreement.

It's a lot easier than it sounds though.

How can I forget the boy who owns my heart?

CHAPTER 1

ELI

F*all*

"You can't make me go to that ceremony," I say with all the confidence I can muster. I want to believe no one can make me go, but deep down, I know the truth.

Our coaches—hell, my entire team is going to make me go to that special ceremony being held tonight before the game starts. The one where Fresno State is honoring Asher Davis by retiring his number. His entire family will be there, and when I say his entire family, I really mean the one family who took him in when he needed support back in the day. The people he considers his family now.

The Callahans.

"You're going to that ceremony," Tony says, his steady voice doing nothing to calm me down whatsoever. "You don't have a choice. Our coaches will kill you. Plus, you should be there just to support Ash. He taught you a lot when you were a baby freshman, or have you forgotten that?"

Fuck, he did. Asher Davis is a true homie. Heck, at one point, I thought he was going to be my brother-in-law.

Yeah, that didn't happen.

We're chilling at my apartment before we head to the field. Diego and Tony showed up bright and early this morning with donuts for all of us. Not the breakfast of champions but fuck it.

That's been my attitude for months. Fuck it.

Fuck. It.

"It won't be so bad," Diego says with an actual smile on his face. Like he truly believes what he's saying. "We'll be together, and we've got your back. Not like Drew Callahan's going to kick your ass out on the field for breaking his daughter's heart."

I tamp down the fury that fills me at Diego's words as Tony sends him an exasperated look.

"Jesus, D. Shut the hell up," Tony growls.

I say nothing, which is killing me, but damn. I refuse to say something I'll regret. I've done enough of that to last me a couple of lifetimes.

I need these guys. I need their support. They're all I've got. I blew the one thing that was good in my life and it's like I can't get her back. We've cut each other off completely.

I don't deserve her anyway. She's too damn good for me. But also...

I'm pissed at her still. For not even trying to fight back. For agreeing with me that we were done. I'm the one who gave her an ultimatum, and it bit me in the ass. If she would've come home and told me she missed me, we would've hashed it out. We'd probably be together right now.

But nope. We talked twice before she left for Spain. One minor argumentative conversation where I hung up on her. Then another big one. Like a massive blow out, yell at each other phone call that wasn't pretty. That time she hung up on me.

I don't even know if she's home from her trip yet. Did she return from Europe? Is she still out there traveling around and meeting other people? Other guys?

Fuck, it's absolute torture thinking of her with someone else.

No one tells me shit either. They're all silent. Abnormally quiet. Someone knows something. I'd corner Grace if I could, but she went and moved recently because of her new job— teaching in the same school district a bunch of us went to as kids. The minute we graduate, Caleb's headed up there too, I guarantee it. Doing what, no one is sure of yet, but he'll figure something out.

Jake's frozen me out completely too—not a huge loss since he's down in So Cal, but totally expected. I did his baby sister wrong and now I'm the mortal enemy again. But this time, I've got his bros defending me as well. They're my friends now too. I'm close with Diego and Caleb, his two besties from high school. In fact, Caleb is watching me right now with the most sympathetic look on his face I think I've ever seen.

"You should try and talk to her," he suddenly says, and I stare at him as if he's grown three heads.

"Hell no," I say without hesitation. "She'll claw my eyes out if I try and approach her."

"You never know," he says with a shrug. "She might be hurting as much as you are."

"I'm not hurting," I say. "I'm too pissed to hurt."

Skeptical looks from each of them for that comment. I'm such an idiot.

"Women," Tony says, shaking his head. "They're the worst, am I right?"

I scoff. "Give me a break. You're so whipped it's not even funny."

"Just as whipped as you were when you and Ava were together," he throws back at me.

"They are the worst," I tell him, because fuck me standing, they are. "Who needs them?"

"Not you," Caleb says.

"Not me," I agree.

I look at every one of them sitting around in my kitchen. They all have girlfriends. Shit, Diego and Jocelyn are practically married. He gave her a ring over the summer, the sucker. But he's doing right by her because she's the mother of their daughter and I get it.

They're a family.

Tony and Hayden are living together and I think he's close to giving her a ring too, which is wild to even contemplate. Jackson isn't around—he's too busy touring the world with Ellie by his side. Those two lovebirds are living the dream. And then there's Caleb.

Caleb the player. Caleb the perv. Caleb the idiot.

Caleb who found himself a good woman—Gracie. The both of them were chasing after other people when they shared a connection with each other all along. He's the one who's blown my mind the most.

A few months ago, my friends' relationships would not have bothered me. I wouldn't have even noticed, too wrapped up in Ava. But now that I'm single and miserable and it feels like something is slowly dying inside of me, I can't help but see it.

Their happiness. All of them are so fucking happy.

And I resent them for it. A few years ago, when most of these guys were still single and I was the one in a relationship and smug in the knowledge that I had a girl who loved me…

I was on top of the world.

Look how far and hard the mighty have fallen.

Because I'm so far from happy…

We eat more donuts—well, I don't. My appetite has been for shit since May. I work out constantly too. I'm in the best physical condition I've ever been in my life. I'm cut, I have an eight pack, I can run fast as a motherfucker because I'm that much lighter, despite the muscle mass I've gained. I'm on fire on the field, and so is the rest of the team. We're predicted to have a great season, and I believe we will.

But it don't mean shit. Not if I don't have my girl by my side.

Once all the donuts have been polished off and Tony and Diego have left, Caleb and I clean up the kitchen, me dumping out the leftover coffee in the to-go cups and Caleb wiping all the crumbs off our tiny kitchen table.

"Has Gracie talked to Ava?" I ask as casually as I can muster.

Caleb finishes cleaning the table and then walks over to the sink, nudging me out of the way so he can run water over the rag he was just using, strangely quiet.

It's like he's trying to come up with something first.

"Yeah," he finally says. "But I don't know if I can tell you about it."

I'm frowning. Hard. "What do you mean by that?"

"They're friends and Gracie has been there for Ava, just like I've been there for you. Let's just leave it at that," Caleb says mysteriously.

Huh. Look at Caleb keeping his mouth shut. This is big for him.

Of course, Gracie and Ava are talking. I should've known. A few years ago, Ellie and Ava both viewed Hayden and Gracie as their sort of big sisters to go to for advice. They would have girls' nights over at Hayden and Gracie's apartment. Jocelyn would be there too. They'd probably cackle and put together voodoo spells on us guys to get us to do what they wanted.

Or maybe not. Shit, I don't know what those girls were up to half the time. I was oblivious. Confident my girl would always want to be with me, just like I always wanted to be with her. Yeah, we had some conflict over the years, especially once she went away to college in San Diego. And yeah, shit got tough sometimes when she was gone. But we were going to make it. Together forever.

Months after we split, and it still hurts so damn bad, I can barely stand it.

"Is she coming to the ceremony tonight?" I ask Caleb.

"Who? Ava?" He shrugs. "I don't know if she's home yet."

"Shouldn't she be? Wouldn't she be in school right now?" We've been in school since late August and it's almost the end of September. SDSU follows a similar schedule.

"From what I understand, her study abroad program went past the beginning of the school year. To the point that she won't be at San Diego State for the fall semester. She'll start back up in the spring," Caleb explains, clamping his lips shut when he realizes he's probably said too much. "Someone mentioned that to me."

"Who?"

"I don't know." He shrugs, but I'm sure he means Gracie.

But I don't call him out on it. They all tread carefully around me, as if they're afraid I'll lash out if they say the wrong thing. Which I totally would, I can't deny it.

"The Callahans will be there tonight," I say morosely. "Not Jake, since he has a game, but the rest of them will be."

And I don't want to see them.

The words hang unspoken in the room. I know Caleb gets what I'm thinking. I can see it on his face. If Ava really is back from Europe and not even enrolled this semester, then I'd bet she's around. Maybe she's holed up with Mommy and Daddy until the end of the year? Or is she back in San Diego having the time of her life?

Too many questions and what ifs and no one will give me an answer. I'd guess most of them don't actually know. The only way I could find out every bit of information is if I spoke to Ava herself. But that's the last thing I want to do.

She left me, just like everyone else important in my life

does. My parents. My brother. Hell, even some of my close friends. I thought Ava was the one person who would never do that to me, but even she let me down.

I need to forget her. Banish her from my life. She made her choice, and the longer I've gone without talking to her or seeing her, the easier it gets.

Somewhat.

Damn, I fucked everything up. But too late now. I'm sure she hates me. But I couldn't take the idea of her just leaving me without discussing it first. I overreacted. Instead of being rejected by the one person who means the most to me, I rejected her first. I thought by doing that, I wouldn't get hurt.

Big mistake. I'm still hurting.

"Yeah. They will be." That's all Caleb says.

"I don't want to talk to them." Actually, I'm dying to talk to them, but I can't admit that.

"I doubt they really want to talk to you either."

Ouch. That was a fuckin' zinger. I rub at my chest, trying to ease the ache there. "Good. Guess we're all on mutual terms then."

"Look, Eli. You don't have to act like a tough guy for my benefit. I know you're suffering. I know you miss Ava, and I get it. I'd miss the shit out of her too if I were you." He leans forward, his gaze imploring. "You might be able to fix this. You could probably talk to her and work it out. I doubt she's over you."

I watch him, my gaze roving over his face, looking for any clue that he might know more than what he's saying. "Have you talked to her?"

Caleb slowly shakes his head.

"Heard it come straight out of her mouth that she misses me and wants me back?"

Another headshake.

No.

"Then I ain't saying shit to her." I rise to my feet, running my fingers through my hair once. Twice. A couple more times, tugging on the ends so hard it hurts. At least I'm feeling something. "Please tell me there's a party after the game tonight."

"Probably," Caleb says with a shrug. "Why?"

He used to live for parties. He was the good-time guy of our friend group. You couldn't take anything he did or said seriously. I used to be that kind of guy too, until I fell completely in love with Ava.

And then she moved away to go to college, and I started to feel bitter.

Resentful.

Pissed at myself for feeling that way.

Under pressure because the weight of this football team seems to settle on my shoulders. If we mess up or lose, I immediately think it's my fault. Even when I know it's not. But I'm their quarterback, their leader, and they all look up to me. I don't want to let them down, especially since this is my last season.

Plus, there's school. Grades. I'm struggling, trying to juggle it all, but all I can give is my best. I don't even know what the fuck I'm going to do when college is over. I thought I had a plan, but it's been ruined thanks to my impulsive actions.

Then there's my family life, which is a joke. My dad isn't around. My mom is flighty. My brother, as usual, is off doing his own thing and leaving it all on me.

"I need to get fucked up." Fucked up so I can forget…

Everything.

CHAPTER 2

AVA

"You have to look your absolute best tonight." Autumn is currently in my closet, going through my clothes meticulously. "Like, knock him on his ass, make him regret every single decision he's ever made in his life, hot."

"I don't want to look hot," I mutter, exiting my closet and flopping backward onto my bed so I can stare up at the ceiling. I'll let Autumn pick out something for me to wear. I'm over it. "I'd rather not go at all. I'm only doing this for Ash. And you."

"He appreciates the support. So do I." Autumn pops her head out of my walk-in closet, contemplating me. "Since his family isn't around, we're all he's got."

She disappears into my closet once more and I close my eyes with a sigh. She doesn't need to remind me about her fiancé's crappy family. That is truly the only reason I'm going —to support him. Though the entire crowd filling the stadium later tonight will be eager to support him as well.

Asher Davis is the hottest quarterback alive in the NFL. He took his team all the way to the Super Bowl his first season—and freaking won. He's amazing. Everyone wants a piece of him. He's fielding a variety of endorsements, and he and Autumn are engaged. The rock on her finger is huge and heavy. I know, because I've tried it on a couple of times, imagining what it would be like if Eli gave me a diamond like that.

The memory tastes bitter in my mouth and I swallow hard.

There will never be any diamonds from Eli for me.

"I forgot you owned this." Autumn exits my closet with a Fresno State T-shirt on a hanger. It's red with the bulldog mascot on the front. Cropped. Cute. "I found it stashed in the back of your closet."

More memories flood me. The last time I wore that shirt, I took Eli to a Bulldog game with the rest of my family. That was his trial by fire, hanging out with all of us for the first time, right when we initially got back together. He came over to the house before the game when no one was home and…

We had sex in my room. Make-up sex, considering we'd had a huge blow-up only a week or two before and things were bad between us.

I'd been so happy that day, confident Eli was back in my life. In the beginning, it was a struggle, and we kept everything a secret, which he didn't like. I didn't either, but felt it was necessary at the time. My brother hated him. My family didn't necessarily approve. Eli went to our rival high school. My friends thought I was crazy for wanting him. Back then, I wondered if I was a little crazy too.

My heart pangs at the past memories running through my mind. I miss him.

Then I remember what he said to me during our last conversation, and my heart hardens over its original shattered shell. I'm mad at him all over again.

Actually, I'm furious.

"I'll wear it." I sit up and snatch the shirt out of Autumn's hand, startling her, especially when the hanger clatters to the floor. "Maybe you could do my makeup?"

Autumn watches me ball the T-shirt up, clutching it in my fingers. "Of course. And I'm thinking you should dress up a little more. I'm wearing a red dress."

"I'm sure I have something more appropriate then." I hurl the T-shirt toward a nearby chair, throwing it with extra force. "He better not talk to me. He better not even look in my direction."

Actually, I will be devastated if he doesn't even bother to look my way. That'll hurt, more than I can bear.

I hate how conflicted he makes me feel. I despise him; I love him. I don't want to see him; I'm dying to get just one look at his handsome face. I want to punch him in the nuts; I want to hug him close and feel his arms come around me.

Throwing myself back on the bed, I continue staring at the ceiling, watching the fan turn lazily above me. Autumn is back in my closet, but I sort of wish she'd leave. She's been such a supportive sister since this all happened. She even came and visited me in Spain over the summer, and we wandered all over the city, checking out the sights and taking lots of photos while eating delicious food.

The entire experience was amazing. A once in a lifetime trip, studying international business, becoming a better Spanish speaker, and learning the ways of another country's culture. I made new friends. Saw new things. Being in Spain was a great distraction from my breakup. If I'd been at home, it would've been so much worse.

But if I'd been at home, Eli and I never would've broken up. We'd still be together.

A sigh leaves me.

I can't win.

———

"Oh, Ava, I love your dress. Is it new?"

I stop at the foot of the stairs, mustering up a smile for my mother. She's watching me carefully, much like she has been since I arrived back home a week ago. As if she's looking for a sign that I'm going to have a psychotic break.

"It's new." I glance down at the navy dress I bought right before I left for Spain. "I got it at Shein."

"Love that site." Autumn appears out of nowhere, offering me a bright smile. "Are we ready to go?"

"I don't know where your brother and dad are," Mom says as she wanders off toward the kitchen. "Drew? Where are you?"

Autumn rolls her eyes. "We need to go soon. I don't want to be late."

"Let's drive to the stadium in your car," I suggest. "I don't even think Beck is out of the shower yet."

Autumn makes a face. Teenaged boys taking too long in the shower is nothing new. We lived with Jake, after all.

"Mom, we're leaving," Autumn calls as she starts for the front door. I follow after her. "Lock up after us!"

"Wait!" We both stop when Mom practically runs back into the foyer. "I thought we'd all go down together as a family. I assume you'll want to take off with Ash after the game, right?"

Autumn and I share a look. She will totally want to leave with Ash. "I'll drive Autumn's car," I offer.

"You sure you'll be up to driving?" Mom asks me, her brows drawn together.

I'm frowning too. "What do you mean? I'll be fine."

"Well, you'll see…you know who tonight."

An exasperated sigh leaves me. "I can handle seeing Eli, Mom. Not like we're going to talk to each other."

Mom and Autumn share a look. One I don't bother trying to decipher.

"Come on," I say to my sister, nudging her out of the way so I can walk out the front door before her. "Let's go."

Autumn follows after me, and we both climb into her

Mercedes SUV, taking off without saying much. I keep my hands clutched together in my lap, my mind running through the infinite possibilities of what might happen between Eli and me if we get a chance to talk after the game.

"Mom's just worried about you," Autumn says, as if she needs to fill up the silence. "She thinks you're not over Eli."

I consider what she said for a few seconds. "I'm not."

Autumn sends me a quick startled glance. "You should hate him."

"I sort of do," I admit. "But I still love him, Autumn. We didn't have any closure. He just—broke up with me over the phone and that was it."

"He's such a dick," she mutters under her breath, but I don't acknowledge her, or agree with her either.

Because yes, Eli Bennett is a complete dick.

But he's also the love of my life. I can't stop thinking about him.

No matter what I do, or where I'm at, he's there. Lingering in the back of my mind, reminding me of what we once had.

And what we've now lost.

"He doesn't deserve your love," Autumn says, her voice stronger. "How he broke up with you was so…awful."

"My leaving him felt like a betrayal," I say, trying to understand where he was coming from. If anyone knows how he thinks, it's me. I've been pretty much it for him over these last few years. "In his eyes, I did him wrong."

"Complete nonsense."

"Not to him."

"Why are you defending him?"

"I don't know," I say with a shrug, staring out the window at the scenery passing by. "I'm trying to understand why he reacts the way he does."

"So you're trying to understand how an asshole behaves?" Autumn retorts. "Don't bother. We can never understand them."

"Hasn't Ash ever done something that's infuriated you? You guys argue, I know you do," I say, wanting her to admit that her relationship isn't perfect. No matter how good it looks to everyone else.

I know my sister. She can be argumentative. We used to have some big fights when we were younger.

"We do, sometimes. It's better lately. I think we appreciate each other more and make our time together count, since we're apart a lot," Autumn says.

"Eli and I used to do the same thing. Until I left him," I say morosely.

"Please. You *temporarily* left for an opportunity you couldn't pass up. What if he got an opportunity like yours? What if he got the chance to do something football-related for the summer that would entail him leaving for three months? You would've supported him, no questions asked," she says.

"I don't know what I would've done," I say, because it's the truth. It's easy for me to say that yes, I totally would've supported him, but maybe I would've been mad. We would've argued. I could've asked him to choose football or me, right?

I frown. Maybe not. Football is important to him. I would never make him choose. I would've made it work, no matter what.

And that's what fuels me for the rest of the drive down to Fresno. Knowing that I would've supported him no matter what, while he's over there making rash decisions and deciding my fate for me.

He's always been impulsive. Emotional. He says things he doesn't mean, and sometimes, those things are hurtful.

Like what he said to me on the phone the last time we spoke. I don't know if we'll ever come back from that.

The more time that passes, the more I'm not sure if I want to come back from it. Maybe we're just done.

For good.

CHAPTER 3

ELI

We stand in a line on the field on the home side with our helmets off and our attention focused on dead center of the fifty-yard line, where our coaches are currently standing, our head coach singing the praises of Asher Davis to the crowd, even though he didn't actually coach him during his time here. Drew Callahan stands next to him, tall and proud as he surveys the sold-out stadium. Only a few minutes ago, he offered up a short speech that was full of praise for Ash, and I can't help but wonder if he has any nice things to say about me.

Probably not.

The crowd is cheering like they can't help themselves, even though Coach is talking, and I wonder what that's like, to have the adoration of so many damn people.

This crowd likes me, but I haven't fully proven myself to them yet, though I'm trying my hardest. I'm having a decent season so far, but I don't want to get too confident. Last season was a shit show of embarrassment. I still can't believe how badly I played.

This season, I'm on top of it. More focused. Angrier when I get on the field, determined not to lose.

Coach thinks the anger is fueling me, and he keeps asking me what the hell I'm so pissed off over, but then he tells me he doesn't want to know. He just wants me mad for the whole season.

What the fuck ever. I'm just trying to get through each game in one piece. I can't afford to lose. This is my last year on this team. I want to go out in a blaze of glory. I'm not going to break records or win awards or even get picked up by a professional team, but damn it, I'm going to bring our team victory as many times as I can, as much as I can control it.

If I don't, I'll feel like a total failure, and I can't have that. I've failed enough these last three years with the team.

I need to end my college football career on an all-time high.

"...and now everyone, please put your hands together for the NFL's reigning Super Bowl champion quarterback and former Fresno State Bulldog, Asher Davis!" the MC announces.

The crowd goes wild, the sound of people cheering and screaming deafening. The rest of the team and I clap politely, a couple of the guys cupping their hands around their mouths and shouting their support. One of them is Caleb.

Of course. That guy can't keep his mouth shut.

My gaze settles on the center of the field, where the entire Callahan clan is heading toward the fifty-yard line, Ash leading the way with Autumn right by his side. She's gazing up at him as if he created the world and he's beaming at the crowd, lifting his arm in greeting. The moment he waves, the crowd roars louder, and Autumn throws her head back and laughs.

You'd think seeing her would remind me of Ava, which she is does. But only in passing. The two sisters don't look much alike. Ava is taller. Thinner. More flat-chested and blonde to Autumn's brunette. Both pretty, but to me...

Ava is beautiful.

I brace myself, catching a glimpse of blonde hair. The swing of a blue skirt. She's in a dress. Of course she is. They're all dolled up in honor of good ol' Ash. Beck is in between Ava and their mom, towering over the rest of them, gazing around the stadium with an awestruck look on his face.

I miss that kid.

When Ava finally comes into view, I'm not prepared for the avalanche of emotion that slams into me. She looks the same.

Yet different.

Wearing a dark blue, short-sleeved dress that cinches in at her waist, the ruffled hem flaring mid-thigh. Her skin is golden, remnants of spending plenty of time in the sun over the summer. Her hair falls down her back in subtle waves, and when I finally allow myself to study her face, I can tell she's nervous.

My heart bubbles in my chest, like it wants to escape. It's reassuring, seeing that she's nervous.

I'm fucking nervous too.

Why, I don't know. Not like I'm going to talk to her tonight. Not like I'm going to have a conversation with her family either. They hate me, I'm sure of it. Even Beck probably does. Thank God Jake isn't here tonight. He'd probably try to smash my face in.

An agitated growl leaves me and Tony, who's standing next to me, does a double-take.

"You look ready to chew through steel," he mutters.

I flex my hands when I realize my fingers are curled into fists. "This sucks."

"It's almost over," he reassures me.

It won't finish fast enough for my satisfaction.

Watching this dog and pony show in celebration of retiring Ash's uniform number is pure torture. Witnessing the family that I used to consider myself part of gather around Ash as they hand him a glass-framed Fresno State jersey with his number and name on the back of it is killing me slowly.

I should be with them, congratulating Ash, standing among the Callahans. Ava by my side and her father going on about how proud he is of all the men in his life. Beck looking up to Ash and me.

Oh yeah, and Jake too, I guess.

My mind starts to wonder. I'm bored. Anxious. Frustrated as shit. Ready to be done with this so the game can start. I glance around the field, up at the stands, smiling faintly when I see a group of girls wearing matching Bulldog T-shirts and holding up a giant sign that says, "You're our #1 Eli!" The words are surrounded by vivid red hearts.

Maybe that's what I should be focusing on. Other girls. Women. I've fucked the same girl for years. I could try and sample something new and different.

Disgust rolls through me. What a shitty thing to think. I don't want someone new and different.

Not at all.

"Your groupies," Tony says, his gaze zeroed in on them too.

"They're cute," I tell him.

He snorts.

Asshole.

My gaze skitters past the cluster of Callahans, who are now taking photos with Ash, the family surrounding him on all sides. I stop on Ava when I realize she's staring right at me.

She doesn't look away.

Neither do I.

I clench my jaw tighter, my entire expression hardening, I can feel it. I narrow my eyes at her, wanting her to see my anger. My frustration with her. With everyone.

She abandoned me. Just like everyone else does. My

mom's gotten better, but she's still flighty. Dad and Ryan could give a shit about me most of the time, though Ryan's busy. I get it.

Not really, but I try to be understanding.

All I've got are my friends, and at one point, I thought I had my girl.

Ava proved me wrong.

And she currently won't stop looking at me.

I tear my gaze from hers first, focusing on the words the announcer is saying. We're about to start the game. The photos with Ash are almost over, thank the good lord Jesus. The team surges forward, crowding around me and I realize —not for the first time—that I'm their leader. They look up to me. They need me to show them what we're going to do next.

My eyes find Ava again and she's still watching me, her lips curved in a barely there smile that gives me the first real glimmer of hope that I've felt in months.

But it's complete bullshit. I have to remind myself of that before I become lost in that pretty smile.

I glance to my left. Then to my right, pretending she might be smiling at someone else. But, of course, I know she's smiling at me.

I send her a *what the fuck are you doing* look and she frowns.

Gives me the finger. Subtly.

I almost want to laugh. This girl…fuck.

I miss her.

So damn bad.

I give her the finger in return and her expression turns cool as she walks away with an extra flounce in her step. Her dress hem flirts with the back of her thighs and I watch her go, hoping to catch a glimpse of an ass cheek.

I couldn't be so lucky.

"What the fuck, Bennett?" Someone shoves me from

behind and I whirl around to see Diego standing there, a defiant expression on his face.

I frown at him. "What's your problem?"

"I thought you two were broken up." When my frown deepens, he makes an exasperated noise. "You and Ava."

"We are."

"I saw the way you two were just looking at each other."

"She gave me the finger."

"Yeah, I don't think she was saying *fuck you*. More like she was meaning, *fuck me*." He starts to laugh just as Caleb approaches with a giant grin on his face, his hand already up and ready for a high five.

Diego gives him one, the two grinning idiots turning their focus on me while I glare at them.

"Don't talk about her like that," I say with a scowl.

"Like what?" Diego's expression turns innocent. "Don't like me knocking on your ex? I thought you were pissed at her."

"I don't like you talking about Ava in *any* way," I say between clenched teeth, my blood running hot.

Diego shakes his head. "You are unbelievable. I was only giving you shit because I could see just how bad you still want her. Why don't you talk to her after the game? I'm sure they're going to stick around and watch."

"Why the hell would they do that? They're here for Ash and no one else," I say, hating how bitter I sound.

"A little birdy told me Ava is staying for the entire game. She's sitting with a bunch of other little birdies." When I don't say anything, Diego sighs. "Jocelyn told me Ava is sitting with the rest of the girls and they're going to watch us play."

Just like old times.

"I don't even know what I would say to her if we did talk." I shake my head. "We're done."

"Oh come on, Eli. You're acting like a damn baby," Caleb says, taking a step back when I turn my scowling face in his direction. He holds his hands up in front of him. "Whoa. Settle down. I'm not coming for you. I've been there for you since all this shit went down."

"Yeah, yeah," I mutter, annoyed that he's right. I'd rather focus my anger and hatred on other people, like these two dickwads.

And not myself.

CHAPTER 4

AVA

"We're having a little get-together after the game," Hayden tells me, her expression unsure. "And…we want you to come."

I glance over at Jocelyn and Gracie, who are both nodding enthusiastically, their eyes bright.

"Will Eli be there?" I ask warily. One part of me hopes the answer is yes. The other part hopes it's a big fat no.

I can't face him.

I don't want to talk to him.

His intensity actually…scares me. And I've never thought that about Eli before.

Ever.

Out on the field earlier, before the game started, I couldn't stop staring at him. At first, he didn't even bother looking in my direction. Just stared straight ahead, his expression like stone. His jaw hard and his eyes glittering with an unfamiliar emotion. The longer I stared at his handsome face, the more I ached to go to him. Though one thing did stop me.

The anger in his expression. In his stance.

More than anything, he looked pissed. Super pissed.

Probably at me.

Hayden grimaces. "Probably?"

My answer is immediate.

"Then no."

"Oh come on, Ava! We haven't seen you in months," Gracie says, leaning forward to lightly touch my arm. "We need to catch up. I want to hear more about Spain."

"Well, I'm home until January, so we have plenty of time to catch up." I smile sweetly at all of them, and Jocelyn actually groans.

"This is ridiculous," she says, shaking her head. "Can't you two just let go of what happened and…make up?"

"Absolutely not," I say firmly, remembering the dirty look he gave me when we finally did make eye contact out on the field. Unable to help myself, I flipped him off.

And then he did the same.

Such a jerk.

Worse? That dirty look he gave me had been kind of…

Sexy.

Okay fine, *really* sexy. Which is stupid because I'm mad at him and hurt. I feel betrayed by what he did, yet I find him sexy.

Talk about conflicted.

But there's something about Eli right now that seems a little rough around the edges. He looks older. Bigger, if that's possible. Madder, which makes sense, since I'm feeling the same emotion. His hair was already mussed up and, even from a distance, I could tell there was scruff on his face, like he hasn't shaved in a couple of days. My baby-faced boyfriend has somehow turned into a full-fledged man over the last few months and just thinking about it leaves me feeling hot and flustered.

"What if he apologized to you?" Gracie asks, pulling me from my thoughts.

I study her, this woman who has become such a close friend in a short amount of time. We texted over the entire summer. We even FaceTimed when I got the chance and we coordinated our schedules. She means a lot to me, but I know she was there for Eli too.

And I don't mind that. He needed someone to listen to him. To give him advice. From the bits and pieces she told me whenever he came up in conversation, I got the sense that she was doing exactly that. Giving him advice. Listening to him.

She would never tell me much, though. I have no idea if he's moved on. If he's found someone else. Or multiple someone else's. I thought about it while in Spain. I was in a different country, all alone, where no one else knew me. Who'd ever discover that I hooked up with a cute Spanish boy?

No one.

But it never happened. I could barely flirt with any guy, let alone allow one to touch me.

"He will never apologize to me," I finally answer, my voice soft.

"How can you be so sure?" Gracie frowns.

"Because in his eyes, he did nothing wrong, so what does he need to apologize for?" I shrug, hating how logical I sound.

"That's messed up," Hayden says.

"Right? But that's just Eli. I know how he thinks." Better than anyone else.

"Well, he thinks like an idiot then," Jocelyn mutters, sounding disgusted. "Seriously, he's going to let you go over something as petty as this?"

"There's no 'going to let me go' about it. He's already let me go. What's done is done," I stress. "I don't want to talk about him anymore."

My friend group respects my wishes and goes silent,

focusing their attention on the field below. The Bulldogs are winning. Eli is playing a magical game. His accuracy is on point and he even ran the ball in for a touchdown, fast as lightning as he streaked through the players, darting into the end zone. Force of habit had me leaping to my feet and cheering for him, my friends watching me in dismay.

I slowly lowered myself back into my seat without a word. Not about to do that again.

I listen as Hayden and Gracie compare teaching stories. Gracie is in an apartment in the same town where my family lives, and teaching at an elementary school that's part of our old school district. The moment Caleb graduates, I know he's moving up there with her.

So cute. They make such a great couple. Thinking about them together is enough to fill a love-starved girl full of envy.

That love-starved girl would be me.

Hayden is teaching at an elementary school here in Fresno while she waits for her boyfriend, Tony, to graduate. I feel like I've known Tony forever since he's one of my brother's best friends. He's quiet and thoughtful, and he would watch out for me at school all the time, even when I didn't realize it.

I don't know what their plans are after Tony graduates, but I have a feeling that whatever it is, they're doing it together.

I envy the confidence all three of these women have in their relationships. Especially Jocelyn, who went through *a lot* with Diego when we were all still in high school, but they're still together. Sharing an apartment and raising their adorable little girl, Gigi, who started preschool this year.

Everything is changing. We're all turning into adults with real jobs and responsibilities.

And I have no idea what I'm doing, or where I'm going next. I feel lost.

Adrift.

I hate it.

"This is dumb," Jocelyn suddenly declares as she turns to look at me. "Please come to the party tonight. It hasn't been the same without you around, Ava. We all miss you. And if Eli shows up, we'll be with you, and we'll support you no matter what. If he wants to talk to you and you don't, we'll tell him to leave you alone."

Gracie and Hayden nod in agreement, their expressions fierce.

I stare at my friends, my heart flooding with love. That they want to support me, no matter what, makes me want to cry.

"Okay," I say softly, earning a loud squeal out of each of them as they all come for me in a group hug. "I can't be left alone, though."

"Never," Gracie says fiercely when they all pull away from me. "I'll walk you into the bathroom if I have to."

"You might have to," I say, shocked I can even make a joke right now.

"He probably won't even show up if he knows you're at my place," Hayden says, trying to reassure me.

But her words don't bolster me whatsoever. He hates me that much that he would completely avoid a party with our friends because I'm there? When he's the one who broke up with me?

What a motherfucker.

"Listen, I'm sure none of you want to answer this question right now, but I have to know—" I hesitate for only a moment, taking a deep breath before I continue on, "Has he… found someone else?"

They're so quiet for so long, I'm a bundle of frazzled nerves in a matter of seconds. Like, I'm literally shaking, I'm so scared of their response.

"No," Gracie finally says. "Not that I know of."

"Like any of them would tell us," Jocelyn says, earning a

hard look from Gracie and Hayden. She immediately appears apologetic, reaching out to lay her hand on my arm. "I'm sorry. You know what I mean."

"I do." And I appreciate Jocelyn's brutal honesty. I don't want flowery words and cover ups. Fake denials and bullshit. I need facts.

Cold hard facts.

"But even with me saying that, I don't think he's been with anyone else." Jocelyn leans in closer to me, her voice low. "They will keep it a secret though, if they don't want you to find out. I don't want you to think Eli's been faithful to you. I have no idea. None of us do."

Her candor is refreshing. Jocelyn doesn't like being lied to, even if it's to protect her feelings. I feel the same way. I trust my friends when they say they don't believe Eli's been with anyone else.

I also know Jocelyn is right when she says the guys would keep it quiet from them if it ever came out that Eli actually did hook up with another girl. For all I know, he's hooked up with countless girls. Using all of them to get over me...

Or maybe it was easy for Eli to get over me. We weren't seeing each other much anyway. The last time we had sex was in February. That's...almost eight months ago now. We never saw each other during spring break because he went to Mexico for part of it with the boys, while I was stuck in San Diego, obligated to stay because of yet another sorority event.

He barely protested when I told him I couldn't see him during spring break, which is so unlike him. I think that's what lulled me into believing he wouldn't be upset when I told him I was going to Spain for the summer instead of coming home. But he surprised me when he exploded with outrage. Screaming at me over the phone. I called him back a few days later, and he immediately knew what my decision was, almost as if he could sense it.

When I told him I hadn't changed my mind, he said, "Guess I know how much I mean to you."

And ended the call.

That was it. That was the very last thing he ever said to me.

"I hope I didn't make you mad," Jocelyn says, pulling me back to the present. "I just didn't want to sugarcoat anything. That gets a person nowhere, if you ask me."

"No, you didn't upset me." My focus returns to the field, zeroing in on the asshole wearing the number one jersey. "He did."

I incline my head in Eli's direction.

Jocelyn slips her arm around my shoulders and gives me a firm squeeze. "It's going to be okay."

"You're right. It is," I reaffirm, wishing I really believed what I was saying.

Because I don't. I don't feel like everything is going to be okay. Not yet, at least. I probably shouldn't have come home. But considering the study abroad program ended in mid-September and I had no housing in San Diego for the rest of the semester, I didn't know what else to do. I took the rest of the semester off, both of my parents encouraging me to do so.

"You need a break," Mom said with a frown. "You work too hard."

"And we rarely get to see you, even when you're home," Dad added. "This way, we can see you more."

The guilt brought me home, though I know that wasn't my parents' intention. I realized rather quickly that things aren't the same anymore. Everyone is down in Fresno, going to school. Ellie and Jackson are currently in London, though they'll be returning to the States soon. She told me she's coming to see me, the moment they arrive in Los Angeles, and I hope that's true.

I miss my best friend.

"And another touchdown thrown by Bennett! He is unstoppable tonight!" the announcer suddenly booms.

The crowd roars their approval, and I automatically clap, watching as Eli thrusts his fist into the air in victory. He's playing a great game tonight. I wish I could take credit for it.

But I know I have nothing to do with his playing skills.

I have nothing to do with him at all.

CHAPTER 5

ELI

took all of that anger and frustration I felt at seeing Ava—having her openly smile at me like nothing happened between us, what the actual fuck—and channeled it onto the football field. I played like a man possessed tonight. Filled with the need to prove to her that I don't need her. That I can do just fine on my own. I'm a skilled motherfucker who knows how to work magic when I'm playing a game.

I proved that too. I had the entire crowd going nuts. Bet they forgot all about Ash Davis tonight. I've been playing consistently since the start of the season. We've only lost one game and it was to a team who has beat our asses every single year for the last ten. Not even Ash could beat them. Other than that, I'm having a pretty perfect season, only throwing one interception so far.

One.

That's pretty damn good.

At least on the field, everything I'm doing lately turns to gold. Tonight's win was fuckin' easy. We're playing an away game next Saturday, and I'm not even worried about it. I just get out there and do what's necessary—and everything falls into place. I feel on top of the world.

Only problem?

I keep thinking about a certain blonde female who I should really tell to kiss my ass.

But then I start remembering how she used to feel in my arms. Her soft, smooth skin. The sweet taste of her lips.

Fuck that. Fuck it.

We're in the locker room after the game when Diego approaches me, slapping his palm against the center of my chest. "Bro-ski. There's a party tonight."

"There's a party every Saturday night," I say with a grin, shoving him away, playing like I'm into it. The last thing I want to do is party.

Though I should. I should drown myself in alcohol and try to forget. I should find some pretty little thing—a brunette with giant titties and brown eyes who looks nothing like Ava —and lose myself in her. Preferably her mouth. A blow job is probably the least intimate sexual act someone could perform on me.

What the hell am I thinking? Sex is intimate no matter what. I'm just fooling myself. Fucking someone else isn't going to take the pain away.

Fucking someone else would ruin everything.

"Nah, this one is different. He's hosting." Diego jerks his thumb toward Tony, who is currently pulling on a clean shirt.

"Why are you talking about me?" Tony asks us both.

"He says you're having a party." I point at Diego.

A panicked look appears on Tony's face for the briefest second, before it's smoothed over and Tony nods once. "Yeah. Just a little get-together. Nothing special."

"There's liquor," Diego tells me.

"Okay." He's acting like we're eighteen and going to a high school party. "We're legal now. We can drink alcohol whenever we want."

"I know that." Diego rolls his eyes. "I'm just excited to get out for a few hours. The grind doesn't stop for me. What with school and work and football, plus Gigi. I'm ready to relax. Have a few drinks with my lady and my friends."

My *lady*? I almost laugh.

"It's a chill event tonight. More for the girls," Tony adds.

Wait a minute—

"Is Ava going to be there?" I ask through tight lips.

Tony and Diego share a look before Tony answers, "Uh, yeah?" He rubs the back of his neck, his gaze not quite meeting mine.

I stand up taller, resting my hands on my hips. "You saying you don't want me there if she's going to be there?"

Is this what it's come to in our friend group? They have to pick sides and shit? I'm the one who's been with these guys and their girlfriends for the last three years. I deserve to keep them more than Ava does.

"No, we're not about that," Tony reassures. "I just figured you didn't want to be around her."

"I don't want to be," I agree vehemently. "But she's not going to stop me from hanging out with my friends."

"Good," Diego says with a nod. "Then come over. You can ignore her, and she'll ignore you. You don't have to say a single word to her for the entire night."

"Sounds like a good plan," I say in agreement. "I'm down."

My gaze finds Tony's, and he's watching us as if we've lost our minds.

"I'll see you guys at my place then," he says, slowly backing away from us. He looks slightly terrified, and I suppose I can't blame him.

But I'm not going to his apartment to cause trouble or start a fight. That's not cool. I can restrain myself.

Somewhat.

———

I go back to my place and get ready. Caleb and I still live together. We found a smaller two-bedroom apartment that's farther away from campus, but we don't mind. It's quieter, the complex is newer and we both get covered parking. A total score when it comes to apartment-living near campus.

Caleb's already at Tony's with Gracie, but I had to come home to take another, longer shower and pick out something to wear. Something that'll make Ava regret every decision she's ever made in her life in regards to me.

Namely, that she let *me* go.

I soap everything up, so I'm as clean as a fucking daisy. Contemplate jerking off but quickly find I'm not in the mood. Once I'm out of the shower, I dry myself thoroughly and pull on a pair of black boxer briefs—Versace baby. I'm a brand whore and I'm over the flashy printed boxers of my youth.

I'm a dignified motherfucker now, don't you know.

Wiping the condensation off the bathroom mirror, I turn my face this way and that, noting the stubble covering my jaw. Should I shave?

Nah. Not like I'll be kissing anyone tonight. Besides, some girls like it.

My girl used to like it. But she's not my girl any longer.

Irritated, I pull on my favorite jeans. Slip a light gray Henley on, liking how it clings to my arms, showing off my biceps. The broadness of my chest. I've filled out a lot over the last year. Been conditioning like crazy, building muscle on muscle and bulking myself up for the season. I feel stronger than I ever have.

I am on top of my game.

Personally, I'm in the fucking toilet, but I push all of those shitty thoughts aside and focus on the fact that I'm going to strut into Tony and Hayden's apartment looking like top fucking dog. I'll make Ava swallow her damn tongue when she sees me.

What sucks is when I strut into Tony's place fifteen

minutes later, no one notices me. Especially not Ava, who's tucked into a corner in the tiny dining room with her back against the wall, surrounded by Gracie, Hayden and Jocelyn.

I send the group a withering stare, despite not a one of them paying attention and saunter into the kitchen, smiling when my friends cheer upon seeing me.

The smile feels fake though. And my shoulders are practically hunched up to my ears, I'm so stressed out.

"You made it." Caleb approaches and we execute our newest handshake. "I thought you were going to bail."

I frown. "Why would you think that?"

"Because of you know who." He tips his beer bottle in the direction of the group of women sitting not too far away from us before taking a swig. "More people should be here soon, though. That'll help."

I glance around the cramped kitchen. "How many more people can we fit in this place?"

"It'll be wall-to-wall baby." Caleb grins, and I can tell he's pleased when Diego approaches with a fresh beer for me. "Drink up. Get some liquid courage."

"I don't need it," I say nonchalantly, just before I take a giant swig.

And end up draining half of it in one go.

"Uh huh," Caleb drawls, a knowing gleam in his eye. He leans in close, his gaze intense as he murmurs, "She's all tore up over you giving her the finger out on the field."

I want to laugh. Such a juvenile move on my part, but it was like I couldn't help myself. "Seriously?"

Caleb nods. "She complained about you to Gracie. Who then, naturally, told me all about it."

"You guys share everything, huh?"

"We don't keep secrets from each other." His expression turns solemn, all traces of his earlier grin gone. "Though I probably shouldn't have told you that about Ava."

I want to roll my eyes, but I say nothing. He already

explained that earlier. Everyone pussy foots around us, and I suppose I can't blame them. We're the first in the friend group to break up—it was bound to happen, but I sure as hell didn't think it would happen to *me*.

People are already careful around me. I can be explosive. I can't help it that my emotions are always just right there, ready to spill out all over the place. I feel everything, and I don't hold back.

I blame my family. Witnessing my parents fight all the time when I was a kid. Ryan retreated while I took it all in, figuring that was the best way to communicate—by yelling.

Such bullshit, I realize now. My parents fucked me up but good.

And that's why my friends don't want to talk about this relationship-slash-Ava stuff with me. They're afraid I'll go off.

Before I can open my mouth to say something, the front door opens and a rush of people push through, most of them guys from our football team. They walk in carrying alcohol and snacks, and Hayden rises to her feet to greet them before she hurries into the kitchen ahead of them.

"You didn't tell me we were having more guests," she says to Tony, a fake smile plastered on her face.

He watches everyone trail into the kitchen after Hayden, blinking at them in surprise. "I didn't know."

"I invited them," Caleb says, earning a dirty look from Hayden for his comment.

"What the hell? Why would you do that?" Tony asks.

"Joey Starr texted me about twenty minutes ago saying the party they were at was lame. I told him ours was too and we needed them to come over and bring the excitement. By excitement, I meant booze and snacks," Caleb explains.

"You thought our party was lame?" Tony actually looks offended.

Caleb shrugs. "No one's really here. And we're divided up like a middle school dance, thanks to—"

He clamps his lips shut, but I know what he was going to say.

Thanks to me and Ava drawing a line in the sand, straight down the middle of our friend group.

Hayden marches up to Caleb, thrusting her finger in his face. "They better not make a mess of this place."

"Don't worry your Joanna-Gaines-farmhouse-loving heart, no one will touch your décor." He taps his finger against some greenery currently poking out of a small glass vase on the dining table. "I'll lead everyone outside."

"Will they fit?" she asks.

"I'll make them. And hey, at least they brought snacks." He points at the haul of chips and dips currently being dumped onto the kitchen counter by our new guests.

"Who the hell is Joanna Gaines?" I ask Caleb, once Hayden leaves us to go organize all the snacks and drinks the guys brought with them.

"Some home designer chick. Her husband is cool." Caleb makes a face. "I kind of hate that I know who they are. Blame Gracie."

My heart pangs, which is so fucking annoying. But I know what that's like. To care about something you otherwise wouldn't give a shit about. And the only reason you care is because your girl shared it with you. Like a makeup brand or one of those romcom movies on Netflix that makes you roll your eyes, but secretly you enjoy watching. Especially because it makes your girl so damn happy to watch it with you.

Share it with you.

"I need another drink," I mutter before I polish off the one I'm currently clutching. Then I head for the kitchen counter, grabbing a fresh beer and downing most of that while chatting with the guys who just showed up.

Eventually we start doing shots and I'm leading the pack, drinking way too much, encouraging them to drink along with me, shouting my approval when they throw back shot after shot. Soon enough, I'm stumbling. Rambling. Shooting dirty looks toward the dining table, my skin practically vibrating because I can feel her presence. We're sharing the same space, the same fucking air, and we're not talking or touching or even looking at each other.

And it's killing me.

Unable to take it any longer, I leave the group while they're mid-shot, but I don't think any of them notice. I push my way through the crowd, my focus on one thing and one thing only.

Ava.

People call my name, but I ignore them. Caleb grabs at my arm as I walk past him, but I pull out of his grip. Tony sends me a warning look when I'm looming behind the group of women huddled around my ex-girlfriend and I glare right back at him. He doesn't intimidate me.

I have every right to speak to her.

They don't notice me at first. They're involved in some sort of deep conversation, their heads bent close together as they speak in low tones. I can't hear exactly what they're saying, and I sort of don't care.

I clear my throat.

They don't react. It's like they don't even hear me. Resting my hands on my hips, I watch them, my focus zeroing in on the familiar blonde hair, willing her to feel my gaze.

Within seconds, she's lifting her head, her startled eyes meeting mine, her mouth forming a little O, clearly in shock. We watch each other, the other three women talking animatedly, their voices rising, oblivious to what's happening between Ava and me. How we're communicating with each other, without saying a word.

Why did you leave me? I ask her for what feels like the thousandth time.

Why did you banish me from your life so easily? she says back to me, the hurt reflected on her face.

Fuck that, I'm hurt too. We both are. It's pretty clear we're miserable without each other.

But I can't just let her back in so easily either. Right?

Finally, Jocelyn glances over her shoulder, doing a double take when she notices me. She nudges Gracie, who also glances back at me, her expression composed since she had a warning.

"Eli," she says, sitting up straighter. "You need something?"

"Yes," I croak. I wave a hand in Ava's direction. I need her, is what I almost say.

But I don't.

"Can we talk?" is what I ask Ava instead, my gaze fixed on her and no one else.

She watches me, so many emotions flitting across her beautiful face. I can read her like a book, and I know she wants to tell me no. More like she probably wants to tell me to fuck off, and I suppose I deserve that. I did her dirty, and I probably don't deserve her forgiveness.

Damn, alcohol is making me see all my faults. This sucks.

"Okay," she finally says, her voice soft. She rises to her feet and my eyes eat her up in that sexy-even-though-it-shouldn't-be dress. The V-neckline offers me a glimpse of her smooth skin along with a hint of cleavage. And the skirt is short enough to show off her long, slender legs.

I clench my hands into fists, restraining myself from reaching for her as she approaches me slowly. Carefully. As if she's afraid I'm about to blow up all over her.

"Privately?" I ask, inclining my head toward hers.

Nodding, she tears her gaze from mine and starts walking. Like the fool I am, I fall into step behind her, following her down the hall as she leads me into a bedroom. I shut the door the moment the two of us are in there, leaning against it as she turns to face me.

"You're drunk," she declares.

Nothing like getting right to the point.

I lean my head back, staring up at the ceiling as I chuckle. My vision swims. "Maybe," I say with a laugh, though I have no clue why I'm amused.

This isn't funny.

A sigh leaves her and I level my head, so I'm staring straight at her once more. "What did you want to talk about, Eli?"

She sounds annoyed. No, more like…exasperated. I'm sure she is.

Well guess what? I am too.

"You and me," I say, not holding back.

But that's all I say. My mind is swirling with all sorts of thoughts and ideas. What could I say to her to fully express what I've been feeling these last six months or however the fuck long it's been since we called it quits?

"What about us?" she asks, crossing her arms. Going into pure defensive mode.

I decide to be truthful. "How could you toss us aside so easily?"

She gapes at me, her mouth hanging open, her eyes blazing with anger. "*What*? I didn't toss us aside. You're the one who gave me a shitty ultimatum and when I made my choice, you told me not to bother you ever again."

I shake my head. "I didn't say it like that."

"You so did. You implied it." She starts pacing the room. Watching her walk back and forth in the small space is kind of making my head spin. "You told me if I left, we weren't together anymore. You said that by me not coming home, it showed that I didn't love you, which is such bullshit. I don't operate like that Eli, and you know it."

"Yeah, well, you were always doing other stuff and forgetting about me! The last time we actually saw each other in person was Valentine's Day, and even then, you weren't into it. You weren't into me," I say, my voice rising.

She stops pacing. "When have I never been into you? I devoted all of my time and attention to you, whenever I could, for the last four years of our lives! School and my sorority kept me busy, you know this, but I still made time for you."

"Barely," I say with a snort. "That shit kept you busy all the damn time! And if you weren't busy, you were always so tired. Yawning in my ear and shit. Like I bored you."

That hurt too. I truly believed Ava was my number one fan.

"Right, but it's okay for football to eat up all of your time? So much of it that all I can settle for are the little scraps of a few hours here and a bye week there? And I'm supposed to be *grateful* for that?" She stomps her way toward me, standing close enough that I catch her familiar scent. It sends a rush of lust through me and I remind myself to keep my shit together.

But damn, an angry Ava has always been a huge turn-on for me. I'm surprised I didn't pick fights with her more often. My girl angry is the hottest thing alive.

"Your double standards are complete bullshit." She stabs her finger into my chest, right at heart level. "So are your ultimatums."

"You not putting me first is bullshit," I retort. "It's like you never gave a shit about me anymore. You were too wrapped up in your own life and there was no more room for me in it."

"You're too demanding!" she tosses at me.

"And you never gave a shit about me enough," I throw back at her.

We glare at each other, our accelerated breaths the only sound filling the room.

This is not how I expected the conversation to go.

"It's always me, me, me," she says, her voice scratchy. "That's all you ever care about. Yourself. What do *I* get out of it? What are you doing for *me*? It hasn't been about us for a while, Eli. It's always you. Swear to God, you're the most selfish person I know. I used to think your arrogance was kind of cute. Even sexy. But now, I-I hate it."

I push away from the door, standing so close to her my feet are practically on top of hers. "You think I'm selfish?"

She nods, her fiery gaze clashing with mine. "You're also an egotistical ass."

Taking a deep breath, I lower my head, until my lips hover above hers. "You never complained before."

"I was blinded to your faults. Distance helped me see what was really going on, and what our relationship turned into." She takes a step back, as if she needs the distance, and releases a shaky breath. "This conversation is getting us nowhere."

It's only making everything worse, if you ask me. "This conversation isn't through and you know it."

"I can smell the liquor on your breath. I'm not talking about this when you're drunk." She places her hands on my chest and gently shoves. I go toppling back, nearly falling on my ass. "Get some sleep, Eli. Text me when you're sober —and not hungover either. I'll talk to you again. But I have to be honest—I don't know if this is going to work out for us."

I'm fucking incredulous just listening to her. "Really? You're going to give up on us that easily?"

"It's never been easy! I've stood by your side for years. With every opportunity you've been handed or earned, I've cheered you on and supported you! I get one chance, one lousy chance at doing something that's just for me, that will only take a few months out of my life, and you had a tantrum and threw our relationship away." She snaps her fingers. "Just like that. Done."

I blink, absorbing her words. The anger and disappointment fueling them. "I'm an asshole. You know this."

"You're an asshole to everyone else, but never me. You always took care of me." She taps her chest for emphasis. "You've changed."

"No, you've changed," I tell her vehemently, shaking my head. I don't want to hear her go on about my faults and where I fucked up when it comes to her. To us.

I know I fucked up. I try to own it, though I don't want to say it out loud. Shouting those words into the universe just makes it all true, and I'm not in the mood to face it.

Not tonight.

"I can't do this." She drops her arms at her sides, frustration written all over her pretty face. "This conversation is over. Text me when you're sober."

Ava tries to walk past me, but I grab hold of her arm, stopping her. My touch is light. She could pull out of my grip easily, but she doesn't. Electricity sparks between our skin the moment we connect and I wonder if she can feel it.

She has to.

"Don't go," I whisper. "Just—hear me out."

I have no idea what to say to her next. Have no plan of action either. But this is the first time we've spoken in months. The first time we've been in each other's presence and I just want to marinate in it for a little bit longer...

"Is there really anything else for us to discuss?" she asks, the disappointment heavy in her voice. "What's done is done, Eli."

"So that's it. You're just going to walk away from me again?"

She stares at me, her expression turning weary. "You're exhausting."

I shift forward, pulling her into me at the same time. She goes willingly, and I wonder if that's because she wants to, or if it's just habit. "You give up too easily."

"I could say the same about you," she returns, her breath catching when I gently squeeze her arm. Yep, she feels it. "I shouldn't always have to prove my love for you. When was the last time you proved your love for me?"

Well, fuck.

When did I not prove my love for this girl? Where the hell has she been the last four years?

Clearly, she wasn't paying attention.

CHAPTER 6

AVA

'm so mad, I'm shaking. Can he feel it, from the way he's gripping my arm? He's so close, his body heat emanates toward me. And all that barely restrained anger contained in his body radiates too. His hazel eyes are greener tonight, as they blaze at me, and when I glance up, I catch him staring at my lips.

As if he's thinking about kissing me.

I don't want him to. If he does, I might not be able to stop him.

"Why does it have to be about proving our love to each other?" he finally asks, his voice low. Husky.

Sexy.

Shit.

I need to get out of here. Being alone in a room with a drunk, pissed-off Eli is not good. He'll most likely try to pounce.

And I won't be able to resist.

"It doesn't," I say. "You're the one who always puts conditions on our relationship."

"That is such crap and you know it."

I say nothing, because I know I'm right. He's always had these expectations from our relationship, and half the time, I felt as if I couldn't meet them. Especially once I went away for college.

That was the kiss of death for us. I see it now. With actual physical distance, we grew more detached. I firmly believed we'd survive just fine. Look at my sister and Ash. She was in Santa Barbara while Ash was here for the entirety of college. Four long years. And now they're engaged and still madly in love. Maybe even more in love than they've ever been. I thought for sure Eli and I were solid. We could survive anything.

But Eli and I are not Autumn and Ash. They were stronger. Ash is definitely more mature than Eli. He's not as selfish either.

I still love Eli, but I meant every word I said earlier. He is truly the most selfish human I know.

"Ava…" His voice drifts and he tugs me even closer, our bodies gently colliding. Heat explodes through my veins, making my skin warm and my body ultra-aware of our proximity. "I miss you."

Those three words are worse than a kiss. They completely devastate me and I close my eyes so I can't stare at his handsome face any longer. "Don't," I say weakly, my body swaying toward his.

It knows what it wants. My mind and my heart can't control anything right now.

"Don't what? Express my feelings? If I don't, I'm going to explode. You should know, Ava. I'm still pissed, but I miss you like fucking crazy."

My heart thumps wildly in my chest at his declaration. I miss him too, but I can't say the words out loud. To do so would make me feel like I'm giving in.

I can't do that. Not yet.

Maybe not ever.

"Do you miss me?" he asks.

He sounds like a scared boy afraid to hear the truth. But when I study his face, all I see is the man he's become. Breathtakingly handsome with those pouty lips and the intense eyes. The sharp jaw covered in light scruff. He tilts his head to the side, waiting for my answer and I suck in a breath, ready to deny it.

Before I can utter a single word, his mouth lands on mine. Soft and still, as if he's asking a question.

Should I do this?

Do you want this?

I yield beneath his lips, mine parting slowly as he pulls away, only to deliver another devastating kiss, taking this one deeper.

Yes, I silently answer him.

I want this.

Within seconds, he's got his arms around my waist and my back pressed against the door, his tongue in my mouth, circling my own. I respond like a woman starved, my arms curling around his neck, my fingers sinking into his hair. It's been so long since we've done this. Since I've touched him. Kissed him.

It feels fresh and new, tingles spreading all over my skin like it's the first time we've ever kissed. A groan sounds from deep in his chest and I answer with a whimper. He pushes against me and I can feel what I do to him. He's already hard.

God, what are we doing? We broke up. We shouldn't be kissing.

But I don't stop. It's as if I can't. We just kiss and kiss, swallowing each other's moans and heated breaths, our tongues twisting, Eli's hands wandering. He catches the hem of my dress and slips his hand beneath it, his fingers lightly running along the outside of my thigh. Goosebumps follow in his wake, I can feel them, and a full body shiver steals over me.

Without hesitation, he grabs hold of me more firmly and next thing I know, he's lifting, my legs automatically going around his hips, my dress bunched up around my waist. He wedges himself in between my thighs, his denim-covered erection nudging against the front of my panties, making me moan.

It's like I can't stop making noise. Can't stop moving with him. Can't stop kissing him. I gasp for air when he breaks the kiss to run his mouth along my neck, his tongue licking, his teeth nipping. I try to pull him in closer, as close as he can get, and he lifts his head, breathing heavily.

My eyes are still closed, but I can feel him watching me. Slowly, I lift my lids and find his gaze on me, his damp lips parted and swollen, the look in his eyes…

Still angry.

I frown.

"You can't deny that," he murmurs, his hand coming up to cup the side of my face. "What we feel for each other still. It's there."

I don't say a word because he's right.

I can't deny it.

"I'm sure you'll walk out of this room as if I don't affect you," he continues, his voice growing stronger, his hand falling away from my cheek. "You'll go back out to your friends and act like nothing happened. Or you'll tell them we got into an argument. They'll call me all kinds of names and you'll agree with them, but deep down, you won't be able to stop thinking about this."

He kisses me deeply, his tongue stroking mine.

"Or this," he whispers against my lips as he thrusts against me nice and slow, his hardness pressing into my softness. I bite back the whimper that threatens to escape, not wanting him to know just how much he affects me.

He has to know though. My panties are wet. Can he feel them? And the way I kissed him. So eager and willing.

I sort of hate myself right now.

"I hate you," I whisper, my throat aching. I don't hate him. Not even close. I hate what he did to me. I hate how he pushed me away and made me feel like utter garbage. I hate more that I'm back in his arms and giving in so easily.

But I also love him. I love him so damn much, it hurts.

I hurt all over.

"Keep telling yourself that," he whispers, his mouth settling on mine briefly before he pulls away. Slowly he lowers me to the floor, where I land on wobbly feet, and he lets me go completely, backing up a couple of steps. "Go."

I blink up at him, trying to control my shuddery breaths.

"Go on, get out of here," he urges, his voice hard as steel. "Before I do something we both might regret."

Scrambling for the handle, I push open the door and stumble out of the bedroom, striding down the hall with my head bent, my hair covering my face. My mind is awhirl with about a million emotions, none of them I can fully comprehend. I don't know how to feel, I don't know what to tell my friends, and I sure as hell don't know how to pretend that nothing just happened between Eli and me.

Somehow, though, I'm able to function. Lifting my head, I find myself in the living room, my friends watching me. They all look worried, especially Jocelyn. I approach the dining table, smiling and shaking my head at a cute guy who asks me if I want a beer. I've never seen him before in my life, but the moment I walk past him, I hear Eli tell the guy, "Leave her the fuck alone."

I don't stick around to hear what else is said.

"What happened? Are you okay?" Hayden asks when I collapse into the empty chair.

"How long have I been gone?" I lift my hand, my fingers

still shaking as I run them through my hair, hoping I seem nonchalant.

"Fifteen, twenty minutes, I think?" Gracie shrugs. The other girls nod their agreement. "Did you two have a fight?"

"Yes. We argued." It's just like Eli predicted. "It was…we got nowhere in our conversation."

Hey, that's not a lie. Our conversation really went nowhere.

Jocelyn touches my arm. "Did he upset you?"

"No more than usual," I say with a shrug. Her hand falls away. "Why do you ask?"

"Your face is really red. Like you're mad or—something." She sends me a searching look and I glance away, uncomfortable with her scrutiny.

I don't want her thinking something else happened. I'm not going to tell them Eli kissed me. And that it was the hottest kiss we've shared in…

Forever.

Nope, I'm keeping that little fact to myself.

I fill them in briefly on the argument, only offering up the main points: he still doesn't think he's done anything wrong. I still think he's a jerk. They all nod in agreement and lightly insult him with the exception of Gracie. Her silence is so obvious that Hayden finally has to say something.

"Are you really not taking our girl's side here?" she asks Gracie.

"Hey, I just lived with him for a year," Gracie says. "I witnessed the demise of their relationship."

I wince. What a way to put it.

"Meaning you witnessed him being a complete raging asshole," Hayden mutters, sending me a 'don't worry, I've got your back,' look.

"He really wasn't that much of an asshole," Gracie admits. "Yeah, he overreacted and should've never made her choose.

That was a dumb move on his part. But he suffered over it. A lot."

I hate hearing that. I want to believe he didn't suffer at all. That I'm the only one who took the brunt of our breakup while he went about his business as if nothing ever happened between us.

It's easier to believe that's how it went down, because I'm the victim in that scenario, which garners sympathy and….

And since when do I want to play the victim?

"Do you regret coming tonight?" Jocelyn asks, her face full of concern.

"No." I shake my head. "I don't regret it at all. That first conversation between us after the breakup needed to happen. Maybe…eventually, we can be friends."

Doubtful. I can't be just Eli's friend. Not after he kissed me like he did.

I don't know what to do about this. About us.

So I'm going to pretend nothing ever happened. It's easier that way.

Safer.

The hairs on my arms prickle with awareness, as if someone is watching me, and I glance over my shoulder to find it's Eli standing with his friends, a beer clutched in his hand and a thunderous expression on his face. He doesn't look away from me. He just stares, as if daring me to do something, to say something.

I stare at him in return, half tempted to go to him. But that would be stupid.

So stupid.

Instead, I turn back around, smiling at something Hayden says, even though I have no idea exactly what it was. I nod and laugh, grateful I haven't had a drop of alcohol tonight. I experienced that kiss with Eli completely sober, and God, it had been so good.

Freaking magical.

It's been a long time since I've been held by someone who isn't my family or a close friend. I crave closeness.

Ugh.

I crave Eli.

Even if I can't have him.

Ever again.

CHAPTER 7

ELI

"Women fucking suck." I chuck the basketball straight at Caleb, who makes a groaning noise when it smacks him in the abs. "Let's go."

I chase him down the basketball court, trying to steal the ball from him, but the fucker is fast. Sometimes we like to play one on one, just to change it up, and our apartment complex has an outdoor court that no one ever uses—except for us.

Like now. On a cool Sunday afternoon, when we should be chillin' or working on homework or what the hell ever. Instead, we're dribbling up and down the court, antagonizing each other playing a sport neither of us are particularly good at, but because we're elite athletes, we're pretty fuckin' good.

I slap the ball out of Caleb's hands and spin, racing toward my hoop, shooting the ball a little earlier than I normally do when, lo and behold, that thing hits the rim and bounces through the hoop.

"Take that!" I yell at Caleb with a laugh.

He grabs the ball and starts jogging to the other side of the court, deceptively at ease. I know the second I lunge for him, he'll probably send me falling on my ass. "Show off," he mutters as he passes me.

I run halfheartedly behind him, not one hundred percent into it. I drank too much last night and woke up hungover this morning. I also can't stop thinking about Ava and her mouth.

All I want to do is kiss it.

My dream girl has turned into my worst nightmare. She wants me still. Last night's entanglement proves it. Fuck, I want her too. But I'm still mad—and I'm sure she is too. We may have talked, but we didn't resolve anything.

Not a damn thing.

I have a good feeling about this though. About us. At the very least, we can use each other for sex for a while.

I frown, stopping in my tracks as I rest my hands on my hips.

What the hell? No, I will not just use her for sex. We're more than that. I love that girl. She lives in me. That sounds corny as hell, even in my thoughts, but it's the damn truth. She's everything to me.

Everything.

Caleb takes the ball all the way to his basket and sinks it into the net with ease, the ball bouncing on the ground. He snatches it from the air, turning to look at me as he continues dribbling the ball.

"You all right?" he asks.

I nod, not even bothering to steal the ball from him, even though it's rightfully mine. "Can I ask you a question?"

He frowns, still bouncing the ball. "Sure."

"You ever uh...just have sex with a girl but not want a relationship attached to it?" I rub the back of my neck, feeling like an idiot for asking.

"Pfft." Caleb makes a dismissive noise, passing the ball straight to me. I catch it before it can do damage to my abs, like I did to him only moments before. "I *invented* that game. Baylee, remember?"

"Oh right." How could I forget? He kept that girl on a string since high school, and only ended it when Baylee told him she was done. We were already halfway through college by then.

"We were total fuck buddies, though I know she caught feelings." He frowns. "I regret how badly I treated her."

"Well, now she's practically married to Carson," I remind him.

"Isn't that crazy? That guy never impressed me much, but they're still going strong." Caleb shrugs. "I'm happy for her."

That's great and all, but I don't want to divert from the real question that's lingering on my tongue.

"How were you able to never catch feelings for her?" I ask, my voice light. Like this conversation is no big deal.

Caleb watches me, his eyes narrowed into slits. "You got someone in mind to be your FWB?"

I frown. "FWB?"

"Friend with benefits," he explains.

I start bouncing the ball, warming up to practice a trick I learned and perfected in seventh grade. "Nah."

"Liar."

"It's true." I shrug and bounce the ball harder, until I flip it into the air and stick my middle finger up, balancing the fucker right on it. "Check this out."

"Not bad," Caleb acknowledges before he runs up and bats the ball away. "Who you got in mind? There are girls lining up to get with you, bro. The pull is strong this year. We're seniors. We could have anyone we want."

We both watch the ball roll across the paved court, until it bounces against the black wrought-iron fence, coming to a stop.

"Do you want anyone else?" I ask him, just to make sure.

"Nah. No way. I'm happy. Gracie is my girl," he says

with boastful confidence. I remember feeling that way. So sure in my relationship. Positive she was going to be mine forever.

Now look at me.

"That's great," I say, and I mean it.

I'm also envious. I want that back.

I want it with Ava.

"After our encounter last night, I'm thinking that's what Ava and I can be," I say. Caleb frowns at me in confusion. "Friends with benefits."

"*What?* You gotta be fucking kidding me." Caleb says, an incredulous look on his face before he busts up laughing.

He laughs for at least a minute. And the longer it lasts, the angrier I get. Until I'm tempted to grab that basketball and throw it in his smug ass laughing face.

"What the fuck is wrong with that?" I finally ask him.

"You're delusional." He shakes his head. "Seriously, what are you thinking? You two were in a relationship for four years, and now you think you're going to be fuck buddies? Unbelievable."

"It could happen." I shrug. Deep down, I know he's speaking the truth. "She still seems into me."

If by being into me, I mean she wants to murder me, then yes.

She's totally into me.

"What went down between you two last night?" Caleb asks, his laughter finally dying.

"We talked."

"And…"

"That's it," I say, realizing at the last second that I don't want to share with him what else Ava and I did last night. It feels too personal to reveal. And a little messed-up. We shouldn't have kissed.

Then again, we should've. It's like we can't help ourselves, and I suppose that's our issue. We still want each other. Our love for each other is deep. We've been through a lot together. It's hard to just—quit that.

"Now you think you two can just randomly hook up, here and there? With no feelings attached?" Caleb raises his brows.

"Oh yeah." I wave a hand like it's no big deal. "We've always had chemistry. I've got no one in my life right now. Neither does she."

At least, I don't think she does. Can't think like that though, or I'll get furious quick.

"Like I said, you're delusional." He jabs his finger in the air, straight at me. "You're still in love with her."

"I still *care* about her," I correct, because no way in hell am I admitting to Caleb that he nailed it on the head.

I'm still in love with Ava.

What if she's still not in love with me?

"Keep telling yourself that," he says with a snort. I've lived with this guy for a while now. How did I not notice how fucking annoying he is before?

Wait, I did. He's just extra annoying at this very moment.

"She's living at home until the spring semester. She'll go back to San Diego in January," I explain. "Why not try and hook up, now and again? We'll run into each other constantly, thanks to our mutual friend group. And it's pointless to hate on each other. I could never hate Ava. Am I still mad at her? Hell yes."

"Is she still mad at you?" Caleb asks.

I remember her blazing green eyes and the things she said. She got some real zingers in too, aiming straight for my heart. And my ego—which she thinks is too big. She even called me the most selfish person she knows, and we know a *lot* of jackasses.

That stung. When it came to her, I was not selfish. As in, I gave her whatever she wanted, whenever she wanted it. I adored that girl. Worshipped her.

I still do.

"Yeah, she's still mad at me," I finally admit.

"Maybe you can fuck the mad out of each other," Caleb suggests, as if that's a perfectly logical solution to our problem.

And you know what? I like that answer. I like it a lot. But would Ava be down?

Probably not.

"I don't know," I say, wincing at how uncertain I sound. That's not how I roll. I'm certain of everything, or at least I pretend to be. "She probably won't agree."

"The good ones usually don't," Caleb says with a slow nod, reminding me of a sage old soul. Which is some straight-up bullshit because I would never describe him in that way. "Just tell her how you feel and make it happen, Eli. I know you can do it. Pretty sure you two can work this out."

"Yeah. Doubtful," I say, my turn to snort this time. "She was still pretty angry with me last night."

"You kind of deserve it," Caleb points out. "You could've survived without her for the summer."

"Maybe not," I say, getting irritated all over again. "She hasn't put me first in a long time, Caleb. And that was just… the final straw."

Caleb is shaking his head, his expression one of pure disappointment. How I wish I had the basketball still in my hands so I could smack him in the face with it. "You've got this all wrong."

"And you don't know shit." I stride toward the fence, snatching the basketball off the ground before I run down the court, jumping high and slam dunking that motherfucker, my fingers curling around the rim.

When I turn, I find Caleb still watching me, his hands on his hips, an annoyed look on his face. "You're acting mad at me, when I know you're really mad at yourself."

"Whatever." I jog toward him cautiously, my gaze locked on his hands. I know how he operates. He'll try and steal the ball from me. "Maybe I should just leave it alone. I've chased her enough."

The moment the words leave my lips, they feel familiar. I remember saying something similar to her when we were first together.

I was such a prick then. I swear I've changed. I've grown-up. Matured. I am solid. On top of the world. I'm not about to let a woman I've loved for the last four years of my life, a woman I've given my all to, run out on me once and for all and never look back. I have to fight for her. For us.

But how do I make this right?

"Hey!"

I turn to see Gracie and Hayden making their way toward us. Dread fills me, settling in my gut and I steel my spine, preparing myself for the verbal blast I'm sure they're going to give me. Gracie is my homie, but she'll side with Ava on this matter, and when she's with Hayden? Forget it.

They'll both come for me.

Caleb takes his advantage, swiping the ball from my hands and dashing down the court like a madman. He sinks the ball through the net within seconds, screaming in victory at the top of his lungs and making me wince.

He loves to rub it in.

"Ladies," I say to Gracie and Hayden as they draw nearer. Their expressions are open, not full of bitterness or hatred and I take that as a good sign. "What brings you out here this fine afternoon?"

"Him." Gracie points at Caleb and I watch as they make their way to each other, Gracie cozying up to him despite the reluctant expression on his face.

"I'm sweaty," he warns her.

"I like it," she murmurs before their lips meet in a kiss.

Gross. I feel like I'm eleven and watching my older brother, Ryan, kiss on one of the many girls he chased after. I didn't understand why any guy would be interested in girls when he had sports and video games—I thought he was crazy. Girls were a mystery to me, one I wasn't interested in.

Fast forward two years and they were an enigma I was dying to figure out.

Still don't have them figured out, if I'm being real right now.

"Hey, Eli," Gracie calls, once she's done slobbering all over her boyfriend.

"Yeah?" I ask warily. My guard is up and I'm fully prepared for her to say something shitty to me about Ava.

"Are you and Ava going to be able to work it out?" She leaves Caleb and approaches me, her expression full of concern.

I shrug, trying to play it off, though I don't know why I'm bothering. Gracie won't give me shit, though I can feel Hayden's assessing gaze on me.

That's the one I have to watch out for.

"Maybe," I say, keeping it purposely vague. Why does everyone want to know our business?

"Do you *want* to work it out with Ava?" Hayden asks.

I swing my attention in her direction, wondering if I have an ally in her or not. I like Hayden. I like all of my friends' girlfriends for the most part, but they'll take Ava's side every time and I know it. Just like I'd take one of my friends' sides every single time. That's how it works when you have your friends' backs.

Unless one of them did something extremely shady or, I don't know—illegal? Then I'd have an issue.

"I do," I finally admit. "But maybe—it should be her turn."

Hayden's face hardens, her mouth turning into a frown. "What do you mean?"

"She has to come to me," I say. "I approached her last night at the party, and it didn't—quite work out. Now the ball is in her court."

Yeah. I like the basketball analogy.

"Really, Eli? You're just going to wait for Ava to approach first?" I turn to Gracie, just in time to see her roll her eyes. "You're so stubborn. All of you are."

"Hey, I tried. Now she needs to make an attempt," I say indignantly.

"You might be waiting for her to come to you forever," Hayden points out.

"That's the chance I'm willing to take," I say, my voice easy. Full of confidence.

But deep inside, I can't deny it.

I'm freaking the fuck out.

CHAPTER 8

AVA

"It's been so nice having you around," Mom says as she approaches the table where I'm sitting. "We've missed you."

It's Monday afternoon and I'm outside in the back yard by the pool, enjoying the cooler weather. A storm is brewing. I can see the dark clouds clinging to the mountains in the near distance, and there's a distinct nip in the air that tells me fall is most definitely upon us.

"Yeah, it's been weird, not having to work on homework or go to class," I say, watching my mother settle into the chair across from me.

I really take her in, noting our similar features, our matching green eyes. My mother is still beautiful, even though she's a mom. But I've always thought Mom was beautiful, and I know Dad does too. He still gets hearts in his eyes when he stares at her too long, and I remember how Eli used to do that with me, too.

Ugh. Eli. Just thinking about him hurts my brain and my heart, yet my body lights up like it wants another chance with him. I still can't forget the kiss we shared Saturday night. It had been months since we'd seen each other, let alone touched. The moment he put his hand on me, my entire body reacted and immediately wanted more. And then when his mouth settled on mine, and the words he said?

Whew. Hot.

The chemistry between us is still there, but is it enough?

"Do you miss school? And your friends?" Mom asks, her soft voice breaking into my thoughts.

We're currently the only two at home. Beck's at school and Dad left a while ago to go join him at football practice. Gracie reached out to me late last night, asking if I wanted to get together for dinner tonight and I said yes. She's the only one of our friends who lives here, since she's teaching at the local elementary school and everyone else is down in Fresno.

"No, not really. The break is nice," I answer. "I do miss Ellie though."

I miss my best friend something fierce. She'll be coming home soon, thank goodness. By Halloween at the latest, she reassured me via text a few days ago. Specifically on Saturday night when I was having a minor freak out after my run-in with Eli and I needed her advice.

More than anything, I needed her to tell me everything was going to be all right. And she did exactly that, calming me down.

"Oh, for a second there I thought you were going to say you miss Eli," Mom says, wincing.

"Ah, no." I shake my head extra hard, as if I need to convince myself. Which, I sort of do, because let's be real.

I totally miss Eli.

"You can be real with me, you know," Mom says, her voice low, her gaze unwavering as she watches me. "I'm sure you actually do miss Eli, even though he hurt you so badly."

"He's a stubborn jackass," I say, not holding anything back. "I saw him Saturday night. After the game."

Mom's brows lift slightly, but otherwise there's no visible reaction to my confession. "And how did it go?"

"Terrible," I say, not about to admit that I kissed him and we basically felt each other up. I'm pretty open with my mother, but not *that* open.

"Did you talk to him?"

I shake my head.

"Not at all?" She sounds skeptical.

"Not enough to make a difference. He's still stubborn as ever." God, I sound bitter.

"So it's over between you two?" Mom actually seems sad.

"How can I work it out with him when he won't even listen to me? He's impossible." He's also ridiculous and hard-headed and…distracting.

Very, very distracting.

"You're still mad at him too, aren't you?"

I nod, not bothering to deny it. "We're uhhh…definitely not seeing eye to eye right now, Mom. And I'm not sure if we ever will."

"You know, your dad and I split up right after we started —seeing each other," Mom admits as she gazes off into the distance.

Why the hesitation over saying 'seeing each other'? The early days of their relationship have always been a bit of a mystery to me, and they rarely talk about it.

"Why?"

"His life was messy. Isn't that what you kids like to say?" She laughs when I make a face. "I sound like an old woman. Anyway, your father was a bit of a mess and I was too, and he tried to cut things off to protect me I suppose, but really? I think he did it to protect himself. He didn't know what to do with me."

"Why do you say that?" And why is she telling me this?

"His feelings for me scared him, which was fine because my feelings for him scared me too. Everything happened so fast between us, it was overwhelming." She's totally lost in her memories, I can see it in her eyes, on her face. "I think sometimes you and Eli overwhelm each other."

"He's overwhelming," I agree.

"But so are you. You're always so passionate when it comes to what you believe in. You don't back down, Ava. Neither does Eli." When my gaze meets hers, she smiles gently. "Maybe you should learn how to back down a bit."

"No way do I want to give first," I say firmly.

Mom laughs. "And you claim he's the stubborn one. I think it goes both ways."

It probably does, but I don't want to admit that.

"I think you two should *really* talk to each other, without any other distractions." She sends me a pointed look. "Like your friends."

"Pretty sure he doesn't want to do that." And I'm too scared to do it. What if he touches me again, kisses me, and we end up getting carried away? Next thing I know, we'll have sex and nothing will get resolved.

"Do you regret going to Spain?" Mom asks, changing the subject.

I shake my head. "It was the best thing I could've ever done for myself at that time, and I have zero regrets."

"Even though you lost your boyfriend in the process?"

"Honestly? I thought maybe we would—be back together by now," I admit, feeling foolish.

Hating that I just said that out loud.

"This is why you should try and talk to him without anyone else around. I know you love your friend group, and they are all so supportive. I wish I had that many friends when I was your age, but sometimes their voices and opinions can get in the way." Her smile is gentle, her gaze sincere.

I know she's right.

"Maybe I'll text him." Oh wait. I can't.

I'm blocked.

I meet Gracie for dinner at Southgate, a local restaurant that is part brew house and has fantastic food. Tourists and locals flock to the place, but considering it's October, there are more locals than tourists currently occupying tables. It's funny how Gracie has turned into a local, though I'm sure she's not necessarily embraced by the community yet since she only started at the elementary school in August.

I remember how reluctant the locals were to accept my family into the fold, and my dad is a freaking NFL Super Bowl champion for the love of God. He won them over by coaching in the youth football league and then at the high school. Only then were the Callahans fully embraced as part of the community.

Gotta love small towns.

"Are you liking it here?" I wrinkle my nose, fully prepared for Gracie to complain. She grew up in the Bay Area, so she's used to big cities. She'd complain that Fresno was too small for her sometimes.

"I love it here. Everyone's so friendly and accepting," she says, her eyes sparkling and a giant smile on her face. We've already ordered drinks and appetizers—no alcohol, since I'm still only twenty, and Gracie drove herself here—and I'm dying to drill her for info on Caleb.

And maybe a little info about Eli too.

"Really?" I didn't expect her to say that.

She nods. "Once they found out Caleb is my boyfriend, I was considered one of them. His parents are an institution in this town. Multi-generational. His grandparents still live here too."

"I forgot about that." I stir my straw in my Coke, then take a sip. "You and Caleb doing good?"

"Yes, can you believe it? Remember how much I hated him?" A sigh escapes her and she's got this dreamy look on her face. It's kind of annoying, only because I recognize it and am currently experiencing a twinge of jealousy.

"I always figured the hate was a mask for all that sexual tension brimming between the two of you," I tease her.

"There was always something, huh? It was hard not to notice." She rests her elbow on the table, her chin propped on her fisted hand. "Just like there's still something between you and Eli."

My cheeks grow warm and I duck my head for a moment, fighting embarrassment. I've told no one about our kiss on Saturday night. Not even Ellie, and I tell her everything.

Can I tell Gracie?

"Did something happen between you two?"

Hmm, sounds like she already suspects.

When I still remain quiet, her eyes narrow and she leans across the table, her voice pitching low as she says, "Something *did* happen. It's written all over your face."

"He kissed me." I shrug, trying to play it off.

"Did you kiss him back?"

"Well, yeah." *Duh*, is what I want to say, but I'm trying to remain mature about the situation.

"And was it good? Better than usual?"

It feels like she's living in my head. "You ask a lot of questions."

"I'm curious, and I'm watching out for you. Eli can be very…persuasive." I'm about to ask her how she knows this when she continues, "I lived with him, which he talked me into doing, by the way, even though I knew it might be a huge mistake. He can convince just about anyone to do something they don't want. He's rather—charming."

"Unless he's pissed at you. Then he's not charming at all," I mutter, making her laugh.

"Says the woman who pissed him off yet kissed him Saturday night."

I ball up my discarded straw wrapper and throw it at her.

It nails her in the cheek, which has me laughing. "He's sexy when he's pissed."

Our laughter dies and the knowing look on her face is almost annoying.

"You think he's sexy."

"Of course I do. I'm still in love with him." I say it like I have a disease. As if I was diagnosed with something terminal and it's killing me slowly. It feels that way sometimes, my love for Eli. Like I'll never get over him no matter how hard I try.

"Then why aren't you doing something about it?" she asks me. When I glance up, I see the sincerity in her gaze. The way she's watching me, as if she's genuinely curious and concerned.

Gracie is a good friend. I need to confide in her.

"You promise you won't say anything about this conversation to Caleb?" I ask.

She nods. "Of course not. He can't keep a secret to save his life. He'd run straight to Eli and report this conversation to him if I told him about it. Not to screw you over, but to help his bro out."

"You do realize when we were in high school, they hated each other," I say, unable to keep that little fact to myself. "One night, Caleb was flirting with me after a football game and Eli about ripped his face off."

"And they call us the dramatic ones." Gracie rolls her eyes.

"Yeah." A sigh leaves me and I decide to be completely real with my friend. "I don't know if I want him back."

"You mean Eli?" she asks. I nod my answer. "Why do you say that?"

"Even after everything that happened between us, I was still willing to go to Spain because, deep down, I thought he'd come around. He'd realize he was being ridiculous, and when I came home, we would be able to talk it out and fix everything, you know?" I was living in a dream land.

"But he hasn't done that," Gracie says.

"He hasn't done that," I repeat with another sigh. "I know he's still in love with me, too. Though I can't confirm if he's been with other girls or not."

My stomach twists just saying the words. I cannot imagine him being with someone else. He had a complete player reputation before we got together. I knew what I was dealing with. But he's been one hundred percent devoted the entire time we've been in a relationship. He was totally into me. Other girls didn't even turn his head.

But we broke up months ago. He can do whatever he wants, with whoever he wants. So can I.

No one else tempts me though. I glance around the room, spotting a cute guy sitting a couple of tables over with a group. He catches my eye, offering me a smile and I look away, not even bothering to smile in return.

Yeah. No one else matters to me. Not right now.

Just Eli.

"I don't think he's been with other girls," Gracie says softly. "But I don't really know either. Not like they would tell me anyway."

Her words don't ease my worry, but I try and shove it into the corner of my mind so I won't focus on it. I can't control what he does, just like he can't control me either.

What if he's been with other women though? Would I be able to forgive him? I suppose there's nothing to forgive, since we aren't together, but if he were able to find someone else so quickly…

I don't know if I could deal with it.

CHAPTER 9

ELI

notice her before I see anyone else. The moment we walk into the restaurant, I spot Ava sitting at a table on the other side of the room, talking intently with Gracie.

I knew it was risky coming to this restaurant. My mom has been harassing me for weeks to meet up with her for dinner, and I finally gave in. She complained that she doesn't like to drive down to Fresno at night, so I agreed to meet her up here, in the same town where I spent my teen years. Where Ava was. *Is*.

Fuck, she's even in the same restaurant. What are the odds?

The hostess leads us to a table, and she keeps giving me flirtatious glances, but I ignore her, keeping my expression steely. Downright unreadable. Mom is talking a bunch of nonsense to the girl as if she knows her and the minute we're seated, I ask her what's up.

"Did you know that girl?" I ask once the hostess seats us.

"Why yes, she actually goes to your old high school. She's a senior. I always see her when I come in here with my friends," Mom says as she snatches up the cocktail menu the hostess left behind.

Worry fills me. She promised she wasn't drinking as much, but I'm thinking she's lying. "Are you really going to order a drink?"

"I'm not driving, so yes," she snaps, her gaze never straying from the menu. If I could snatch it out of her hands and fling it across the room, I so would.

Great idea, Mom, coming to this place so you can booze it up and oh yeah, look at that. There's Ava.

It's like I can't escape her pretty ass.

Fucking sucks.

I bite back what I really want to say and flip open the menu, my gaze sliding over the options, though I don't actually comprehend what I'm reading. My emotions are turbulent. Rising and falling within me, fighting for domination. I'm equal parts frustrated and stressed and nervous, all because of a certain someone who I'm currently sharing air with.

"Eli."

I glance up when Mom whispers my name. "What?"

"Isn't that Ava over there?" She tips her head in the direction of Ava and Gracie's table.

I nod, training my gaze on the menu. I refuse to look over at her. "Yeah."

"She's back in town?"

I nod again, my appetite fleeing.

"Back from Spain?"

"Yes, Mom." I slam the menu shut and drop it onto the table. "She's back from Spain."

"Why isn't she in school?"

"She took the semester off."

"Are you two speaking?" Mom knows about our breakup, but that's all she knows. I gave her no details, which was probably a mistake because now she's full of questions and I don't want to talk about Ava.

"Not really." I steal a glance in her direction, unable to

help myself. Our gazes meet, and she looks away quickly, as if she's embarrassed she got caught watching me.

I don't look away though. I'm willing her to return her gaze to mine, hating all the old, uncomfortable feelings coming back to me. It's like I'm seventeen again and I'm in love with a girl who doesn't want to give me the time of day. I'm annoyed with my controlling mother and frustrated with this beautiful girl who doesn't want anyone to know we're actually seeing each other.

That was the Eli of old's struggles, and I hated feeling like that. I hate worse feeling like that now.

"I always thought you two would get married," Mom says wistfully, as if she's already dreamed up the wedding. "Such a shame it ended."

"Yeah well, we've both moved on," I say, relief flooding me when a server approaches our table and asks for our drink order. I only ask for water. Mom orders a glass of wine.

"You can drink with me, you know," she says once the server leaves. "You're of legal age now."

"Gee thanks for giving me your permission," I say sarcastically, hating the wounded look that crosses her face. I exhale loudly and scrub my hand over my jaw. "Sorry. I don't want to drink and then have to drive home."

"You could stay the night. Your room is still pretty much intact," Mom suggests.

"Still don't want to risk getting behind the wheel after a couple of beers. What if I got a DUI?" My college football career would be over. Wrecked because I threw a couple back with my mother.

No thank you.

One thing I've noticed—people with a drinking problem don't like to drink alone. In social situations, Mom is always encouraging whoever she's with to drink. I didn't understand it when I was younger, but now I get it.

She doesn't want to be the only one, and when she is, it

makes her feel like the spotlight is on her. When other people drink with her, it makes her drinking feel more socially acceptable.

We make small talk. She asks me about school. I ask her about her friends. She tells me how they took a girls' trip to the coast. I let her know how the football team is doing. We dance around other subjects, like me and Ava, or her and Ryan. My older brother barely texts her, let alone calls her, and she's upset about it. I try to tell her Ryan's off doing his own thing, but she won't listen to me.

I think she enjoys being mad at him.

"Have you spoken to your father lately?" Mom asks, after the server brings us our meals. I got a cheeseburger, but I can already tell I'm not feeling it. I'm not that hungry, too fuckin' aware of the girl still sitting in this restaurant, ruining my vibe.

I shake my head and munch on a French fry. "Not in a while."

"He's the worst," she practically spits out. "Off galli-vanting with other women when he should be working and spending time with his children."

I withhold my eye roll. She's always harping on the fact that Dad is dating other women. She hated him when they were together. She hates him more now that they're apart. It's frustrating.

"The children are both grown, Mom," I remind her. "He doesn't need to spend time with us."

"He didn't much when you and your brother were young either. You have to admit you're not close to him," Mom says.

I'm not. And we're even more distant. We're *all* distant. I tolerate Mom because she's got no one else beyond her friends, and they have lives. They can't coddle her all the time. Ryan doesn't want to deal with her because she always ends up getting angry at him. I think he reminds her of Dad.

My family life sucks.

I think of the Callahans and how fucking wholesome that bunch is. They're a family who truly love each other, and who accept each other unconditionally. I liked being a part of their family. It killed me that I couldn't celebrate Ash's jersey retirement with them. I didn't even speak to her parents, too worried her dad wanted to beat my ass or her mom wanted to give me a bunch of shit for treating their daughter terribly.

It hurts, what happened between Ava and me. Losing her —and her entire family. It hurts worse that she's sitting with Gracie across the room and I can't talk to her.

I feel like I'm slowly dying inside.

When Mom spots the server and orders another glass of wine, I decide to let my feelings be known once he's gone.

"You told me you weren't drinking as much anymore," I say, my tone accusing.

She lifts one shoulder, her expression impassive. "What's a couple of glasses of wine?"

"For you, it's a sign you're probably drinking too much again," I say.

Her eyes narrow. "Don't you judge me. None of you are around anymore. I'm lonely. What else am I going to do?"

"Take up a new hobby? Binge watch something on Netflix? Exercise? Hang out with your friends?" I suggest. "There are a lot of other things you can do besides drink."

She waves a hand, dismissing my words. "A little wine never killed anybody. In Europe, they consider drinking a glass of wine every day good for you."

"That's a glass with dinner. Not four." Or an entire bottle, which she's been known to do.

"I don't need you judging me for my choices."

"Why not? No one else does."

A sigh leaves her. "I don't want to fight with you, so stop. Let's finish our meal."

We do so in silence, and I quietly watch as Ava and Gracie leave the restaurant. Ava doesn't bother looking in my direction. Gracie glances over her shoulder at the last second, right before she exits the place, and offers me a quick little wave.

I lift my hand in acknowledgement, hating how my stomach churns. I barely ate my dinner and I feel like I could throw it all back up.

"You look sad," Mom says, and I realize she saw Ava leave the restaurant too. "You should try and work it out with Ava."

"She doesn't want me," I say morosely, not knowing for sure if that's true, but going with it anyway.

"Oh, you're just saying that. You two were together for four years. You don't just stop loving someone after that long," Mom says.

She should know. Despite her hatred for my father, she still loves him too.

That's half the reason she hates him, I think.

"Don't let yourself become bitter," Mom says, pulling my attention back to her. "Don't let yourself become me."

I stare at her, noting the vulnerability on her face. This is the realest she's been with me in a while. "You're not bitter—"

She laughs, and even it sounds bitter. "Don't lie, Eli. It's not becoming. My favorite trait of yours is that you're always truthful. Even when it hurts or is rude. You at least always tell it like it is. I need that from you, son. I need it from you more than you know. And that's why I'm trying to be truthful with you."

"I just worry about you," I admit, my voice low. "When you drink—"

"I know," she interrupts, pushing the wine glass away from her. "I shouldn't drink as much. And you shouldn't be so stubborn. Go to her. Talk to her. Tell her you're sorry."

"I'm not so—"

"Eli," she interrupts again. "Don't lie to yourself, and don't lie to me either. Talk to Ava. Send her a text and tell her you want to meet up or whatever."

I can't. I blocked her ass from everything months ago, like the impulsive dick I am. It was easier to block her. That way I didn't have to see her posts when she was in Spain, looking beautiful and having the time of her life. I didn't have the temptation to call or text her and admit that I missed her. Blocking her was saving my sanity.

And ruining my chances to ever make it right between us.

I think about what my mother said the entire drive back to her house. After dropping her off, I don't head to Fresno. I turn my car around and head north, back up the mountain. Until I find myself driving slowly through Ava's parents' neighborhood, shutting off the headlights on my car as I pull in front of her home and park. I stare up at the massive house the Callahans live in for a moment, my gaze automatically going to Ava's window.

The light is on. A couple of windows down, another light is on.

Beck's room.

No lights are on downstairs and I check the time. It's past nine, still pretty early, meaning her parents could be awake. Tucked into the couch in the family room, snuggled up together as they watch something to end their night, which is their usual ritual.

Should I chance it? Or just go home?

Fuck it, I'm doing it.

I slip out of the car, as if I'm in pure stealth mode, shutting the door quietly and sneaking across the front lawn, heading for the side of the house. I'm keeping with the 'I feel like I'm seventeen again' mood and come to a stop in front of the trellis that's attached to the wall, leading right up to the second story.

Right up to Ava's bedroom window.

I crawled up it a couple of times when we were in high school. Sneaking into her room like a crazy asshole, and she loved every minute of it. We would hook up anywhere we could when we first got together. In the back of my car or hers. In that old cabin Jackson's uncle owned. Her bedroom. My bedroom. That one night after she won homecoming princess and was still wearing the crown when I fucked her the first time.

She was my princess then. She's still my princess now, if she'll let me into her room.

Reaching out, I give the trellis a firm shake, ignoring the worry streaking through me. I'm bigger than I was at seventeen. I'm more muscular, I'm taller and I weigh more. This is risky shit right here.

But I'm not one to let risk hold me back, so I grab onto the trellis and start climbing the wall, wincing when I hear something snap. Bracing myself for the inevitable fall.

Luckily, I'm still in one piece, attached to the wall like a modern-day Spider-Man.

Once I'm at the base of her window, I knock lightly. Three times with a pause in between knocks, like we used to do. I wait, clinging to the wall, my arms starting to shake.

She doesn't come. Doesn't lift away her curtains to peek outside, nothing.

Fuck.

I knock again, before whispering her name.

"Ava. It's me."

Still nothing.

I readjust my position on the trellis, the wood creaking beneath my weight as a piece breaks away from the wall. Quickly I glance at the ground, realizing if I fall it's a long way down until I hit grass, and I pray to God that if I do fall, I won't break a fucking bone.

Why the hell did I think this would be a good idea again?

Deciding I don't give a shit, I raise my voice and let myself be heard.

"Damn it, Ava, let me in," I practically yell, wincing when my voice carries in the quiet night.

The curtains are pushed open and there she is, standing in front of her window, her expression full of shock as she takes me in.

My eyes eat her up, my entire body breaking out in a sweat. Her hair is pulled up into a sloppy bun on top of her head and she's wearing an oversized red Fresno State T-shirt that's old and faded.

She's beautiful.

When she opens the window, and I see her face, I realize she's also really pissed.

"What the hell are you doing here?" she bites out, sounding hostile.

"I came to talk to you," I say, keeping it casual. Like it's no biggie that I climbed up the side of the house to do so.

"Can't you call like a normal person?"

I don't bother answering. The trellis trembles beneath my hold, letting me know it can't take my weight much longer, and I reach a hand out to her, grateful the screen is still off her window. Can't believe her dad never had it replaced. "Pull me in before I fall to the ground and break my arm."

She grabs my hand, both of us ignoring the electricity that sparks between us as she braces her feet and tugs with all her might. I help her, pushing my way through the window, until I'm tumbling onto the floor of her teenaged bedroom.

Being inside this room is giving me major flashbacks, all of them pleasant. Nothing bad happened between us in this room, and that gives me hope.

"You need to leave," she says as soon as she shoves the window closed.

I remain where I'm sitting on the floor and tilt my head, trying to catch a glimpse underneath that giant T-shirt she's wearing. I don't see shorts. All I see are her long legs, which tells me she might have some panties on under that thing and nothing else. "But I just got here."

"I don't want to talk to you tonight." She turns to face me, irritation written all over her pretty face when she catches me staring. "And stop trying to look up my shirt."

My girl knows me so well.

I hop to my feet and start pacing, unable to stop myself. Pacing helps me think, I swear. "I need you to hear me out."

"No. I don't have to, Eli. We're not together anymore. You can't boss me around and you definitely can't march back into my life as if you never left it." She stomps straight toward me and thrusts her index finger into my face, wagging it like a pissed-off teacher. "You broke my heart. I can't forgive you so easily for that."

"You broke my heart too, you know. It's like my feelings didn't even matter in your decisions," I throw at her.

"I'm starting to wonder if you even have a heart," she tosses back as she takes that weaponized index finger and pokes me in the chest, like she's trying to find it. "I don't miss you, Eli. Not one. Single. Bit."

She pokes me every time she says a word and damn it, that finger hurts.

"You're such a fuckin' liar, Princess." She winces when I call her that and before she can drop her hand, I grab her wrist, holding it to my chest. "You miss me so damn bad. I haunt your dreams. And your nightmares. You probably touch yourself in the middle of the night while you think about me. Am I right?"

Her green eyes are wide and blazing with an emotion I don't really recognize, which I don't like. What is this girl thinking? I've had her so figured out the last few years, and now she feels like a mystery again.

"You're disgusting," she whispers.

I tug her closer, her body colliding with mine. "You really believe that? I'm disgusting? Such harsh words for the guy who stole your cherry."

"That right there is why I think you're disgusting." She

makes a face, a shuddery breath leaving her. "Who calls it a cherry?"

"That's what I took though, right? My virgin girlfriend who hasn't been with anyone else. You were all mine. You belonged to me," I whisper, my grip on her wrist lessening as I gently stroke her skin with my thumb. "Do you still?"

She jerks her arm from my hold, taking a step back. As if she needs the space. "That's none of your business."

Anger floods me, ripping through my veins, simmering beneath my skin. Has she actually been with someone else while I'm over here saving myself for her like a chump? "What kind of answer is that?"

"The kind of answer you deserve, considering you're not my boyfriend anymore," she says, her voice hard.

I can't help myself—I chase her around her bedroom. Around her bed. She shrieks when she glances over her shoulder and spots my intense expression. Anticipating her every move, I lunge for her when she tries to make her way toward the walk-in closet and end up tackling her onto the bed.

I'm on top of her and we're both breathing hard, my face in hers. She doesn't have a lick of makeup on and she smells fragrant, like her favorite body lotion. Memories come back of me exploring all that smooth skin with my mouth and fingers. How good it always was between us, even when we argued.

Sometimes it was really fucking spectacular after we argued.

"Get off me." She bucks her hips against mine in a weak attempt to get rid of me, but I'm huge compared to her. It does nothing but remind me of how soft and pliant she is beneath me. "I'm going to knee you in the balls if you don't get up, Eli. I mean it."

"I'd love to see you try." I lower my face to hers, our mouths aligned, our gazes locked. "Fuck, you're sexy when you're mad. I miss you, baby. So damn much. Why are we fighting this?"

Her expression hardens, her lips thinning. "You're the one who broke up with me."

"You left me."

"I was coming back," she reminds me, and I close my eyes, pressing my forehead against hers.

"This is stupid. The back and forth shit is getting old," I whisper. "You want to be with me?"

She's quiet, as if she doesn't want to admit it first.

I get it. I don't want to say it first either.

Restraint slipping from me, I lower my mouth to hers. That first moment they touch, sparks fly between our lips and the kiss immediately turns explosive. It's seeking tongues and low gasps and sweet moans. It's my hand slipping beneath the hem of her T-shirt to find she's only wearing skimpy panties and tracing the crease where her thigh meets her hip. It's the whimper that escapes her when I do that.

It's everything. How responsive she is. How we reach for each other as if we've never stopped. Her hands beneath my shirt, stroking my back, pulling me closer on top of her. We kiss each other hungrily, as if we're starving and we're the only ones who can satisfy each other. It's frantic. Sloppy.

And then it's as if she's filled with otherworldly strength and she's shoving me off of her and I have no choice but to roll over onto my side, watching in confusion as she scrambles off the bed and starts pacing the room like I did only moments ago.

"Please leave," she says shakily as she touches her mouth with trembling fingers. "I can't keep doing this, Eli."

Sitting up, I run a hand through my hair. My fingers are quaking too. My entire body feels as if it's buzzing, surges of adrenaline coursing through me. "Ava..."

"No." She shakes her head, that loose bun on top of her head tipping to the side. "Don't try and convince me. You're right, I can't handle all of this back and forth stuff either. It's too—hard on me."

I watch her pace, her expression a mix of emotions—serious concentration, accompanied by a healthy dose of total confusion.

And I feel her on every level.

I rise to my feet and try to approach her, but she holds both hands out, warding me off. "Don't get any closer."

I frown. "Why not? Afraid I'll give you cooties?"

Ava rolls her eyes. "You're being ridiculous. I'm just—if we get too close to each other, we do things we might regret."

I don't regret shit when it comes to Ava, but I do regret how we ended things. "Fine, whatever. I'll keep my distance. Let's talk."

"Not tonight. I'm tired. I'd prefer if you distanced yourself completely and left." She tilts her head toward the window.

My mouth drops open. "You really expect me to leave out the window?"

"You came in that way, right?"

"The trellis will collapse under my weight."

"Maybe you should lose some weight."

I bark out a laugh. "It's all muscle, baby. I'm a lot bigger than I was at seventeen."

Her gaze skims me from head to toe, lingering on my chest before it guiltily jumps to mine. "Yeah, you are."

Normally I'd puff up my chest and tell her to get her ass over here, but she won't respond well to that. "Talk to me."

She shakes her head. "Not right now."

"Come on." I won't beg.

I won't.

"What else is there to say? Are you here to apologize? Or are you here because you want to fuck me?"

I actually flinch. "Maybe I want—both."

Ava crosses her arms. "You can't have it all. Not yet. We need to talk about—things first."

"Then let's talk."

"Not tonight. Some other time." She lifts her chin. Little miss stubborn. "You should go."

A ragged exhale leaves me.

Fine.

I'm out.

CHAPTER 10

AVA

"Would you like to hear how my evening went?" I ask cheerily.

I'm in my room the next morning after my run-in with Eli, on the phone with Ellie. She goes quiet for a moment, as if I asked her a trick question and she doesn't quite know how to answer. "Um…okay?"

"Great! All right, picture it. I'm in my room, minding my own business and about to go to bed, so I can waste an hour on TikTok before I fall asleep, when I hear a knock. On my window. Mind you, I'm on the second floor," I say.

"Oh, I know." She sounds amused. Not freaked out or worried for me, which makes me guess she probably knows who it was knocking on my window.

"I throw back my curtains and I see Eli, just his head. He climbed up the trellis, Ellie."

"Just like in high school," she says, though I don't need the reminder.

A sigh leaves me and I fight against the warm memories of Eli climbing the trellis and sneaking into my room back in the day. He was so bad.

And I loved every stolen minute I spent with him back then. It was thrilling.

Exciting.

"What did you do when you saw him?" she asks.

"I let him in. I had to. It was either that, or he could've plunged to his death," I retort.

She laughs. "I doubt he would've actually died, but he might've broken a bone and ended his football career forever."

Frowning, I shake my head. I didn't even think of that. He is such an impulsive idiot sometimes, putting himself at risk in such a foolish way. All because of me.

You're worth it, is what he would've said.

Before we ended things.

"He's crazy," I murmur.

"Yes, he is," Ellie readily agrees. "So tell me. Did you guys…do anything?"

I think of the kiss, how hot it was. How easy it would've been to succumb to it. To give in to him. He's got very persuasive lips.

Persuasive everything.

"No."

"Really?" She sounds doubtful.

"We kissed," I admit, closing my eyes. I'm still in bed, in my room, and it's almost ten in the morning. I'm not one to sleep in, but I had a hard time falling asleep last night. I kept running over what happened. What he said. What I said. The taste of his lips. His hard body on top of mine…

I finally drifted off to sleep only to dream of him. Of course. When I finally woke up, confused and sweating, I realized quickly the house was quiet. Pretty sure everyone is gone and I'm glad. I know Beck is at school, but I don't know where my parents are, or even when they actually left.

It's okay, though. I'd rather not face them this morning.

Not that they have any clue that Eli "stopped by" last night, but I'm still frazzled by his brief visit.

"Oooh, you guys kissed? Not surprising. How was it?" She sounds like the Ellie I knew back in middle school, when we were so young and silly and gossiped about boys and the popular group and who was going out with who.

"It was terrible," I lie.

No, it was amazing. Even better than I remember. Is it my mind playing tricks on me? I go without for months, so any little show of attention from Eli sets me on fire? Am I that pathetic?

Or is it just that fiery between us still?

"You're a liar," Ellie says, not holding back.

Busted. "Fine. It wasn't terrible. But I'm still so frustrated with him, Ellie. He says the worst things."

"He always has," Ellie points out.

Hmm. My best friend knows Eli better than I thought.

"Did he apologize yet?" she asks.

"No, of course he didn't."

Instead of forcing him back out my window, I opened the door of my bedroom for him, so he could exit the house like a normal human being. I asked if he wanted me to walk him to the front door and he said he knew where it was, I didn't need to bother.

So I didn't.

Even though I wanted to.

I waited a few minutes after he left, closing the curtains immediately but sneaking looks out the window to see if his car was still parked out front. He sat in that car for a while. I don't know what he was doing. Thinking? Contemplating coming back into the house and talking to me?

I stood by the window with my heart in my throat, my stomach twisted in knots, secretly praying he would come to his senses and march back into the house, up the stairs and into my room and tell me he was sorry and that he loved me more than anything in the world.

But he did none of that. He eventually started the car and pulled away from the curb, disappearing into the night. I went downstairs, locked the front door, went back into my room and cried my eyes out into my pillow.

"Are you two ever going to be able to fix this?" Ellie asks.

"I don't know," I say honestly. "Is it best that I just let him go and we move on? First love doesn't always last forever."

"No, it doesn't," she agrees. "But I thought you two were special."

So did I, not that I want to admit it now.

"Clearly he's too wrapped up in his own ego to see what he's doing," I say, sounding like a bitter old hag. "I think I should move on."

"Really?" Ellie squeaks. She sounds surprised.

"Yes," I say with a nod, even though she can't see me. "I need to go out with friends. Meet someone new. Maybe lots of someone news."

That's never going to happen with the friend group here. Eli is part of it. And I have no single friends here.

Right now, I wish I was in San Diego. I suppose I could go down there if I really wanted to, though I really have nowhere to live. I bet Mom and Dad would rent an apartment for me, and then I could eventually find roommates for the spring semester.

The problem is, my old roommates are in their place for the school year, so I can't live with them. I really don't want to live with strangers. And I really don't want to live on my own either. Sleeping in my own apartment at night, every night sounds...

A little scary.

Not that I would admit that to anyone. I'm supposed to be an independent woman who can handle anything. I'm twenty years old, for the love of God. Years ago, women my age were already married and having children.

I'm definitely not ready for all of that responsibility. Living on my own, being my own person and not attached to someone else—that's overwhelming too. I was comfortable being part of a team. Ava and Eli.

Eli and Ava.

Now I'm just Ava.

And I'm terrified. Despite everything we've gone through, I'm afraid to be on my own and do my own thing.

It's almost as if I don't know how.

My experience in Spain was amazing, but I was accompanied by someone the entire time. The host family I lived with had a daughter two years younger than me, and we became fast friends. I also made friends with others who were involved in the study abroad program. We would all see the sights together. I never, ever felt alone, and I was experiencing so many new things, I didn't have time to think. Or worry. Or wonder what Eli was doing without me.

Okay, that last part is a lie. I definitely thought about Eli, and wondered what he was doing. But then I'd shove him out of my head and focus on what *I* was doing and experiencing. I could worry about him later.

Like now. It's all I do. Doesn't help that he pushes himself upon me every chance he can get. It's like he can't leave me alone, and I get it.

Even though he frustrates me and I'd love to sock him in the nuts like I threatened him when he snuck into my room last night, I still can't resist him either.

I'm just as bad as he is.

"…and you never did explain how Eli ended up at your house, you know," Ellie says, her words bringing me back to the present.

I tell her about seeing him at Southgate.

"All the restaurants in town and we both pick that one," I say.

"Not like there are a lot of options," Ellie says.

She's so right. "Is it ever going to hurt less? Seeing him?"

"Yes," Ellie says, her voice soft. "I know it hurts right now and feels overwhelming, but eventually, it's going to lessen, and it'll get easier. And someday, you'll most likely forget all about him."

"Doubtful," I automatically say because I can't imagine ever forgetting about Eli Bennett.

"I know. The fucker," Ellie mutters.

We both laugh at that. Then I change the subject, asking about her podcast. When she was starting out, I was one of her first guests and we had so much fun and talked so much, she had to edit it down from three hours to one, which we found hilarious.

Back when I could laugh easily and was so confident. I was on top of the world and secure in my relationship with Eli. Even when I was down in San Diego and we had the occasional rough patch due to us living so far apart, I never worried about us. We were strong. We could make it through anything.

Everything.

"I'll be at my parents just before Halloween," Ellie says, pulling me out of my thoughts yet again. "Anyone doing anything?"

"If they're not, we should plan something," I suggest, suddenly excited at the possibilities. "We should host a costume party!"

"Where would we have the party? Oh wait…" Her voice drifts and I can tell she's thinking. "I wonder if Jackson's uncle still owns that cabin."

"Oh, no way," I breathe. I can't imagine having a party there again. Talk about a flashback.

"I think he does. Wouldn't it be fun to have a party there?

We had a lot of good times back then," Ellie says, her voice wistful.

"Yeah, you dreamily watching Jackson while he strummed his guitar for his fans," I tease her.

"I was his number one fan though," she says cheekily. "Even back then."

"And especially right now."

"It's still hard for me to believe sometimes that we're actually together and living this—life." She hesitates for a moment. "I'm sorry. I don't mean to rub it in your face or whatever. I'm just really happy."

"And you deserve to be," I tell her gently. "It's okay to express your happiness. You deserve it."

"It was worth it. Sometimes, we have to go through shit to get to the good stuff on the other side," Ellie says, my oh-so-wise friend. "Maybe that's what's happening with you and Eli, Ava. You're going through tough times to get to the good again."

"Yeah. Maybe," I say, but I don't believe it.

I'm starting to think our good times are over.

Forever.

CHAPTER 11

ELI

"Thanks for taking the time to talk to us today, Eli," says our new head coach Jeff Harris. He took over in the summer, and it's been a pretty seamless transition. I'd been worried, at first, that a new coach would fuck up our team mojo, but if anything, Harris seems to have helped it along.

That and my internal rage that pushes me on and urges me to destroy every team we play. That helps a lot too.

"Sure, of course." I settle into the chair on the other side of the table where Coach is sitting. We're in one of the smaller workout rooms that our team doesn't really use. And every single coach on staff seems to be sitting at this six-foot table, all of them smiling at me.

It's kind of intimidating.

"We wanted to talk to you privately and let you know what's going on." Coach settles his clasped hands on top of the table, leaning over it. "Scouts have reached out to us, son."

I frown. "What kind of scouts?"

"The ones who come from the NFL."

"NFL *teams*?" I ask, sounding like an idiot.

"Yeah, of course," Coach says.

"Which ones?" I need names. Facts.

"Like the Ravens and the Eagles and the Falcons."

All bird teams. Huh.

That's kind of weird.

"Other teams too," Coach adds.

I lean back in my chair, taken aback. "Seriously?"

A few of them chuckle. "Seriously," Coach says. "I've reviewed your past tapes, looked over your stats, and compared to last year, you're on fuckin' fire."

I nod, overcome by what they're telling me. My head is spinning with all the possibilities.

NFL scouts? I never believed that was in the cards for me. I was an adequate quarterback in high school, but nothing spectacular. Even though it kills me to admit it, I'm no Jake Callahan. That fucker is an *amazing* quarterback. So was his father. Jake will go on to the NFL for sure, but me?

Nah.

"The office has fielded a few calls," Coach Harris continues. "And there are people coming to watch you at this weekend's game."

Shit, shit, shit.

"We don't want to put pressure on you, Eli," says the offensive line coach. Todd Donovan's been with us since my freshman year and I love this guy. He was a Bulldog back in his day too and he has a special love for the team that no one else on the coaching staff does. He gets us. "Just keep up what you're doing and you'll be fine."

"May I ask you a question?" Harris says.

I sit up straighter at his formal tone. "Sure."

"What's gotten into you this season that has you playing so well?" He squints at me, as if he's trying to figure me out.

Should I tell him the truth? I broke up with my girl-friend and now I'm out to crush anyone who gets in my way on the football field? Because that's the truth. I'm channeling all of my anger into each game and it's keeping me on point.

It's kind of wild. I've always been an emotional player, and usually I let my emotions get the best of me. Last season was a shit show because of it.

This season, though? Once I'm on the field, I'm in complete control of my emotions, my throwing, my accuracy, hell, even my running game is better than it's ever been. I'm stronger, I'm tougher, I'm more focused...

Huh. Maybe having a girlfriend fucked with my head and made me a worse player over the last three years. Now there's something to consider.

Though even I can admit to myself that sounds like a load of horse shit.

"Maturity," is what Todd says, answering for me. His gaze meets mine. "Our boy is a senior. He knows what he's doing out on that field and it shows."

"Thanks," I say, grateful for the compliment.

"You keep this up, I'm thinking you could get drafted," Coach says.

We talk a little more about the possibilities and the potential. There are other teammates of mine mentioned in passing that have NFL interest too, including fucking Diego Garcia, which is unbelievable, but then again not. They've already talked to him about it. They saved me for last.

By the time I'm exiting the room, I'm still in shock, blown away by what the coaching staff told me. The NFL? Really? I can barely wrap my head around it.

And I have no one I can tell. No one to share my exciting news with and celebrate.

My first instinct is to call Ava, but...yeah. No. She's not the first person I run to anymore, and I miss her like fucking crazy, but this is not the way I should approach her.

Not now.

Hmm. My dad? He never answers my calls. Barely responds to my texts. Why set myself up for disappointment?

Mom? She's probably taking a nap, sleepy after a late boozy lunch.

There's only one person who I can reach out to who would understand, but I don't know if he'll actually be interested, let alone if he'll even talk to me.

Fuck it. I text him anyway.

Me: **Can I call you? I have some questions about scouts and the draft.**

I shove my phone back in my pocket and make my way out of the, mostly empty, locker room, disappointed none of my teammates are around. We'll have to get together later so I can tell them the good news.

Man. I shake my head, still blown away. I head outside, grimacing against the dim sunlight, making my way to the parking lot when my phone buzzes.

Nervous, I pull it out of my pocket and check to see I have a notification.

Drew Callahan: **Call me now.**

I fumble with the phone, nearly dropping it before I come to a stop and call my ex-girlfriend's dad. He answers on the first ring, his voice friendly, like it's any other old day and we're talking about football like we always do.

"Hey," I say, hating how nervous I sound. "Thanks for taking my call."

"I only have a few minutes, but what's up?" Drew asks.

"I just talked to my coaches. I, uh, I have interest from the NFL. They think I have a good chance of making the upcoming draft," I explain.

"Eli, that's fantastic. Congratulations." He sounds like he means it too, which makes me feel like maybe my ex's dad doesn't hate me after all.

"Thanks. I, uh, I didn't know who else to call," I confess, withholding the exhale that wants to escape me.

I probably shouldn't have admitted that. I sound pathetic. Like I have no one else. Ava's gone and my friends aren't around right now. They'll be excited for me and we'll probably drink ourselves stupid over it tonight—and for Diego too—but I really need someone to actually *care* about me right now.

In this moment.

Someone who matters to me.

"I'm honored that you wanted to tell me," Drew says, and he sounds like it too. "You're an excellent player, Eli. You've been amazing all season. I'm not surprised you're being considered."

"I'm sure Jake is too," I say, because of course he is.

"Oh yeah. It's definitely happening for him," Drew says, and I can hear the pride in his voice. He's proud of his oldest son, and he should be.

I wish my dad could be proud of me, but he's too busy fucking some random ho he picked up on a dating app to care.

"That's awesome," I say. We hated each other years ago, Jake and me. And he might hate me now after what I did to his sister, but there was a point in my life when I could consider Jake Callahan my friend.

And I liked it. I liked him. I like all those Callahans, damn it.

"Eli, if you ever need to talk, you can reach out to me anytime you want, you got it?" Before I can respond, he continues, "I know you don't have a lot of parental support, and I know you and Ava are—finished, but I'm here for you if you need anything."

"I appreciate that," I tell him, hating how tight my chest feels. Like I could cry or some shit.

And I don't cry. Like ever.

"Anytime," he repeats. "I'm proud of you. You've put in the work, and it shows. I think you're about to be rewarded."

Drew Callahan's words stick with me as I drive back to my apartment. They stay with me as I walk through the parking lot. No one ever tells me I make them proud. Ava would tell me she was proud of me all the time, but that was different.

It's nice to have an adult see your potential. See all the years and the sweat you put into something.

Hearing Drew's praise was the huge boost that I needed— knowing that an adult actually gives a shit...

Means a lot.

Despite everything that's happened over the last few months, I feel pretty good right now.

Actually, I feel on top of the damn world.

The moment I walk into the apartment, I'm greeted by the loud roar of my friends and a couple of teammates. Caleb and Tony are there as well as Diego, who is grinning from ear to ear. A few other guys too, all dudes I've become close with over the last year. They're all congratulating me and squeezing my shoulders. Someone slips a beer into my hand and I chug it, basking in their praise. They're pumping me up and when I lock eyes with Diego, I reach for him and give him a bear hug.

"Excited for you, bro," I tell him when we pull away from each other. "You're on your way."

"So are you," he says with a grin, clanking his beer bottle against mine. "We're on top of our game!"

"Literally," Caleb says with a smile as he slaps hands first with Diego, then me. "You guys are making the rest of us look like chumps."

"Never," I say, and I mean every word. Glancing around the room, I take in the familiar faces of my teammates who've been with me this season. Some I've been with for years. Every one of them in this room I consider my friends. My brothers. "I need every single one of you out on that field. This isn't the Eli show. Or the Diego show."

Diego laughs and points at me. "Hell yeah!"

I can't help but laugh too. We all do.

"We're a team. And we all play an important part. We support each other. We get the job done." I scan their faces, giving a firm nod before I take a giant swig from my beer then hold it above my head as if I'm about to offer a toast. "Now let's celebrate and get fucked up!"

The roar in the room is deafening. Caleb calls in a giant pizza order, my treat. Tony leaves to buy more beer. Diego goes out on the patio to call Jocelyn and give her a better rundown on what's going on.

Nothing might ever come out of this. Our NFL potential could come and go in the blink of an eye, but it's fun to dream. Exciting to think about all the possibilities.

And that's what I'm going to do tonight. I'm going to forget my troubles. Forget my worries. I'm going to get fucking drunk, and I'm going to eat fucking pizza until I feel like I'm going to burst.

Everything else can wait until tomorrow.

CHAPTER 12

AVA

We're at the Bulldog game the Saturday before Halloween and we're actually tailgating. It's me and the girls—Hayden, Gracie and Jocelyn—and my parents, who aren't at Jake's game this Saturday because he has a bye week. Beck and Jos's sister Addison are with us too. I guess they're friends? I don't know what's going on, but I see the way Beck looks at Addie sometimes, and I wonder if he has a little crush.

I'll have to ask him about it later.

Dad doesn't make his beer butt chicken anymore. Instead, we're having Mom's "world famous" (quote from Dad) chicken wings. She marinates half of them in teriyaki sauce and the other half in spicy hot sauce overnight. Then Dad barbecues them, and I have to admit, they smell amazing. Usually I don't like eating wings—a lot of work and mess for little reward—but Dad is so excited for us to try them, I'll do it just to make him happy.

Hayden and Gracie always act a little starstruck around my father. Gracie admitted once she thought he was a total DILF and that's just…ew. I can't imagine my dad with anyone else but my mom. And those two still act like teenagers in love sometimes. When I was younger, I thought it was embarrassing.

Now I watch them and I feel sad. I think of Eli and how he ruined everything.

The jerk.

That I'm here tonight to watch him somehow feels wrong. I should boycott this game. Really I should be at some frat party in San Diego right now with my friends, flirting with a cute boy who won't give me a bunch of shit for my life choices.

But Dad has box seat season tickets and we always have more than enough room in that thing to have lots of people come watch the game. My dad didn't go to Fresno State, but because we live so close, he likes to support the team. Plus, they're a D-1 school and maybe someday Beck will play here. Jake was always meant for greatness. Not that Beck isn't a great player, because he so is. He just has a different attitude about football.

For Jake, it's life. He took it seriously from the time he was six and started playing in the youth leagues. Beck has been playing just as long too, but he doesn't live for it. Not like our big brother.

Eli has much the same attitude as Beck. He could give or take football, though playing for the Bulldogs through the years, I noticed he started to take it more seriously. He's their leader this year, and he's having the best season of his college career, which is perfect, considering he's a senior. I've watched highlights on ESPN and YouTube. The boy is on fire. He's throwing perfect spirals that land most of the time in Diego's outstretched hands and it's truly a sight to witness.

"Do you need any help, Mr. Callahan?" This comes from Gracie, who is currently watching my father with adoring eyes.

Oh boy.

"I'm good, Gracie." He flashes her a smile from over his

shoulder and I swear I just heard her sigh. "And I don't know how many times I have to tell you, but call me Drew."

"Okay—Drew." She giggles.

So does Hayden.

I roll my eyes.

"I think your friends have a crush on your father," Mom whispers to me.

I make a face. "It's kind of gross."

Mom waves her hand. "It's harmless."

"You really don't mind?" I meet her gaze, noticing how unbothered she looks.

"If I had an issue with every woman who's had the hots for your dad over the years, I'd be long gone by now," Mom says with a laugh.

Her confidence in my father is staggering, but then again, it's not; they truly love each other and nothing can keep them apart.

I remember feeling like that with Eli...

My phone buzzes and I pull it out of the back pocket of my jeans to see I have a text from Ellie.

Where are you?

I send her a quick reply.

Me: **Tailgating before the game. Where are YOU?**

Ellie: **Wouldn't you like to know?**

Hmm. What's up with that?

I watch my friends fangirl over my dad while Beck and Addie are making semi-awkward conversation, as Jocelyn looks on with amusement. Mom is going through the food in the giant ice chest that currently sits in the back of her brand-new Range Rover and I go to help her, shrieking when cold fingers suddenly touch my bare arm.

Whirling around, I let out another, much louder scream when I see Ellie standing before me with a giant smile on her face. I pull her into my arms and clutch her close, fighting the tears that want to spill. I can't cry. Not right now. But I'm so happy my best friend is here—it's been months since I've seen her—that I squeeze her extra hard, worried I might never let her go.

"I've missed you," I tell her, my voice shaky.

"Surprise," she murmurs as she gently pulls out of my embrace, though she still keeps hold of my arms. Her smile is kind, her eyes brimming with tears just like mine. "We kept our coming here a secret."

"You suck," I say with a sniff, giving her another quick hug.

"But aren't you glad?" She laughs, wiping beneath her eyes. "We only just got here about an hour ago."

"Did you drive or fly?"

"Drove." Ellie rolls her eyes. "Jackson wanted to go over the Grapevine with the windows down on the Porsche, blasting the radio."

"So old-fashioned," I tease. "Tell me he was at least streaming."

"Nope." Ellie shakes her head. "He wanted the radio on. Said something about keeping it authentic? He's so funny sometimes."

I take a step back, really drinking her in. She's wearing jeans and a navy Bulldogs sweatshirt. Her hair is longer than usual, and the ends are wavy. Her dark brown eyes sparkle and there's a flush to her cheeks. I give her yet another hug. "You look so happy, El."

"I'm really happy." She drops a kiss on my cheek. "You look sad."

"I am," I say, being completely honest. We separate from each other again, though we're still standing close. "It probably wasn't a good idea, coming to this game."

"It'll be fun. We'll all be together, watching the boys. Like old times," she says.

"Right, but now it's my turn to be the one watching the

boy who won't have anything to do with me." I wince. "Sorry. You know what I mean."

Yeah, I'm actually referencing how Jackson used to be. She existed only when it mattered to him. Otherwise, he'd ignore her or just treat her like a friend.

Now though? Their relationship is true goals. He adores her.

I glance around, looking for Jackson, but he's nowhere to be found.

"Where's your boyfriend?" I ask Ellie.

"With the team, can you believe it? The special teams coach always had a soft spot for him and Jackson still has his phone number. He arranged to show up in the locker room as a surprise," Ellie explains.

"I don't know how they let him in. They're usually pretty strict about that stuff."

"When you're a celebrity who used to play for the team, no matter how briefly, I guess they'll let you in." Ellie beams.

Gracie and Hayden join us and they both hug Ellie, all of us chattering and playing catch up with each other. Jocelyn eventually joins our group as well, her little sister tagging along, listening to all of us as we talk about college and men and the future. Addie's eyes get wider and wider the more we say, which is kind of amusing.

"Boys are nothing but trouble huh," she says, after everyone listens to me complain about Eli, and they insert their two cents.

We all laugh.

"They are," her sister agrees. "But some of them are also worth the trouble."

"Sometimes," I add.

Everyone's focus turns to me.

"What's going on with you two anyway? And don't give us a bunch of bullshit," Gracie says. "Caleb says Eli has the NFL looking at him."

I feel like I've been socked in the stomach, I'm so surprised. "Really?" I squeak out.

She nods. "Isn't it awesome?"

"Diego too," Jocelyn adds. "Those two are having a phenomenal season. Scouts are here this weekend. I'm pretty sure they're both going into the draft in the spring."

I'm stunned. Happy for Eli and Diego. Extra happy for Eli, despite everything. But this is the opportunity he never believed he could have. From the time we first started dating, he always said he wasn't going to be a big football star. He loves the game, but he never fully believed in himself.

"That's amazing," I finally say, when it feels like they're all watching me, waiting for my reaction. My gaze goes to Jocelyn. "I'm so happy for Diego. For you too."

"It's exciting," she says with a smile. "But Diego warned me not to get my hopes up. Nothing may come of this, but we both can't help but dream of NFL stardom."

"How is Eli dealing with it?" I ask my friends. Ellie shrugs because, of course, she doesn't know.

The other three women though? They should know.

"Caleb says he's excited," Gracie says.

And that's it. That's all she offers. Hayden and Jocelyn nod in agreement, and then they change the subject.

I can't stop thinking about it though. I go through the motions and fill my plate with food when my parents declare it's ready, but I don't really eat any of it. I sit with Beck and Addie, half-listening to their conversation while my friends all sit with my parents and talk about football, something I'm not interested in discussing.

I just want to sit in my thoughts. Eli's life is moving forward at an accelerated rate while I'm over here stalled. I wish I was celebrating with him. Celebrating him. I can't help but be proud of him.

So proud.

Who's in his corner? His friends, of course. The women

who are with me right now—minus Ellie, who will always, no matter what, be in my corner. Do his parents know and more than that, do they care? What about his brother, Ryan? What does he think? Has Eli told him yet?

Sighing, I get out of my chair without a word to Beck or Addie and make my way over to a garbage can, dumping my mostly full plate of food. Mom spots me, and she must've noticed my plate.

"You weren't hungry?"

I shake my head, saying nothing.

She frowns. "You all right?"

"Did you know about Eli and the NFL?" I blurt.

Her expression barely shifts. "Yes."

I gape at her. "And you didn't think to tell me?"

"I don't know how to bring him up in conversation with you right now," she admits. "And I figured you might not even care."

"My problem is I care too much," I stress. "I wish you would've told me. Gracie mentioned it and I about fell over, I was so surprised."

"He called your father," Mom says, her voice low. "Right after he found out."

"What?" I say it so loudly, everyone swivels their head in our direction. My cheeks turn red with embarrassment, but thankfully they all look away and resume their conversations.

Mom nods. "Your father mentioned it to me that night. I guess Eli had no one else to share it with and wanted to tell your dad."

"Was Dad nice to him?" They haven't always had the best relationship. My father used to actively dislike him. Didn't help, that one time Dad caught Eli in the back yard with me in the middle of the night.

We were young and in love and no one was going to stop us. Not even my father.

Just like with Jake, my father eventually came around. My

mom always had a soft spot for Eli. She likes broken boys though.

And Eli Bennett is definitely a broken boy. He used to be *my* broken boy.

Now I'm the ex who finds out his important life events second-hand.

"Yes, he was nice," Mom answers.

"Huh." I wish he would've called me. I wish I was the first person he wanted to tell.

"Kind of risky, considering how your father feels about him," Mom continues.

"What do you mean by that?"

"Your father doesn't approve of the way he treated you when you went to Spain. I don't either. But he said all of the right things to Eli and told him that he's proud of him. That's all Eli really wanted."

Just as I suspected, Eli still doesn't have any familial support. It's so badly fractured he had to talk to my dad to get an adult's approval.

"Why didn't he tell me?" The moment the words leave me, I feel pathetic. He didn't tell me because we're not together. I don't deserve to know. I'm out of his life, just as he's out of mine. I don't tell him what's going on with me, why should I expect him to let me know about the NFL?

"You're not his girlfriend any longer," Mom reminds me gently. "And you're still mad at him, right? He probably thought you didn't care."

Probably. Has he already moved on? Maybe he just wanted to brag.

See Drew Callahan? I'm worth it. I'm worthy of you and your family. Your daughter. I have potential, even though you never really believed in me.

I can hear Eli say those exact words in my head, though he'd never repeat them to my father out loud.

Bet he thought it though. I know how he works. How he thinks.

I know Eli Bennett better than anyone else on this planet. But I don't have to worry about him anymore. He's not mine.

No matter how badly I secretly want him to be.

CHAPTER 13
ELI

"Eli, you played a fantastic game tonight. This season you've been incredibly consistent. What do you credit that to?" The female reporter thrusts the microphone she's holding into my face, wearing a pasted-on smile.

For about a second, I consider telling her the truth.

I blame it on breaking up with my girlfriend. Really helped me focus on the game instead of worrying about her pretty ass all the time.

Instead, I smile and incline my head toward hers as I say, "I'm having a good season, but it's not all me. We've really come together as a team this year and we're working well together. We've got a rhythm going, but uh, you know." I chuckle, reaching behind my neck to rub it. "I don't want to say too much or I might jinx it."

She laughs, but it sounds fake. "Dreaming about the NFL yet, Eli?"

I hate how she keeps saying my name, like she knows me. She doesn't. "I don't want to get too far ahead of myself."

"The rumors are out there saying you have an excellent chance at being an early draft pick. What do you think?"

Early? I've not heard that word used before. "If that happens..." I shrug. "That would be amazing."

"So nonchalant." She's teasing, but damn it, I don't want to look like an egotistical ass. Which is really saying something because most of the time, I live for this shit.

"Like I said, I don't want to get ahead of myself. I need to stay focused on the team and finish out the season. Right?" I smile, and it's just as fake as hers.

"Of course. Thank you for speaking with me tonight. And congratulations again on the win." She turns to her cameraman and signals him to end it before returning her focus to me. "It wouldn't make you look bad if you spoke about your NFL chances, you know. I could help you get more publicity."

"It's all good," I tell her. "But thanks for the tip."

I turn away from her before she can say another word, irritated. Like that chick could help me. She's some no-count local reporter, how can she help me? If she was from ESPN, then I could at least believe her. Not that I want any 'help'.

Help is never offered for free. They'd want something in return, and right now, I don't want to owe anyone a damn thing.

Curling my fingers through the face guard of my helmet, I keep striding across the field, nodding and smiling at people as I pass them by. Most of them offer their congratulations. A group of girls giggles when I smile at them. A couple of girls from the cheer team approach, their expressions flirtatious, and I humor them for a few minutes, basking in their praise and accepting their invite to a party tonight.

Doubt I'll go, but right now is not the time to discount options. I'm a free agent. I can do whatever the hell I want, with whoever I want, when I want.

Putting a little strut in my walk, I lift my chin at a cluster of people, surprised when one of them darts out toward me, waving her hand so that a man with a giant video camera follows behind her.

That's when I notice the mic she's holding says ESPN on it. I come to a stop, waiting for her to approach.

"Eli Bennett." She smiles. She's a lot more attractive than the other reporter. Her hair is long and dark, and her brown eyes sparkle as she takes me in. "Just the man I was looking for."

I hold my arms out, my helmet still dangling. "I'm all yours."

She laughs. "I'm sure. Have a few moments to speak with me?"

"For you? Anything," I tell her, brimming with confidence.

She asks the same questions as the local reporter, though she's not as pushy. The conversation flows easily, and I give credit to my team, to the coaches, to the entire Bulldog football program. This school should fucking love me come Monday morning. I'm praising them so damn much, I bet the athletic director will jizz in his pants when he sees my interview.

"You're a real team player, aren't you?" the reporter asks when our conversation is over.

"I try," I say with a modest shrug. Even a year ago, I didn't necessarily get it. I was brutal on myself, believing our games rested purely on my shoulders. Mentally beating myself up every time I screwed up, which was often. I had a shit season my junior year because of my behavior, and I was ready to give up on myself and the team.

The one person who convinced me not to was…

Ava.

She's here tonight. I haven't personally laid eyes on her, but Caleb warned me she was coming with her family and the girls. Jackson showed up unexpectedly right before the game, which made my fucking night. He's half the reason I played so damn well. I wanted to look good for him.

And Ava's the other half—I wanted to look good for her too.

I linger on the field for way too long, hoping for a glimpse of Ava or maybe even her father, but I don't ever spot them. I finally give up and head for the locker room, where I'm welcomed with lots of shouting and cursing, Jackson leading the pack, the fucker. He's grinning when I approach him, holding his hand up, which I clasp. Instead of giving him some complicated handshake we made up when we were still in high school, I yank him in for a hug, slapping him on the back.

"What did you think?" I ask after we quickly let go of each other.

"You were on fire tonight," he says with a nod. "No wonder the NFL wants you."

"They don't want me," I say, trying to brush it off. I played well for the scouts too, can't forget about that.

Though I sort of did. Forget about them. I was too wrapped up in Jackson and Ava being here tonight and wanting to impress them.

"Don't give me that bullshit," Jackson says. "They want you. We should celebrate your win tonight."

"What do you have in mind?" I ask warily. Jackson is a partier of the highest degree. The rock-star life is perfect for him.

"There's a party happening after the game. Watson over there invited us." He points at one of the seniors on the defensive line. The guy is as big as a house and stronger than fuck. "His girlfriend is throwing it. I guess she's a cheerleader?"

That must've been the party the other girls from the cheer team invited me to. "If lots of women are there, I'm down."

Jackson laughs. "You looking to get laid?"

"Sure. Yeah." I shrug, hating how the thought of being

with another female, that's not Ava, doesn't appeal to me at all. "I want to celebrate. I've been on the grind all season."

"You've been on the grind the last three and half years," Jackson reminds me. "When was the last time you partied?"

"A couple nights ago," I admit. I got shit-faced drunk that night when I found out about my NFL potential. "Paid the price with a massive hangover the next day too."

"Well, you're not doing shit tomorrow so let's go for it. I'm sure the girls will join us." Jackson pauses, his expression turning worried. "Just Ellie and the rest of the girlfriends."

"No Ava?" I decide to be the one who says her name first. I'm guessing Jackson wouldn't mention her for fear of upsetting me.

"I don't think so. She can go home with her mom and dad." He laughs.

I don't. He shouldn't make fun of her, but I don't call him out for it. Not my place anymore.

"I don't care if she's there." I shrug, trying to play it off.

"You sure about that? I hear she takes the wind out of your sails," Jackson says. "Ellie will want to bring her."

"Ellie can do whatever she wants." My voice is calm.

That's my mode tonight. Calm in the face of Ava.

"All right. Cool." Jackson nods.

"Listen, I don't want Ava ruining my vibe, but if I avoid her, she'll avoid me. We'll be fine." I grab his shoulder and give him a light shake. "I'm on top of the world right now, J. I feel fuckin' good. I had my best game of the season, and people want to talk to me. They keep mentioning the NFL and it's blowing my fucking mind. I just want to bask in this for a while. That's all I'm asking for."

"I get it," Jackson says with a nod. "It's your night, bro."

"Yeah, it is, isn't it?" I smile, but deep inside, I sort of do want to talk to Ava. Feel her out. See what she wants.

See if what she might want is...

Me.

———

By the time we all shower and change, it's nearing midnight when we arrive at the party. We coordinated it so the majority of the team would arrive at the house together and the moment we walk through the door, we're greeted by enthusiastic party-goers, most of them female. I smile and nod as they talk to me. Say thank you when one girl with huge tits brings me a beer, then bats her extra-long fake eyelashes at me.

But I'm just going through the motions. Pretending to be excited when I'm really not.

I find Diego, Caleb and Tony huddled together in the back yard and I immediately go to them, letting down my guard when I settle into a chair and we start talking about the game and who we're playing next week.

"Where are your girlfriends?" I ask them, when there's a lull in the conversation.

They send each other a look before they turn their focus on me.

"Around," Caleb says vaguely.

My gaze meets Tony's, who shrugs. They act like they're hiding something.

Or someone.

If she's here, I think I'd feel it. My Ava senses would be tingling. But I feel nothing at all, which is almost worse. To numb myself further, I drink more beer.

Do shots with a group in the kitchen.

Chat up a few of the newer members of the team, filling them with hope and telling them not to give up. I remember sitting on that bench the majority of my first season and I was nothing but a ball of frustration the entire time.

"It gets better," I tell them, enjoying the way they watch me as if I can do no wrong, hanging on my every word. I remember staring at Ash Davis with the same dumbstruck look on my face. "Stick it out. If you're good, you'll succeed."

I'm buzzing. Feeling high—and I didn't even partake in the blunt a group of dudes was passing around earlier. I'm high on the attention, on the way people who are complete strangers seem to know exactly who I am. It feels good. It's heady shit.

But real life eventually calls.

As in, I gotta take a piss.

Making my way through the house, I find the hallway where I assume the bathroom is. I spot a blonde girl leaning against a wall, her back to me. Her hair is long. Reminds me of Ava's.

Every blonde woman I see reminds me of Ava. This is nothing new.

It's the way she holds herself that's familiar. My gaze drops to her ass and I know in an instant it's my ex.

I'd recognize that ass anywhere.

A groan leaves me, louder than I intended, and she whips around, proving that yes indeed, it's Ava. Her gaze narrows when she spots me and she drops her hands to her sides, her phone clutched in one of them.

"It's you." My tone is accusatory, though I knew she'd show up. I'm just being dickish about it.

"What are you doing here?" Her tone is accusatory too.

We say this at the same time.

Always friendly, aren't we.

"I didn't think you'd show." I point at her.

She frowns. "Well, here I am."

My gaze sweeps down the length of her, lingering on the best parts. "Looking pretty fine tonight, too."

Her lips twist. "Eli."

"What? Just statin' facts." I let my gaze wander yet again. "Don't like me checking you out?"

"I'm not sure how to feel about it." She sounds almost...amused.

And that sounds like progress.

"Why'd you come tonight?"

"Ellie wanted me to." She stands up straighter. "She thinks I need to let loose and have fun."

"I need the same thing," I say, going for the bathroom when the door suddenly swings open and a guy I've never seen before walks out.

"Hey," Ava yells, dashing in front of me. "I was next."

"Gotta move faster than that, babe." I slip into the bathroom before she can and shut the door in her face, twisting the lock extra loud. I laugh when she pounds on the door and then go handle my business, smiling when I hear her call me names through the thin wood of the door.

I really do love a pissed-off Ava. She's fun to mess with.

Once I'm finished and I've washed my hands, singing "Happy Birthday" under my breath, because I know it takes a long time and I'm just trying to piss her off more, I finally go to the door and slowly open it.

She's standing where I left her, looking furious. And gorgeous. She shoves past me and strides inside the bathroom, going straight to the sink and turning on the water.

"You just wanted to wash your hands?"

Ava lifts her head, our gazes meeting in the mirror. "So?"

"Lame," I tell her, thinking she had to pee or whatever. "Now I'm glad I cut in front of your ass."

"You're rude." She soaps up her hands and starts scrubbing them vigorously, like she's going in for surgery.

I ignore her insult. "You like it."

"Not really." She rinses her hands off, her gaze still on me. "You played a good game tonight, Eli."

I try to shrug off the pleasure filling me at her compliment, but I can't. It feels good, that she said something.

"Thanks—why'd you come?" I shut the door when someone approaches, locking it once more.

I don't want anyone barging in on us during what I think could be an important conversation.

"I came with my parents. They have season box tickets." She drops her gaze, watching her hands as she continues to run them under the water. She gives a little jerk and shuts the water off, reaching for the hand towel hanging on the hook nearby.

I approach her, which means I take approximately three steps, since the bathroom is so damn small. I'm standing directly behind her, my body so close it's almost brushing hers and I will her to look into the mirror so our reflections will meet once again. When her gaze finally lifts, I say what's been on the tip of my tongue since she answered me.

"You didn't come to watch me?"

Her green eyes are big, eating me up. My heart is racing. Being close to her always amps me up. More than any alcohol I can drink or any dynamic play I make out on the field. Nothing makes me feel like Ava Callahan does.

Nothing.

"Not really," she whispers, her gaze never straying from mine.

I raise a brow. "Really?"

She rolls her eyes. "Fine. Yes, I came to watch you."

My blood warms and I stand a little taller. "Knew it."

"You're having a terrific season."

"You actually keep track?" I'm surprised.

"I can't help myself. I still root for you out on that field, Eli."

"You don't root for me anywhere else."

Ava's quiet. And I know what that means. She's trying to come up with something to say. Guess I stumped her.

Always used to love it when I did that.

"I heard about the NFL thing," she finally says, bracing

her hands on the bathroom counter in front of her. "Congratu-lations."

A thousand things want to fall off my tongue.

Can you fucking believe it?

I have a real chance, babe. A solid chance of being drafted.

All of my secret dreams are coming true.

I couldn't do any of this without you.

I say none of that. What's funny is she's the reason why I've had such a fantastic season. Losing her helped me focus.

"Thanks," I say, my voice scratchy. I clear my throat, not wanting to seem vulnerable to this girl, who could say a couple of choice words and completely devastate me.

Being in this tiny bathroom with her right now was a bad enough choice. I should probably get the hell out of here.

But I don't. Instead, I settle my hands on her slender shoulders and she does the craziest thing.

Her eyes fall closed and she hangs her head, her hair sliding forward. She doesn't shrug me off or tell me to stop touching her. Swear to fucking God, it feels like she leans toward me, her head swinging my way, though her neck is still bent.

She's not looking at me. Which is good because she'd see shock and pleasure written all over my face, at the same time.

With shaky fingers, I brush the hair away from her face. Drift my fingers across her neck, my gaze snagging on her face. She presses her lips together, just before she turns around and lifts her gaze to mine, those big green eyes taking me in, telling me everything she's feeling without her having to say a damn word.

My mind blanks and my gaze zeros in on her mouth. Those plump pink lips I still want to kiss despite everything we've gone through together.

Big mistake, my brain tells me. *Don't do it. Don't do it!*

Leaning in, I mentally tell my thoughts to fuck right off.

CHAPTER 14

AVA

realize mere seconds before his mouth finds mine that Eli is going to kiss me. And like the weak, pathetic creature I am for him, I don't protest. I don't tell him to stop and I don't push him away.

Nope.

Instead, I pull him in, my arms circling around his neck, my hands sinking into his soft, thick hair. His mouth moves over mine, tasting of beer and harder liquor, though I can't decipher what type exactly. He kisses me in that mind-numbing, body-humming way of his, and I light up like a Christmas tree, eager for more.

I'm so predictable, it's painful.

He doesn't pull away either. I think he's enjoying the kiss as much as I am, and I throw myself into it, pressing my body fully against him, my tongue matching the same rhythm as his. I show a little aggression and he becomes even fiercer, a growl leaving him just before he kisses me like he really means it. He backs me up against the counter, somehow lifting me so my butt is sitting on the edge, my legs falling open as he steps right in between them as if he belongs there.

Eli does belong there. Here. With me. Why do we keep

fighting this? Yes, I'm still upset and frustrated with him, but I can't deny my feelings.

And my feelings are screaming that I'm still in love with this man.

The kiss goes on and on, his hand settling on my hip, keeping me in place, as if he's afraid I'm going to run away. I kiss him hungrily, trying to communicate through my lips that I'm not going anywhere. I'm already exactly where I want to be.

There's a soft knock on the door, but we both ignore it, our mouths too busy to do anything else but continue kissing each other. A whimper leaves me when he breaks away from my lips to trail his mouth down my neck. He licks and nibbles, his other hand shifting, resting on my waist before slowly moving up higher.

Higher.

Until his hand is on my breast, lightly resting there, asking a silent question.

Yes or no, Ava? Can I do this?

I don't pull away. I say nothing. I lean into his palm.

Yes, I say.

Yes.

His thumb drifts over the front of my shirt. My bra. Slowly rubbing back and forth, again and again, making me sigh into his mouth. There are layers between his hand and my flesh and still my nipple hardens. My core tightens.

My body missed him.

There's another knock on the door, more insistent than the last time. I remove my hands from his hair and touch his shoulders, pushing him so he has no choice but to lift away from me, his brows furrowed in confusion.

"We should go," I whisper.

He watches me, his lower lip damp, his tongue sneaking out for a lick and making it shinier. A jolt of lust races through me and my breath hitches.

"You really want to leave?" he asks, the sound of his deep voice settling right between my thighs.

"No." I shake my head, and I'm rewarded for my honest answer with another sweet, drugging kiss.

Now the knocking is nonstop and a male voice booms, "Come the fuck on! I gotta piss!"

Eli pulls away from me, his gaze meeting mine. "You want this?"

What exactly is he referring to? I'm about to ask, but realize we don't have time to pick this moment apart. I go on full instinct, nodding my answer instead.

He offers me the slightest closed mouth smile, one side quirked up. Otherwise, there's no reaction. "Give me thirty minutes."

I frown. "What do you mean?"

"Give us thirty minutes. You go back out to that party and so will I. Talk to someone else. Talk to a bunch of guys, I don't care. See if any of them interest you," he says.

What in the world? "Eli, I—"

He rests his fingers over my lips, silencing me. "Flirt with other guys. Take forty-five minutes if you need it. But don't drink another drop of alcohol. I won't either. Let's see how we feel about each other at the end."

"Give me an hour," I tell him, because I could probably convince myself this is a bad idea in an hour. I could definitely flirt with other guys. Talk to my friends and tell them what's happening—they will talk me out of this, I know they will. Leaving with Eli is a bad idea and I'll end up sabotaging this entire night, like I'm so good at doing lately.

"Perfect. We can set a timer." We both pull our phones out and do exactly that, setting our timers at the same exact time. The guy is still pounding the door, making me feel guilty that we've been in here so long. He must really have to use the bathroom. "Let's go."

We exit the bathroom, the beefy looking guy easing up

when he spots Eli. "Hey man. Sorry to interrupt your hookup."

"No problem," Eli says easily, not bothering to correct him. We walk down the hallway side by side, as if we're still together, and I search the room for my friends, glancing over at where Eli was just standing when I realize he's gone.

Huh. Well, that only took two seconds for him to abandon me completely.

I spot him immediately, not too far from where I'm standing. Surrounded by a group of women, but he's talking to just one.

My heart sinks.

She's pretty. Blonde like me. About my height. She's smiling at him as she talks and he nods at whatever she's saying, appearing completely into her. He never once looks in my direction. The longer I watch, the angrier I get. Not even three minutes ago he had his hands all over me and his tongue in my mouth, and now he's flirting with some random chick.

Fine. Two can play at that game.

I wander around the house, my gaze searching as I seek out a guy. *Any* guy. Preferably one I find attractive, which shouldn't be difficult.

I spot my friends and I wave but don't stop to talk to them. I feel like a shark swimming in the ocean, searching for my next meal. Diego makes eye contact with me when I enter the kitchen and I wave at him but otherwise don't stop to talk to him either. He's with Caleb and Tony and all three of them are looking at me with pity in their eyes.

No thanks. The last thing I need is Eli's 'boys' watching out for their bro and telling me I need to leave him alone.

"Ava."

The voice is deep. Male. He says my name like he knows me and when I glance over my shoulder, I see a guy standing there, leaning against the wall, surrounded by friends. They're all laughing and talking, except for him.

He's watching me.

I turn to fully face him, squinting at his familiar face. Dark brown hair. Handsome, rugged features. Pretty sure I went to high school with him.

"You remember me?" he asks, sounding amused.

His name comes to me from out of nowhere. "James, right?"

He nods and smiles, revealing deep dimples bracketing each side of his mouth. His hair flops in front of his forehead and he sweeps it away, his blue eyes sparkling as he takes me in. He's really cute. "You do remember."

"We went to school together, of course I remember you. You're a year younger than me, right?"

"Yeah. You're not gonna hold that against me, are you?" His smile widens.

I'm actually blushing, and I immediately feel guilty. Why, I don't know. Eli and I are not together. We haven't been for months. Who cares if we just made out in a bathroom? He's the one who wanted to do this in the first place. But why? To test ourselves? To see if what we really want is each other?

God, sometimes he's so frustrating.

"I'm definitely not holding that against you," I tell James, my tone extra flirtatious as I slide in closer to him. I can feel eyes on the back of my head, and I guarantee Eli's friends are staring me down. I hope they go report me talking to this dude. "How are you? I didn't know you were going to Fresno State."

"I didn't know you were going here either," he says, his gaze eating me up, not hiding it whatsoever as he sweeps those blue eyes up and down my body.

"Oh, I don't. I go to San Diego State," I correct him.

"Here visiting for the weekend then?" He lifts a brow.

"I was in a study abroad program over the summer that

ended in September, so I'm taking the rest of the semester off. I'll go back to San Diego in January," I explain.

"Ah." He nods. "You've been hanging out with Bennett then?"

Everyone knew we were together my senior year of high school. I made it super obvious and told anyone who would listen that he was my boyfriend, proud of the fact that I was dating someone older, someone in college. If anyone followed my social media, they'd know I was involved with him the last few years as well. I posted him—and us—constantly. James' assumption makes sense.

"Actually, we broke up," I admit.

"Really?" His expression changes. As if everything just got a little more interesting. "Just to warn you, he's here tonight. I saw him walk in."

"I know," I say with a little shrug, playing it off. "It's fine. We share a lot of the same friends, so I knew we'd run into each other. It was bound to happen eventually."

I'm not about to admit to James that I kissed Eli in the bathroom. He'd walk away so fast my head would spin. And this is what I'm supposed to be doing, right? Flirting with someone else? Testing myself?

I hear familiar laughter coming from behind me and my heart pangs. I know that laugh anywhere. It's Eli. And it is followed by a female laughing too, which makes my heart ache even more.

"You don't have a drink," James says, inclining his head toward my empty hand. His voice is really deep. "You want something?"

I shake my head. "Thanks, but no. I've had enough already."

"It's still early though." He mock pouts. I love how we're talking while surrounded by his friends, who are all too involved in their own little conversations with other people.

"I can't get too drunk," I tell him. "I want to remember tonight, you know?"

He laughs. "I know exactly what you mean, but I haven't hit my limit yet. Come to the back yard with me? I hear there's a fresh keg out there."

"Sure," I say, falling into step beside him once he's pushed away from the wall. We head through the kitchen, my gaze scanning the area, searching for stupid Eli.

I don't see him anywhere.

We stop in the kitchen and James slaps hands with a friend of his. They make easy conversation about the party, the game, the class they share. I stand there essentially ignored and already bored, wondering if I made the right choice.

But then I remember Eli asking me to do exactly this and I realize I need to make the most of this moment. Even though what we're doing makes no sense and I don't even know if we're going to leave this party together or whatever, I'm at a loss.

What do I do now? I'm so out of practice flirting with someone, I feel...inept.

"Ready to go outside?" I ask James when there's a lull in their conversation, flashing him what I hope is a beguiling smile.

"Yeah, let's go." He grabs hold of my arm and steers me away from his friend, who he never introduced me to, by the way, but whatever. We head for the back door and within seconds, we're outside, the cool air washing over me and making me shiver.

There's a cluster of people standing around a keg and we head over to them, me asking questions about people in James' graduating class. He tells me what they're doing now, and the conversation is flowing easily, just like the beer from the keg. James fills his cup and while I wish we were back inside, he doesn't seem in any hurry to get back in there, so I keep up the conversation outside, trying to ignore the cold seeping into my bones.

"You really broke up with Bennett?" James asks me at one point.

Frowning slightly, I nod. "Yeah. I already told you that."

"It's just—he's watching us." He tilts his head slightly to the left. "Don't turn around and make it obvious. He's on the back patio talking to some girl, but he's not listening to her."

"How do you know?"

"He's too busy watching us. You," James stresses before he takes a giant swallow of his beer. "I don't want any trouble."

"You're not in trouble."

"He looks like he wants to tear me apart, and he's a big dude." James sounds the slightest bit scared, the wimp.

Unable to stand it any longer, I glance over my shoulder to find Eli's smoldering gaze on me, his mouth tight, his jaw clenched. A fresh wave of lust washes over me, just seeing the look on his face. Angry Eli is intimidating.

Sexy.

I smile at him. He asked for this. Did he think I wouldn't talk to another guy? If so, he completely underestimated me. Which I think has been his problem for a while. I'm just as stubborn as he is when I want to be.

Like right now.

Eli glowers at me in return, the woman shifting closer to him, her hands moving in tandem with her mouth. She's a very animated talker, but I can tell he's not even listening to her. Just like James said.

He's too focused on me.

She's still talking as he walks away from her without saying anything in return, heading in my direction. I whirl back around, sending an apologetic look at James and he just shakes his head.

"I knew I shouldn't have bothered trying with you. You

two are still wrapped up in each other. It's pretty obvious," he says, and I'm so stinking grateful he doesn't sound pissed, I do something completely impulsive.

I hug James.

"Thank you for being so understanding," I murmur as I pull out of his arms...

And collide with Eli.

"Oh." I glance up at him to see he's glaring at James as if he wants to murder him. My stomach flutters. Clearly, I have issues. "Hey."

"Great game tonight," James starts, but the look on Eli's face shuts him up.

"Keep your fucking hands off her," Eli says fiercely, his wrath aimed at the innocent guy I just hugged.

Maybe I shouldn't have done that.

James throws his hands up in front of himself. "She hugged me first. I'm not interested."

"Keep it that way, asshole," my obviously jealous ex-boyfriend spits out at him.

"Eli," I start, but he turns that glare on me, and I take a step back from the force of it, wary. He must see my wariness because his gaze softens, as does his voice.

"You got a minute?" Eli asks me, not waiting for my answer. He wraps his fingers around the crook of my elbow and guides me away from James.

"What are you doing? Our time isn't up yet," I tell him, wishing I could grab my phone and see how many more minutes we have left.

"I couldn't take it anymore," he says through tight lips, not smiling or acknowledging anyone as we pass by the party goers. Everyone is watching us, which is kind of awkward, so all I can do is smile and wave at the few people I actually do know.

Like my friends who are currently watching us with shock all over their faces.

"Couldn't take what?" I ask.

"Watching you with that asshole," he grits out.

"You're the one who talked to someone else first," I so kindly point out like the mature, responsible adult that I am.

"She called me over. I know her. We have classes together," he says irritably.

I tamp down the jealousy rising within me. "I know James too."

"James." Eli makes a disgusted face, as if the guy's name completely offends him. "How do you know that prick?"

"I went to high school with him. He's a year younger than me."

"Going for babies now, huh? That's just great, Ava."

I jerk my arm out of his hold, suddenly infuriated. "Don't you dare insult me when you're hanging out with groupies, knowing they'd all die for the chance to hook up with you."

He smiles, the asshole, and if I could smack that smug look off his face, I so would.

"You're right. They're all *dying* for a piece of me." He leans in close, his nose almost touching mine. "Except for you. You could give two shits about me."

We glare at each other while standing in front of the door, and I swallow hard. I could walk out of this house right now and never have to deal with him again.

"You're wrong," I whisper harshly. "I'm still in love with you, and that's my problem. You're the one who wanted to pretend we're interested in other people in the first place. This weird, go flirt with other guys for forty-five minutes thing that makes no sense. *You* make no sense, Eli. Why didn't we just leave together after the bathroom? Why did you want to do this? Were you testing me? Is that it?"

Without thought, I place both of my hands on his chest and give him a shove. Of course, he doesn't move a muscle. He's as solid as a tree and that infuriates me even further.

Worse, he doesn't speak. He only stares at me like I've lost my mind.

Well, maybe I have.

"I'm sick of the back and forth. If you still want me, Eli Bennett—" I take a step closer to him and poke him in the chest with my index finger, "fucking prove it."

CHAPTER 15

ELI

I feel like a dick. A jealous, enraged, out-of-control asshole. I had her right where I wanted her. In my arms, in the bathroom, her body pressed to mine. She would've left with me right then, no questions asked.

But I had to go and test her and myself by putting that stipulation on us first. Why the hell did I do that? Why did I torture myself and her too? I thought it would be no big deal, watching her flirt with other guys.

Truly? I didn't even think she'd do it. I was thinking she'd hang out with her friends and wait me out. That was my original plan—to wait this out. See if I still wanted to take her home. If the occasional female approached me, I'd chat her up but never take it too far. I'm not interested in anyone else.

Just Ava.

Then someone had to call me over and Ava witnessed it. I forget sometimes she can be just as stubborn as me. She went right out and found a guy and I couldn't stand it. I showed all my cards with that reaction.

Such a jealous fuck. I can't take it.

"You want me to be real with you?" I ask her.

She frowns, nodding slowly. "For the love of God, *please*."

"You're right. I was testing you."

"I knew it." Her eyes narrow and she crosses her arms. "Did I fail?"

"No, you passed with flying fucking colors." I contemplate her, drinking in her beauty and her anger and everything that makes her the Ava I love so damn much. I've got nothing to lose, so I'm shooting my shot. "Come home with me."

My heart stops. If she so much as hesitates—

"Yes," she says, without any hesitation whatsoever. "Let's go."

I take her hand, lacing my fingers with hers, and we exit through the front door. Race down the walkway and hit the sidewalk that lines the street, our steps brisk. We don't look at each other. She doesn't say a word, and neither do I, because I'm fucking overcome right now. She said yes.

She's leaving with me.

It feels like it takes ten years to get to my car, especially since we're still not talking, both of us too intent on arriving at our destination. I unlock the doors with my key fob, opening the passenger door for her like a fucking gentleman. She climbs in, without a word, and I shut the door, afraid to look at her face. Worried I'll see disgust or regret written all over it.

I don't think I could take that.

Rounding the front of the vehicle like the road is on fire, I slip into the driver's seat in seconds, breathless. I can feel her eyes on me as I lean toward the dash to start the car, and that's when she comes at me.

Next thing I know she's straddling my lap and I'm scrambling, reaching for the side of my chair to push the seat back, her lips crashing on mine, her hands cupping my face, keeping me still as she basically devours my mouth. I let her take complete control, my hands slowly going to her waist and pinning her in place, afraid she might run.

I don't think I could take it if she ran. Or told me to stop.

She throws herself into the kiss, her lips insistent, her tongue wrapping around mine. She grinds that fine little body of hers against me, and I can feel the heat of her pussy pressing against my dick, even through her jeans and mine. In seconds, I'm hard as a rock and dying to get inside her, but I can't push. I can't rush.

I want to savor her. I want it all.

"You are so infuriating," she whispers against my lips right before she nips at them. "Seriously, Eli. Why are you like this?"

"It's my natural charm." I can't help but joke, even during such a serious moment. More than serious.

This moment could be life-changing.

Her fingers slip beneath my sweatshirt and graze my stomach, the lightest touch setting me on fire. "Baby, slow down," I tell her when those hands slip lower, her fingers playing with the button on the front of my jeans.

"No," she whispers as she undoes the button, then gently pulls down the zipper. Fuck, her fingers are so close to my dick, I'm afraid I'll come if she so much as barely touches me. "Do you want to do—this in the car?"

"Do what? Fuck?" I toss the harsh word out on purpose to gauge her reaction.

Will she be offended? Old Ava wasn't fazed by my filthy mouth whatsoever, though I never brought it to its full potential when we were naked.

Major regret.

Her eyes flare with heat and she brushes her mouth lightly against mine, her lips tickling me when she speaks. "Is that what you want to do? Fuck me in your car, Eli?"

Both of my hands are on her ass as I pull her in close, letting her feel exactly what she's doing to me. "What do you think?"

She reaches inside my jeans, her fingers brushing against

my dick. "I think you should quit talking and start fucking, if you want this to happen."

What the hell?

Realizing she means business, I stop talking and get down to it, just like she said. She helps me along, shoving my jeans down before she slips her hand into the front of my boxer briefs. Her fingers curl around my erect cock and she gives it a squeeze, nearly making my eyes cross.

I kiss her, fumbling with her jeans until I've got them shoved down far enough that it becomes incredibly awkward. She removes her hand from my boxers and takes care of them, discarding the jeans onto the floorboard of my car before she thrusts her face in mine once more. "Maybe we should take this to the back seat."

"It'll be uncomfortable," I warn her.

"For you. I'll be fine." She smiles. "Fuck me in the car or let me go forever, Bennett."

Damn, this girl. What is she saying? Let her go forever?

Fat-fucking chance of that ever happening.

"I'll make it work." I drop little kisses along her slender neck, her skin breaking out in tiny goosebumps. "I'd do just about anything to get inside you."

She rises up, resting her hands on my chest, sitting right on top of my dick. Her hair is mussed and her eyes are heavy as she watches me, licking her upper lip. I watch her, completely entranced.

I've missed her so damn bad. More than I even wanted to admit to myself.

"Anything?" She raises her brows as she slides her hands under my hoodie once more, trailing her fingers along my stomach. "Would you get naked for me in the front seat of your car?"

I glance out the window, my heart racing. No one's around at the moment. "Take it off," I tell her, as I meet her gaze once more, waving at my sweatshirt.

She pushes the fabric up, revealing my abs. My chest. I lift my arms, and she tugs the hoodie up and over my head, taking my T-shirt along with it before she tosses both items toward the back seat, landing God knows where. Her gaze roves across my shoulders and chest, lingering on my abs. "You look more muscular."

"I work out a lot more," I tell her, distracted by the feel of her pussy pressed against my dick. Her panties are thin. Black. My fingers itch to slip inside and test her. See how wet she is.

I bet she's fucking soaked.

"This is probably a mistake," she murmurs, just before she leans over me, her mouth finding mine. She sucks on my lower lip, my dick growing harder with every pull of her mouth, I swear to God. "I shouldn't fuck you. My friends say you don't deserve me."

The mistake remark hurts, more than I want to admit, even to myself, but I say nothing. Just bury my hands in her hair and pull her mouth closer to mine.

"But I've missed your hands on me, Eli," she continues, a hiss leaving her when I remove my hands from her hair and grip her heart-shaped ass. "Oh God, I could probably come like this."

I shift her back and forth across my cock, creating friction. She moves her hips, pressing downward as a gasp escapes her. Her thighs squeeze and I lift up at the same time I pull her downward.

We're basically dry humping in the driver's seat of my car. Someone could catch us at any second. I look out the window once more, realizing just how on display Ava is while I'm lying back in the seat and no one can really see me.

"Let's take this back here," I mutter, indicating to the back seat with my head.

She shakes her head, her hips still rolling. "Not—" her breathing hitches, "—yet."

Oh fuck. She's getting off on me. Like, actually getting off. I rest my hands on her hips and help her move, watching as she leans her head back, exposing her throat, her hands braced on my chest.

So hot.

"I'm—oh God." A jolt seems to run straight through her and her body shakes, an agonized moan falling from her lips. I hold her tight against my erection, surprised she came so fast.

Can't help but be a little impressed.

Ava lifts her head and opens her eyes, smiling lazily down at me. "I just came."

"I know."

"It wasn't a very big one." A shiver steals over her. "But it was good."

"I can make you come harder," I say, my voice laced with promise.

She continues to move, her hips slowly rolling back and forth. "Really?"

"You doubt my abilities? I've given you multiple orgasms over the years," I remind her. "But we need to get in the back seat. Anyone could see you, babe."

"No one's paying attention to me." She leans in and brushes a kiss against my lips. "Except for you."

The kiss turns filthy in an instant. Sloppy. Our tongues tangle, my fingers slipping beneath her panties, so I can touch her bare ass. She groans into my mouth and I break away from her first, my breathing ragged. "Back seat," I demand.

She climbs off of me and practically throws herself back there. I follow after her, my intent clear as I grab her by the waist and roll her over so she's facing me. Her eyes are huge as she stares up at me, her breathing rapid, her cheeks flushed from the earlier orgasm. "I like how bossy you are."

"Really?" I lift a brow.

Ava nods and reaches out, her fingers curling around the

open flap of my jeans, her knuckles brushing against my dick. "It's hot."

Hmm. Interesting.

"Take the panties off," I tell her, my voice firm. I usually prefer taking them off for her, but it's been a while and I'm down for changing our normal routine.

Her eyes flare with heat as she reaches for the thin waist-band of her panties and slowly pulls them down, lifting her butt, tugging the thin black fabric down her thighs. Over her knees. Falling down her calves until they stop at her feet. She already took her shoes off earlier, and she slips off her socks, then starts to kick off her panties. I reach for them at the last second, pulling them off and bringing them to my nose.

Like a sick fuck, I inhale, her familiar scent hitting my senses like a punch to the gut. She smiles, shaking her head.

"Eli," she says softly.

"Ava," I return, hovering above her, discarding the panties. She's still got her sweater on but nothing else. And the sweater is so long I can't really see anything, but I can smell her. I tug on the hem, suddenly impatient. "Take this off."

CHAPTER 16

AVA

He's different. Moodier. The demanding thing is new and super-hot. Everything about him is hot tonight. From the gleam in his hazel eyes that are greener than usual, to the determined set of his jaw. His mouth that can say the worst things but then kiss me so softly, I almost want to cry.

"Ava." His deep voice is full of command. "Take it off."

I sit up, my body brushing his, his breathing becoming deeper as I reach for the hem of my sweater and pull it up, then over my head, tossing it aside. Next, I reach behind me, my eyes never leaving his as I undo the snap of my bra and rid myself of it. Until I'm sitting completely naked in the back seat of his fancy car, breathless with anticipation over what he might do to me next.

Of course Eli doesn't disappoint. He steals a kiss, leaving me breathless as he runs his mouth down my neck. Across my chest. His tongue and lips are hot, setting my skin on fire and I run my hands down his back, marveling at the muscle I feel shift beneath my palms. When his lips find my nipple, I whimper, melting into the seat when he pulls and tugs on it, just before sucking deep.

I've missed this so much. I've missed him just as much. That we're doing it in the back of a car is so unlike us. Yeah, we did that sort of thing in high school, but we gave it up once we were out on our own.

But why? I know it's uncomfortable and awkward, but it's also hot and exciting and thrilling. Just like his mouth as he slides farther down, his knees hitting the floorboard as he runs his warm lips across my stomach. Lower.

Lower still.

All the air sticks in my throat when his big hands smooth over the top of my thighs before going inside and spreading them wide.

Oh shit.

And when his mouth drifts even lower, his lips finding me where I'm wet and ready, I lift my hips. Slide my hands into his hair and hold him to me.

Swear to God, he chuckles, as if he knows I might murder him if he leaves this spot.

He laps at my flesh with his tongue, searching, finding all the spots he knows will set me off. His tongue slides across my clit, setting off a fresh dose of sparks cascading through my body. I close my eyes and throw back my head, trying to get into a more comfortable position, but fuck it.

His mouth works me over. When he slips a finger inside of me, I moan. When he starts working the finger in and out of me, I may as well just give up and die, it feels so damn good.

He whips me into a frenzy in a matter of minutes. Until I'm a gasping, shaking mess, begging him to never stop. He says nothing. Just makes encouraging noises and growls against my flesh, which feels amazing. I figured since I already came, it would take a while, but nope.

I'm coming again. My limbs shaking as my brain goes completely blank and I'm lost to the sensation of his lips sucking my clit, his fingers fucking me as wave after wave of pleasure washes over me.

Jesus God, if I end up in heaven, at least I went with a smile on my face.

His mouth gentles as the tremors slowly subside, as if he knows it'll be too much for me if he continues. Which he does. He knows me so well.

Better than anyone else on this earth.

"Baby," he murmurs against my thigh, just before he drops a kiss there. "That was fucking hot."

I can't speak. My eyes pop open and I stare up at the ceiling, trying to control my breathing. My body. But it's as if my bones have turned to liquid and I can't move. I can't even remove my hand from his hair. I thread my fingers through the silky strands when he lifts his head, and I can feel his gaze on me.

Finally, I turn my eyes onto him, breathless at the expression on his face. The way his lips shine from just going down on me. The sweat clinging to his forehead. I offer him a small smile and it's as if it spurs him into action.

He yanks down his jeans, kicking his shoes off before he can get rid of everything. The boxers are next—black and designer, of course. His cock is huge and my gaze drops to it, my eyes widening the longer I stare at it.

Damn. It's bigger than I remember. It's been a while since we've been together and I worry—

"Come here." His voice is soft. Sexy. I rise up and go to him, letting him pull me onto his lap, his arms going around me and holding me tightly so we're skin on skin. He's so warm and firm everywhere and I briefly rest my hands on his shoulders, his erection poking at my ass. "Put my cock inside you."

My clit actually tingles from the underlying command in his tone and I tilt my ass up, grabbing hold of the base of his erection at the same time, positioning him before I slowly lower myself onto him until he's fully seated inside of me.

We remain still, staring into each other's eyes, our chests

brushing, our mouths so close I can feel his breath waft across my face. "Ava…"

I press my mouth to his before he can say anything else. Whatever he was going to say, I don't want to hear it. Not yet. Not now. His words…

They scare me.

I communicate with him with my mouth. My tongue. My body. I start to move, riding him, lifting until he almost slips out before I slide back down, engulfing him completely. It's awkward in the car, but it doesn't feel awkward with him. He's the only boy I've ever been with. The only one who's touched me like this.

Fucked me like this.

Is it easier to think of it as fucking? If describing what we're doing in more intimate terms, does that make it somehow more meaningful? I can't put too many expectations on this moment. That'll only make it more devastating when he disappoints me.

And knowing Eli, he will eventually disappoint me. By something he says, or the way he reacts.

Right now, though, he's not disappointing me at all. It feels so good, his thick arms around me, his thick cock inside of me. Driving me wild. We might be mad at each other and can't come to terms about what happened to break us up in the first place, but when we're like this together, we're perfect.

"Fuck," he whispers against my lips when I come down hard on him, taking his erection as deep as I can. He slips his fingers into my hair, tugging on it, making me wince. "Faster baby. Ride me."

I increase my speed, our sweaty skin slapping, the scent of sex filling the car. We're both completely naked in the back seat, and I swear to God, I hear a group of people walk by, their muffled conversation sounding like they're right outside the BMW.

My movements still, but Eli's not having it. He guides my

hips with his hands, urging me to continue and I lean in close, my mouth at his ear. "Someone's right outside," I whisper.

He stops moving, his eyes cracking open as he turns his head in the direction of the people standing outside his car on the sidewalk. "The windows are tinted. They can't see inside."

"They might hear us." He lifts his hips, nudging a spot deep inside me that has my eyes falling closed, a dizzying wave of pleasure crashing over me. "Stop."

"You don't want me to stop." He thrusts. "You want me to keep." Another upward thrust. "Going."

Every time he does that, he hits something deep that has me seeing stars. I wrap my arms around his neck and tip my head down, my mouth finding his as we start moving in tandem once more. The car might be rocking. Eli is groaning. Can those people outside hear us?

I don't even care anymore.

Their voices drift as they walk away and that's when we start fucking in earnest. It's a race to see who comes first. I'm guessing him since I've already had two orgasms, but I can already feel another one forming, everything inside of me tensing up in anticipation. It's going to be good. Sooooo goooood…

Eli grabs hold of me tightly, a moan sounding deep in his chest as he starts to come. Mine follows soon after his, my pussy milking him, wringing out his orgasm even more until we collapse on top of each other in a heap, his face buried in my chest, mine pressed in his hair.

We sit like that for a while, the only sound, our harsh breaths. My heart feels like it's going to pump out of my chest and when I finally crack open my eyes, I stare out the back window, grateful to see no one around.

"Uhhh…"

I frown.

Something about Eli's voice sounds all wrong. Like, terribly wrong.

"We probably…"

I pull away from him slightly to see his face.

He won't even look at me.

My heart drops.

"We probably what?" I ask quietly.

"Maybe we shouldn't have done that?" His gaze finds mine, and he winces.

The motherfucker actually *winces.*

I pull off of him, ignoring the sensation of semen spilling down my thighs. Ignoring the sympathetic look on his face. Immediately wishing I could forget this entire encounter. If I could punch him, I would.

I would! Right in that smug, beautiful face of his.

"You're a dick," I say through clenched teeth as I reach for anything I can pull on to cover myself. I feel naked. Vulnerable. Shaky.

Should've known this was going to happen.

"What are you doing?" he asks.

Ignoring him, I stumble upon his hoodie first, so guess what?

I steal it, yanking it over my head, grateful it covers most of my body, it's so large. Smells just like him too, which is distracting and annoying.

"Come on, Ava. You have to admit what just happened was pretty—impulsive. And we're not even together anymore."

I stare at him, incredulous. I thought this was our shot to get back together. He's the one who asked me to leave with him. I believed he was going to apologize and we could've continued on. A couple once again. Eli and Ava.

Ava and Eli.

"You were never going to apologize, were you?" I ask, my voice deadly quiet.

He should be careful right now. How he answers could make everything worse, or better.

"Apologize for what?" he asks with a frown.

A sigh leaves me. Eli is *never* careful. That's what I both love and hate about him.

I'm such an idiot. Seriously. He probably just used me for sex. That's it. He doesn't want to be with me.

Not really.

"I'm wasting my time." I spot my phone lying on the floorboard and snatch it up. Find my Vans and slip them on my feet. Forget the socks and my jeans and my sweater and the bra. Though I do wish I had my underwear, at least. "Where are my panties?"

He glances around, still sitting there naked, his cock at half mast, like he could be raring to go again in a few minutes. The guy always had terrific stamina. "I don't know."

"Last time I saw them you were *sniffing* them." My voice drips with disgust. It's my turn to grimace as I scan the car one last time. "Forget it. I don't need them. I'm out."

"Ava." He grabs my hand just as I go to open the back door and I turn to glare at him and his stupid pleading face. "Don't leave. Talk to me."

"There's nothing to say. You think what just happened was a *mistake*." Heavy emphasis on the last word out of my mouth.

"You're the one who said that first," he reminds me.

"Well, clearly you agree," I retort, hating that he threw my own words back in my face. I guess it's what I deserve.

"Hear me out." His fingers tighten. "You can't go outside like that. You don't have any clothes on. Let me drive you home. We can talk on the way."

"No. There's nothing left to say. Besides, I have this." I jerk out of his hold and tug on the hem of his hoodie. "It's the least you could give me after such a shitty night."

I open the door, the blast of cool air coming in making me

shiver. I climb out of the car and slam the door before he can say or do anything else. Though I don't know what he could do, considering he's buck naked.

A cackle leaves me and I can't help it. I'm laughing as I launch into a jog, the air whooshing straight up the oversized hoodie, extra cold on all my damp parts. I run toward the house where the party is still happening, reaching inside the hoodie's front pocket to pull my phone out. Pausing, I type out a quick text and shove my phone back into the pocket before I hurry toward the house, the laughter long dying on my lips.

When I feel the wetness dripping down my face, I realize I'm crying. The tears are flowing nonstop, extra cold thanks to the wind. A sob escapes my mouth and I press my hand to it, throwing my head back and squeezing my eyes shut.

Squeezing out a few more tears too.

I hear someone say my name. A female someone. I don't move, a gasp leaving me when I feel a set of arms wrap around me. Then another. And another. It's as if I'm being gently tackled on all sides.

It's my friends, and they've formed a circle around me. I can't tell who's who at first but when I finally open my eyes, I see each of their faces. The concern etched in them.

"What did that asshole do?" Ellie asks, her voice the fiercest I've ever heard it.

I shake my head, unable to find any words.

A collective disappointed sigh leaves the group and I hiccup a sob, so grateful for these women.

I need them now more than ever.

CHAPTER 17

ELI

The moment the ball is hiked to me, I'm looking everywhere. Left. Right. Left again. None of my receivers are open. And defense is running toward me, feral expressions on their faces as they draw closer.

I panic in my hurry to get rid of the ball.

"Fuck," I bite out, throwing the ball too wide. It lands in Caleb's hands as if that was meant to happen.

The problem is he's currently playing on the defensive side while we practice. Someone knocks into him, taking him to the ground, but I can hear his laughter. Hate how he pops back onto his feet as if it's no big deal.

"That was shit, Bennett," he calls, the smile on his face way too big. "I just intercepted your ass."

"Again," someone else pipes up.

I give the whole lot of them the finger, disgusted with them.

Disgusted with myself most of all.

Despite it being the end of October, we're experiencing a weird, yet not so weird heatwave this week. California weather is so freaking unpredictable, and the high today was predicted to be ninety degrees. With the way I'm currently sweating, I don't doubt that temp at all.

It's a couple days before Halloween for the love of God. This is all kinds of fucked up.

What else is fucked up? My throwing arm today. I can't get it right. After being on top of my game all season, throughout every practice and game, I'm playing terrible. Like some sort of fumbling rookie who's terrified of his own shadow.

Maybe it's because I didn't sleep well over the weekend.

Or maybe it's because I spent most of Sunday afternoon working on a fucking paper that was due today.

I try not to let myself think about Ava or the fact that we had sex for the first time in months, and how great it was…

Until it wasn't.

I haven't had sex with freaking anyone since that last weekend in February we were together, and I've been playing great ever since.

Is *sex* ruining me? Is sex with Ava the issue?

I shove that crazy thought out of my head as I stride off the field, ignoring my team's razzing and insults. I know they don't really mean it. They're just giving me shit.

But their words ring in my head and make everything worse, swear to God. I can't let them get to me. Even more, I can't let them know they're getting to me. Then they'll never let up.

"You all right?"

I turn to find Diego approaching me, his expression concerned.

"I'm great," I grit out before I whip my helmet off and drop it on the ground. I really want to throw it down the side-lines, but the coaches don't approve of violent outbursts. If they let it happen during practice, we're more likely to do it during games and we could get in trouble.

"Really?" Diego scratches his chin. "You're kind of a mess today."

"No shit?" I send him a wide-eyed look. "More like I suck complete ass."

"Something bugging you?"

It's his tone. The way he's looking at me. I get the sense Diego knows exactly what's bugging me. Not that I'm going to mention it to him. Not out here during practice.

After Ava fled the back seat of my car Saturday night in just my hoodie, I sat there for a few minutes, naked and stunned. Then I pulled on my clothes, jumped into the driver's seat and got the hell out of there before anyone came out to find me. Ended up lying awake in my bed for hours after I got home, reliving the moment with Ava. How good it felt with her, how fucking right we are together.

How I freaked out immediately after it happened, afraid she might be full of regret once she realized what we did, and how I decided in a millisecond to beat her to the punch. She's the one who told me it was probably a mistake, and that word kept repeating in my head, over and over again. Even while I was fucking her.

That's why I said all that bullshit about how we shouldn't have done it. Was it a dick move?

Hell yes, but I've been known for making dick moves here and there. It shouldn't have surprised her.

But it hurt her. More than I thought it would. Worse, it made her mad. Really mad.

What I said ruined any progress we might've made before that. That's why I couldn't sleep. That's why I wrote a shit paper. That's why I can't throw a ball to save my life today. I fucked up and I know it, and I don't know how to fix it.

Haven't mentioned shit to the guys either, but I'm thinking Diego knows what's up. Which means all those dick-heads know what's up. And they probably think I'm a giant prick, thanks to their girlfriends calling me every name in the book.

I suppose I deserve the name-calling. The hate and the wrath. I'm an insensitive asshole. It's like I can't help myself.

"I'm sure you already know what it is," I say to Diego, annoyed when one of the coaches calls a water break.

That means I have to talk to Diego even longer. With my luck, Tony and Caleb might join us. Sounds like a good time.

Not.

"Jocelyn mentioned something to me, but she didn't go in to too much detail," Diego says.

I turn to see Caleb making his way toward us. "Gracie told me that you fucked Ava in the back seat of your car and then told her it was a mistake."

I scowl. "Say it louder. I don't think the entire team heard you."

Caleb grins, the fucker. "I could scream it if you really wanted me to." He cups his hands around his mouth, like he's actually going to do what he just said, but Diego smacks one of his arms down. "Ow. I was just fuckin' with him."

"I don't think he's in the mood to be fucked with," Diego says, his expression serious. "Unless it's with Ava."

The devilish smirk that curves his lips reminds me of the Diego of old. When he was a real asshole and no one liked him. Not even his best friend, Jake.

"Don't talk about her like that," I snap at him.

Caleb sends Diego a look. "Yeah, bro. Show some respect."

"Says the dick who can't keep his mouth shut," I mutter, my anger now focused on Caleb. "How about we don't talk about her at all?"

"How about you figure out what your problem is, and why you're playing so shitty?" Caleb throws back at me, Diego nodding in agreement. "That girl walks back into your life and throws you completely off balance."

Caleb's not wrong, as much as I hate to admit it. I'm really starting to think the problem is…

Ava.

Which is stupid, I know it is. I need to get my shit together and stop making excuses.

Tony approaches us, his expression thunderous. "Leave him alone. Seriously, you two assholes need to take a hike." He jerks his thumb over his shoulder and like a pair of kids who just got busted, Caleb and Diego stomp off, sending matching, sullen glares in my direction as they glance over their shoulders.

"Please tell me you're not going to rip into me," I say, hating how whiny I sound, but shit. I don't think I can take a lecture right now.

"I'm not." Tony's voice is firm, but there's genuine concern in his gaze. Doesn't seem like he's here to give me a bunch of shit. "You seem to be struggling."

"You don't need to sugarcoat whatever you have to say. I'm sure Hayden filled you in on what happened between Ava and me Saturday night." I throw it right out there so neither of us has to pretend.

Tony winces. "She mentioned a few things. Didn't go into too many details."

"You don't know about that mole at the base of my dick then?" I squint at him, mentally daring him to keep a straight face.

Tony's always been a tough nut to crack. He doesn't so much as offer up a smile. "I don't know those intimate details, no."

"Whew." I mock wipe sweat off my forehead. "Thank God."

"Listen, you can act like this is a big joke to those other assholes, but I can see you're hurting. You don't have to pretend with me," Tony says, taking a step closer. "I know we haven't always seen eye to eye in the past, and we've never been that particularly close compared to the other guys, but I'm worried about you. And I care a lot about Ava. I've known her a long time."

"I'm worried about her too," I admit, my voice lowering. "I fucked it up royally with her Saturday night. That was the last thing I meant to do."

"When you left the party with her, what was your plan?" Tony asks.

"I don't know." I shrug, defensive. "Get her back to my place and get her naked?"

Tony doesn't say a word. Just crosses his arms and waits me out.

It's unnerving.

"I had no plan," I admit, throwing my hands in the air. "I didn't know what I was going to say or do. I was just fucking thrilled she left with me."

"She wanted an apology."

"Still? I thought we were past that." And why didn't she say so?

"Are you?" Tony arches a brow.

"Yeah. Yeah, I am past it. Even though she didn't choose me. No one *ever* chooses me," I say, frustration making my voice raspy.

Or maybe that's emotion. I don't know.

A whistle blows. Back to practice we go.

"We're not finished with this conversation," Tony says, once I grab my helmet and we're jogging back out onto the field. "Let's go grab a beer somewhere after practice. Or dinner. We can talk some more."

"Fine," I mutter under my breath.

Blah blah blah. He'll want to talk about our feelings— excuse me, *my* feelings. Tony shouldn't get a business degree. He should become a damn therapist. This guy is always trying to fix everyone.

Maybe that's why I've kept my distance from him. I don't

dislike Tony. He's a stand-up guy. Great football player. Solid friend, though he's right. We've never been particularly close. Out on the field and with the team, he's got my back and I've got his. But those probing dark eyes of his sort of freak me out, and I'm not looking for a confessional.

I can deal with my own fucking problems, thank you very much.

The rest of practice goes by in a blur. I continue to play terribly. To the point Coach pulls me off the field and puts in the second string. "Just to see what he's got," Coach tells me, his tone reassuring.

Marshall Hatfield has a tremendous arm, and he shows it off like any second string would when offered the chance to step up. The guy throws an eighty-yard pass on his first play. Everyone claps and whistles.

I sit on the bench like a pouty baby, scowling as I kick my helmet. Hating the world.

Tony just shakes his head every time he glances in my direction. Diego and Caleb steadily ignore me. I think I scared them.

Good. They're supposed to be my friends. And friends aren't supposed to make you feel shitty.

By the time we're long finished with practice and we're done showering, Tony approaches me, his damp hair hanging across his forehead and practically covering those all-knowing eyes of his.

"You ready?"

I shut my locker door before turning to face him. "Where are we going?"

"Pizza? Doghouse? I don't care." Tony shrugs. "I'll drive if you want."

"How about I follow you."

We decide on pizza—Doghouse Grill will just bring us unwanted attention since so many Fresno State students go there, especially on me. And I'm not saying that to brag.

Everyone knows my face in this area, if not the whole damn town, and people will approach me. Ask questions about the team, the season, my future prospects. It's happened before, and usually I revel in it.

I'd rather be anonymous tonight. And I think Tony senses that.

Once we arrive at the restaurant, we walk in together and I'm glad to see it's mostly empty. We give our order, splitting a pitcher of beer, and once Tony pays—what a guy—we make our way over to a table in the farthest, darkest corner of the place. Tony sets the pitcher carefully onto the table while I plunk down the glasses.

"Hatfield looked pretty amazing out there," Tony says, after we sit down and he starts pouring me a glass of beer.

Great way to start the conversation. Like rubbing salt in an open wound.

"He'll do great next season," I say as casually as I can.

"It's okay to have an off-day." Tony pushes the full mug of beer toward me. "You're allowed one every once in a while."

"I can't afford them." I take a drink of beer and slurp up nothing but foam, grimacing.

"You put too much pressure on yourself."

He's just preaching to the choir.

"Everyone's looking at me right now. Just waiting for me to fuck up. Then they can point their fingers and say, 'See, I told you so. He's a fluke.'" I shake my head. "I know how the so-called fans think."

"You are so bitter today," Tony marvels. "I prefer egotistical Eli to everyone hates me, I want to die Eli."

"Trust me, I prefer that version of myself too," I mutter.

"You two need to just talk it out." When I send him a questioning look, he continues, "Ava. You need to talk to her."

"I don't know what to say." I glance down at the old, scarred wooden table, my vision growing hazy, my thoughts full of the beautiful green-eyed girl who's turned my world completely upside down. I miss her. I'm furious with her. I love her. I don't want to look at her.

It's confusing as hell.

"I don't know what to do. Every time I open my mouth, I ruin it. No one's on my side. They're all on Ava's. Even you guys," I say miserably.

Tony sighs. "Look, regarding Caleb and Diego. All this trouble between you and Ava reminds them of high school. When it was very much an us versus you mentality. Don't forget, we were all Jake's friends first. You mess with Ava, you mess with us too. That's how we used to roll."

"That's how you guys *still* roll." I curl my hand into a fist and lightly tap the edge of the table. "I've lived with Caleb the last couple of years. He's one of my closest friends. And that guy is still going to take Ava's side over mine, thanks to his friendship with Jake."

"He was just giving you shit." Tony brushes it off, waving his hand. "Don't let him get to you."

"That guy is full of golden advice when he wants to give it." It's surprisingly true. I've heard many a wise word fall from Caleb's lips, but not lately.

"Right. But he can also be an idiot who says whatever comes to him at any given moment. Don't let him bring you down. And don't think he doesn't have your back. He does. We all do." He pauses. "Even me."

I decide to be brutally honest. "Feels like it was difficult for you to say that."

"It wasn't." He runs a hand through his hair, pushing it off his forehead. "I like you, Bennett. But more than anything, I *respect* you. You did a complete turn-around this last year. You went from being an emotional player who let every little thing get to you, and turned yourself into a focused QB with solid leadership qualities. The team admires you. They want to please you like you're our dad or something, and it's pretty incredible."

I just stare at him, trying to wrap my head around what he's saying.

"You're having an off moment, and you're letting all of those emotions get in your head again." He taps his temple with his index finger. "Everything's living right there, messing with your focus. Your game. What's going to fix it?"

"I was starting to think having sex with Ava was fucking with my game." The words fall from my lips without thought. "I mean, look at me. We do it in the back seat of my car and now I can't play for shit."

Tony chuckles. "I really doubt having sex with Ava is ruining your game play."

"Whatever. It's possible."

I'm being ridiculous.

I think of us in the back seat Saturday night. How eager I was to get her naked. Get inside of her. And how I ruined it all after we were done. She haunts me to the point of madness. I can see her face right now, just after she pulled on my hoodie, all sex-rumpled and gorgeous, and hurt.

So fucking hurt.

All because of me.

"I'm a dick," I say, then blow out a harsh breath. I prop my elbows on the table and hold my head in my hands. "I don't know how to fix this."

"Talk to her." He keeps saying that, everyone does. But it's not that easy. A conversation isn't going to fix us.

"I tried that." I lift my eyes to his. "I ended up fucking her in the back seat of my car and making everything else worse."

He doesn't even flinch. God, if I had even fifty percent of this guy's calmness, I'd be a totally different person. "You love her?"

"Yes," I croak, sounding like I was just diagnosed with an incurable disease.

"Are you *in* love with her?"

I lift my head and drop my arms onto the table. "Of course I am. I've been in love with that girl for what feels like forever. She lives inside of me." I rest my hand against my chest like some dramatic emo kid.

"Then why can't you say sorry for being a jackass and move on? The longer you keep this up, the more you're driving her away."

I absorb what Tony just said, watching him drink from his glass. Watching still as he checks his phone. He taps out a quick text, his lips curved into a barely-there smile, and I know immediately who he's texting.

Hayden.

"You love her?" I tilt my head toward the phone still in his hand.

The expression on his face softens as he thinks of his girl. "Yeah."

"What if she told you she was going to leave for four months instead of spending her summer with you?" I ask. "Put yourself in my shoes. I rarely saw Ava the last couple of years, thanks to her being in San Diego. We didn't spend a lot of time together. The college she chose to attend is a six-hour drive away. I snapped up every minute I could with that girl, yet she still wanted to bail on me."

"She didn't want to bail on you, she wanted to do something for herself. Something that was important to her. An opportunity that could've changed her life and allowed her to see a different part of the world. All she ever wanted was your support, Eli," Tony says, as if he's speaking on Ava's behalf.

"Did the trip to Spain change her life?" I ask, not bothering to wait for his answer. "Because it sure as hell changed mine. I ended up losing her in the process and now I'm all fucked in the head."

"That's your own damn fault. And you're too stubborn to

see it." He takes a swig of his beer before slamming the glass down onto the table. "I thought I might be able to talk to you and make you see what you've done, but here you are, bringing up all that old shit when I thought you were moving past it. You're impossible."

I open my mouth, about to protest, but Tony keeps talking. "It's not always about you, you know. You can't put your abandonment issues on her. She wasn't abandoning you. She was going somewhere else for a couple of months. That's it. I don't know how many times we all have to tell you this."

"I don't put my issues on her," I protest, offended. "And I don't have abandonment issues."

"Ha!"

That's all Tony says. *Ha!*

I glare at him. He drinks his beer, calm as ever. I remember what I said to him earlier at practice, like a little baby. How everyone leaves me.

My big mouth proving his point.

"Hey guys! Here's your pizza."

We both swivel our heads to find a cute blonde standing at the end of our table, holding the pizza high above her head. She slides it onto the table, then drops a stack of paper plates next to it.

"Need anything else?" she asks cheerfully, her gaze swinging to mine. Her eyes widen the slightest bit, as if she might recognize me, and she says, "Aren't you…"

"No, he's not," Tony says, his voice short and rude as hell. "And we don't need anything else. Thanks."

"Uh…you're welcome." She shoots him a confused look before she wanders off.

"That was mean," I say, as I reach for a paper plate before I drop a slice of pizza on it.

"I don't know if I could handle watching some hot blonde who gives off vague Ava vibes fawning all over you and you giving her your number." He grabs his own slice of pizza before taking a giant bite out of it, plopping it onto his plate.

"I wasn't going to flirt with her." I didn't even realize she had vague Ava vibes. "And I definitely wasn't going to give her my number."

Tony snorts. "Right."

"Hey, I'm a free agent. If I want to flirt with a babe, I can," I tell him.

"You're not a free agent. You're hopelessly in love with Ava, like you just told me." He shakes his head and I hate seeing the disappointment on his face. Now I feel like this guy is my dad and all I do is ruin everything.

Sucks.

"Man up, Eli," Tony continues. "You're almost done with college. You have a chance to play for the NFL, which I know excites you, no matter how much you try to blow it off. Like I said, Man. The. Fuck. Up. Tell her you love her. Tell her you want to be with her. Tell her you're fucking sorry, bro. Before you lose her for good."

CHAPTER 18

AVA

What does one do when she's super frustrated with her ex, who has sex with her and then expresses doubt over the entire hookup?

She rage cleans her childhood bedroom, that's what.

I've been in pure demolition cleaning mode for the last couple of days. Going through my closet was a project long overdue, and so overwhelming, I almost quit multiple times.

But I powered through. It helped to keep my focus on other things and not allow myself to think about Eli.

Which I'm doing right now. He needs to go. Vanish. Poof.

It's hard not to think about him when I find specific clothing items that I wore with him. Like the dress I wore at the homecoming ceremony when I won junior princess—the same dress I wore the night he took my virginity. I wanted to put it in the donation pile so badly, but like a sentimental fool, I hung onto it.

Then I stumbled upon the jersey I wore to Bulldog football games last year—the few that I could actually attend. The one with his number on it and his last name emblazoned on the back. I was so proud of that jersey, letting everyone know, who would listen, that he was my boyfriend. I was fully prepared to carry that name myself eventually.

Ava Bennett has a good ring to it.

It's when I start going through my old jewelry box that I have a difficult time. So many sentimental items. A lot of them from Eli. I put them all together in one little drawer. A pair of earrings he gave me. A silver bracelet with a tiny heart charm. A necklace with a small diamond pendant.

And then I find *the* necklace.

The one that belonged to him with the #1 pendant on it. My brother tore it off his neck when they got into a fight in our back yard a long time ago, and I found it. Kept it. Never gave it back to Eli, and when he discovered I was wearing it, he said it belonged to me.

"I like seeing my number on you," he said one night, when I was lying there with nothing else on but that necklace.

The tears form and I clutch the stupid necklace in my fist, tempted to throw it away.

But his dad gave it to him a long time ago, and I know it has sentimental value. Does he even remember that I still have it? Would he want it back?

I'm thinking yes. He'd definitely want it back.

I find a little envelope that I saved for whatever reason and drop the necklace inside, sealing it with the metal closure. I suppose I could mail it back to him. That's the sort of impersonal treatment he totally deserves.

Or I could write him a letter and express all the pain he's brought upon me. Would he read it? Would he understand what I was trying to say to him?

Probably not.

Heaving a big sigh, I drop the envelope on my dresser, right when there's a knock on my door and then it swings open.

"Hey," Ellie strides in, all sunshiny bright with the

mustard yellow sweater she's wearing and that giant smile on her face. "How are you?"

We're all going to pretend what happened Saturday night never happened. I'd been an emotional, underdressed wreck when they found me, and they all rallied around me so hard. It felt good, basking in their love and care, even though I was the saddest I think I've ever been in my life.

They reminded me there were more important things in my life than just Eli, and I needed that. More than I realized.

"I'm good," I say, smiling at her in return. "Just...cleaning."

Ellie's gaze scans the room, her expression slowly morphing into surprise, along with a hint of dismay. "Wow, it looks like a bomb went off in here."

"A bomb made of clothes." I go to my bed and sweep a bunch of clothes off of it, not caring that they all fall onto the floor in a heap. "It's a big project."

"I'll say." She perches on the edge of the bed, glancing around. "What are you doing with all of this?"

"Donating most of it. Some things I'm tossing. If they're faded or ripped or whatever." I gesture toward a garbage bag sitting next to my desk full of items I'm throwing away. "I own a lot of stuff, so it feels good to get rid of most of it. It's a cleanse."

"Like a metaphor for your entire life right now," Ellie says dryly.

I shoot her a look. "True."

Her expression turns serious. "Are you doing okay after what...happened?"

I nod. Shrug. "Yeah. I mean, it is what it is. I can't change any of it."

"Have you heard from him?"

I shake my head.

Her expression turns sour. "He's the worst. Seriously. He can't even *text* you?"

"We've blocked each other in every way you can think of. He has no way of getting a hold of me," I explain, feeling stupid.

"And how old are we again? This is some early high school shit if you ask me." Ellie hops to her feet and starts wandering around my room, dropping down to go through a pile of old flannel shirts I don't want anymore. She glances up at me. "Do you care if I take some of these?"

"Have at them," I tell her. "You can take whatever you want."

She starts making her own stack of clothes. "I have good news about Halloween."

I appreciate her change of topic. I really don't want to rehash what Eli and I did. And how he reacted afterward. What's done is done. I can't change any of it, and while I regret the conversation afterward, I don't regret us having sex. I've missed him. His body, his mouth, his words, being close with him, having him in a way that no one else ever does.

"What do you mean?" I ask, when I realize Ellie is waiting for me to say something.

"Jackson rented a cabin on the lake." She grins. "And wait until you see it."

"Pretty nice?" I raise a brow.

Ellie rises to her feet. "It's huge. Three stories with two giant wraparound decks that face the lake. It's been recently remodeled, right down to the studs, whatever that means. And we're having a massive costume party there Friday night."

She's grinning from ear to ear, she looks so pleased with her announcement, and while I bet the house is amazing, and the party will be fun, I don't know if I want to go.

Okay, for real? I *really* don't want to go.

"Sounds fun." I fake it for my friend's benefit, since she

seems so excited. But I'm sure Eli will be there, and he is the last person I want to see. "I'll probably have to pass."

"Oh come on, Ava." Ellie's face falls and she puts her clasped hands up in front of her chest. "Don't say that. I want you there. We'll have so much fun. We can decorate the house all scary and wear funny costumes and get shit-faced drunk. It'll be everything we wanted to do in high school, only we're older, and we can get away with it now."

That does sound like a good time. I wouldn't mind getting shit-faced, just to forget my troubles. I'm always down for a costume party, since Halloween is one of my favorite times of year. I'd have a blast helping her decorate the house.

"Jackson was able to convince the homeowners that it was cool if a rock star had a party at their place? They really don't mind?" I ask.

"Money talks," Ellie says. "Seriously, I think he paid an outrageous amount to rent it, plus the deposit. But Jackson told me it wasn't about the money. He just wanted us to have a good time—and he knew this would make me happy."

Oh swoon. With a hint of gag. They're total relationship goals while I'm totally single.

"You two are adorable," I say with a sigh.

"You think we're gross," Ellie says with a laugh. "I'm sorry."

"You're fine." I smile at her. "I'm happy you're happy."

"I wish you were happy, though," Ellie says, her voice small. "That's all I want for you, Ava. And I feel like he destroys your happiness every time you see him."

"Is *he* going to be invited to this party?" I love how neither of us say his name.

"I can't tell Jackson he's not invited," she admits, sinking her teeth into her lower lip. "Though I wish I could. But Eli is his best friend. He loves that guy with his whole heart."

"Then maybe I shouldn't go," I say. I go to the dresser and

pick up the envelope, contemplating what I'm going to do before I turn to her and stretch my hand out, the envelope clasped in my fingers. "Can you give this to Jackson to give to Eli?"

Ellie frowns. "What is it?"

"Just take it." I wave the envelope at her and she snatches it from my fingers. "Open it. Look at it. I don't care."

Her gaze stays on me for a moment before she opens the envelope and peeks inside, then pulls the necklace out, the pendant dangling from the chain.

I avert my gaze, hating how my chest literally hurts just looking at that stupid #1 pendant. Wishing I could focus on the fact that he's such an egotistical asshole he chose the number one as his jersey number. "Yeah, I'll make sure he gets it back."

"Thank you." I exhale loudly and then paste on a smile. "Nothing like getting rid of old memories that just drag you down, am I right?"

"For sure," she says with a firm nod, shoving the necklace back into the envelope before she drops it into her purse, which is resting on my bed. "Ava, fuck that guy."

"Right. Okay. Fuck that guy." I nod and smile, but inside, my heart is cracking. Even when I think it can't break anymore, he still manages to shatter it into a million pieces.

Completely destroying me.

———

"Did you have a nice visit with Ellie?"

I come to a stop at the kitchen counter, watching as my mom washes her hands at the sink. "I did," I tell her back. "She took some of my clothes."

"Great. You have a lot. I'm sure you won't miss them." Mom turns off the faucet and dries her hands before she turns to face me. "She should've stayed for dinner."

"She wanted to get to Jackson."

"Ah." Mom nods, understanding written all over her face. "They're still going strong."

"Oh yes. I guess he rented a house on the lake for the weekend. They're having a Halloween party Friday night," I tell her.

"How fun. Are you going?"

"I don't know." I shrug. "Eli might be there."

"You're going to let him control your social life?" She crosses her arms in front of her. "That's not like you."

"No, I just—I don't want to run into him." I didn't tell her about my most recent "run in" with Eli last weekend, because how do you tell your mom you had sex with your ex in the back seat of his car?

You don't.

"How about you come with us then? We're going to Santa Clara Saturday and staying the night, then we'll be at Ash's game Sunday afternoon. His team is playing the Niners," Mom says, her face brightening. "Autumn will be there. The three of us can go shopping Saturday—I bet retail therapy could pull you out of your funk."

"Mom, I'm cleaning out my room. The last thing I need is retail therapy. I'm trying to get rid of stuff, not add more," I protest. "And what about Beck and Dad?"

"They'll be fine. They always find something to do. Come on, you should go with us. It can be like old times. We'll only be missing Jake," she says, her smile sad.

She misses Jake something fierce. We don't see him much and Dad's coaching schedule at the high school with Beck doesn't allow them to travel often to make it to Jake's football games.

"I don't know…" My voice drifts. That doesn't sound like much fun. I'm not in the mood to shop. Or listen to my sister ramble on about her great relationship and what a piece of shit Eli is. I'd almost rather stay home and be by myself. That actually sounds really nice. "Maybe?"

"Think about it," Mom says, never one to push. "Though I understand if you don't want to go. I will say this though."

"Say what?"

"Don't let Eli stop you from going to that party Friday night. If you want to hang out with your friends and let loose and have fun, do it." She smiles. "If he's there, be polite and say hello. Then ignore him the rest of the night."

I can only imagine what he would do if I did that.

"I suppose I could," I say with a small, sad smile.

"It could also be a great opportunity for you two to sneak away and talk," Mom says, sounding hopeful.

"Mom." I sigh. "I'm afraid we're passed that. I don't see us getting back together."

"I'm sorry to hear that. I know he's hurt you, but I never thought it was on purpose. He tends to get a little...wrapped up in his own problems sometimes," she says.

"Don't make excuses for him. He's a selfish asshole most of the time," I say, sounding bitter. "But he's not my selfish asshole anymore, so I don't have to worry about him, you know?"

"Was he really that selfish, though? He sure did love you," Mom says.

"In a toxic way," I add.

"Oh, Ava. Really?" The pointed look she sends me has me recoiling a bit. "I'm serious. I know you're upset and he's hurt you terribly, and I'm not saying your feelings are invalid. But there were a lot of good times between you two as well. Don't they outnumber the bad?"

They do. They so do.

"I'm going to stay here," I tell her before I change my mind. "I appreciate the invite, but I don't mind staying alone. And I think I will go to that Halloween party."

Mom smiles. "Good. You should. You'll have a great time. You'll be with your friends. You can wear a fun costume. It'll be nice."

She sounds like such a mom right now. I'm about to go to her and give her a hug, when the door from the garage opens and Beck comes stomping in.

"I'm starving," he announces.

"Well hello to you too," Mom says, patting him on the back as he walks past her and heads straight to the fridge. "Don't snack on anything. Dinner will be ready in twenty minutes."

"Twenty minutes?" He peers inside the fridge, pulling out a plastic container of God knows what. "I'm snacking."

Mom rolls her eyes at me, then turns her attention to the door when it swings open and in walks my dad.

His eyes find her and he smiles. She goes right to him and he embraces her, one hand on her butt as he drops a long kiss to her lips. I turn away, embarrassed I caught my dad copping a feel, but then again...

It's sweet, how much they love each other. I want that so badly for myself. It's the kind of relationship I've been chasing after, before I even became aware I was chasing it. Their undying love for each other is total life goals.

My phone rings and I check it to see it's Ellie FaceTiming me. I go to the family room and take her call, making a frowny face in the camera so that's what she sees when the call connects. She laughs.

"Uh, didn't you just leave my house?"

"Word on the street is that Eli is definitely going to the party," she announces.

"Really?" My tone is hopeful, and I clear my throat.

She nods. She's still driving, the phone propped up on her dashboard, which probably isn't safe. "I just talked to Jackson, and I asked him if Eli was coming."

"Didn't you already figure the answer was yes?"

"I needed confirmation. And I don't want that to deter you from coming," she says.

"It won't," I say firmly. "I'm going."

I'll do what my mom said. If we run into each other, I'll be polite and say hello, then ignore him the rest of the night.

Easy peasy.

"Yay," Ellie cheers. "Let's go shopping for costumes. One of those Halloween superstores. What do you think?"

"Definitely. Let's go tomorrow. Unless you have plans."

"I'm as free as a bird," she sing-songs.

I laugh. "So am I."

So am I.

CHAPTER 19

ELI

P ractice for the rest of the week went a lot better. There was no need to call Marshall back out onto the field to show me up. My friends were all proud of me, and we were all in sync once more. It felt good. I felt good. Jackson mentioned a Halloween party, and while I agreed to go, I was starting to have second thoughts. Maybe I needed to cut back on the partying.

I need to get serious and focus on football and nothing else. Get through the season with a clear head and a clean—and impressive—record. Even though I told everyone I was going to the Halloween party, I was starting to consider backing out without telling anyone.

Not because of Ava, but because of me. I wanted to help myself. Fix myself. Once I'm fixed, then I can repair my broken relationships, right?

But then Jackson had to call and tell me who else was coming to the party.

"You will never fucking believe it," he says to me, like it's some big surprise.

"Who?"

It's Thursday night and I'm kicking it in my room after

taking a shower. I'm exhausted, ready to crash, but Jackson texted me asking if I could talk.

"Brenden."

I sit up in bed. "You mean Brenden, my old best friend, Brenden?"

We were close since freshman year, but then things kind of got weird thanks to his girlfriend at the time, and then I got closer to Jackson, which I think made Brenden jealous. We even got into a fight. Verbal and physical. God, we were stupid back then.

We made up, but our friendship was never really the same. He spent all of his time with that chick, and I was spending every free moment I had with Ava.

We graduated; Brenden went to college up north and I went to Fresno State. We ran into each other once, about a year out of high school. We still follow each other on Instagram, but he doesn't post much.

"Yep, that Brenden. Weirdest thing. I stopped at the Dollar General to buy some Muddy Buddies or whatever the fuck they're called for Ellie, because she's craving that shit constantly lately, and I ran into him while I was wandering the aisles," Jackson explains. "We got to talking and he said he'd dropped out of college and came home to help his mom out. I guess his parents got a divorce or some shit. I don't know. Anyway, I mentioned the party to him and he said he'd be down and I told him you would be there."

"No shit." I'm silent for a moment. "What the fuck are Muddy Buddies?"

Jackson laughs. "I'll send you a pic of the bag. Ellie says they're delicious. Anyway, you have to go to the party since your friend will be there. You two haven't seen each other in years."

"Yeah, okay. I'm down. I'd love to see Brenden," I say, meaning every word. I'll get to spend time with my old high school friend.

I'm actually looking forward to it.

Jackson blows out an exaggerated breath. "All right. Cool. I'm glad you're going."

"Yeah, me too."

I think about running into Ava at the party. Will she talk to me? Listen to me? Or will she ignore me?

She'd break my heart if she ignored me.

Damn it, I want Ava. I want her to be mine again.

"I'm already at the house so whenever you can, come over. Oh, and it's a costume party," he adds.

"I'm not wearing a costume," I say firmly.

"Come on, it'll be fun."

"Not in the mood for fun." If that isn't the truth, I don't know what is. Lighthearted fun is not in my plans for the foreseeable future.

"You need some, my friend. Whether you realize it or not," Jackson says, his voice lowering. I hear a door opening in the background, and then it's quietly shut.

"The night before a big game? I can't get too shit-faced." We don't have a strict no drinking policy for the team, but our coaches all frown upon it. They know we'll be up to no good and sneaking it if they flat-out banned alcohol, but they always give us little speeches about "thinking smart" and "not fucking up our chances with a few extra drinks the night before."

In other words, they're not big fans of us partying during the football season, and I get it. I've seen more than one guy on the team stumble and eventually get kicked off the team or they drop out because partying has consumed them completely. I like to party, but I'm not about to let alcohol control my life.

I've witnessed too much of that thanks to my mother.

"You won't," Jackson says, because he has all the faith in me that I wish I had in myself. "I want you to see this place. It's fucking awesome. I'm thinking about buying it."

"Is it for sale?"

"I don't know, but I bet for the right price, I could make it mine. Ellie loves it. It's close to where her parents live, and it's been completely remodeled. Sits right on the lake. The view is spectacular. With a huge wraparound deck. We've already fucked around out here." He chuckles.

"No details, please." I sound like a damn prude, but shit. I don't want to hear about his great sex life with Ellie.

Jackson sighs, sounding put out. "Just—get your ass out here when you can, okay? The sooner, the better. I know you don't have class tomorrow."

"I've got practice."

"Friday practices aren't as intense. Coach doesn't want to overwork you all," he reminds me. A little detail he knows because, hell, he used to be on the team.

"Come up when you can. I miss you, bro. We can shoot the shit for a while before the party starts. It'll be like old times," he says, his tone smooth. Like he's trying to charm me or something.

"Where will Ellie be?"

"I set her up with a spa visit, but she doesn't know about it yet. Girl thinks she's going to decorate the house tomorrow for the party." He laughs. "I hired someone to come and set it all up. It's going to be fucking spooky as shit. Can't wait."

"Sounds like you're sparing no expense." And just for a Halloween party.

"Anything to make my girl happy," he says. "She really wanted to have a party with our friends. So here I am, blowing a bunch of cash on a party for you assholes, who won't even appreciate it."

We both laugh. "You're so pussy-whipped, Rivers."

"Yeah, you don't hear me complaining though, do you?" He doesn't wait for me to reply. "I'm going to marry that girl. Just you watch."

I've barely ended the call when there's a knock on my

door. Caleb doesn't wait for me to say come in or fuck off. He just opens the door and barges in, his expression full of…

Despair?

"I'm sorry," he says, without hesitating for even a second. "I feel like a dick for what I said to you a few days ago and it's been hanging over me ever since. I just talked to Gracie about it, and she told me I should apologize."

"So you're apologizing because your girlfriend said you should?" I'm not letting him off the hook so easily. We've been there for each other the last three years. I've gotten into it with him a few times, but he feels like a brother to me. And brothers fight sometimes. Ryan and I used to all the damn time when we were kids.

"Nah. I've wanted to, but you've been icing me out ever since it happened." He looks butt-hurt, when he's the one who said all that shitty stuff.

"I accept your apology," I tell him, watching as his shoulders sag with relief. "It felt like you were taking Ava's side. And that you weren't taking my pain seriously."

He steps farther into the room, settling in the chair at my desk. "You sound really dramatic right now. It's taking everything inside of me not to make some crack about your so-called pain, but I'm restraining myself."

"Gee, thanks." I grab one of my pillows and toss it at him, nailing him right in the face. "Asshole."

"I know you're hurting," he continues. "And I'm here for you, bro. But don't make me turn on Ava. I can't take sides. I love you both."

I suppose I could make a crack about him using the word love in reference to me, but I do him the same favor he did for me and I refrain from making a joke of it. "You going to Jackson's party tomorrow?"

His face breaks out in a smile. "I wouldn't miss it."

"Let's go together? Or are you going with Gracie?" I do my best not to make a face.

"You know, they're all going up early to get ready with Ellie. I guess the place they're staying at is like a palace," Caleb says. "So yeah, I'll go with you. You wearing a costume?"

I finally give in and make a face. "No way."

"Really? I am." He puffs out his chest.

I'm scared to ask. "What are you going as?"

"A pimp." He starts laughing. "Gracie found some cheesy ass costume online and ordered it for me. It's fucking fabulous. I can't wait to wear it."

I laugh too because that is going to be something to see. "You got gold chains and shit?"

"You know it." He nods, still smiling. "A cane. A hat. The shirt doesn't even have buttons, so my chest is completely exposed. Wish I had a giant fur coat. That would be a nice touch."

"You're ridiculous," I say, shaking my head.

"And I'm sorry." His expression turns serious again. "Seriously. I feel the need to say it again because I was a dick out on the field, but I was just trying to lighten the mood."

"Way too soon, bro," I say, my voice quiet.

"Totally realize that now." He rises and takes a few steps closer to the bed, holding his hand. "We good?"

I take his hand and we perform some elaborate handshake that's automatic. "We're good."

––––––––

I whistle low as Jackson takes us onto the third-floor deck of the house they're staying in for the weekend. The scent of pine trees hits me hard up this high, and the sky is a crisp blue, the sun shining on the water just in front of us. "This is pretty fucking nice, Jackson."

"Right? I don't ever want to leave." He takes a deep

breath and holds it for a moment before exhaling loudly. "Kind of big for just two people, though."

"Plenty big for a party," Caleb says as he goes for the black metal railing that lines the entire deck. "This view is unbelievable."

"I know." Jackson wanders around the deck, his head tilted back as he takes in the towering trees surrounding the house. It's quiet outside, the wind whispering through the pines. There are a few birds chirping in the distance and I can hear the low hum of a boat's engine on the water. "I need to write for my next album and I haven't been able to concentrate long enough to work on lyrics. Ellie suggested staying here for a few months."

I don't want to get my hopes up at the thought of having Jackson here for a couple of months. Having him around always makes me miss the fucker. "You seriously considering it?"

"I am," he says with a nod. "This place could end up covered in snow in a few weeks. Talk about beautiful."

"I hate snow," Caleb says, turning to face us. "Wait, I take that back. I loved a good snow day when we were kids and didn't have to go to school."

"I have nowhere else to be for the next few months," Jackson says. "And I owe the label an album."

"The pressure's on," I tell him, and he nods in agreement.

We're all dealing with pressure. It's not just me and the football team or Jackson and his record label. Caleb has his own pressure, trying to figure out what to do with his life. Or Tony and his dad trying to convince him to join the family business. I've always had suspicions they were involved in the freaking mafia, but maybe that's just me being overly dramatic.

I remember my dad telling my brother, a long time ago, that everyone has stress, it's how you handle it that makes the difference. Most of the time, his advice is bullshit and I can't take it seriously. Mostly because he never follows his own damn advice. The way he handles stress is running away from his problems. My brother is much the same.

I frown, realization hitting me. I don't run away from my problems. I blame other people and can't admit when I've done something wrong.

That's kind of fucked up.

No, that's actually *really* fucked up.

"Where are the girls?" I ask, wanting to get it out of the way. I have a suspicion Ava is with them.

"At the day spa at Tenaya Lodge," Jackson says with a grin. "All the ladies are getting special treatment today, thanks to me."

"Showoff," Caleb mutters. "Making me look bad."

"I doubt that. Gracie looks at you as if you can do no wrong," Jackson tells him, shaking his head. "Still can't believe you two are together."

"I love her," Caleb says simply. "She makes my life better. I don't know why I denied wanting a girlfriend for so long."

"You were waiting for her ass," Jackson says, like that explains everything. "That's how I feel about Ellie, at least."

I think of Ava and how I chased after her. Was that the wrong move? I'm not a chill dude. I can't wait for things to happen to me. I'm the one who's always making it happen.

And maybe that's where I fucked up with Ava. I forced myself on her and she had no choice but to be with me.

Maybe we were never meant to be.

"How many people are coming to this party tonight?" I ask, desperate to get my mind off Ava.

"I don't know. A lot." Jackson grins. "We invited at least fifty, and told them to invite their friends. With over five thousand square feet, this place can accommodate them."

"Damn, that's a lot of potential people." Caleb glances around. "They could fuck this place up."

"I'm not worried," Jackson says easily. "If it ends up a mess, I'll hire someone to clean it."

"Must be nice to not have to worry about money," Caleb says.

"You have no idea," Jackson says. "You'll be there some-day, my friend."

Maybe Caleb will, maybe not. I don't think any of us will know what it's like to have the sort of money and fame Jackson has.

"You've got us all beat," I tell Jackson. "Mr. Fancy Leather Pants Rock Star."

I will never let him live down the leather pants he wore in a music video last year. So tight I swear I could make out the outline of his junk, which he denied, but come on.

Women went nuts for those leather pants. He has legions of female fans.

"Shut the fuck up," he says good-naturedly. "You're just mad you'd never look as good as me in leather pants."

"What the hell ever," I mutter, all of us laughing.

"And don't count yourself out. You're about to embark on an NFL career," Jackson says.

"True," Caleb adds.

"Maybe." I shrug.

I don't know if it'll actually happen. I'd love to play for a professional team, but could I stand the pressure? Could I actually make it onto the team? All that old doubt resurfaces like it always does and I try my best to shove it away, but it's hard.

Tomorrow's game is important—we need to clench our position in the playoffs, and every game matters. This means we're drawing closer to playing in a college bowl—with me as the quarterback. The last time that happened, Ash Davis took us. This season, it's on me. It's my last shot for glory. I don't want to choke up and lose. What if I keep losing? What if my chance at a bowl win is lost? All thanks to me?

I can barely stomach the idea. I need to focus. No drinking tonight. They all say I need to get fucked up so I can forget my problems, but fuck that.

I'm having a calm evening, catching up with Brenden and the rest of these assholes, and I'm going to crash early. Jackson offered me a bedroom to stay the night in and I took him up on it. I can leave first thing in the morning with plenty of time to get to the stadium for the game. It's all set up perfectly.

I can't let anyone distract me from the end goal. Not even Ava.

Especially not myself.

CHAPTER 20

AVA

The house where Jackson and Ellie are having the party is so large that it's been relatively easy for me to avoid Eli all night. I only spotted him once since the party started. We made eye contact in the crowded game room on the ground floor, his gaze flickering up and down my body, not bothering to hide that he was checking me out.

My skin heated and I stood taller, thrusting my chest out. Wanting him to get a good look at what he's missing out on. Me dressed as a cowgirl in extra-short denim shorts, a tank top that barely contains my breasts, with an old flannel I dug up in my closet thrown on over it and tied at the waist. The cowboy boots I'm wearing I borrowed from Gracie and they're pinching my feet, but damn it, I look good. I feel powerful. Pretty.

Sexy.

He looked away when I thrust my chest out, some girl standing next to him said something and he focused all of his attention on her.

While I stood there and stewed, furious.

Jealous.

I hate when I feel like this.

I didn't bother retaliating though. There are no boys here that I want to talk to. Despite Ellie pointing out a good-looking one every time she found one, and yeah, I can't deny that there are a lot of attractive guys here tonight, I'm just not interested. The last thing I want is someone new. I don't even want to flirt or hook-up, none of it.

I just want to be by myself for a little while.

Ellie dressed up as a cowgirl too, and Jackson dressed as a cowboy—wearing leather pants. They're tight and more than a little ridiculous but somehow Jackson can pull them off so I don't say anything as the three of us take endless photos together at the beginning of the party. I just smile and stand at his side, silently admitting he doesn't look half bad in them.

Caleb's in a pimp costume and Gracie is dressed as a police officer. She keeps slapping the fake handcuffs on him and pretending she's going to haul him out to her police car. At one point, they were nowhere to be found for about a half hour, and I wondered if they hooked up in her car.

Probably.

There are a lot of creative costumes, though most of the females are wearing a sexy variation of something. A lot of the guys didn't even bother dressing up, including Eli.

The spoilsport.

The house is decorated perfectly. Dark and spooky with scary music playing in the background and a fog machine pumping out scented fog into the game room, filling it with mist. Most of the regular lightbulbs have been replaced with black ones, so everything is dim and dark.

It's a total mood.

I wish I was in a better one, so I could really enjoy this.

Jackson had the party catered and the food is to die for, but I'm not that hungry. I nibble on a few appetizers. Drink one too many witches' brew cocktails. Make conversation with the girls. Let Gracie and Hayden introduce me to some of their friends, women I've never met before who are a little older than me and seem so put together. They talk about their careers, their futures and their boyfriends. One of them is engaged. Another is trying to get pregnant because she doesn't want to be an old mom, preferring to be a young, cool mom.

Direct quote.

I just nod and smile, feeling as if I have nothing in common with any of them, though I don't dislike them. Not at all. I just feel very young and inexperienced. Even Ellie can hold her own, chatting with them about her life with Jackson and how much she's traveled. I don't bother mentioning my dad is a retired NFL star and that we traveled the world when I was young. Most trips I don't really remember because I was just a kid and I didn't appreciate what we were doing.

That's not my story to tell. It's my parents'. All I've ever done is gone to college for a couple of years and partici-pated in a study abroad program in Spain. I learned a lot during my time there. I went to quite a few cities and explored the country. I enjoyed spending time with my host family and I interned with an established textile company, learning the ins and outs of the family-run business, all while working on my conversational Spanish. It was a great experience.

But it's kid stuff compared to these women and what they do. I've done nothing special. I let myself get wrapped up in a relationship with a man who was doing far more interesting things than me. Does that make me pathetic?

I'm starting to think it does.

Or maybe those are my own insecurities bringing me down.

I drown my disappointment in myself with more Halloween-themed cocktails, this time sipping on a witches' heart. It's purple and red and the cute bartender served it to me in a martini glass. I don't bother telling him I'm underage —another pitiful detail about me—and I take another one, my head spinning as I feel the alcohol coursing through my veins, warming me from the inside.

"Ava."

I nearly jump out of my skin when I hear my name, the drink sloshing from the glass as I whip around to find Ellie watching me with concern filling her dark gaze. I smile and raise my glass in a toast to her, right before I take a sip.

"Are you okay?" she asks me.

I shake my head. "Never better."

Her frown deepens. "What's wrong?" She takes a step closer, her voice lowering as she reaches out and grabs my free hand. "Did Eli say something to you?"

"No, he's been ignoring me all night." I say the last few words so loud, more than a few people swivel their heads in my direction. "Ellie, do you think I'm enough?"

"What are you talking about?"

"Me. Am I enough? Or am I a pathetic little girl who's accomplished nothing in her life and never will?" I'm on the verge of tears. I can literally feel them trembling beneath my eyeballs, so I squeeze them shut, willing them not to fall. Once they do, the waterworks show will be officially on and I won't be able to stop it.

It's supposed to be a happy time. We're at a party. We should be living it up and having fun. Instead, all I want to do is drown in my misery with tears.

"Oh, Ava. You are totally enough." Ellie squeezes my hand. "Why would you even think like that?"

"Hayden and Gracie introduced me to their friends and they're all so accomplished. They've done things for themselves, you know? They've graduated college and started careers and they've got something to talk about." I dip my head, staring at the boots on my feet. "I've got nothing."

"You're only twenty," Ellie points out.

"So are you." I lift my head, my gaze meeting hers. "We're the same age and you've done so much more already."

"You've done a lot too, thanks to your father."

"*Only* because of my father," I correct. "What I've done doesn't count because it wasn't me. It's all my father. And my parents, together. Me? I'm just lucky enough to be his kid. That's it. I've accomplished nothing so far, and I already feel so behind in experiences. In life. I've wasted so much time."

"Ava, that's not true. You've always said you wanted to change the world," she starts, but I cut her off with a look.

"How, though? I have no plan. I'm majoring in international business, but I don't want to be a business woman." I say the last two words as if they're dirty. "I don't care about any of the classes I'm taking. When I'm at SDSU, I'm a good little student, the perfect sorority girl. Always helping out. Getting involved, but for what?"

"You're allowed to have fun," Ellie says softly.

"Meh. I'm just some dumb blonde lost in the crowd. A girl who wasted the last four years of her life loving a boy who so easily gave her up because she wanted to do something for herself." The tears do come now, sliding down my cheeks as if I can't control them. Which I suppose I can't. "How do you do it, Ellie? How do you become an individual when you're so connected to Jackson?"

"I just make sure I never stand too deep in Jackson's shadow." She smiles, before pulling me into a hug, holding me close. "You are a star, Ava. A big, bright, shining star and I don't want you feeling like you're not important enough. You're going to go on and make something of yourself. It's okay if you don't know what that is yet. You still have plenty of time to figure it out."

I cling to her, the drink dangling from my fingers, and I'm careful I don't spill it on either of us. "I'm scared. What if I fuck something up?"

"If you do, it's okay. It can be fixed." She smiles reassuringly.

I slowly pull away from her. "You really believe in me that much?"

"I've *always* believed in you," she says, leaning in so she can press her forehead to mine. "Now let's dump that drink and go outside so you can get some fresh air. I think you need to slow down on the alcohol consumption for a little bit."

We end up on the top floor of the house, Ellie leading me out onto the deck. Even at night, the view is magical. There's a full moon, so the silvery light glints off the lake, the towering pine trees shrouded in shadow. There are strings of orange and purple lights overhead, strung across and attached to poles in a crisscross pattern. There are overstuffed outdoor couches and chairs strewn about, surrounding wood-burning firepits. Up here it's quieter, a lot less people, though there are still plenty of them around. The women sitting are draped in thick, cozy blankets and I shiver, wishing I had one wrapped around me.

Ellie finds us a bowl of chips and we nibble on them as we sit by one of the firepits, the warmth of the fire warming us up. She found a bottle of water for me and I sip from it every few minutes, feeling better already.

"I'm too emotional," I tell my best friend. "I need to get over myself."

She fiercely shakes her head. "No, you're not too emotional. You have every right to feel this way—you've been through a lot. It's like the seven stages of grief or whatever. Right now, you're sad. And picking on yourself."

"I need to stop. Maybe he's the one I should be picking on, you know?"

"How about we just stop talking about him?" She lifts her brows. "You're wasting your energy, worrying over what he's doing, or worse, getting mad at him. Forget him, Ava. If he's really going to let you go so easily, then he never deserved you in the first place."

Ellie's right.

So why is it so hard to let him go?

Oh, I know. It's because I just glanced up and there he is, sitting on a couch across the deck from us, Jackson on one side of him and...

I squint, trying to make out the other guy sitting next to him. His face is familiar, but I can't quite place him.

"Who is that with Eli and Jackson?" I ask Ellie.

She glances up, her expression changing when she spots them. "Damn it, Ava. I didn't mean to bring you outside with Eli sitting over there. I didn't realize he was—"

"It's okay," I interrupt. "But who is that guy? He's familiar to me."

"It's Brenden. He was Eli's best friend back in high school," she says.

Oh, I totally remember him. They got into a fight at one point, pretty soon after Eli and I got together. Something to do with Brenden's girlfriend at the time, if I'm remembering correctly.

"Guess Jackson ran into him somewhere a few days ago and invited him to the party. I'm glad he showed up," Ellie says, her gaze sliding to mine. "Keeps Eli occupied since he wants to catch up with an old friend."

"Better he stay involved in conversation with his friends than flirting with other girls." I raise my brows.

"You said it, not me," Ellie says with a faint smile.

Despite Ellie's advice—and her constant chatter in trying to distract me—I can't stop watching them. We keep snacking on chips, Ellie telling me some story I'm barely paying attention to because I'm too distracted, staring at Eli's profile. His strong jaw, the light scruff I see there, even from this distance, which means it's not so light after all. The way the side of his mouth ticks up, every once in a while, as if he's smiling or laughing about something. How animated he is when he talks to his friends. His hands everywhere, his expressions exaggerated. I can only guess what sort of boastful story he's telling, but Jackson and Brenden are both laughing, getting into it and adding to Eli's tale.

My heart pangs. They're having fun, and I'm glad to see it. Even though I'm miserable. Despite my best friend's efforts and her sweet words. Even with everyone else rallying around me trying to pump me up and remind me of my worth, I'm still miserable.

I want him. No one else. Just him.

"Ooh, someone just left behind one of the blankets," Ellie says as she rises to her feet. "I'm going to go grab it so we can share it."

"Okay," I say absently, watching as she walks in the opposite direction of where Eli and Jackson are sitting.

I wait a few minutes, my gaze still glued to Eli, and without thought, I stand, making my way over to the couch, the sound of their voices getting clearer the closer I get.

"...and then you fucking hit me. Remember that?" Eli asks Brenden.

I pause, holding my breath as I wait for Brenden's response. I mean, Eli doesn't sound mad but, I don't know.

Maybe he is?

Brenden throws back his head and laughs. Jackson and Eli do too. "I can't believe I did that," Brenden says, shaking his head. "I don't even know where I got the balls to punch you. What the hell was my problem?"

"You were pissed off, that's why," Jackson adds.

"Well, I sure as hell wouldn't do it now," Brenden says once his laughter has calmed some. "You're a big motherfucker, Eli. It's kind of scary."

Jackson laughs, glancing around the deck, his gaze snagging on me. He does a double take, his smile falling a little, and Eli notices.

Glances over his shoulder.

And spots me.

CHAPTER 21

ELI

Come the fuck on. I was having a great night. Laughing with my boys, catching up on old times and forgetting about my bullshit problems. And now Ava's standing behind us, looking cute as hell—and sad as hell too, can't lie—and probably wanting to start some shit.

I'm not in the mood for it.

"Gimme a minute," I tell the guys, before I get off the couch and head over to where Ava is standing. I can hear someone call her name—Ellie, who sends me a glare that would probably slay me dead if her eyes were actual weapons—but Ava completely ignores her.

Her eyes are on me. Only for me.

"I don't want to fight—" I start, but she cuts me off.

"Me either," she says hurriedly, taking a step forward.

My gaze drops to her chest. That tank top stretches tight across her tits and they are plumped up more than normal. Frustration ripples through me.

I don't want all the assholes here looking at her tits.

"What do you want from me then?" I ask warily, lifting my gaze to hers.

Her big green eyes seem to eat me up. "I miss you," she

whispers, a scowl crossing her face the moment the words leave her. "I kind of hate that I just said that, but I do. You're an asshole."

I stiffen at her insult, not in the mood to deal with another teardown.

"You're arrogant and sometimes you're insufferable, but damn it, you're *my* asshole." She taps her fingers against her chest, right on her cleavage. I don't mean to stare but…

I do.

"You're also the most stubborn person I know. And I'm pretty stubborn too. Most of my family is." Her laugh is soft. "Maybe that's why you fit in so well with us."

I can't let her words get my hopes up. She probably just needs to get this all out so we'll be…what?

At peace?

I'll never be fully at peace if I can't have Ava.

"Everything you said is true." Her eyes widen when I make that admission. "You're right. I'm a stubborn asshole. You fuck with my head, Ava. You come back into my life and you're right there, yet I can't touch you. I can't have you."

I wave a hand in her direction and she takes another step closer.

"What happened last weekend in my car…" My voice drifts, and I hesitate. This is delicate territory. I say one wrong thing and I'll set her off. Hell, I could probably say something truthful and it would set her off. Everything is so damn unpredictable between us right now and I hate it.

"I called it a mistake first," she admits, her voice barely above a whisper. "If I should be mad at anyone about that, it's myself."

I stare at her.

She stares at me in return.

Jackson approaches, letting loose an uneasy chuckle. "You two kids okay over here?"

I send him a look. "We're just talking."

And we really didn't need the interruption.

"Just wanting to make sure," Jackson says, pasting on a fake smile. "Looking cute, Ava."

"Thanks, Jackson."

"Shut the fuck up, Jackson."

He full-blown laughs now, the jerk.

"Just sayin'." He backs away from us a few steps before he turns on his heel and returns to the couch, rejoining Brenden, who's watching me and Ava with curiosity in his eyes.

I return my attention to her, gesturing toward her open flannel shirt. "You look cold."

Ava frowns. "What are you talking about?" She glances down at her chest. "Oh."

The look on her face when her gaze finds mine, once again, is all-knowing. As if she just realized the power she still has over me and is reveling in it.

Because yes, I was referring to her hard nipples poking against the tank top. She must be wearing the thinnest bra ever. Those babies are on full display and now I'm really irritated by them.

Stepping forward, I reach out, grabbing both sides of her flannel shirt and yanking them forward to the center of her chest, so that they meet.

Covering her nipples and the tops of her breasts completely.

"There," I say as I take a couple of steps back, staring at her, now covered, chest. "Much better."

She rolls her eyes. "You don't have to worry about those anymore."

"Hard habit to break." I smirk, both hating and enjoying how easy this is between us. So easy, it's downright painful. "Ava, what the fuck are we doing?"

"You want to know what I'm doing?" She raises her brows.

"Tell me."

"Waiting for an apology."

I contemplate her, knowing she wants that apology from me. What I've done, how stubborn I've been, has only made me suffer. I've made Ava suffer as well, and that is getting us absolutely nowhere.

Well fuck it. I need to rectify things between us.

Now.

"I'm sorry," I murmur.

Her expression alights with hope. "For what?"

My girl is going to make this hard for me, isn't she?

"For making you choose. For not being supportive. For being an asshole. For ending us, all because of my selfishness. For making you miserable. For making both of us miserable." I could rattle off a few more reasons, but Ava doesn't let me.

She's too busy tackle hugging me.

That's it. That's all she does. Just wraps those arms around my middle and clings to me. I return the hug, my arms coming around her as I rest my face in her fragrant hair. The scent of her shampoo is familiar, sending a wave of reassurance through me that tells me I did the right thing.

I've got my girl back in my arms.

She presses her face against my chest, all snug and warm. We stand there for I don't know how long, just holding onto each other, until finally, slowly, she pulls away so she can look up at me. She keeps her arms around me and I do the same to her.

"Thank you. That's all I needed to hear."

Then she does the craziest thing.

Ava pulls out of my embrace completely, a mysterious little smile playing upon her lips. She turns and starts to walk away, my gaze falling to her ass, watching it shift and move beneath the denim shorts that show off her long, sexy legs. She glances over her shoulder, her expression sexy as fuck, her eyes full of mischief.

Just before she faces forward and keeps walking.

Away from me.

What the hell?

I run a shaky hand through my hair, mind boggled. I spot Ellie sitting on a couch alone, Ava passing right by her, and Ellie watches her go with confusion clouding her face. Looks like I'm not the only one who's thrown.

Like the pussy-whipped fucker I truly am, I follow after Ava, losing sight of her for a second when I get into the house, only to spot her pretty blonde head start for the staircase. I go to the stairs myself and race down them, my heart pumping, my skin literally tingling with anticipation.

My girl is making me chase her, and fuck me, I like it.

She walks into the main living area, which is crowded with a variety of bodies, many of them in costumes. Some of them even wearing masks. I hear people call out my name, but I ignore them, too intent on keeping track of Ava. Not wanting to lose sight of her for even a second.

I stay back as I trail her, though all she has to do is turn and see me. She never does, though. It's as if she can sense my presence and is confident that I'm right there, following her every step.

Which I am. She has me all figured out.

Ava heads into the kitchen, where she's embraced by Hayden and Gracie, who are settled in at the giant granite kitchen counter. They offer her a drink, and she declines. They pass her some weird looking appetizer and she takes a bite, her tongue sneaking out to lick a stray crumb still clinging to the corner of her lip.

My body aches at seeing her tongue. Hearing her laugh. Watching her flip her shiny hair over her shoulder.

But I'm patient—a word no one ever uses to describe me. I wait.

She glances quickly in my direction, flashing me a smile before she turns away. My heart starts to race, and I wonder if I'm getting played.

Getting played for something good, is what I'm hoping.

After delivering more hugs to her friends, she takes off, leaving the kitchen. I do the same. She walks down the hall, passing by a bathroom, where people are waiting to use it. She talks to one boy in particular, resting her hand on his chest briefly before she departs.

My chest burns. That motherfucker is lucky he didn't do something stupid, like touch her. I send him a glare as I walk past him and he immediately throws up his hands, looking confused.

Dick.

The hall makes a sharp turn right and I panic for a moment when I pass the corner and still don't see her. It's nothing but closed doors, two on the left, three on the right. I keep walking, my steps slow, my gaze whipping back and forth, just waiting for one of those doors to open.

But there's nothing.

The hall turns left and I keep going, stopping short when I spot Ava at the end of the hall, in front of a set of closed double doors. She smiles when she sees me, her hands going to her hips.

"You're so predictable."

Some might take that as criticism, but I don't. She likes that she can count on me.

"I call it dependable," I tell her as I slow down, putting some swagger into my step.

Her eyes flare with interest and a smile plays upon her lips. "Are we playing a game, Eli?"

"Life is a continuous game," I say as I make my approach. She's leaning against the doors, her hips thrust forward some, those long legs catching my attention. "And you know I'm always up to win."

"I am not your prize."

"Really?" I raise a brow. "Could've fooled me."

I grab hold of her hips, making her gasp, and pull her into

me, our bodies flush, a shaky breath leaving her when we're face to face. "What's behind the doors?"

"I-I don't know."

I lean in closer, my mouth about an inch from hers. Maybe closer. "Liar."

"One of the main bedrooms," she whispers.

"Meaning there's a nice big bed inside?"

She nods.

I reach around her, testing the door handle and it opens with ease. Jackson is such a dumb fucker. If this was my place, I'd be locking every door I could to keep the riffraff out. "Come on," I tell her, releasing my hold on her hips, so I can take her hand and lead her into the bedroom. "Let's check it out."

Ava follows me inside, and I turn, firmly shutting and locking the door while she hits the switch on the wall, illuminating the room in soft, golden light. It's huge, like twice as big as Ava's bedroom and her room is impressive. There's a massive, what looks to be, custom bed sitting dead center with a cream-colored duvet cover on top and a massive faux fur throw blanket tossed across the end of the mattress.

"Looks comfy," she says.

I stop just behind her, slipping my arms around her waist and nuzzling the side of her face with mine. "Let's test it out."

She melts into me, resting her hands over mine. "I think this is where Ellie and Jackson are sleeping."

"They won't mind." I push her hair aside with my face and press my mouth on her neck. "Come on."

"Not yet," she breathes, when my lips find that particular spot behind her ear. "We should go back to the party."

I chuckle. "You're the one who got me to follow you down here, Princess. Don't forget that."

I feel a buzzing in my back pocket that can only be my phone. Reaching for it, I check out the screen to see an unfamiliar number. I put my phone away and return my attention to Ava. "I've missed you so damn bad."

"You were just with me last week." There's amusement in her tone, thank God.

"Yeah and I kind of fucked it up."

"So did I," she admits, hanging her head, her fingers tightening on mine. "But we can fix this. Fix—us."

"I know we can," I whisper against her neck, feeling her shiver. "I've been a complete asshole to you, Ava. I hate that I've hurt you."

She dips her head to the right, a little sigh leaving her when I kiss her neck. "All I've ever wanted is your support. I give it to you unconditionally, no matter what. That's what I want in return."

"I'm here for you, baby. Whatever you want, I'll give you." As much as I can, considering the intense football season. My focus is always Ava, but right now, football is really fuckin' important to me.

She knows this. And she understands it too. Look at her family. They live and breathe the sport.

I squeeze her hips when she remains silent, savoring the feel of her pressed against me, her ass rubbing my growing erection. Doesn't take much to set my body off when it comes to this woman, and having her so close is a total distraction.

As in, all I can think about it is getting her naked and in that massive bed.

"Eli." Her voice is so soft, I can barely hear her.

"What baby?" I rest my mouth at her ear, nibbling on the lobe.

"I want to spend the night with you," she admits, her voice low.

Sexy.

My body tightens in response. "That's all I want too."

Ava turns in my arms so we're facing each other, those big

green eyes twisting me up inside as stares up at me. "I want it to be good between us again."

"It will be," I say with confidence. How can it not? All is right in the world. I've got my girl back in my arms and we're on the same page.

"I'm sorry if I've been stubborn," she murmurs.

I can't help but chuckle, leaning in so I can rest my forehead to hers. "That's all I've ever been. I'm the one who should be apologizing. Over and over again."

Her face is full of wonder. "Who are you and what did you do with my Eli?"

My chuckle deepens and I give in to my urges, kissing her.

She opens to me immediately, her tongue meeting mine and it's on. I drop my hands to her ass, squeezing and kneading as our kiss deepens. She slides her hands up my chest, circling her arms around my neck and I haul her in closer.

As close as I can get her.

Ava moans my name and fuck. That's all I need to hear. I run my hands up, beneath her shirt, ready to start stripping her—

My butt buzzes again, and I go still.

So does Ava.

"Is someone trying to call you?" she asks, her lips moving against mine.

"Ignore it." I kiss her again but she pulls away so our gazes meet, her brows lowered in concern.

"You should check who it is."

"It doesn't matter." I lean in close but she shakes her head.

"It might," she says. "Check who's calling. Then we can get back—to business."

Grinning to hide my momentary sexual frustration, I let go of her to pull my phone out of my back pocket once more, frowning when I see that the call is from Ryan this time. My brother.

And he never calls me.

I answer him, impatience in my tone.

"Great timing," I practically growl. "What's up?"

"It's Mom. She's been in a car accident," he says.

I whirl away from Ava, so my back is to her. "*What?* What do you mean? How did you hear—"

"Someone at the hospital called me. Said they tried to get ahold of you first, since you live closer, but you didn't answer," he says accusingly.

Shit. That must've been the hospital calling me a few minutes ago.

"Is she okay? What happened?" Nerves make my stomach clench and I feel Ava approach. She rests her hand on my shoulder and I send her a quick look, seeing the concern in her gaze.

"I don't know all the details yet. But I believe there was just a single car involved, and she's the only one who was hurt. Thank God," he mutters.

"What do you mean by that?"

"She was drunk. The cops want to arrest her for DUI," Ryan says, his words filling me with dread.

"What are you saying?" I ask, confused.

"The cops who found her said the interior of her car reeked of alcohol. No one has the official blood test yet, but it was fairly obvious Mom was above the legal drinking limit," Ryan explains, his tone serious. "I think she's in serious trouble."

CHAPTER 22

AVA

can only make out snippets of his conversation with his brother, but from what I can tell, Eli's mother was in a car accident.

And she might've been...drunk?

"Okay yeah. I'll call you when I get to the hospital and talk to someone." He ends the call and turns to me, his face white. He looks like he's in shock. "My mom's been in a car accident."

"Where?" I ask gently. I take his hands in mine, noting that they're ice cold. "Where is she, Eli?"

"Saint Agnes. I need to go." He lets go of my hands and starts for the door. I chase after him, surprised at how fast the man can be, though I guess I shouldn't, considering how quick he is on the field. "I'll call you."

"Eli." I follow him down the hall, having to run extra fast to keep up with him. "Eli, I'll go with you."

It's as if he doesn't even hear me. He walks through all the people still mingling in the living room and goes for the front door, throwing it open. I follow him out into the chilly night, shivering when the breeze off the lake hits me. My feet in the cowboy boots are killing me as I keep running, falling behind as Eli's determined steps take him to his car. It's only when he stops to fumble in his front pockets for his keys that I get a chance to catch up to him, calling his name.

He blinks at me, looking shocked. "I thought you were staying here."

I shake my head. "I want to go with you."

"I don't know how long it's going to take. I could be there for hours."

"I don't care. I want to be there for you," I say firmly.

A faint smile curls his lips and he dips his head to press a soft kiss to my lips before he digs for his keys again, pulling them out and unlocking the doors. I slide into the passenger seat and he gets behind the steering wheel, starting up the car.

"You okay to drive?" I ask, hoping that he is. I've had too much to drink. He seems fairly sober.

"I had a beer a couple of hours ago, but that was it," he says, as he puts the vehicle in reverse and starts to back out of the space. "I'm fine."

It's a tension-filled car ride the entire way. Eli's worry radiates off of him in waves, and his brother calls about thirty minutes into the journey, frustrated that we aren't there yet.

"Where the fuck were you anyway?" Ryan asks, sounding furious.

"Up by the lake at a costume party," Eli tells him, his voice ragged. "The house was over an hour away from the hospital. We're halfway there."

"We? Who are you with?"

"Ava came with me." He sends me a quick look.

"I thought you two were broken up."

Eli winces. "We're—back together."

I don't correct him because I feel the same way, even though we didn't actually say those words to each other. I don't do anything but stare straight ahead, curling my hands into fists, hating how shaky and nervous I feel. I need to be strong for Eli right now. He needs me. I can't be all worked up over what his brother is saying and how he's treating Eli. He's just worried.

"Well, what the fuck ever, just call me when you get there and find out what's going on with Mom, okay?"

"Will do," Eli says, his voice determined.

They end the call and, once again, there's silence. But I don't think I can stand it. I want to ask questions, but should I? I don't want to upset Eli more.

I'm curious though. I want to know.

"Do you know what happened? With the car accident?"

He nods. "She was by herself. And her blood alcohol level was over the legal limit so I guess the cops want to arrest her. Even though she hasn't done anything or hurt anyone but herself. Fuck, I don't know. I guess we'll find out."

"What are the extent of her injuries?" I ask.

"That I don't know. Ryan didn't say much, so I guess we'll find out." His jaw hardens. "She'll be fine. She has to be."

I hope so. The relationship Eli has with his mother has always been described as volatile, but I know he'd be devastated if something horrible happened to her.

Completely devastated.

We make small talk, but it's forced. Eli is completely distracted. Worried. And I don't want him so preoccupied he gets us in a car accident as well, so I stop trying to keep up the conversation. By the time we're at the hospital, it's late, yet the parking lot is crowded. Eli finds a spot to park and whips into it, shutting off the car and climbing out without waiting for me or talking to me at all.

I feel invisible as I follow him into the emergency room. My phone dings with a notification and I check to see it's Ellie, who I texted right after we left to let her know what's going on.

Ellie: **You at the hospital yet?**

Me: **We just got here.**

Ellie: **Keep me updated, okay? When you get a chance.**
Me: **Will do.**

"She's in a room," Eli says to me after he's spoken with someone at the front desk. "The nurse didn't go into detail, but she said we could head up to the second floor. That's where she's at."

"Let's go," I say, going to him and taking hold of his hand. "Come on."

I take the lead, finding the elevator, the two of us standing close as we wait for it. We stand even closer as we ride the elevator. I wish I could comfort him. My arms literally ache to do so, but he's so tense, his body practically vibrates.

All I want to do is make him feel better.

We exit the elevator and approach another desk, and this time, the nurse is full of information. I stand right next to Eli the entire conversation, wanting to hear what she has to say.

"Your mother is okay." The woman scans the computer screen in front of her. "Lacerations to her face, most likely caused by the airbag. Ummm…" She taps at the keyboard, squinting at the screen. "Looks like she has bruised ribs and a possible concussion. They're keeping her overnight for observation."

"That's it?" Eli asks hopefully.

The nurse glances up at him. "Injury wise, she came out fairly unscathed, which is normal when it's a drunk-driving case."

Eli's entire body tenses up. "Are you sure she was drunk?"

"Alcohol level noted at .09, almost a .10. Yes, she was legally intoxicated." The nurse's expression is not particularly friendly. "Does she drink and drive often?"

"I don't know. I don't control her," Eli retorts.

I place my hand on his arm, trying to calm him. He sends me a questioning look but otherwise doesn't say anything. "What room is she in?"

"Two-thirty-six." The nurse points down the hall. "But it's not currently visiting hours."

"Don't really care," he says, as he pushes away from the counter and heads down the hall toward her room. I send the nurse an apologetic look and follow after him, stopping short when he enters the room, without hesitation, marching right up to the bed she's lying in.

He's standing at her bedside when I walk inside the room and pause at the foot of the bed.

"Mom," he whispers, his voice rough with emotion as he stares at her face. There are bruises already forming, and tiny cuts on her face too. One laceration is so large, she has a giant bandage covering it. "Mom, wake up."

She doesn't react at all. I haven't seen his mother in a while, but she looks really thin. Almost gaunt. She's lying flat on her back, her arms at her sides, her entire body eerily still.

It's a little freaky.

Eli settles his hand on top of her head, his touch gentle as he drinks in her beat-up face. I see the pain cross his own face, the way he frowns and swallows hard. He strokes her hair carefully, his voice louder.

"Mom, it's me. Eli. Wake up. I want to talk to you."

She makes a noise, like a little groan, turning away from him. He keeps speaking, his tone low and soothing until her eyes finally flutter open and she turns to look at him.

"Eli," she says, her voice full of wonder. "What are you doing here?"

"I came as soon as I heard," he says, trying to smile at her, but it comes out looking forced, so he gives up. "You okay?"

"It hurts." She averts her head, her eyes falling closed. "My whole body."

"What happened?"

"Swerved to avoid a rabbit that darted out into the road." She shakes her head, grimacing. "Hit a tree."

Eli's silent as he takes in what she said. So am I, feeling

helpless. I can't do anything or say anything. Why did I come?

To be here for Eli. To give him support when he needs it the most. He's hurting. And probably doesn't know how to deal with this.

I'll help him the best that I can.

"I always tell you to just hit those little fuckers," he says ferociously. "Now look, you got in an accident over them."

"Eli, language," she says on a gasp, a soft bit of laughter leaving her. "It's okay. I'm okay. Not so sure about the car though."

He sends me a look before he returns his attention to his mom. "Did you talk to the cops?"

"The cops? Yes, the police were there, but...why would I talk to them?" She frowns, a little crease forming between her eyebrows.

"Mom." He brushes his fingers through her hair again, seeming at a loss. "They said—they said you'd been drinking."

"I had a few glasses of wine. No big deal." She waves a dismissive hand, wincing. It's as if every little movement pains her.

"The nurse said something about the cops possibly pressing charges."

"I'm harmless."

He makes a disgusted noise, then immediately contains it. "We'll talk tomorrow."

"Are they keeping me here overnight?" She tries to lift her head, glancing around the room. "I don't want to stay overnight."

"The doctor wants to keep you for observation." He reaches for her hand, giving it a gentle squeeze. "They're just doing what's best for you."

She nods, turning her head in my direction, her eyes going wide when she spots me. "Ava, is that you?"

I send her an awkward wave, feeling dumb. "Hi."

Her gaze goes from me to Eli, and then back to me. "I thought you two were broken up."

"We're working on it," Eli says, his voice clipped.

He won't look at me, and it kind of hurts, but I know he's not mad at me. He's in pain. Confused and conflicted. I'm sure he's scared for his mom, and mad at her too; she did this to herself. I thought she'd stopped drinking so much.

Apparently not.

"Aw, that's nice. Always did like you," his mother tells me, her eyes sliding closed.

Eli makes more small talk with her while I text Ellie and keep her up-to-date on what's going on with his mother. She says all the right, supportive things and I can't help but think I lucked out in the best friend department.

She's such a good friend to me. I don't know what I'd do without her.

We're in his mom's room for over an hour when Eli suddenly approaches me, his expression serious.

"I want to stay, but I don't think she'll know whether I'm here or not." He waves a hand in the direction of the bed, where it appears his mother is sleeping peacefully.

"She'll be safe here. We can leave her and you can go home and get some sleep yourself. Then come back in the morning to pick her up and take her home," I suggest.

He nods, his expression grim. "You don't think she'll be upset when she wakes up and I'm not here?"

"She'll be okay," I reassure him. "You can call her first thing in the morning. She'll understand you wanted to go home."

"I have my game tomorrow." He makes a face. "I won't have time to pick her up from the hospital. Guess I'll have to miss the game."

Alarm races through me and I touch his arm. He can't

miss tomorrow's game. Too much is at stake for him—like his future. "I can pick her up for you."

He frowns, his gaze locked on me. "You would do that for me?"

"I want to help. I don't mind." I smile at him, suddenly feeling a little shy. I don't know why, considering I would've done this before, when we were together. And now we sort of are again, so it makes sense. Right? "Are you ready to leave?"

Eli glances at the hospital bed, watching his mom for a moment before he turns back to me. "Okay, yeah. Let's go."

We leave the hospital in a hurry, both of us acting as if we can't wait to get out of there. The antiseptic smell clings to my nostrils, even after we've both climbed into the car and we're back on the road. From the hospital, we're still almost forty minutes from Eli's house, and even farther to mine.

I'm kind of hoping I'll get to stay the night at Eli's, though I don't want to push. But where else am I going to go? Plus, he's exhausted. I'm sure he just wants to crash into bed, not drive me all the way back to my parents' house an hour away from here.

"Thank you for coming with me," he says, as he's pulling out of the parking lot.

"Of course," I tell him softly. "I don't think I did much, but you're welcome."

"It helped just knowing you were there." He glances over at me, his gaze meeting mine. "It always helps, knowing you're in my corner."

My chest grows tight at his admission. "I will always be in your corner, Eli. Even when we were broken up and you were being a jerk, I was still totally in your corner. Always supporting you."

He's quiet, returning his concentration to the road, his hands gripping the steering wheel tightly. I watch him, noting the exhaustion lining his face. His hair mussed from him running his fingers through it. Faint lines bracket either side of his mouth, and for the first time ever, I realize he looks so much older.

And so tired.

"You want me to take you home?" he asks, his voice quiet.

When he looks in my direction, I slowly shake my head. "I want to go home with you, Eli."

CHAPTER 23

ELI

'm stunned by Ava's request, but then again not. We did just pretty much make up back at Jackson's party. I was about to take off her clothes too, until the phone call.

Still can't believe my mom crashed her car into a damn tree, all to save a stupid rabbit.

I shake my head, frustration mixed with anger making my blood simmer. Her car accident was stupid. I can think this because she didn't badly hurt herself, thank God. It could've been so much worse. She could've wrecked with another car. She could've killed innocent people—

No. I can't think about it. Something needs to change. It's going to be a hard conversation to have with her but, damn it, my mother needs to lay off the booze once and for all.

And it's all on me to make her stop.

I head into the turn lane, grateful when the light turns green almost immediately and I'm able to whip a U-turn, heading back the way we came until we pass the hospital and we're on the way to my apartment.

Caleb won't be home. They're staying the night up at Jackson's rental. That had been my plan too, until this.

I scrub a hand over my face, trying to tamp down my frustration.

"I guess you're okay with me coming home with you?" she asks, amusement lacing her tone.

"Definitely," I say gruffly, reaching out to settle my hand on her bare knee, my fingers sliding upward along her thigh. If I was in a better mood, I might try to get her off while driving, but my mood is actually for shit and I'm exhausted.

So I lift my hand from her thigh and settle it back on the steering wheel like a boring ass chump.

By the time we're pulling into the parking lot of my apartment complex, my eyelids feel like they have concrete blocks sitting on top of them, they're so heavy. We climb out of the car and I lock it, then Ava follows me to my apartment building.

"This is nice," she says as she looks around, a shiver moving through her since it's so late at night and pretty fucking cold, especially considering what she's wearing, which isn't much. "Looks brand-new."

"It is," I tell her, leading her right to our front door. I unlock it and let her inside first, following after her and shutting and locking the door behind me. I don't bother turning on any lights. I just head straight for my bedroom and Ava falls into step behind me, hurrying along.

The moment we're in my room I close the door, toeing off my shoes almost immediately.

"I'm exhausted."

"I'm sure," she murmurs, watching as I collapse on the edge of the mattress and pull my shirt up and over my head, dropping it onto the floor. I undo the fly of my jeans and rise to my feet, once more, tugging them off. Until I'm just standing there in only my boxers and my socks, wishing I was in the mood to take this in a different direction.

But I'm not. I need sleep.

I just want to forget what happened tonight with my mom. At least for a little bit.

"Come on." Ava approaches me, her fingers curling around mine. She turns me to face the bed, then reaches for the comforter and tugs it back. "Get into bed."

I let go of her hand and crawl under the covers, rolling onto my back at the same time that she covers me with the comforter, pulling it up to my chin. "Taking care of me?"

Her smile is faint. "You're letting me so…yes."

She shrugs out of the flannel shirt and I watch her with heavy-lidded eyes, my gaze eating her up. That fucking tank top should be illegal. Her tits appear ready to pop out of the neckline at any moment. She plops her perfect butt on the edge of my bed and kicks off the cowboy boots, a pleasurable little moan leaving her after she removes each one.

I shouldn't find that sound arousing, but I do.

"My feet were killing me," she announces as she stands once more, her hands going to the front snap of her denim shorts as she slowly scans my room. "Do you mind if I take a shower?"

"Go for it," I murmur, anxiously waiting for her to drop those shorts.

I might be tired, but I'm not dead.

She lets them fall, revealing that she's wearing pale pink panties with thin white stripes.

Fuck.

Ava kicks off the shorts and makes her way back over to me, bending over so her tits half hang out of her top, pressing her mouth against my forehead. "Go to sleep," she murmurs against my skin before she lifts away from me.

She's standing in my room in a skimpy tank and a pair of panties, every one of my wet dreams coming true, and I'm so exhausted I can barely move.

Fuck my life. Seriously.

"Grab a T-shirt from my closet," I tell her, pointing to where it's at. "To wear to bed."

"Okay," she chirps as she turns toward the closet, flashing her mostly bare ass to me, since those panties are really nothing but a skimpy thong.

Jesus. I might have a heart attack.

My eyes close as I hear her rummage through my closet. God knows what she's finding, but damn it, I have nothing to hide. This girl knows everything there is to discover about me. I have no secrets.

She leaves the closet and then I hear the gentle closing of the bathroom door. The sound of water turning on as she starts her shower. My mind starts to drift, filled with pleasant, sexy images of Ava in her undies and tank. Of her perfect breasts straining against the fabric when she leaned over me. If I'd been more awake, I would've nipped at her. Grazed my teeth against her nipple. Tugged the fabric down farther and exposed her completely.

Yeah. Did none of that. All I can do is smile as I drift off to sleep, secure in the fact that my girl is back.

My girl is mine.

———

Something's tickling my nose.

I wrinkle it, trying to get away from whatever it is touching me, but it's right there. Surrounding me. I don't want to open my eyes or check my phone. I'm warm and sleepy and I don't want to know what time it is. Not yet. That might ruin everything.

I drift back off to sleep, but the tickle returns, even worse now, making my nose itch. I reach up, batting at whatever it is that's bothering me.

Hair. Soft, silky hair, then I remember.

Ava.

She's in bed with me.

My senses rouse, becoming more aware of my situation. She's right next to me, her back to my front, her ass lodged against my cock.

My very erect cock.

I press my face into her hair and close my eyes, breathing deep as I slip one arm around her waist. She's so warm and soft, and my T-shirt she's wearing has ridden up, so my fingers make contact with her stomach.

My hand wanders up, my fingers brushing the underside of her left breast, skimming upward until I encounter her hard nipple. I lightly circle it with my thumb.

She squirms against me, pressing her ass against my dick.

I cup her breast, testing the weight for a moment, before I let it go, my hand drifting down along her side, tracing her ribs, the dip of her waist, the flare of her hip. She doesn't have panties on. She's bare-assed naked under the shirt so I cup her pussy.

A little moan leaves her, and she shifts, her thighs opening for my fingers. I take my advantage and slip them farther, encountering wet heat. She arches against me and I shift, her head falling back on my shoulder, a shuddery breath leaving her when I begin to slowly stroke.

We don't say a word. It's so quiet and dark in my room. And she's so damn wet, I can hear my fingers as they move inside her pussy. The accelerated pants of her breath. She winds her arm around the back of my head, turning toward me at the same time I turn to her, our mouths meeting in a hot, sloppy kiss.

I need this, I think as I feast on her mouth, my tongue gliding against hers. I need her.

I need her so damn bad.

We end the kiss, Ava rubbing her ass against me invitingly, and I know what she wants.

I want it too.

Removing my hand from her pussy, I place it on her hip, readjusting myself so my cock is right where it needs to be. I grip the base with my other hand and slowly push forward, filling her up inch by inch, until I'm fully inside her.

We lie like that for a moment, both of us catching our breaths. Adjusting to the position. I don't remember us fucking like this much before. I always wanted to be face to face with her, so I could look at her. Watch her as the pleasure washed over her. I got off on those expressions, knowing I was the one who made her feel so damn good.

This is hot too, though. It's so dark, we can't see each other anyway.

I start to move, withdrawing almost all the way out of her body before I plunge back in. I keep the pace slow, driving myself out of my mind, but damn, it feels so good. I want to stretch the moment out for as long as possible.

A moan leaves her when I nudge even deeper. I keep doing it, hitting that same spot over and over, a grunt leaving me every time. Suddenly impatient, I pull out of her, ignoring her cry of protest as I kick the covers away and rise up on my knees, repositioning her until she's lying on her stomach. I reach around her, my hand splayed on her abdomen as I haul her up into position.

On her hands and knees.

She glances over her shoulder at me, her hair covering most of her face, but I can make out one glittering green eye. Pouty lips. The expression on her face is telling me everything she's feeling without her having to say a word.

She wants this. She wants me.

I hold onto her hip as I slide inside of her, dropping my gaze on the spot where our bodies connect. I watch in total fascination as I slide in and out of her body, that familiar feeling racing down my spine and settling deep in my balls. I could come like this. So easily.

Too easily.

Wrapping my hands around her waist, I pause, my fingers pressing into her flesh, my cock all the way inside of her, throbbing. Anxious to blow.

Not yet, I tell myself. Not yet.

She moves with me, to the point that I don't have to do anything but watch as she slides up and down my dick. It's fucking hot. Everything about this moment is heightened. Charged. The air seems to sizzle the faster we fuck and a cry falls from her lips, just as her pussy grips me in a stranglehold.

Ava's coming, her pussy milking my dick, drawing the orgasm out of me almost involuntarily. A groan leaves me when it hits, my entire body stilling as my cock throbs, spilling semen deep inside her.

We collapse onto the bed together, me sliding up so we're face to face. I kiss her. Devour her. She turns more fully toward me, her arms slipping around my neck as she presses her body to mine.

I love her. I love her so much, and I thought I'd lost her. Hell, at one point tonight, I thought I was losing my mom, too. My life. It's been a tumultuous six months and I don't know how I've kept my head in the game.

Foreign emotions hit me, making me feel heavy as I cling to her, my arms wrapped tightly around her waist. She winds her legs around my hips, her mouth finding mine once more. We kiss as if we're never going to stop and I roll her over so she's beneath me. Her thighs spread, allowing me to settle in between them and the more we kiss, the harder I get.

Until I'm slipping inside of her again, fucking her hard. Harder. Holding nothing back this time around. She takes it, whimpering every time I slam into her, and I kiss her, stealing that sound. Her breath. Wishing I owned her very soul.

I know she owns mine.

I'm feeling everything. All of it. Her and me. Our connection. How good it is between us. How right. I can't let her go after this. If she pulls some shit on me again, I don't know if I'll be able to survive it.

She's my world. My princess.

Hell, my queen.

"I love you," I whisper against her mouth, my thrusts hard, jolting her up the mattress with every push of my body. "I love you so fuckin' much, Ava."

"I love you too," she murmurs, her fingers pulling on the hair at my nape, forcing me to open my eyes. She's watching me with those beautiful green eyes, her swollen mouth tilting up, waiting for my kiss.

I deliver it, lingering there, tasting her. Drinking from her. "You drive me fucking crazy."

She laughs, the sound vaguely evil. As if she gets off on making me insane. "You like it."

Ava's right.

I do.

CHAPTER 24

AVA

wake up confused at first, momentarily forgetting where I'm at. I'm all alone in the bed, completely naked. Throwing my arms above my head, I stretch, a soft groan leaving me when I feel the ache in my muscles. As if I've been pleasantly abused.

That's when it hits me.

Last night with Eli at the party. Making up with him. His mom's car wreck. Going to the hospital. Coming home with him.

Getting thoroughly fucked by him in the middle of the night.

A smile crosses my lips and I close my eyes, pressing my face into the pillow.

It smells like him and I breathe deep, feeling like an addict with a serious issue.

I hear a voice. Deep and male. He's talking. Eli. But I only hear one side of the conversation, so I assume he's on the phone.

"…I don't know if I can come get you. Don't you have some friends you could call? I have a game—" He goes silent.

Rolling over, I crack my eyes open and push up into a

sitting position, shoving my hair out of my face. I don't know where he's at, but his bedroom door is partially open, so I can only assume he's out in the hall.

"Fine," he says, sounding desolate. "Yeah no, it's cool. I'll come pick you up. Give me some time. I need to call my coaches first—"

He goes silent again and my heart pangs for him. He doesn't want to miss his game, and he shouldn't have to. Despite how terrible her accident was, his mother brought this all on herself.

It isn't fair, what she's asking him to do.

"Okay, see you in a bit. Bye." A ragged breath leaves him and I can only assume how he's feeling, what he's thinking.

And then he's there, standing in the doorway, wearing a pair of gray sweatpants and nothing else.

Hmm. Women go nuts over men in gray sweatpants on the internet and I can suddenly see why. There are entire hashtags devoted to the cause. I think there might even be #graypantsTikTok and I always blew it off because, come on.

It seems kind of silly, right?

My mouth goes dry the longer I stare at him. The sweatpants hang extremely low on his hips and I swear I see a hint of pubic hair, which is…

Yes, it's hot. So hot.

Plus, it's obvious he's not wearing boxers under those sweatpants, so his junk is free.

My cheeks heat at the mere thought.

"You're awake." He hesitates and I can feel his gaze roving over me.

I drop my head, hoping he doesn't notice my blushing.

"Why is your face so red?"

I lift my gaze to his once more, playing it off. "Nothing. Good morning."

He smiles and it's sweet and soft. I haven't had him look

at me like that in so long, my stomach actually flutters. "Good morning."

"Your mom wants you to come pick her up?" When he frowns, I continue, "I might've overheard your conversation."

"Yeah, total pain in my ass. My coaches are going to be so pissed at me." He makes a face, running his fingers through his hair, his biceps bulging with the movement.

Be still my throbbing heart, goodness.

"I'll go get her," I tell him, sitting up straighter and letting the comforter fall to my waist. "I told you I would last night."

His gaze drops to my bared chest. "You don't have to do that," he tells my breasts.

"I already offered. I want to help you. I know how important the game is to you and how much you don't want to miss it," I say. "She doesn't need you to come get her. I can do it for you."

His smile is still soft as he fully enters the room, approaching the bed. Approaching me. He stops right in front of me, bending down to kiss my lips. The kiss is soft yet purposeful, and my entire body tingles when he pulls away.

"You're cute when you're mad," he whispers. "Especially on my behalf."

"I'm not mad," I say, sitting up straighter.

"Right," he drawls. "You're distracting as fuck, I'll tell you that. Sitting there with your tits out." He waves a hand at my naked chest.

I flip my hair out of the way so he can get a good look at them. "You're enjoying the view. And you're distracting too, with those sweats on."

He reaches for the waistband, tugging them down some. Not enough to expose himself, but now there's even more pubic hair on display. "You're enjoying the view," he mimics me with a grin.

I shove the covers out of the way and rise up on my knees,

my hands going to the waistband of his sweats and pushing his hands away. "Let me," I whisper.

Just before I shove them down.

His cock is already mostly erect. It doesn't take much, I think, as I wrap my hand around him and start to stroke. He hisses out a breath, thrusting into my hand all while shaking his head. "We shouldn't."

"We are." My voice is determined.

"I need to text my mom."

"Uh uh. Don't tell her you're not coming to get her. And let's stop talking about her." I lean in, delivering an exaggerated open-mouthed kiss to the tip of his dick. His mouth drops open when I do, his gaze zeroed in on that very spot. "We have other matters to take care of first."

"Baby." He sounds in pain. "I gotta take a shower and get the hell out of here. It's already late."

"You have a few more minutes," I say before I wrap my lips around the entire head and begin to suck.

His hands sink into my hair as I work my mouth up and down his cock, his mouth hanging open slightly, like he's in shock and can't believe this is happening. I keep my gaze locked on his, my fingers wrapped tightly around the base as I suck him deep into my mouth.

I've given Eli Bennett quite a few blowjobs since we've been together, but most of the time, they're done in the dark. Not that I'm shy or anything when it comes to him and us, but...

I don't know, I always felt like I was lacking in the BJ department, especially when we were first together. I was young and had zero experience.

"Keep looking at me like that and I'm going to come," he warns, as if it's a bad thing.

I cup his balls with my other hand, taking him deeper into my mouth. I want him to come. In our relationship, he's always been the giver. I give too, but a lot of the time, it would feel imbalanced.

Right now, I want to give. Give and give and give.

"Ava." He says my name as a warning.

I release my hold on him, sticking my tongue out so I can trace the flared head before slipping down and running my tongue along the thick vein on his cock. His hands loosen in my hair and I wish he'd pull it tighter.

"Babe." His tone switches in an instant, turning pleading. "You gotta sto—"

I pull him back into my mouth, sucking so hard my cheeks hollow out. He grants my wish, his fingers curling into my hair as he starts to fuck my mouth, thrusting in and out. I let him use me, applying pressure to his cock, my fingers squeezing the base, tasting the precum on my tongue.

And then it's not precum at all. He's full-blown coming, groaning long and low as his semen fills my mouth and I swallow it down, every last drop.

I usually pull away at the last second and have him come all over my hand, which he enjoys watching. My Eli is very visual.

"Fuck," he grits out when I finally pull away, wiping at the corner of my lips with shaky fingers. "What made you do that?"

I sit on the edge of the bed on my knees, staring up at his handsome face. He seems shocked, which tells me our relationship really lacked excitement near the end. "Was hoping to ease some of your tension."

His smile is naughty. There is no other word for it. "I appreciate it. I'd appreciate it even more if you took a shower with me. That would help ease a lot of tension."

"I thought you had to get ready to leave," I point out, warmth spreading through my body when he cups my cheeks, staring at me as if I'm the prettiest thing he's ever seen.

"I do. But I've always got time for you." He leans in and drops another one of those deadly soft kisses on my lips. I never want them to end. "Come on. Let's go take a shower."

He kicks off his sweats and offers his hand to me. I take it, letting him help me stand and we walk to the bathroom together. He lets go of my hand at the last second, his palm finding my ass and giving it a smack, making me dart into the bathroom, laughing.

I haven't felt this happy in a long time.

———————

After we took a sex-filled shower, Eli threw an old pair of my leggings at me, along with a hoodie that had shrunk in the wash and was now too small for him. I got dressed and borrowed a pair of Adidas slides from Gracie that I found in the living room that she must've left behind.

Or they belong to Caleb and he has really small feet, which I doubt.

I rode with Eli to the stadium and he delivered a heart-stopping kiss to my lips before he took off, leaving me with his car. Since it's so similar to my old BMW, I have no problem driving it and I cruise to the hospital, dismayed at the lack of parking. It's as if every spot is already filled.

Once I find parking in the deepest, farthest part of the lot, I make my way to the hospital, grateful the morning is cool and cloudy, so I don't feel overheated. The Fresno State sweatshirt Eli gave me is thick and warm.

I take the elevator to the second floor, exiting as soon as the double doors open, ready to walk past the nurses' station and head straight for Eli's mother's room when I do a double take.

There's a guy standing at the nurses' station, his arms propped on the desk's ledge, a charming smile curling his lips. He's tall and golden haired, just like my Eli, and I realize it's freaking Ryan Bennett standing there.

Flirting with the nurses.

I come to a stop and clear my throat, catching his attention. He does a double take as well, his smile falling a bit when he sees me. The jerk.

"Ava," he says as he pushes away from the desk and approaches me. "What are you doing here?"

"I came to pick up your mother," I say, unable to keep the accusing tone out of my voice.

"I'm taking care of it, since Eli wouldn't," he says, sounding vaguely bitter.

My mouth pops open. "What? He was totally going to come get her. He fully planned on giving up his game today to come here, but I volunteered to help him out."

"I didn't think you two were even together," he says.

"Well, we are," I say, lifting my chin, sounding snotty, which I really don't mean, but there's something about Ryan Bennett that makes me mad.

Maybe it's the way he keeps ignoring Eli, when all he wants is his big brother to call him every once in a while. Acknowledge him.

Yet he doesn't. It hurts Eli, not that he'd ever admit it. He stuffs those feelings way down, where no one can see them.

But I can. I always have.

"Great. Good for Eli. Life seems to be going well for him," Ryan says, his tone vaguely sarcastic.

I glare at him, a nasty insult on the tip of my tongue, but I swallow it down. He's dealing with his own problems and battling his own demons. We all handle our issues differently, and I shouldn't judge. I don't know him that well.

I just wish he would be a better brother to Eli.

"He's doing very well. You'd know that if you called him more often." Oops, a dig slipped out after all.

His lips thin but, otherwise, he doesn't acknowledge my

comment. "I've got my mother handled, but I appreciate you coming by."

He starts to walk away, heading toward his mom's room and I call out to him, "Do you really?"

Ryan pauses, glancing over his shoulder. "What did you just say?"

"Do you really appreciate me coming here?" I follow after him, dying to hear his answer. "Because you don't seem like you're happy with me showing up at all. You haven't spoken to Eli today?"

"I came straight here after I got the call from the hospital last night. I've been driving ever since." He turns to face me, resting his hands on his hips. He reminds me of Eli, though I can't help but think my boyfriend is way cuter. Of course, Ryan also looks super tired with the dark bags under his eyes, but he is undeniably handsome. And right now, I can tell he's irritated with me.

Well, that's great. I'm irritated with him too.

"And you didn't call your brother," I say as I catch up with him.

He sends me an irritated look. "No, I haven't. Why would I?"

"Why *wouldn't* you?" I ask incredulously. "You knew he came to the hospital last night. Don't you think you should've checked in with him and see what he had to say?"

He comes to a stop right before her room, glaring at me. "He's not even here this morning."

"He has a game to get ready for," I return, crossing my arms.

"Football is more important to him than our mother. Noted." He nods once, his expression flat as he starts for the door.

I step in front of him, getting in his way. "That's not true. You have no idea what's going on in his life, or what he needs to do. He was perfectly willing to not play today and come pick up your mother, but I told him I would take care of it. If he'd known you were coming, he wouldn't have to worry at all, but you can't even bother to send him a quick text to let him know what's going on."

Ryan says nothing and I shake my head, letting my frustration pour out.

"I don't understand any of you. Seriously." I step closer, lowering my voice. "Your mother has a drinking problem, and Eli doesn't know how to fix it. She keeps playing it off like there's nothing wrong, and he doesn't know what to do. He needs your help. Your support. But you're too busy doing whatever it is you're doing, while you run away from your family and your problems."

"You don't know what my problems are," he accuses, his brows furrowing.

"No, of course I don't because you don't talk to *anyone*. You don't tell anyone shit. You just let it build up and it resides right there." I poke at his chest with my index finger. "Weighing on your heart. You can't run away from your problems, Ryan. They're always there, sitting on your heart, reminding you of how much you've messed up your life."

He glares at me, absently rubbing his chest. "Eli has mentioned you've got a mouth on you."

"I don't hold back," I say proudly. "Now I'm going to go in there so I can say hi to your mother, but it's on you to get her home. Step up and actually help out for once. That woman needs you. So does your brother."

I huff out a breath and turn on my heel, walking straight into the room and hitting their mother with a bright smile when our gazes connect.

"Good morning," I say as I approach the side of her bed. Her face is more bruised this morning and she looks tired. "How are you feeling?"

"Beat up," she says with a small smile. "The nurses

warned it would hurt more the morning after, and they were right. I ache everywhere."

Reaching out, I gently pat her arm, grateful she doesn't wince when I touch her. The last thing I want to do is hurt her. "Are they ready to release you?"

"Yes, soon." She frowns. "Where's Eli? I thought I heard him outside?"

"I volunteered to come get you," I say. "But I just ran into—"

"Mom." Ryan strides into the room with a giant smile on his face and an equally giant bouquet of pink roses in his arms. "Are you all right?"

Where the hell did those come from?

He practically shoves me out of the way to get to his mother's bedside, and I step back, letting them have their moment.

Still lingering around though, so I can watch this show unfold.

"Oh, Ryan, you came!" He sets the roses on a nearby table before he bends over her and wraps her in a careful hug, all while she gushes. "I was so hoping you would be here, and that you would be the one who picked me up. I've missed you so much."

Okay maybe I don't want to watch this. I'll just get irritated and feel insulted on my boyfriend's behalf.

Can I think that? That Eli is my boyfriend once again?

I'm going with yes.

"Looks like you've got this covered," I tell Ryan.

They both swivel their heads in my direction, as if they forgot I was even there.

"I'll take her home," he says, going into authoritative, oldest child mode. I recognize it well, thanks to my sister pulling that on us all the time, especially when we were younger. "But thanks for coming."

And then they start speaking in low tones, his mother

launching into an explanation of what happened last night. I can already tell she's trying to downplay the drinking and the severity of the accident. Does he know about the police involvement? How they want to arrest her for DUI?

I flee the room before the irritation becomes unbearable.

Guess I'll let him figure all that out on his own.

CHAPTER 25

ELI

'm distracted again. Playing for shit on the worst possible day.

Game day.

And an important one too—but aren't they all important?

I can't have this happen. Not here, not now. I'm having total flashbacks to last season, when every little thing would take me down and I would make mistake after mistake. To the point that it became ultra-obvious to everyone, including the spectators and the other teams and worst of all, the media, that I was turning into a shit quarterback who allowed his emotions to rule him.

That was almost a direct quote by some local reporter who gleefully did his best to knock me off my pedestal. The asshole.

It's the beginning of the third quarter and I couldn't manage to score when we had the ball, so now I'm leaving the field, disgusted with myself, knowing I'm the sole reason why we're playing so shitty.

"Hey! Bennett!"

I turn as we're almost off the field, watching as Tony

approaches me, his dark eyes locked on me as he draws nearer. "What?" I ask wearily.

We come to a stop on the sideline, in front of the bench. The defense is shuffling past us, jogging out onto the field for their turn, including Caleb who watches us as he runs past.

I ignore him, concentrating on Tony, praying he isn't going to give me a bunch of shit.

"Don't let it all get in your head." He thwacks his fingers against the side of my helmet. "You're living in there right now when you need to be out on this field."

He's right. I know he's right. But I can't help but be distracted. I'm worried about my mom. Her problem hangs over me like a dark cloud, because she needs help, yet she's in full denial. It's hard to help someone who believes they've got everything under control.

And I don't have time for her. I mean, I'll make time. I have to. She's my mom, after all. But I've got school and football and homework and Ava and I don't know how I'm going to manage it all.

Then there's the sex thing. As in, Ava and I did it last night. Early this morning. In the shower. It was amazing. Better than it's ever been between us. She's so responsive and extra bold and I'm fucking digging it.

But…the sex thing seems to mess with my playing abilities, which sounds like a bunch of shit. Yet here I am, fucking up out on the field. I threw an interception in the second quarter, which about sent me to my knees.

My coaches' glares on the sidelines were the only thing keeping me from falling completely apart. That and they didn't turn it into a touchdown. Just a field goal, but still. They're up by ten, and I hope to God we can pull out the win.

"Yeah, I know," I say to Tony, my voice clipped. Truth hurts and all that. "I need to focus."

"Focus on the game. Don't let your Ava issues distract you." Tony slaps the back of my helmet as we make our way to the bench, both of us collapsing onto it, sitting right next to each other.

He has no clue what's really going on. Ava and I are in a good place—I think. We should be, considering how much we were all over each other last night and this morning. When she'd given me the blow job after I got off the phone, damn. She was sexy as fuck, turning those big eyes up to me with her mouth full of my dick.

A shudder moves through me and I force it away. I can't get distracted. I need to focus, like Tony said.

"What's your problem?" Diego comes out of nowhere, standing in front of me with his index finger doing that aggressive pointing thing that's usually my schtick. "You're playing for shit."

"Diego," Tony starts, but Diego whirls on him, his expression fierce.

"What? You know it's true. He's distracted or some shit. I thought halftime would help clear his head. That little speech was a rouser." Diego sends me a disgusted look.

Coach Harris went off on us during halftime in the locker room, and while I agreed with everything he said and wanted to get back out here in full ass-kicking mode, I still couldn't manage to score a touchdown, thanks to my terrible accuracy.

"I'm trying," I tell him. "And I don't need your shit coming at me right now. You're not what I would call motivating."

"And you're not what I would call NFL material, but I guess we'll have to agree to disagree," Diego retorts.

I leap to my feet and shove at his chest, blind anger taking over me. "What the fuck did you just say to me?"

He thrusts his face in mine, his dark eyes blazing with anger. "Touch me again and I'll fucking kick your ass."

"I'd love to see you try," I throw back at him, our faces so close I can actually feel his breath.

"Guys, come on. Knock this shit off," Tony says, glancing over his shoulder.

I look in the same direction Tony is, realizing the coaching staff is watching me. Us. Coach Harris marches right up to me, his expression fierce. "You're benched." He jerks his thumb over his shoulder. "For the rest of the quarter."

I gape at him. "What the hell? Are you *serious?*"

"Deadly serious. And if you keep arguing with me, I'm benching you for the rest of the game. I'll let Marshall prove to us what he's got." Coach strides away, not even waiting for me to answer.

I flop back into the space I vacated, not even a few minutes ago, my mouth tight, my thoughts turbulent. Fucking Diego.

I'm to blame just as much as he is, though he is the prick who started it.

I'm tempted to say something, about to go in search of Coach when Tony grabs my sleeve, keeping me from leaving. "Don't bother."

"Don't bother what?"

"Doing whatever you're thinking of doing. Don't go defend yourself or cause more shit with Diego. He's under enormous pressure right now, just like you are."

I didn't even think of that. He's actually under just as much pressure as I am. Maybe even more because he's got a family to take care of and nothing to fall back on. Me? At least I have fairly wealthy parents who can bail me out of pretty much any situation.

Diego doesn't have that luxury.

"Whatever." I slump against the bench, my legs spread, my shoulders hunched—as much as they can be hunched in all the pads and protective gear. "This is some bullshit."

"Give yourself a break," Tony says. "Use the rest of the quarter to clear your thoughts and focus on the game. The only person you're damaging right now is you."

"And the rest of the team," I remind him.

"We're good, bro. Marshall Hatfield is going out there and he's going to annihilate them. I can almost guarantee it. That kid is fierce." Tony shakes his head. "But don't worry. He doesn't have your polish and expertise. He's a little messy still. But he can get us through the third quarter."

Tony gets up and saunters off, and I watch him go, his words on repeat in my head.

Polish and expertise. Polish and expertise.

The more I think about those two words, the better I feel. Tony's right. I have polish and expertise. I've been doing this for a long time. I lead this team. They look up to me.

I need to be an example, not an out-of-control asshole.

"Hey D," I yell, when I spot Diego standing nearby only a few minutes later.

"What?" His jaw clenches and his eyes are still ablaze as he glares at me.

"I'm sorry, man. I didn't mean to unleash on you," I tell him, my voice dripping with sincerity.

He walks over to the bench, stopping directly in front of me. "I'm sorry too. The pressure has been weighing on me and it's been—tough."

"I get it." If any two players on this team right now can understand each other, it's us. I stand up and offer him my hand. "We good?"

Diego takes my hand, giving me one of our endless homie shakes. "We're all right, Bennett. Even if you're a pain in my ass sometimes."

We chuckle, and the pressure sitting on my chest eases some.

Not enough to make it easier to breathe though. I'm still twisted up in knots, anxiously watching the game, my gaze never straying from the field. I keep my fists clenched on my knees, bent forward, so my ass is perched on the edge of the bench as I track everything happening. Our defensive line is strong and they keep the opposing team from scoring yet again, which gives me hope for the first time the entire game.

"Good luck," I tell Marshall, just before he's about to run onto the field.

He stops short, sending an appreciative look my way. "Thanks."

I realize Marshall seems terrified. His brown eyes are wide and unblinking, and for such a big dude, he's giving off major scaredy cat vibes.

"You've got this," I tell him, my voice full of confidence. "Show them what you're made of."

He nods once, his helmet wobbling on his head. "Will do. Thank you."

I watch as Marshall jogs onto the field and I go to where the coaches are standing, hoping one of them will talk to me.

"You all right, Bennett?" Coach asks me.

I nod once, staring out at the field. "I fucked up. Sorry."

"We can't be perfect all the time." He slaps me on the back, smiling faintly. "Take a breather. Let Marshall do his job."

"We're down though. Now is not the time to put in the second string," I remind him.

"Better to send Marshall out there than put even more pressure on you and watch you fail," he says, blunt as always.

"True," I mumble.

I watch my offensive line and Marshall play pretty damn well. To my surprise, they drive the ball down the field fairly quickly and end up scoring a touchdown, plus the extra point.

Now we're only down by three.

Glancing toward the crowd, I can't help but wonder if Ava is here. Is she watching? Or is she still with my mom? I have no idea what's going on, because I don't have my phone and there's no way for her to get in contact with me until after the game.

I wonder if she'd be down for us being celibate at least through playoffs. I blew off the sex thing fucking with my head as a one off. Looks like it's an actual thing, which is crazy, but I do remember when Tim Tebow was around and everyone said that guy was a virgin.

Maybe that big ol' fucker actually wasn't getting pussy on the regular and it kept him on top of his game. I've heard weirder shit.

And athletes are a superstitious lot. My dad had an ugly ass Forty-Niner Velcro wallet that he got in high school and he swore the one season he stopped using it, the Niners didn't make it to the playoffs. He started using it again, and they were, once more, on top of their game.

Like my dad's wallet had anything to do with their season. Just goes to show that superstitious behavior carries over onto the fans' too.

Somehow our defense keeps the score the same and the third quarter is over. Coach indicates with a wave of his finger that he wants me to go back in and so I do.

Hopefully we can score and make this game our bitch.

CHAPTER 26

AVA

Considering I didn't have to take Eli's mom back to her house, I was at a loss for what to do. All of my friends were still up at the cabin Jackson rented. Like...all of them. I didn't want to drive all the way up there, only to have to turn around and head back down the hill to get Eli's car to him.

Then I realized they were all going to the football game since most of their boyfriends are playing, so I made plans to meet up with them at Hayden's apartment so we could get ready together. Killing some time before they arrived, I went to the mall real quick and bought a new pair of jeans, some panties and a really cute sweater at American Eagle.

They always come in clutch when I'm needing something new to wear.

By the time I show up at Hayden's apartment, I'm sleepy and in need of a nap. She takes one look at me, clutching my AE bag in one hand and a Starbucks in my other hand, and her expression turns suspicious.

"What have you been up to?" Hayden's brows shoot up.

I stride into her apartment when she opens the door

wider, waving at Gracie, who's sitting on the couch. "Where's Ellie?"

"Still with Jackson. They're coming to the game later. Together." Gracie rolls her eyes. "Those two don't do anything without each other."

"I think it's cute," I say, automatically defending my best friend.

"Oh, so do I. I guess I'm just jealous since Caleb's been so busy with football lately. Though she should know about sitting on the sidelines watching her boyfriend perform." Gracie laughs. "Ignore me. I'm acting like a jealous troll."

I set my bag on the floor and collapse on the couch, feeling the exhaustion settle deep in my limbs. "I'm so tired."

"Why, hmmm?" The look Hayden sends my way tells me she's not going to let this go. She definitely suspects I've been up to something. "Where did you disappear off to last night?"

I go over the events from last evening. The call Eli received about his mom. How we went to the hospital and she was injured but nothing too serious. I don't mention the potential drunk driving charge. Why bring that up when it might not even happen?

"Ellie didn't mention anything to you guys?" I ask them. "I texted her after we left to let her know."

"No. But she disappeared with Jackson eventually too so..." Gracie shrugs. "Everyone was up to something except for me."

"I was at the hospital," I stress.

"All night?" Hayden asks.

"Eventually we went back to Eli's apartment."

"Is that why you're dressed like that?" When I frown, she laughs. "Like a hobo wearing her boyfriend's old sweatshirt and socks and some ratty-ass leggings he dug out of the bottom of his closet that you owned like...three years ago?"

I burst out laughing. "You pretty much nailed it." I kick

out my foot toward Gracie, waving the Adidas slides. "These belong to you. Snagged them out of Caleb's room."

Gracie shakes her head. "Those are my 'I have nothing else to wear on my feet' shoes."

"They've worked out pretty well. And this is why I went shopping earlier. I needed something to wear tonight to the game."

Eli mentioned he'd leave tickets for me at will call.

Can't wait to watch him play again.

Gracie snatches up the bag and peeks inside, pulling out a blue and green printed thong. "Nice," she says, twirling them on her finger. "Wearing them for Eli later?"

"Why do you need new panties, hmm?" Hayden asks. "I'm guessing you're not wearing any at the moment."

"No bra either," I confirm with a laugh. "Might've had an —encounter or two with Eli last night. Well, more like the middle of the night."

And earlier this morning. Oh and right before we left the apartment.

"Are you two back together or what?" Gracie asks.

"We are." I bite my lower lip. "I mean, it's not official or anything. We haven't labeled our relationship yet."

Hayden's brows shoot up. "I would say if you two are having sex, you're back together."

"Unless it's hate sex, which can be fun," Gracie adds.

I think of the night in the back seat of his car. That was definitely pent-up, I want you but I hate you sex.

"He told me he loved me," I confess.

"When he was inside you?"

"Gracie!" Hayden yells.

Gracie shrugs. "Just asking. That's when they tend to say it the most."

"Yes," I admit. "That's exactly how it happened."

"Ugh, men." Gracie shakes her head.

"You're not allowed to be mad at men in general. You're

the one in a solid relationship with the reformed horn dog," Hayden tells her best friend.

"We're not talking about Caleb and me," Gracie says, her gaze on mine and her cheeks the faintest pink. "We're talking about you and Eli. Just—be careful, my friend. Eli is a great guy. I adore him, but he's also impulsive. I don't want him to hurt you."

"He won't. I know what I'm doing when it comes to Eli," I say assuredly.

Her words of warning linger in my brain as we start to get ready, though. I take a quick shower and change into all-new clothes, right down to the thong and a new bralette. I even bought shoes—a pair of new slip-on black Vans, which I've been wanting to replace my old ones for a while.

"You're not wearing Bulldog gear," Gracie chastises when she sees me in my jeans and new black sweater.

"I refuse to buy a new team T-shirt or sweatshirt when I have so many at home," I say, as I walk up to the standing mirror sitting in the corner of Hayden's bedroom. "I like my fit. I'll wear this sweater on repeat all through winter."

"It's cute," Hayden agrees, coming up behind me. She's got on a white Bulldog sweatshirt and jeans, her hair pulled into a high pony. She's grown it out over the last year and it falls past her shoulders now.

"More for Tony to grab," she joked with us, which made me laugh.

And blush.

I think about it again. Eli has pulled my hair a few times during sex, but never hard enough to really hurt.

That sounds kind of fun.

Any type of experimental sex with Eli sounds fun. I feel much bolder with him this time around. He really enjoyed that blow job earlier this morning. Again, he's all about the visual. I could put on a little show for him tonight, if he's not too tired.

I could ask him to do a few things with me. *To* me. He might be interested.

Knowing Eli, he'll be extremely interested.

By the time we make it over to the stadium, the first quarter of the game has already started. Considering we have seats in the reserved section for the girlfriends and wives—crazy that some of the members of the team are married, but a few of them already are—we don't have to worry about where we sit, and we always have great seats.

We grab some snacks and something to drink, since none of us have eaten much today. Once we're settled in our seats, I immediately find Eli on the field, and I can tell, even from the distance, that he's not happy.

My heart sinks and my appetite disappears. An unhappy Eli on the field means an unhappy and potentially angry Eli off the field too. And that's the worst. I've dealt with his moods before. I was almost glad I wasn't around much last season—his worst season by far. He was constantly beating himself up.

The team gets into position, Eli getting ready to throw the ball, and I notice his frenzied movements. As if he doesn't know who to throw to. Diego is trying to catch his attention, but he's also being blocked by a big dude from the other team.

Eli throws the ball and it sails high into the sky, landing…

In that big dude's equally big hands.

"Oh shit!" Gracie exclaims, clapping a hand over her mouth when she catches me looking at her.

His disappointment is palpable. He's mentally beating himself up. And it's like this the entirety of the game. At half-time, I have high hopes he can readjust and get his head back into the game.

But it doesn't work. And at one point early in the third quarter, I swear it looks like he's about to get into a fight with…Diego?

What the hell?

My mood—as well as my friends'—becomes more and more somber. We toss most of the food we bought, too upset to eat it. By the time we're nearing the end of the fourth quarter, I'm completely discouraged.

We're going to lose. The second loss of the season—and it's at home.

I'm sure Eli is devastated.

Somehow, during the final seconds of the game, our boys are able to drive the ball down the field, but unable to score a touchdown. They're close enough for a field goal, which the kicker makes.

Now we're tied.

Holy shit.

"We're going into overtime," Hayden says. "Oh my God, I hope we can win."

I say nothing. It's like I can't. I'm too choked up and filled with worry. We *must* win.

We have to.

The game ends with the score tied, and after a few minutes, the team captains walk out onto the field for the coin toss. I watch Eli and Tony walk out together, my chest expanding with pride. Hayden reaches out and grips my hand, not saying a word, but I can tell she's nervous.

So am I.

We win the coin toss and they choose the opposing team to receive first. Perfect. I sit perched on the edge of my seat, my entire body tense as I watch our defense play. Gracie is rowdy, constantly screaming for Caleb, which makes me and Hayden laugh, but it's nervous laughter. We can't fully get into it.

We're both too stressed out.

The other team gets a field goal, which devastates me. If our boys can't score, they'll lose. The pressure just turned up even more, and from what I've seen today, Eli isn't handling it well.

At all.

"He did this last week," Gracie announces, causing both Hayden and me to look at her.

"Who did what?" Hayden asks.

"Eli. At practice though. He messed up again and again and their coaches pulled him off the field. They had the second-string quarterback play for a while, and Caleb said he was pretty good." Gracie nods toward the field. "That's why they probably had him play earlier. Just to test him out."

"They usually never do that sort of thing when they're losing and they're only in the third quarter," I say, busting out some of my coach's daughter knowledge.

"True that," Hayden says with a nod.

They go out on the field and...I don't see number one out there.

"Oh, Hatfield went out," Gracie says, her voice full of disappointment.

My gaze frantic, I spot Eli on the sidelines, his helmet off, his expression one of bitter disappointment as he stands next to Caleb, their gazes on the field.

I'm dying to know what happened. But then again...

I'd rather not know anything at all.

CHAPTER 27

ELI

We lost. By a mother fuckin' field goal.

I told Coach Harris to let me out on that field, but he wouldn't hear it. Said the pressure was too much and it would get to me. He was afraid I'd choke. Worse, I think he believed I'd choke so badly that I'd throw an interception and let the other team score. Like he's lost all faith in my ass, all because of one bad performance.

I guess that's all it takes to ruin everything.

Marshall does his best, as does the rest of the team, but they can't manage to get the ball down the field. They barely get it close enough for a field-goal attempt, but they try anyway, and the kicker misses it. It was too far anyway and would've broken a record if he'd made it, so no surprise he didn't.

Can't believe we fucking lost. So fucking frustrating. I can't blame anyone else for the loss either. I sucked ass out on the field today and I don't know what went wrong. I haven't seen our fans this disappointed since last season. We were on a winning streak. I was their golden boy.

Now I'm an utter failure.

I storm off the field as fast as I can, the moment the clock turns zero, not wanting to stick around and talk to the media. I hear coaching staff yelling my name as I make my escape, but I don't look back or respond. I know what they want. Me to stand out there and look grim while talking about missed opportunities and coming back stronger next week.

Fuck that. I'd rather say nothing at all.

The rest of the team stays out there for a while longer, I'm sure earning the approval of Coach, while I'm in the locker room taking a shower, eager to get the fuck out of here.

No luck though. The second I walk out of the showers with a towel around me, there's Coach, his arms crossed and his eyes narrowed as he contemplates me.

"You left."

"What was I supposed to say? Sorry I fucked up, better luck next week?" I go to walk by him, but he steps in my way, blocking me. "I know you wanted me to talk to reporters. I'm afraid I would've said something shitty and made it worse."

He nods, respecting my explanation, only because he knows it's true. I went off a few times last season and made an ass of myself. "You still should have talked to them. A couple of losses in the seasons won't ruin your career, Bennett."

A sigh leaves me. "I've been under a lot of pressure."

"I know. Both on the field and off. Heard about you and your girl getting back together." He raises his brows. "A coincidence?"

"No," I spit out. Anger rises within me and I tamp it down. I don't want him blaming Ava for any of this—even though I've blamed her for some of it. Funny how every time I have sex with her, my concentration goes to shit.

"You can't let the personal stuff get in your head and mess with your game," Harris says, his voice lowering, his gaze serious. "Don't you want to be in the NFL?"

I nod. Of course I do. He knows this.

"Then don't let your emotions spill onto the field. From

what I've seen, you've really improved this season compared to last and your focus is razor sharp—until today. Straighten up, Bennett. You've got this. You've had it all season, every game day. We're so close to the end goal. Don't get distracted now," he continues.

"Yeah, I know. Listen, it's been a rough twenty-four hours. Some stuff is happening with my mom," I admit. "She got in a car wreck last night."

"Oh no. Is she all right?" I see the concern etched in his face, and it's reassuring. He's a good guy. Hard on us sometimes, especially me, but he means well. And I think I need someone to be hard on me sometimes to keep me in line.

"She's good. I think. I need to call her." I haven't talked to anyone in hours. I have no idea how it went with Ava getting her. I didn't even bother checking my phone when I got in the locker room, I was too intent on getting the hell out of here.

"Definitely check up on her, she's your mom. And let me know what's going on. But—maybe ease up on the relationship stuff, you know what I mean?" He sends me a look and I frown. "I don't mean to get in your personal business, son, but I have to when it's impacting our team. Seems to me you were playing at your best when you were single. And now you're back with that girl who broke your heart and you're a mess. Think about that."

Coach walks away before I can protest or argue, and his words stay with me. Sink into my brain. Seep into my bones.

I don't like what he's saying, but I can't deny it either.

Coach is right. If I want to get into the NFL, I need to stay focused. I need this for my future—my future with Ava. Everything I'm doing right now is for her.

For *us*.

She'll understand if I need to focus on football for the next few weeks. It'll be tough, but worth it in the end. Especially if I get drafted. Damn, if that happens…

My future with Ava is set.

And that's all I want. My girl by my side, forever. Loving her and taking care of her in the best way I can.

As I start getting dressed, the team trickles in, all of them looking as dejected as I feel. I offer them encouraging comments and they do the same for me, not a one of them calling me out.

I'm waiting for that to come from my best friends. Those fuckers won't hold back.

After tugging on my shirt, I finally check my phone and find a bunch of text messages, mostly from Ava and my mother and…Ryan?

Ava: **Your brother showed up to the hospital. I kind of chewed him out, I'm sorry, but I couldn't restrain myself. I'm glad he came though. Your mother was glad too.**

Mom: **Ryan showed up and brought me home! He said he's going to stay for as long as I need him, the sweetheart. Call me when you can. Good luck on your game. Love you.**

Ryan: **I'm with Mom and took her home. She wanted me to pour her a glass of wine but I wouldn't do it. I think her problem is worse than she's letting on. Text me when you get this message.**

I roll my eyes at my brother's text. *No shit, Sherlock* is what I want to respond with, but I don't.

I'll call him in a few. I need to be in a certain mood when I deal with him and now is not it.

Ava: **I'm at the game. Hopefully we can meet up after. Gracie can take me home if you're too tired to drive.**

She sends me a string of red hearts and my own heart throbs, hating that she witnessed my shitty gameplay.

I feel like a failure at all the things. Football. School. Family. Ava.

All of it.

Why can't I have it all? Why can't shit go right for once?

"Hey."

I turn at the sound of Caleb's voice, which is more subdued than I think I've ever heard it. He's full of as much bravado as me most of the time. But when I see his somber expression, and note the matching expressions on Tony and Diego as they stop just behind him, all three of them watching me, I realize they feel bad. Not just for themselves, but also for me.

They're worried about me.

Because they give a shit—and that means a lot.

"You doing okay?" Tony asks.

I nod, working my damnedest to keep a brave face. "Yeah. Sucked, but what's two losses, right?"

"We'll kick ass next week," Diego says fiercely.

"Hell yeah, we will," Caleb adds.

I nod, appreciating their faith in me. In us. "We'll do great. Work harder at practice."

"It's an away game, but we always beat San Jose," Diego says. "And at least it's not too far."

"Thank God," I mutter, shaking my head.

"Want to get the fuck out of here?" Caleb asks me. "I rode with Gracie, but she said she wanted to get home after the game."

"Ava dropped me off," I admit. "She still has my car."

"Perfect. She could leave with Gracie. Unless she's staying the night with you?" He raises his brows.

She shouldn't. I should send her pretty ass back to her parents' house, and we can reconnect later.

Like at the end of the football season?

I banish the thought.

But it sticks with me still as my friends talk and I mostly listen. As we exit the locker room and head for the place where we always end up meeting up with the girls, I remember how I used to depart before they'd get to the girls, when I was broken up with Ava, and seeing them all greet their boyfriends made me sad. Made me miss her.

Now she's probably there waiting for me and I almost dread seeing her. I mean, I want to, but I also think…

Maybe we should take it slow—like *really* slow until the end of the season. I'm willing to do just about anything to stay on track and finish out the season on top. Everyone's right, another blip, another loss isn't going to ruin everything, but what if this keeps up? I stay with Ava, keep having sex with her and keep having shit practices and lose more games. Lose my shot at the chance to win a bowl.

Lose my shot at getting to the NFL.

My heart feels like it seizes in my chest and I rub at it absently, recognizing it as anxiety. I can't risk it.

I can't risk fucking up our entire future because I'm not doing this just for me—this is all for her too. I love that girl more than anything. She loves me too, and she'll understand. She will. She comes from a football family. If anyone should get what I'm doing and where I'm coming from, it's her.

When I finally do see Ava, I can't help the smile that appears. She smiles in return, her eyes full of sadness. All for me.

Damn, this woman. She has such a big heart.

She comes to me, stopping just in front of me and resting her hands on my chest. "You okay?" Her voice is quiet, just for me.

I nod, leaning in to kiss her because, damn it, I can't help it. And it might be the last time we kiss for a while.

But she can sacrifice for me, can't she?

Just for a little while.

"Are you sure?" Her fingers curl into my shirt, tugging me down so I have to kiss her again. Not a hardship. "You seemed really upset earlier. You didn't even stay on the field for the reporters."

"So they can ask me endless questions and make me feel like shit? No thanks," I mutter, slinging my arm around her shoulders and pulling her into my side. "Let's get out of here."

"Are you tired? I can go home with Gracie if that's easier on you," she suggests, nibbling on her lower lip.

"I want to take you home. I want to talk to you about a few things and maybe I could stop by and see my mom and Ryan, see how she's doing," I tell her.

"Okay." She nods, still looking worried. I don't like seeing that expression on my girl.

Just wait until I tell her what I'm thinking. She might flip the fuck out.

We chat with the group for a little bit, but we all want out of here, so we part ways in the parking lot, me following Ava, since I have no clue where she parked my car.

"Do you want me to drive?" she asks when we're finally approaching the car and she's pulling my keys out of her bag.

"I'll drive. I don't mind," I answer, taking the keys from her.

I'm quiet for the first few minutes I'm driving, maneuvering myself out of the parking lot and away from the stadium and campus. Traffic is shit on the main streets and by the time we're on the freeway headed north, I'm exhaling with relief.

Traffic stresses me the fuck out. Hell, lately, everything stresses me out.

Ava remains quiet too and I know she's doing it for me. She's concentrating on her phone, tapping away on the screen and I wonder who she's texting.

This makes me remember I need to text my brother and I punch the steering wheel in frustration, startling Ava.

"What's wrong?"

"I was supposed to call Ryan."

"Have you talked to him at all today?"

"Nope. I bet he's pissed at me about it too."

"It's the least he could've done, show up and help out

with your mom. He leaves everything on you," Ava says bitterly, always running to my defense.

"He doesn't live here anymore, how can I expect him to help out when he's not around?" I ask her.

"What's he doing anyway? I follow him on Instagram. He travels a lot and doesn't seem to really work a steady job," she says.

I shrug, unable to answer. Ryan's turned into a bit of a nomad. When I was younger, I envied his freedom. He didn't have roots anywhere, and that appealed to me.

Now I realize, he's lost. He doesn't know how to settle down. And that must suck, not being able to figure out what you want or who you are.

"I'm just glad he showed up," I say wearily. "Him being here will be a big help."

"I guess so." She crosses her arms in front of her, looking pouty.

Cute.

Sexy as hell.

"Aw, don't be mad, Princess. Don't let him get to you." I learned a long time ago if I let every little thing Ryan did bother me, I'd be pissed for all eternity. And who does that really suck for? Me, while Ryan's off doing whatever it is Ryan's doing.

Better to let that shit go.

That I'm even able to let shit go is monumental. I'm not known for that.

"How did my mom seem?" I ask, changing the subject.

Ava visibly relaxes in her seat. "Good. Sore. Really glad to see your brother."

"She's always liked him best, even though they fight all the time and he reminds her of Dad," I say.

Ava gapes at me. "Are you serious?"

"She definitely prefers Ryan over me." I shrug. "Don't your parents play favorites?"

"No." She shakes her head. "Absolutely not. They love us all in different ways, but I never feel like my mom loves one more than another, and same with my dad."

"Aren't you lucky with your perfect family." I can't help my snarky comment.

A sigh leaves her. "Are you trying to start a fight? I'm not in the mood, Eli. I'm tired, and so are you. I know you're frustrated about the game, and that's why I was trying to leave it alone. But it's like you're picking on me, and I don't like it."

"I'm not picking on you," I tell her, feeling like a dick. "I just—I'm under enormous amounts of pressure right now. The team, the games, my mom, my brother, all of it is getting to me, and I don't think I'm handling it very well."

She's quiet, so I remain silent too. I've said my piece. There's more I should admit, but is this the right time to lay it all out?

I guess it's either now or I stretch it out longer and make it harder for me to leave her alone.

Keeping my distance from her will only be for a short period of time. No big deal in the long run. Though damn, I did just get her back in my life...

"I know you're under a lot of pressure," she finally says, her voice small. "I just want to help you, Eli. In any way I can. I'm not in school right now, so if you need me to help your mom out, I can totally do it."

I want to take her up on it. I desperately need her support, and of course, I want to be there for her and support her as much as I can too.

But I can't right now. Later.

After the football season.

Yeah, we'll be good after that. Everything will come together like it's supposed to.

"Here's the weird thing," I start, hating how nervous I sound. She can sense it too. I can tell by the odd way she's currently looking at me. "Feels like when we uh, have sex, I play terrible. The time we hooked up in my car? I played like shit during practice and everyone noticed. My teammates, the coaches. They put the second string in and he did great."

"I heard about that," she admits.

"You did?" I'm shocked.

She nods. "Gracie mentioned it. Caleb must've told her."

I'm quiet for a moment. Maybe she'll be more understanding since she already knows I'm having an issue.

"It happened again today. We have sex and my concentration is for shit. I can't throw a ball to save my damn life and I lost the game."

Now we're both quiet, but I can feel her gaze on me. Assessing. Questioning.

"What are you trying to say?"

I clear my throat, searching for the right words, so this doesn't sound completely shitty. "I'm wondering if we should —take a break for a little bit. See each other again during playoffs. Or even after playoffs. Like after the bowl game. If we get a bid for one."

"What?"

She screeches the word, making me wince.

"It's only for a couple more months, if that—"

"You're talking until mid-December," she says.

"Not that far off. It's practically November. Come on, Princess." My tone turns pleading. "We can make the sacrifice, right? This is our future we're talking about here."

Ava bursts out laughing. "Oh, this is good. My God, can you even see what you're doing to me right now?"

I know she's so mad, I'm fucking grateful we're getting closer to her house, that's for damn sure.

"It'll be tough. I'll miss you like crazy, but it's for the best for my future, babe. For *our* future. It's like your pussy is made of magic or something and it zaps all my skills right out of me."

"If I could hit you right now, I so would, Eli. You're being ridiculous." She's shaking her head, her face crumpling.

Oh shit, like she's going to cry.

"Baby." I touch her thigh and she jerks away from my hand. "Come on. I was hoping you would understand. I'm doing this for us."

"Like you understood when I told you about my chance to go to Spain for the summer? Like that? It's only for a few months. A small sacrifice for my future. For *our* future. Those are words I said to you at some point and now you're repeating the same shit to me about your football season, which is somehow getting fucked by us…fucking? What the hell?"

"Don't say it like that," I start, but she interrupts me.

"You can't tell me what to say or how to think. If you could just see the irony of this situation right now, my God." She shakes her head, her eyes watering. "I asked you to wait for me, and you wouldn't."

She says nothing for the rest of the drive to her house. And it's at least another twenty minutes before we even get there. I want to speak, but every time I'm ready to say something, I snap my lips shut, second-guessing myself.

I'm sure my remaining quiet is for the best. I'll just say something else that pisses her off and that's the last thing I want to do, though I've already done it.

My girl is furious. I can tell. Steam should be coming from her ears. She's crying too, which also breaks my heart. Angry crying. Every time a tear dares to leak from her eyes, she furiously wipes it away like she's disgusted.

I did that to her, I remind myself. I'm the one who made her cry.

But then again, what else is new? I do that a lot lately.

Makes me feel like absolute garbage, too.

Finally, we're in her neighborhood and she starts gathering her things, as if she's going to jump out of my car before

I've got it fully stopped. I watch in disbelief as she puts the American Eagle shopping bag in her lap, along with her purse. Her head is averted and she won't look at me.

"Ava," I say quietly, as I apply the brakes, not coming to a complete stop.

I'm afraid if I stop, she really will leap out of the car.

"What?" She turns to glare at me.

"Can't you understand where I'm coming from?"

"No," she spits out. "Because you never understood where I was coming from. I know it's petty and childish to react this way, but damn it, Eli, you can't work a double standard on me. You broke up with me for going to Spain for a couple of months because you believed I abandoned you. Now you want me to stay away from you for the rest of the season so you can keep your head in the game and not get distracted by my—*vagina*. It's such a bunch of bullshit!"

I blink at her, surprised by the hostility in her tone. "I figured coming from a family of football players, you'd totally understand."

"The football players I'm related to aren't as emotionally driven as you are. My father knew how to separate the game from his personal life. So does Jake. Even my uncle Owen was good at that, though he's probably the most emotional out of the three. The most like you," she explains.

I always knew Owen Maguire was my own personal hero.

"This is different. This is *temporary*," I stress. "All I want is to secure my chances to get into the draft. That's it. I'm doing this for us, baby. For our future together." I'm brave enough to pull in front of her house and throw the car into park. If she runs right now, I don't know what I'll do.

Or how we'll ever come back from it.

She gapes at me. "It's different yet exactly the same, and if you can't see that, then I'll never be able to explain it to you. You are so frustrating, Eli. Seriously. I love you. But if you need distance, fine. I'll give it to you. I'll give you all the distance you could ever want."

Now it's my turn to stare at her with my mouth hanging open. "What exactly do you mean?"

She shrugs. "Maybe we'll end up together, maybe we won't."

"So what? That's it? I ask for one favor, and you tell me there are no guarantees that you'll stick around for me." My heart aches, and I tell the son of a bitch to man up.

I can't believe she's saying this.

Ava hangs her head, staring at that goddamned shopping bag in her lap. "You still don't get it."

My anger sends me right over the edge. "What is there to get?" I roar, making her jump.

The tears flow down her cheeks and she doesn't bother wiping them away this time. No, my girl lets them fall and she is the saddest I've ever seen her. Mad too, I can tell by that angry glow in her pretty eyes.

I am fucking everything up, when all I want to do is to fix this. Fix us and our future so I can guarantee her that I'll always be there, taking care of her no matter what.

"You're asking me to make sacrifices for you when you wouldn't do it for me. How is that fair?"

"I'm only asking you for one thing—" I start but she shakes her head, the look on her face rendering me silent.

"And I only asked you for one thing too, but you couldn't give it to me. Our relationship feels like a double standard and I'm tired of you trying to convince me to do what *you* want." She taps her chest with her finger, a sob leaving her. "I'm choosing me, Eli. And when you're ready to choose us for real, then talk to me. But until then, leave me alone."

I don't say anything, her words shocking me still. She's so upset.

Again, all on me.

She starts digging in her purse, pulling out a small envelope and setting it on the dashboard. "That's yours."

"What is it?" I ask warily.

"Open it. Maybe it'll give you the luck you're looking for, for the rest of the season," she says.

I grab the envelope and peek inside, shocked to see my old necklace with the number one pendant hanging from it.

Damn, I wondered where that went. It feels good to have it back, though my favorite place to see it was always around Ava's neck.

Her giving my necklace back to me feels so...

Final.

"Go ahead and worry about your football season and your future and your career with the NFL. Clearly, I'm a burden, not an asset. So have fun by yourself, Eli. See you later." She opens the door and starts to leave. I reach for her, my fingers slipping from her arm as she gets out of the car, taking that stupid shopping bag with her. She slams the door extra hard, the entire vehicle rattling with the force of it, and she storms down the walkway toward her parents' house, never once looking back.

Look back, Princess, I think to myself as I clutch my old necklace in my hand, my gaze watching her as she grows smaller and smaller. If she looks back, we'll be fine. And she's going to look back. I know it.

I know her.

But she doesn't.

CHAPTER 28

AVA

ne month later

"You look pale."

I stop in the open doorway of my bathroom and stare blankly at my sister, rubbing my fingers over my lips. I just brushed my teeth because my mouth tasted horrible, and I've been feeling gross all morning.

All week really.

I blame it on Thanksgiving coming up. While I like the holiday and love that my family always gets together for it every single year without fail, I've never been a huge fan of Thanksgiving food. Mom has been cooking up a storm with my Aunt Chelsea. She and Uncle Owen arrived yesterday morning along with my cousins, and while it's been fun to see everyone and hang out, I'm still sad.

I've been sad for almost a month now, and nothing anyone does for me changes my mood.

"Ava, what the hell is wrong with you?" Autumn asks me when I still haven't said anything.

I shrug and enter my bedroom, throwing myself on my bed. "Nothing. I'm fine."

"You're lying." She lies next to me, her gaze never leaving my face. "Are you even sleeping right now?"

"It's all I do. Mom thinks I'm depressed."

"She said the same thing to me," Autumn admits, her worried gaze meeting mine. "She also said you won't really talk, you don't really eat and you barely leave your room. You don't spend much time with your friends either."

"They're all busy with their boyfriends and their lives, while mine is on hold," I say, my thoughts already focusing on the future. There's been no word from Eli, which is no surprise. Not really. The longer I go without hearing from him, the easier it will be to leave.

San Diego beckons. I can't wait to go back and I'm headed there early. Mom helped me line up an apartment and next month I finalize my school schedule.

I'm desperate to get out of here.

"Your life isn't on hold," Autumn whispers, reaching out to take my hand in hers. "You could still be enjoying your time here, hanging out with Beck and Mom and Dad. Or your friends. They're never too busy for you, and you know it."

"Says the woman who's living her best life with her NFL playing fiancé," I say, sounding like a spiteful old hag. "Traveling everywhere with him, having a great time and being with the man you love. Supporting him because he supports you just as much."

"I don't know about that," she says with a little laugh. "Right now our lives are all about Asher Davis, NFL quarterback."

I bet he still supports her more than Eli could ever support me.

"Have you even tried to talk to him?" she murmurs.

"Who, Ash? Your fiancé is kind of busy right now," I tease her because it's easier to focus on anyone else than Eli.

"I'm not talking about Ash."

A sigh leaves me. "No, I haven't tried talking to Eli. He sent me a few texts right after our last fight, but I didn't respond."

He was trying to convince me to talk to him, but I wasn't in the mood. I'm still not. And I didn't block him again. Not on any social media, and he didn't block me either. We're readily available to each other at any moment, but I'm not ready to reach out.

I guess neither is he.

He's having a great football season. The Bulldogs made it to the playoffs, and if they win this weekend's game, they'll play in the Mountain West conference championship the first weekend in December. And if they win the championship, the Bulldogs will receive the opportunity to play in a bowl game in mid-December. By the time he's finished with his last college football season, I'll be packing up, eager to escape. I'm leaving for San Diego the first week in January.

I'm out of here. And I'm not looking back this time around, or waiting for someone to realize they fucked up.

"You two are so stubborn," Autumn mutters.

"I told you everything that happened between us, you know why I'm being stubborn." And I'm not backing down from it either. The man is infuriating.

"Listen, I think he's a little prick, you know this. I don't have a soft spot for him like Mom, or see all that potential in him like Dad. But I don't hate him like Jake does whenever Eli does you wrong."

"Jake still hates him?" He'll be home this afternoon and he's bringing Hannah with him. I can't wait to see them, though I don't want any "I told you so" lectures from my big brother either.

"Any excuse he can get for hating Eli, he'll take," Autumn says. "But what I'm trying to tell you is that I will always be on your side no matter what. You're my baby sister. We have to stick together."

There's something she's not saying.

"But?" I prompt.

"But...you're only torturing yourself by cutting him completely off. Eli just—he gets wrapped up in his own head and makes *really* emotional decisions."

"That end up hurting me," I remind her.

"Right. You're so right. He does things and never thinks about the consequences. Look, I've been with Ash for a long time, and I understand the pressure he's under—as much as I can, considering I'm not the one who's actually dealing with it. But I know it's a lot."

I remain quiet, her words sinking into me. She knows better than anyone what it's like, dealing with a boyfriend who plays for a college team. Mom knew, but that was years ago.

"And I really think the pressure just got to Eli and he exploded, believing you were the easiest thing to temporarily remove from his life. That's because you're the one person he can count on more than anyone else. He figured you would be there and show up for him when he needed you," Autumn explains.

Her words are killing me. She's probably right, and it's tough to hear.

"It's not fair, how he treated you," she says. I lift my gaze to hers, seeing all the sympathy swirling in her gaze. "I'm not saying what he did was right, I'm just trying to figure him out."

"I know," I murmur. I am the one person he believed he could count on more than anyone else. Everyone disappoints him. Or he disappoints other people—that's the way he feels, at least.

Never me, though. I'm supposed to love him and stand by

him no matter what. Instead, I told him he's a selfish ass who doesn't deserve me.

So where do I go from here?

"I'll support you no matter what you do. If you're over him, then good. Be done with him," Autumn says fiercely.

A frustrated huff leaves me and I glare at the ceiling, kicking at the mattress like a toddler having a tantrum. Autumn lets me, not saying a word or chastising me for my lame behavior. I need to get it out and she's letting me, thank God.

"I'm not the bad guy in this situation," I tell her.

"Neither of you are."

I jump off the bed and start pacing around my room, kicking clothes strewn about the floor out of my way. My room is a mess. I can't remember the last time I cleaned it. And it's so dark in here. The blinds are drawn, as well as the blackout curtains and I go to one of my windows, yanking the curtains open before I draw up the blinds.

The sun smacks me right in the face, and I squint, surprised to see nothing but clear blue skies and a few white fluffy clouds. "It's beautiful outside."

"I tried to get you to go on a walk with me," she says, like the bossy big sister she is. "But you said no."

I turn to look at her, watching as she sits up on my bed, smoothing her hair away from her face. "I'm tired of being sad," I say.

She smiles. "If I'd known my talking to you would've pushed you out of your perpetual bad mood, I would've done it sooner."

Rolling my eyes, I stare out the window once more, spotting my dad in the front yard with my uncle, my cousin Knox and Beck. They're throwing a football back and forth, all of them football gods in their own right.

Which, of course, makes me think of Eli and everyone else. Even Ash.

"Where's your fiancé?"

"He's flying in tonight. Then he flies back out first thing Friday morning. He has a game," Autumn explains.

"Are you staying longer?"

"I'll stay as long as you need me, baby sister."

My gaze narrows. "Did Mom say she wanted you to stay?"

"Maybe." She shrugs, brushing it off. "You need to get out in the sun. You're really pale, and giving me serious *Twilight* vibes. Plus you look like you've lost weight."

"Depression over a breakup is a great diet," I say sarcastically, though I mean every word I say.

Autumn joins me at the window, glancing down at the yard. "Remember when we used to throw the football with them?"

"They humored us."

"Ha," she barks. "I don't know about you, but I always had a pretty good arm. Dad used to say I was better than Jake."

Her laughter grows, and so does mine.

"That made him so mad," I say, comforted when Autumn wraps her arm around my shoulders and pulls me into her side.

"It did, and there is nothing better than making Jake angry."

We both laugh at that.

"Let's go out there and show them what we've got."

I glance down at myself in the old T-shirt I'm wearing—one of Eli's, of course, because I like torturing myself. "Let me change first."

"Okay." She pulls me in for a hug. "And hey, it's going to be all right. It'll all work out like it's supposed to."

After Autumn leaves, I go into the bathroom and brush my hair. Splash water on my face. Stare at my reflection, noting that I'm actually very pale, even my lips. My hair hangs limp and I can't remember the last time I washed it. I haven't worn makeup since I don't know when and I haven't gotten dressed up. It's mostly old T-shirts and sweats. And my appetite has completely left me.

Deciding to brush my teeth, I put some toothpaste on my electric toothbrush and start, scrubbing my back molars vigorously.

Too vigorously.

I gag, pulling the toothbrush out fast and stand there gasping for a moment.

Carefully, I start up again, but this time the gagging happens much faster than the first time and I actually vomit.

Not much since I really don't have anything in my system, but still.

That was weird.

———

"You look better," Dad says as he comes to stand next to me on the lawn. "Got a little pink in your cheeks."

We've been playing catch with the guys for at least an hour, and while I'm over here panting, ready to be done with all the running around since I'm woefully out of shape, nobody else looks in a hurry to wrap this up. My cousin Knox is standing on the other side of my dad, tossing insults at his father and my brother and sister, which is cracking me up and making me forget my troubles, at least temporarily.

I love Knox. He's funny. Reminds me of my uncle.

"Fresh air will do wonders for a person. Isn't that what you always used to tell us," I reply, hoping he won't ask me too many questions. He hasn't since the re-breakup went down, thank God, but I'm sure he knows why I'm sad.

Mom probably filled him in with all the details, though I didn't tell her every single one.

"It is." Beck sails the ball right at Dad and he catches it

with one hand. Impressive. "And it's true. You've been locked up in your room for weeks, Ava. You're worrying me."

Parental guilt is real. And while my parents aren't the type to lay it on thick, when they do say stuff like what Dad just did, well…

They succeed in making me feel bad.

"I'm okay," I say with the smallest smile. "I just need to get over myself."

Dad makes a harumphing sound. "More like you need to get over someone else."

"Do you hate him?" I ask, despising the worry in my voice. I don't want my father to hate Eli. A few months ago, yes, I wanted it. But right now?

No. I don't understand why either. This entire situation between us has been so confusing.

"Time out," Dad calls to everyone, holding his hand up before he returns his attention to me. Everyone else ignores us and starts throwing the ball to each other, taking us completely out of it. "No, I don't hate Eli Bennett. I just hate what he's done to my daughter."

I swallow hard, telling myself not to fall apart and cry. It's difficult, though, when you've got your daddy, your original protector, standing in front of you with concern etched all over his face, sounding like he's still my knight in shining armor. "We've done the same thing to each other, and it's so stupid."

I realize this. I realized this almost instantly after our last conversation. Two wrongs don't make a right. But how can I be understanding and supportive when he didn't do the same for me? Should I have been the understanding girlfriend and given him what he wanted as an example of how to really be?

Maybe.

Though I can't regret what I've done. It's too late to change it now.

"Your mother and I were younger than you two when we

first got together." His smile is faint. "And we did some really stupid shit."

I can't help but laugh, which makes him chuckle too. "Mom has mentioned a few things."

"Really?" He lifts his brows. "Well, whatever she's said, I'm sure it was actually ten times worse. I was a complete dumbass who ran away from my feelings."

Eli is always too much in his feelings. He doesn't want to run away from them. He wants to soak in them and rehash them over and over again.

"And I tried my best to distance myself from your mother to protect her," he continues. "Didn't work. She forced herself back into my life."

"You wanted her to though," I say to him.

"Oh yeah. I definitely wanted her to, though at the time, I didn't see it. She was the light to my dark. And I used to be—really dark," he admits.

I can't even fathom it. My father is the most loving, protective man I know. Even when we were little and he wasn't around much, thanks to his NFL career, he always made time for us. Made each of us, and our mother, feel special.

"I don't believe it," I tease him.

"It's true. I was dealing with my personal demons and your mother helped me get through it," he says with a nod. "Eli has his own demons to battle. He's a different kind of player than I ever was. Much more—"

"Emotional," I finish for him. "His emotions are a blessing and a curse."

"Exactly. They get him in trouble. Like he's in trouble with you right now."

It's true. And I want to fix it, but I don't know how. Or where to start. I'm terrified if I wait for Eli to make the first move, he just…never will.

And that'll be it. Everything over between us. Done. Finished.

"I can't even believe I'm saying this, since it sounds like I'm defending him, but I have played with a variety of guys during my football career. Professionals, who never acted out, were always on time and excellent players. Ones who had the skills but lacked the passion. Those types didn't go far. I could go on and on. Eli has the skillset *and* the passion, he just needs to learn how to rein the passion in so it doesn't overwhelm him. And to leave his troubles at home or wherever they belong, and bring the skills and the passion onto the field. If he can get that under control, he will rule the world," Dad says.

"What kind of player were you?" I have my own feelings, but I want to hear his.

"I had the skillset and eventually the passion, but at first, I was more of a machine. I knew how to get out on that field and get the job done. Your mother helped me find my love for football. Before her, I was just going through the motions," he explains.

The love of a good woman changed him, I guess.

"Your brother is much the same. He channels his anger onto the field, which helps," Dad continues.

"I think Eli was doing that after we broke up. Then we get back together and his anger disappeared," I say, not about to tell my father how Eli called my vagina magical and said it zapped him of his powers.

Talk about ridiculous.

"He probably was. Don't take it as an insult that you throw him off. Just—maybe he just needs to figure out his shit?" When I send him a look, he shrugs. "I don't know."

Hmm. I don't know if I have the patience to wait for Eli to figure himself out.

For all I know, he's already moved on.

CHAPTER 29

AVA

t's Thanksgiving afternoon and I've mostly avoided the chaos that is my house. Family and friends everywhere. The annual football game with the fam—I begged out of it, said I wasn't feeling good.

Which is true. I feel like crap. I think I'm coming down with something. I'm tired all the time, can barely keep my eyes open, and I try to eat, but I just want to barf it all back up so I stop. Which means I'm cranky, because I'm hungry, yet everything sounds disgusting.

A vicious cycle.

I'm getting lots of sympathetic looks from family members and my Aunt Chelsea has asked me if I was okay at least one hundred times since she arrived a couple of days ago, which tells me I must look really bad.

Autumn texts me it's almost time to eat and I throw a sweater on over my T-shirt and leggings combo, ready to head downstairs when there's a knock on my door and then Jake's busting through it, his expression determined.

He comes to a stop and looks me up and down, his brows drawing together. "You look worse than yesterday."

"Gee, thanks." I try to push past him, but he grabs hold of my arm. "If you came in my room to make me feel bad about myself, good job. You succeeded."

"That wasn't the plan, but everyone's concerned about you, Ava. Are you like legit depressed over this Eli Bennett thing? He's not worth your stress," he says with a scowl.

Talking about Eli with Jake is never smart. "I thought I was depressed, but I feel awful. I think I've caught something."

Jake releases his hold on me and takes a big step back as if I'm contagious. Which I might be. "Whoa. Like what?"

"I don't know. A virus? A bug? The flu?" I touch my forehead, but I can't tell if I have a fever.

"You achy all over?"

I shake my head.

"Feverish?"

"I don't think so."

"Throwing up, coming out both ends?" He winces.

"Gross. And no. Though I do feel nauseous."

"Pregnant?" Jake laughs.

I don't.

Oh shit.

Pregnant?

His laughter dies when I don't react the way he wants me to. "Nah."

I meet his gaze, then shrug.

"Ava, no."

Um, I can't remember the last time I had my period. The times with Eli, we never used a condom. Because I've been on the pill for pretty much the entirety of our relationship.

With the exception of the last few months. I kept forgetting to renew my prescription, so they could send me the pills via mail and I eventually thought, screw it.

Not like anyone was screwing me.

But someone has recently. Quite a few times.

With no condom.

"Damn it, Ava, you can't be pregnant with that asshole's baby." The look on my brother's face is nothing short of horrified.

"Don't call him an asshole." I fall heavily onto the edge of my bed, staring off into space. I use an app on my phone to track my period, but lately, I haven't even opened it. I used to obsessively check it to track my cycle, but after a while—and being on the pill for so long—I rarely saw the need. And I was still regular like clockwork.

Grabbing my phone, I go into my app, ignoring Jake who's huffing and puffing and muttering over Eli, and I check when I should've had my period last.

Over two weeks ago.

I immediately text Autumn.

Me: **Could you come to my room please?**

"You should go," I tell Jake, who stops his pacing to glare at me. "Tell Mom and Dad I'll be down in a few minutes."

"That's it? You're going to drop a bomb on me and then expect me to act like nothing's happened?" Jake rakes his hands through his hair, clutching the back of his head.

He looks really stressed out.

"I think we're both overreacting." It's amazing how calm and level-headed I feel in this moment. I don't know what's come over me. "Seriously, I think it's just the flu."

"If you say so." He sounds doubtful.

I jump to my feet and go to my brother, sending him an imploring look. "Don't utter a word of this to anyone, okay? It's probably not even true, but I don't want you starting rumors or whatever among the family. You can't even tell Hannah."

His expression turns pained. "I tell Hannah everything."

"You can't tell her this. Besides, there's nothing to tell. I don't even believe it. I'm sick," I say firmly.

"I would never tell anyone about this, even if it was true.

That's your news to tell," he says, now looking offended. "I know how to keep a secret."

"I know. I'm just—there's no way it's possible."

Another skeptical look from my brother, but at least he's smart enough to keep quiet. "I'm starving so I'm headed downstairs. See you in a few?" He starts for my bedroom door.

I nod. "Yes—and Jake?"

Pausing, he glances over his shoulder. "Yeah?"

I go to him, throwing my arms around his waist and giving him a hug. He returns it, holding me tightly. "Thank you."

"For what? All I did is freak you out."

I laugh against his shirt front. "Just for being there for me. Even though you're irritating sometimes, I do appreciate you."

He chuckles, dropping a quick kiss on top of my head before he lets me go. "Come downstairs before they send me back up here to get you."

"I will," I tell him as he leaves my room.

Autumn takes a while to come up here and I'm pacing around my room, gnawing on my lip as I consider all the possibilities.

No way am I pregnant. I'm not that girl.

My stomach roils at that exact moment, and I cover my mouth, pausing to study my reflection in the mirror above my dresser.

Yeah, I don't look good. I could rectify that. A little makeup, maybe curl my hair…

I don't have time for all that. A quick fix will have to do.

Hurriedly, I change clothes, putting on a pair of jeans instead of leggings. Slipping on that cute black sweater I bought a few weeks ago. I go into my connecting bathroom and brush my hair, hating how staticky it looks and throw it up in a quick bun instead. I'm applying mascara to my lashes when Autumn finally barges into my room, sounding out of breath.

"Why aren't you downstairs at the table?"

"I'm getting ready." I turn to look at her, noting how adorable she is in the dark green, flower-printed dress she's wearing with tights and boots, her dark hair perfectly curled. She looks like she walked straight out of a photoshoot.

"You look better," she says, her gaze kind. "Are you feeling better too?"

I nod, trying to ignore the nauseous wave taking over me. "Yes."

"Good. You must have some weird twenty-four-hour thing," she says.

I drop the mascara into the drawer and shut it before turning to face her. "I was wondering if I could possibly be…pregnant."

Autumn's mouth drops open and she reaches out to grip the bathroom counter. As if she needs to or she might topple to the floor. "*No.*"

"I don't know," I whisper. "I haven't had my period in weeks."

"You're on the pill."

I slowly shake my head.

Her mouth drops open even more. Not sure how that's even possible. "Ava, really? What the hell?"

"It's hard to explain." I wave my hand. "And I can't worry about that. But I'm wondering. Or maybe I'm just sick."

"Stress can cause you to skip your period," she kindly points out. "Going off the pill can too."

"I've been off it for months."

Autumn doesn't bother asking why, thank goodness. I can give her all the details later. "You should take a pregnancy test."

My stomach dances with nerves. "I can't do that."

"Why not?"

"That'll make everything so…real." I grimace. "What if it's positive?"

"What if it is?"

"What will I do?"

"I don't know…what will you do?"

"Autumn, you sound like a damn parrot. Stop." I stride toward the window and stare outside, wondering what Eli is doing for the holiday. Is he with his family? Is his brother still hanging around? Or is it another lonely Thanksgiving at the Bennett house? The last few Thanksgivings he's always come here. He'd bring his mom too.

We were like one big happy family.

"You two aren't together," Autumn reminds me.

I actually laugh. "Oh, I know."

"Will he want to get back together if you're pregnant? I'm sure he will."

"I am too." I can only imagine what he'll think, what he'll want.

"But what about you? What will *you* want?"

I envision myself pregnant, waddling around. Eli wanting to take care of me. Rubbing my belly. Talking to the baby. Proud as hell and praying for a baby boy he can toss a football to.

I'd rather have a girl. He'd go into pure protective mode and it would be the most adorable thing ever.

Oops. I think I'm getting ahead of myself.

"I don't want to think about any of that until I know what's going on," I say, thinking that is the most mature response I can come up with. "But I can't worry about that now. Let's go downstairs and eat."

My stomach makes a noise of protest at me saying "eat."

Figures.

"Are you really going to be able to eat?" Autumn sounds doubtful.

I roll my eyes as we exit my bedroom. "I'm fine. Really. Don't worry about me."

We head downstairs, and I immediately regret my decision to wear the sweater. It's so hot down here, it's practically sweltering.

I follow Autumn into our dining room, the mingled scents of all the food hitting me at full force.

Oh God, that smells disgusting.

I rest a hand on my stomach, hating how it pitches and roils like I'm a boat in the middle of the ocean. I gaze at everyone sitting around the table. All of the people I love and care about, my family.

"Ava." Mom slowly stands, her brows knit together. "Are you okay?"

Autumn turns to me and I blindly reach out, grabbing at her arm.

I miss and sink to the floor.

Into nothingness.

———

I crack my eyes open at the commanding way someone—my father?—says my name.

Yep, there he is, his face in mine, his blue eyes swimming with worry. He glances up and speaks to the rest of the table. "She's awake."

"Thank God." That's my Aunt Chelsea.

I roll my head, realizing I'm sitting in someone's lap. Autumn's. She's brushing my hair away from my forehead. "You fainted."

Mom rushes into the dining room, kneeling down with a glass of water in her hands. "Can you sit up?" she asks me.

Nodding, I lift up slowly, my head woozy. "I can't believe I fainted."

"When was the last time you ate?" Dad asks, his voice stern.

"I don't know." I take the water from Mom and sip it.

"Not too much," she warns, making me feel like I'm five and I just threw my guts up all over my bedroom floor.

That might've been an actual experience I'm referring to.

"Ava," she murmurs. "You can't stop eating just because your relationship ended. You need to take care of yourself."

I don't want the lecture. I know I should take care of myself. But I'm pretty sure this goes beyond a break-up issue. I'm starting to think I'm really sick.

"I'm going back up to my room. I need to lie down."

"Can you take her upstairs?" Mom asks Autumn.

My sister nods. "Of course. You want to wait a few more minutes? Or are you ready to go now?" she asks me.

I want to get away from everyone's watchful gaze as soon as possible. They're all staring, and it's making me uncomfortable. "Let's go."

I stand on slightly wobbly legs and let my sister lead me back upstairs, mute. She doesn't say a word either. Not until we're in my bedroom and no one's around to hear her.

"When I get a chance, I'm leaving to go pick up a pregnancy test," she announces.

Reality smacks itself right in my face. "You think I should take one?"

She nods firmly. "Oh yeah. I don't know if you're sick, but we need to figure this out. While you still have time to make a tough decision."

"Um, if you're referring to an abortion, there is no way in hell I would ever do that. This is mine and Eli's baby," I stress.

"Right, and he's a prick."

"A prick that I'm still in love with," I retort.

"Fine, okay. You're right. You can't do that. But you need

to figure out what's going on with your body, because if you're sick, then you need to go to the doctor. You haven't been well for at least two weeks," Autumn says, reaching out to gently squeeze my arm. "I'm worried about you."

A sigh leaves me, and I appreciate her concern.

I'm worried about me too.

CHAPTER 30
ELI

There are four words strung together in the English language that I hate more than any others out there on the planet.

We need to talk.

I received a text from Ava that said exactly this on Thanksgiving night. We'd just played a game—yeah, one scheduled on Thanksgiving, which I was kind of glad for, considering I was sad I wasn't spending it with Ava and her family—and I checked my phone long after the game was over, when we were on the bus headed home.

Ava: **We need to talk.**

That's it. That's all she said. No, *how are you?* or *Happy Thanksgiving* or *I'm thankful for you*-type texts. None of that shit. I get the ultra-nerve wracking, *we need to talk* instead, and it sucks ass.

But then I shove all my worry and anxiety out of the way because at least the woman wants to talk to me, am I right? I texted her immediately upon seeing the text.

Me: **I'm on a bus coming home right now. Want to call me?**

She doesn't respond.

Of course she doesn't respond. It's late. Maybe she's in bed? My girl is more of a night owl, but maybe she's exhausted after a busy holiday with her family.

Man, I have the best memories of Thanksgiving with the Callahans. They all show up. They play football and eat lots of food and laugh and joke the entire time. They watch movies together and they have dessert contests like who can make the best pie, and the afternoon football games with all those greats out on the lawn are the absolute best. I've played football with Owen Maguire and Drew Callahan—who can say that?

Me. I can say it.

I've brought Jackson with me. Jake would have Diego over. One time Caleb came over for dessert and played. It was a blast.

I miss my girl. I've missed her since our last stupid fight, when I knew it was all my fault, but part of me doesn't regret the move, because it helped keep her away from me for a bit so I could get my head on straight. I was a mess, letting my emotions take over me and screw with my head, my game.

Not any longer. Something clicked recently, though I can't quite put my finger on it. Maybe it was intense practice after intense practice, Tony right there by my side almost at all times, convincing me I was on track. Shutting out all the negativity and bullshit that fucks with me, thanks to his soothing voice praising me and reminding me that I've got this. Tony and I have become closer and I'm thankful for that guy. I always believed his quietness meant he was hiding something.

He's not—he's always listening. Thinking.

Reminding me that I'm doing this for me. For Ava.

For our future.

It also helped that Ryan has stuck around and is staying with Mom. He got a job as a bartender at Southgate and is killing it with tips. He talks about finding somewhere to live close by, once Mom seems capable of being on her own once more, and we don't have to worry about her trying to hit the bottle.

She did have DUI charges brought on her, and that's a whole other mess we still need to figure out, but one I'm not necessarily having to deal with at the moment. Ryan promised me he'd help. Mom has a lawyer friend and she's already hired him. They're taking care of it.

For the first time in what feels like forever, it's not all on me, and that's a huge relief.

Sure wish my girl would call me back, though. I want to hear her voice. Tell her what's going on. Will she listen to me? Or is she just calling with bad news? I don't know if I can handle any more bad news this year. It's been a rough one and I'm ready for it to be over.

I'm just about drifting off to sleep when my phone buzzes, jolting me awake. I fumble to check my phone to see I have a text.

Ava: **We should talk in person.**

I frown, rereading what she said, hating the nervous feeling that socks me in the gut.

Me: **I'm free tomorrow.**

Ava: **Want to meet somewhere in the morning? Or will you be too tired?**

Me: **I'll meet you whenever you want, wherever you want.**

There. That shows I'm willing to do whatever she wants. Because I am.

Anything for my Ava.

I stare at the little gray bubble with the three white dots, anxious for her answer, grateful no one is paying attention to me. This late at night, most everyone is snoozing or messin' on their phone.

Finally, she responds.

Ava: **Tomorrow at 10?**

Me: **Grab some breakfast somewhere?**

Ava: **Okay.**

We go back and forth for a little bit, discussing where to meet and I can tell she really doesn't care where we meet. I make a suggestion, she agrees, and that's it.

We're meeting tomorrow morning. I wonder what she wants to talk about.

Hopefully it's nothing too serious.

———

I enter the restaurant at 9:55 to find her already there, sitting alone at a table with a glass of water in front of her, wearing a thick sweater that swallows her up and makes her look tiny. I stop short when I catch sight of her face. She looks...

Worried.

Scared.

Pale.

Tired.

So damn tired.

I rush to the table, ignoring the hostess who calls out to me, and sit across from Ava at the table, leaning across it, my voice low as I ask, "Princess, you okay?"

She blinks at me, then rolls her eyes. Sassy as ever, even when she looks low. "So many people have asked me that exact question the last couple of weeks."

"You look a little...beat." I wince the moment the words leave me. I'm trying to make things right with her, not make her feel worse.

Ava sighs. "I know. It's—how are you? How'd you do at the game yesterday?"

I notice her change of subject but decide not to push it. "Good. We won. I played well. Didn't throw an interception."

Her smile is small. "I'm glad. I didn't know you guys played on Thanksgiving."

"It's a new thing, I guess. We've never done it before." I shrug, turning my attention to the server who stops by our table to ask if I want coffee. I ask for a water and then pick up the menu, casually scanning it and suddenly nervous as fuck when Ava speaks.

"I need to tell you something."

I glance up at her real quick before my gaze returns to the breakfast specials. "Shoot."

"I'm pregnant."

I drop the menu with a clatter, my gaze going to hers. She's watching me, her expression absolutely petrified, her eyes so wide it's like I can't see anything else. "What did you just say?"

Nervous laughter leaves her and she shoves the menu out of her way, as if it disgusts her. "I'm pregnant. I took a pregnancy test last night. Actually, I took three. And they all came up positive."

I'm speechless. All I can do is watch her, my brain scrambling to come up with words.

I'm drawing a complete blank.

"Don't you have anything to say?" she prompts.

"H-how did this happen?"

Yeah, *that's* the first thing I manage to say to her.

"I think you know how it happened, Eli." Her voice drips with sarcasm. "It was the whole us having sex thing, if you haven't figured that out yet."

I look around, but there's no one nearby. We chose a restaurant not too close to shopping centers because they're all packed, thanks to Black Friday specials. "I thought you were on the pill."

"When I came back from Spain, I kept forgetting to order a refill. And then I just—never got back on it." She bites her lower lip, her eyes starting to well up. "So I guess it's my fault that it happened."

"Hey, hey, hey." I don't even think, I just do. Next thing I know, I'm sitting on her side of the booth, my arm around her shoulders, and she's leaning into me, her hair tickling my mouth as she sobs into my sweatshirt. "This is no one's *fault*. It's gonna be all right."

She's crying so hard, her shoulders are shaking. The waitress chooses that moment to approach our table with my glass of water and I shake my head. She nods in understanding, sets the glass on the table and keeps walking.

"Ava." I reach for her face with my other hand, my fingers coming underneath her chin and tilting her head up. Her watery gaze meets mine, her cheeks covered with tears and I gently wipe at them with my thumb. "Are you sure?"

"Three tests, Eli. Three positives." She hiccups and swallows a sob. "I've felt like crap for weeks."

Concern laces through me. "What do you mean?"

"I'm tired. I can't eat because I'm too nauseous. All I want to do is sleep." She shrugs. "It's been awful."

"Why didn't you call me sooner?"

"I didn't want to mess with your game mojo." The words she says are slightly bitter, but her tone gentles with the next sentence. "I know you're dealing with a lot, and at first I just thought I was sick."

My chest hurts at hearing her say that. "I'm never dealing with so much that I can't think about you. You're the most important thing to me in this world."

Ava sniffs. "You wanted to take a break."

"I'm a fucking idiot." I shake my head once. "I don't know what I was thinking. I need you. I love you."

I'm not holding shit back. Not anymore.

"This..." Her gaze briefly casts downward before it returns to mine. "This will change everything."

I can't help it. I drop my hand from her face and settle it over her flat stomach, my touch light. "You're for real right now."

She nods. Smiles faintly. Maybe she can feel my excitement because, yeah, I can't deny it.

I'm excited.

I'm going to be a dad. And Ava is my baby mama.

Another server walks by and I announce, "We're having a baby."

"Sshh," Ava says, hitting my arm.

The lady is older, there's gray in her hair and wrinkles around her eyes. She stops when I say that, a big smile forming on her face. "That's wonderful. Congratulations."

"Thanks." I'm beaming. I can feel the smile stretching my face so wide, it almost hurts.

The woman walks away and Ava sends me a chastising look. "You shouldn't have done that."

"Why not? We're going to be parents, Ava." I tip my head back and laugh. "Can you freakin' imagine? You and me, Mom and Dad?"

She smiles, and it's like the clouds have broken and the sun is shining through them, thin beams of golden light falling on the two of us. I lean in and touch her face, sweeping my thumb across her cheek. Her skin is so soft, and she's a little pale, but damn if she isn't the most beautiful thing I've ever seen.

And she's going to have my baby.

"Aren't you scared?" she asks, her lips trembling.

Leaning in, I kiss her. It's soft and light and I hope she can feel what I'm feeling, because yeah, I'm scared. But with her by my side, we're going to be fine.

"Yeah," I admit. "I'm excited too, though."

She grabs hold of the front of my sweatshirt, fisting the fabric. "I'm still mad at you, Eli."

"I'm a dick," I say immediately.

"It's going to take more than that for me to forgive you." She shakes her head. "You pushed me away so easily."

"It was a mistake. I'm just—I don't know what the fuck is

wrong with me. There's been so much going on, so much pressure coming in on me from all sides." I press my forehead to hers and stare into her eyes. "I didn't know what to do. I'm sorry."

"We can't keep doing this to each other, especially now. We have someone else to think about."

Oh fuck.

I lift away from her, needing the space for a moment. I lean back against the booth, waving at the server as she approaches us. "You serve liquor here?"

She cackles out a laugh. "No, we do not, young man, and especially not in the morning. How about a strong cup of coffee?"

"Done," I tell her.

"Are you sure you don't want a cup of coffee?" the woman asks Ava kindly.

She shakes her head. "No, thank you."

I send her a look when the waitress leaves. "You live for that shit. Coffee. Starbucks. Whatever."

"Caffeine isn't good for the baby," she admits softly.

I whistle low, marveling at what she just said. At how she just changed my life completely with only a few words. "This is crazy. You're *pregnant*."

"Right?" She glances helplessly around the mostly empty restaurant. "I agree."

"I can't wait to tell everyone," I start, but clamp my lips shut when she shakes her head. "What? You don't want me telling anyone?"

Fuck, I'm going to burst if I have to keep this to myself for long.

"Not yet," she admits. "Let's wait a bit first."

"Why?"

"I don't know." She shrugs. "Maybe I want to keep it just between us right now."

"Do your parents know?"

"No, but Autumn does," she admits.

"But you don't want me to tell anyone?" I'm a little offended.

"She's the *only* one who knows, besides you and me. She ran out on Thanksgiving night and bought me the pregnancy tests," Ava explains. "My sister has been a huge help to me. I don't know what I would've done without her."

"I get it, yeah." I nod, not wanting to upset the mother of my unborn child.

Need to keep my girl and our baby healthy.

"I'm scared to tell my parents about the baby," she admits, her voice the barest whisper. "What if they get…mad?"

"They won't," I reassure her. I can't imagine them being anything but happy.

Well, maybe they won't be happy *I'm* the one who got their daughter pregnant.

"Didn't they have Autumn really young?" I ask.

Ava nods. "Doesn't mean they'll like it. They always want more for us. They tell us that a lot. And what am I going to do about school? I just signed a lease and I'm leaving for San Diego right after New Year's."

My heart drops at her admission. "*What?*"

"That was always my plan," she admits, her voice small. "I thought it was best to go back to school."

"You can't leave," I say fiercely, telling myself I won't get mad. Though I can't believe she made plans to go back to San Diego, it's not surprising. I'm sure that was always the plan, just as she said. "I want you to stay here with me, Ava. I want to take care of you. And our baby."

She gazes at me, her expression soft and open. All I want to do is hug and kiss her, but she wants me to listen to her right now, so I restrain myself. "We really, *really* need to talk everything through."

"We will," I say, slipping my fingers around her chin and tilting her head back, so I can kiss her. My mouth lingers on hers as I kiss her once. Twice. Three times. Trying to pour all of my love for her into this simple connection of our lips. "Let me eat breakfast first, though. Daddy's hungry."

Ava cracks up, pulling away from me. "Okay, that was a little gross."

"You liked it." I smile at her.

She smiles back.

Yeah.

She liked it.

CHAPTER 31

AVA

fter I watch Eli eat—I only munched on his sourdough toast, which caused him to order more toast for himself—we head back to his apartment to talk. God, I was so scared to tell him about the baby, but he responded really well.

In fact, I can tell he's excited, which I didn't expect.

I don't know what I expected from Eli. That's the best and worst thing about him. His impulsiveness, never knowing how he's going to respond to…whatever.

Last night after I took the pregnancy test and saw the almost immediate results, I told Autumn it had to be false. So I drank a bunch of water and took another one.

Positive. Again.

The look my sister sent me practically dared me to deny it.

I'm really good at denial though. It's like my brain couldn't compute it. Pregnant? Me?

Impossible.

Luckily enough, she bought three tests, so I drank even more water and two hours later, I took the final test.

Still positive.

I cried. Autumn held me and said soothing words while I

sobbed all over the front of her pretty dress, always careful not to get snot on it. I felt weak and stupid for getting pregnant. Really, really stupid. I'm only twenty. I should've known better. I was on birth control and let it lapse like a dumbass and then like an even bigger dumbass, I let my exboyfriend—which is what he still is if we're keeping things real—come inside me.

Multiple times.

It's like I forgot. We've gone for years without condoms and I was totally used to not using them. He was too. We just fell back into old habits and while it was amazing as always, the sex resulted in me getting pregnant.

Pregnant.

I'm going to have a baby.

Eli's baby.

Wow.

Still in a little shock over the whole thing.

Pretty sure I know when it happened—the night we went back to his place after his mom was in the car wreck. When he woke me in the middle of the night and we ended up having sex. It had been downright magical.

Magical enough to make a baby? Maybe.

A shiver steals through me at the thought.

When we walk into the apartment, of course Caleb is there kicking it on the couch playing video games, and he sits up straight when he spots me, his blue eyes wide as he hits pause on the controller before greeting me. "Ava. Long time, no see."

"Hey, Caleb." I wave at him, feeling awkward.

His gaze goes from Eli to me, and then back to Eli again, a little frown on his face. "You two good now?"

"We're fucking great." Eli snags my hand and I send him a look.

One that says, *don't you dare open your mouth further.*

He goes silent, his lips curled in a mysterious smile.

Caleb frowns. A silent Eli isn't normal, and he knows it.

"That's great," Caleb finally says, his gaze settling on me. "Gracie will be glad to hear this."

"Uh huh." My response is noncommittal because I don't know what's going to happen after this discussion, and I can only imagine what Caleb will tell Gracie.

Honestly? I refuse to get my hopes up. Every time I think we're good, Eli goes and does something to prove we are absolutely not good at all. I'm tired of it. I need stability, now more than ever. I need confirmation that he'll love me no matter what. I need him to be responsible, to support me and our unborn baby.

More than anything, I need to know he's going to step up and be a good father. A solid boyfriend. A man who's going to stand by my side and not be so damn selfish all the time.

He's got it in him. I *know* he does. He just needs to grow up a little more first. Maybe having a baby will help make that happen.

"Come on," he says, pulling me out of my thoughts. I wave at Caleb and follow Eli into his room, settling on the chair at his desk as he shuts and locks the door.

"Don't want him to just barge in," Eli says as he turns to face me. "Caleb's been known to do that."

Right. "I'm not having sex with you, Eli."

"What? I don't expect you to have sex with me." He almost looks offended. "I know you want to talk."

"I do."

"Let's talk then." He settles on the corner of his bed, facing me. His legs spread wide, feet planted firmly on the floor, his chest and shoulders looking extra broad in that black hoodie he's wearing. He looks good.

When does he not?

I exhale loudly and settle my hands on my knees. "Okay. By my calculations, I think the baby is due in early July. Though I need confirmation from a doctor, I guess."

He grins. "A 4th of July baby?"

I wish he wouldn't smile. It's so distracting.

"Maybe. I don't know. I'm thinking I could probably go to school for the spring semester and then take a leave of absence. Once I'm moved in, I'll find a doctor down in San Diego, though I plan on having the baby here. I'll come home when school's done, and deliver the baby in the summer. It'll work out perfect." Eli is shaking his head, his expression full of annoyance. "What?"

"I don't want you going to San Diego for the spring semester."

He says it with such finality I can feel my irritation rising. "Why not? I need to go to school, and I'll be out by May. At least six weeks before the baby is due. Then I come home and have the baby here. The timing is perfect."

"Yeah, no. I don't think so. That's not gonna work."

"Why the hell not?" I snap.

"What about me?" He taps his chest. "Where do I fit into your plan?"

"What about you?" I retort. "I'm the one who's carrying the baby for the next eight months or so. Delivering the baby. You're not too involved except at the beginning."

Okay, that was a little mean, but he's being so bossy.

Truth? I want to give in to him. I'd rather put school on hold and revel in being pregnant. Enjoying the time with Eli while we prepare for our future.

But is that what he wants? Can he step up and take care of me?

Can he handle the pressure?

"I take offense to that." He crosses his arms. "I want to be involved in all of this. Every little thing. That's my baby inside of you. Don't forget."

As if I could.

"How's that going to work? You're here." I wave my

hand, indicating the room. "And I'm going to be down there for school."

We're quiet for a moment, my words hanging between us and I cross my arms too, feeling a little defensive.

I don't know why I'm saying all of this. I don't really want to go to San Diego and be alone, going to school while I'm pregnant with my first child. Even my mom would tell me that's a ridiculous idea. My dad would probably stop me from leaving. Autumn would do her best to talk me out of it. They all would.

If Eli made me the right offer, said the right things, I'd agree to chuck the San Diego plan forever and stay with him.

"Is that what you really want to do?" he asks with a sigh.

No, I want to say. *No, I want to stay here and I want to make a little family with you. That's what I really want. I don't care about anything else. Just you and our baby growing inside of me.*

Like a chicken shit, I don't say any of that. I need to be real with him and tell him how I feel. How important he is to me, despite everything that's happened between us.

I know we can make this work. We have before. We did for years.

We can make it work again.

Parting my lips, I start, "It's a smart pla—"

"Because it's not what I want," he interrupts. "I can't stand the thought of you being pregnant, and like, hundreds of miles away from me. What if something happens to you, Ava? What if you need me? It'll take me hours to get to you, and I'd probably lose my mind in the meantime. I can't do it. I won't."

I drop my arms at my sides. "What do you want to do, then?"

Eli does the craziest thing.

He falls on his knees and crawls over to me, grabbing my right hand and holding it in both of his. "I love you, Ava Elizabeth Callahan. I love you more than life itself. And I love that you're going to have my baby. That we're going to be parents."

I stare at him, swallowing hard. I'm speechless.

"I've made some mistakes. Big ones. I was a selfish asshole and ain't gonna lie, I'm probably *still* a selfish asshole, but I'm going to work on it—for you. For our baby. For us, and the family we're going to become. I'm sorry that I keep fucking up and hurting you, but you need to know just one thing This asshole loves you with all his heart." He pauses for the smallest moment. "I want you to marry me."

I gasp. "Eli—"

"Hear me out," he says, squeezing my hand in between both of his. "It makes sense, us getting married. I know we're young, but we're in love and I'm on my way to possible stardom in the NFL. I don't want to make you give up your dreams of completing college, but what if you put it on pause for a little while? We can get married and move in together. By the time the baby's born, we'll know if I get drafted or not, and we can move wherever we need to go. Just you and me and baby Bennett. It'll be great. I can take care of you. Give you whatever you need, and our baby too. Watch out, Patrick Mahomes and your cute little girl and baby mama. We'll break the internet with our cute as shit baby and put them to shame."

I can't help but laugh.

"Come on, babe." His hazel eyes glow as he contemplates me, on his knees for me, his expression so serious. No smile. No cocky Eli in sight. Just a man asking for my hand in marriage—literally. "I love you so damn much. I'm sorry for all the mistakes I've made. I never meant to hurt you, and I'm bound to make more mistakes. You know I'm not perfect."

"I'm not perfect either," I murmur.

"But we're perfect together." He brings my hand to his mouth and kisses the back of it. "We don't make sense when we're apart, Ava. It hurt my heart so fuckin' bad, not having you in my life for those months. Not being able to talk to you. Look at you. Be with you in every way I can."

His voice lowers with the last sentence, making my skin warm.

"Marry me. Be my wife. Let me take care of you, Princess. Make me the happiest man in the world and say yes."

I can't help but waver. We haven't talked enough yet about our situation. There are so many things I still need to say. Things I want to ensure. I want him to promise he'll put the baby first. And me first too. It can't always be about himself anymore. There are other things to consider. Other people involved now. It's not just about him.

It's never going to be just about him again.

But I can't resist this man. I love him. Deep down, he knows it.

He's got me.

"Eli…"

"Just say yes." He pauses. "Please."

This is a man who never says please for *anything*.

Except for me.

"Yes," I whisper.

The smile that curls his lips is blinding. Beautiful. He tugs on my hand as he rises up on his knees, his mouth finding mine in a sweet kiss. "I'm going to do whatever it takes to prove to you that I love you, Ava," he murmurs against my lips. "And that I love my baby growing inside you, too. I'm going to do right by you and the baby. Just you watch."

I believe him.

I do.

CHAPTER 32

ELI

Ava wraps her arms around my neck, and I deepen the kiss for a moment before I pull away, so I can stare into her beautiful eyes. "We're really going to do this?"

She nods slowly, shifting so she can trace my left eyebrow with her finger. "Yes. We are."

"I can't believe you're pregnant," I whisper, my gaze eating her up. This woman—she is my everything. I need to tell her that more often. I used to all the time, when we were younger and first falling in love.

She's always been my everything.

"I can't either." She draws her finger down my nose. "You have freckles."

"Barely."

"They're there, though." She lightly draws her finger across the bridge of my nose. "They're cute."

I make a face. "When I was younger, they were worse."

She leans in, dropping a kiss just below my left eye and on the side of my nose. "I wonder if our baby will have them."

My heart floods with love for this woman and I wrap my arms around her tightly, pulling her in as close as I can get her, considering I'm on my damn knees and she's sitting in my desk chair. "I want a blonde baby with green eyes."

"I think that could happen," she whispers. "Your eyes look extra green right now."

"Ava," I whisper, suddenly overcome.

Her eyes fill with tears. She can feel it too. The emotion welling between us.

The love.

"Come to bed with me," I murmur, leaning in to gently press my mouth to hers. "I just want to hold you."

I pull away from her slightly to take her hand and she stands with me, coming willingly to the bed, letting go of my hand so I can take off my sweatshirt. I toe off my shoes and so does she. She tears off her sweater too, revealing the T-shirt she wears beneath it. Then I pull back the comforter and we're both crawling onto the mattress. I tug the covers over the both of us and pull her to me, holding her as close as I can get her. She tangles her legs with mine, her head tucked beneath my chin, her breath fanning against my neck.

Making me hard, but what else is new? She looks at me and I want her. I always want her.

But I'm not going to push. She flat out said she's not having sex with me and I'm not going to look like some horndog who only cares about getting in her panties.

I love getting in her panties, but right now she needs something else from me.

I rub my hands up and down her back, noting how she melts into me the more I stroke her. I press my lips to her forehead, delivering tiny kisses. She soaks it up as if she's love-starved and maybe she is. I'm sure she's overly emotional since she found out she's pregnant, which is just…huge.

Life-changing.

I'm going to be a dad.

"I fucked this all up before between us," I whisper against

her temple. "And I hate that I did that. I was selfish and stupid. But I promise, Princess, I will never do that again. Everything I do from now on, forever, is for you and our baby."

No response. She's so quiet, I start to worry.

Until I realize from the sound of her deep breathing that she's fallen asleep.

My poor exhausted baby.

I kiss her temple. Brush her hair out of my face. Tighten my arms around her, comforted by the way she snuggles closer, even in her sleep. I meant every word I just said to her, even if she didn't hear me. I will do whatever it takes to make it right between us. I need to get over my issues and stop trying to put them on her. She is by far the most important thing in my life.

More important than football.

Than my family.

She *is* my family. My life. My light.

My everything.

———

I wake up to a pretty girl staring at me, her cheeks flushed, her eyes sparkling.

"Hi," she murmurs.

"Hey." I'm groggy. "How long have we been sleeping?"

"I don't know, but I'm starving." She leans in so close her lips move against mine as she says, "I want pizza."

A chuckle leaves me. "You're actually hungry?"

She nods. "Maybe you have magic powers."

"You know I do," I return, unable to keep the arrogance out of my voice.

"Kind of like my magical vagina?" She lifts her brows.

I place a hand over her mouth. "Such an unsexy word."

"What? Vagina?" Her voice is muffled beneath my palm.

"Yes," I tell her, removing my hand from her mouth so I can kiss her.

"It'll be in full working order when I give birth, doing its job," she says. "Are you prepared for that?"

"Of course. I will be right there front and center, nudging the doctor and nurses out of the way so I can catch our baby," I say with authority, envisioning the moment in my brain.

"Our baby is not a football," she says, sounding amused.

"It'll be small like one. I'll tell you hike, and you can just push the baby out right into my hands." I laugh.

So does Ava.

"Can we order a pizza?" she asks. "Or go somewhere to eat?" She makes a face. "I really don't feel like going anywhere."

"Let's have one delivered then." I reach over to grab my phone from the nightstand. "What do you want on it?"

"Pepperoni and pineapple. Oh, and olives," she says. A little crease forms between her eyebrows. "Maybe some red onion?"

"Ava." I grimace. "That sounds disgusting."

"I think it all sounds good. Like...*really* good." Her eyes widen. "Maybe I'm having a craving?"

"If that's your craving, it's kind of awful."

She rolls onto her back, her head propped on a stack of pillows as she stares up at my ceiling. "Thin crust. Light sauce. God, the pineapple sounds so delicious right now, and I don't even like pineapple on my pizza normally. But I'm willing to try it."

I open up my phone and go to the local pizza place's app. "I hate pineapple on pizza."

"But you'll eat it for me?" She turns to look at me with the sweetest expression on her pretty face.

"For you, I will do anything." I lean over and kiss her. "Except eat pineapple on my pizza."

She mock frowns. "You're no fun."

"I'm going to order you your own, plus one for me." I shoot Caleb a quick text, asking if he wants pizza too. "Not sure if I want to try yours."

"What if it's awful?" She sits up, running her fingers through her hair. "It won't be. I just know it."

I sit up next to her, pushing her hair away from her neck, so I can kiss her there. "Baby, you are sexy when you're pregnant."

She shoves me away, a giant smile on her face. "Shut it. You're just saying that."

"Nah, it's true. But I think you're sexy all the time so…" I kiss her neck again, dropping my phone on top of the comforter, so I can reach for her, slipping my hand under her T-shirt so I can touch her. My fingers drift from her stomach to her ribs, to her breast, tracing the lacy edge of her bra.

Ava shivers. "What are you doing?"

"What does it look like?" I feel good. Invigorated. That nap with Ava in my arms helped, I'm sure.

"Eli…" Her voice drifts and her eyes fall closed when I kiss along her jaw.

"Hmm?"

"I'm hungry," she whispers.

"I'll give you what you want," I tell her, cupping her breast fully.

"For food. Pineapple pizza."

I pull away from her and lie back down, grabbing my phone. I notice that I have a text.

Caleb: **Yeah, I'm down for pizza. Whatever you want to get.**

"I'm ordering right now," I tell her, and she starts bouncing and clapping her hands like a little kid. "Caleb and I are going to share one."

"Can you get breadsticks too?" Her expression is hopeful. "I don't know what happened, but it's like my stomach opened back up and is ready for business."

I shake my head as I add an order of breadsticks. "Done."

"Maybe being with you made me hungry." She leans over and kisses me, her tongue sliding in briefly between my lips. "For all the things."

I hurriedly finish making the pizza order before I toss my phone aside and reach for her. "It'll be here in forty-five minutes."

She comes into my arms with a laugh, her eyes glowing, her mouth landing on mine greedily. I roll her over onto her back, me on top of her as we devour each other, a low moan falling from her lips when I shift to kiss and lick at her neck. I'm suddenly overwhelmed with love for this woman. I can't get enough of her. I want to show her what she means to me. Show her how much I love her and our baby.

Within minutes, our clothes are gone. I gather her breasts in my hands and press them together, sucking one nipple, then the other, making her gasp. She watches me, her gaze never leaving me as I map her skin with my lips, lingering on her stomach. Kissing her gently. Reverently.

Ava runs her hand through my hair, her lips tipped up in a barely there smile.

I shift lower, kissing the inside of her thighs. The backs of her knees. She whimpers, wanting my mouth on her pussy and I deliver, licking her clit, licking her everywhere. Swear to God, she tastes different, and I wonder if it's because she's pregnant.

Chills race over me, just knowing she's going to have my baby.

I can't get over it.

I suck her clit in between my lips, rubbing my index finger up and down her pussy before I slowly push it inside, trying to be careful. She's wet and slick, so fucking hot and I curl my finger inside her, aiming for that one spot I know that gets her going, increasing my rhythm on her clit.

She cries out, a jolt rippling through her as I destroy her

with my mouth and finger. She's coming, her entire body stiffening before she falls apart, her pussy clenching and releasing around my finger, her clit pulsating against my lips.

Once her trembling has calmed, I lift away from her to find her gaze on me. "That was quick," I murmur, dropping a kiss just above her pussy.

"You make me horny," she admits shyly.

"Welcome to my world." I move up, so we're face to face and kiss her, slowly sliding my tongue against hers, so she can get a good taste before I pull away. "I'm horny for you all the time."

She slips her hands to the back of my head, pulling me back down for another kiss. It's filthy and sexy as fuck and my cock is throbbing, I want inside her so damn bad. She spreads her thighs and it would be so easy to slip inside, but something stops me.

I break away from her seeking lips, panting as I ask, "You think this will hurt the baby?"

Her smile is knowing, and full of womanly power. There is no other way to describe it. "No. Our baby is about as big as a grain of rice right now."

I thrust against her nice and slow, and she arches against me. "So I won't bump his head or anything?"

"No." She giggles. "And *his* head? You think it's a boy?"

"I don't know what it is." I thrust my hips again, slipping just the head of my cock inside of her. "But I don't want to hurt him. Or you."

"You won't," she whispers. "I want you inside of me, Eli. Please."

I will give my princess whatever she desires. No hesitation.

I reach in between us and guide my cock inside of her, watching her face the entire time I push into her. Her eyelids flutter. Her lips purse. A sigh leaves her and her eyes close, her mouth curved upward. "I feel like I'm home," I tell her.

"Every time I'm inside of you, Ava, it's like I belong here. With you. Us. Together. We're meant to be with each other."

"Yes." She shifts beneath me, sending me deeper, the both of us groaning. "I feel the same way. We belong together."

"I love you," I tell her as I start to move. It's like a wave of calm has washed over me. Having my girl back in my life for good. Knowing she's going to have a baby. *Our* baby. I think about the upcoming playoff game, and the championship game after that. If we win, we'll play in the Las Vegas Bowl, and I just know…

I've got this. I've got everything.

"I love you too." She winds her legs around my hips, holding on. "I love you so much."

Ah this girl.

She will be the end of me.

CHAPTER 33

AVA

"Eli." We're sitting at the tiny table in their dining room, and I'm watching him eat. I'm already stuffed full of pizza—it was so delicious—and now I'm perfectly content watching my man munch on a breadstick that he keeps dipping in ranch. He's so attractive, even when he eats and I exhale softly, caught up in my thoughts.

The father of my future child. Crazy, isn't it? I was so scared when I found out I was pregnant, and now I'm over-whelmed with love for this man.

"Ava." He grabs his water bottle and takes a long swig. "What's up, babe?"

I'm also full of doubt. My thoughts ping pong back and forth, leaving me second guessing every choice we're making. "Are you sure we're doing the right thing?"

We're the only two in the apartment. Caleb left a while ago to go hang out with Gracie for the evening. It's the perfect time for me to say something to Eli in the hopes he can reassure me the decisions we're making are the right ones.

"About what?" he asks with a frown.

"About you and me, and...the baby."

His entire expression lights up. I think he loves the idea of having a baby, and I was so scared to tell him, unsure of his reaction.

I shouldn't have been scared over telling him.

"We're definitely doing the right thing," he says firmly.

"And we're not going to get into another stupid argument and act selfish toward each other?" I sound scared, only because I kind of am.

After everything we've been through, I can't help but be a little worried.

And full of doubt over everything too. All of it. My future, which I thought I knew was certain. I had a plan. One that didn't include Eli, and I told myself I was okay with it. I could survive without him.

Until I realized I was pregnant and I knew I didn't want to raise a child alone.

Am I wanting to be with him because I truly love him or because I didn't want to do this alone? I don't know.

I'm so confused.

And I hate it.

My love for Eli is real. I can't deny that, but I also still feel really alone. And with nothing else to occupy my mind, when everyone else is busy living their lives and being productive, I'm quietly freaking out, soaking in my emotions and feeling like a failure.

God, I really need to get over myself.

"Oh, we'll definitely get into arguments. Can't deny that," Eli says with a chuckle. "But I won't be selfish with you."

"You won't?" My voice is so small, I sound pitiful.

He slowly shakes his head, pushing his empty plate away from him. "I love you, Ava. And I love that baby growing inside of you too. Like you said earlier, it's not just about me anymore. It's about *us*. And our future. I'm going to work my hardest to make sure I can give you and the baby whatever you need. I'm going to take care of you and our family. I promise."

His words ignite a flicker of hope in my chest. I watch him, at a loss for what to say. He's acting right, and saying the right things, but is that only because I put those things into his head?

And since when have I ever doubted Eli so much before? This isn't normal for me.

Maybe I'm just hormonal.

"I've been thinking." He sits up straighter, resting his forearms on top of the table, his hands clasped together. My gaze settles on those big hands of his, wishing they were touching me right now. "Maybe we should get married right away. Like before the end of the year."

My mouth drops open. "Wh-what?"

The proposal was sweet. I know he meant every word. But get married in the next five weeks? That sounds…

Impossible.

"Something small. Maybe up in the mountains? At one of the resorts? We could have a winter themed wedding, or a Christmas one."

"Eli…"

"And we could find our own place to live around here. Caleb will understand. Maybe he could even move in with Gracie and you could move in here with me. Wait it out until I know what I'm doing with the NFL or whatever." He shrugs, seemingly brushing it off. The NFL draft was the most important thing to him, and now he acts like it's not his number one focus. "And once we know what's happening, we'll move to wherever we need to go and begin our life together. As a family."

My heart feels like it just cracked open, I'm so overwhelmed. "Is that what you want to do?"

"More like is that what *you* want?" He leans over the table, his expression earnest. "I just want to make you happy, baby. That's it. I love you. And now that you're back in my life for good, I'm going to do this right."

"What if you don't get into the NFL?" I ask, my voice low.

"Then I don't." He shrugs, seemingly unbothered. "I've got something even more important happening this summer, if you didn't already know."

Eli grins and I can't help but smile back.

"You'll get drafted," I tell him, my voice brimming with confidence. "I have faith in you."

"At least someone does." His smile doesn't fade. In fact, it seems to grow even bigger and I bask in the warmth of it for a bit. "I refuse to do wrong by you, Ava. I've made enough mistakes to last a lifetime. I won't do it again."

Emotion sweeps over me, making my eyes sting with tears and the next thing I know, I'm crying. Eli leaps out of his chair and comes to my side of the table, nudging me over so he can settle into my chair before pulling me into his lap.

He's big and warm and when his arms come around me, I sink into him. My face is pressed against his neck and my eyes are closed. I breathe him in, trying to control the gentle sobs making my entire body shake.

"Baby, *please* don't cry." He sounds in agony as he runs his hand up and down my back in comfort. "Seriously, I hate seeing your tears."

"Why?" I ask, my lips brushing against his neck.

"They make me wanna cry too. Plus, when you cry it feels like I hurt you."

I pull away so I can look into his eyes. "I'm not crying because I'm sad. I'm happy."

The relief on his face is brief. "Then why are you crying? Why do you look like I just kicked your puppy?"

"I'm—overwhelmed." My smile is tentative. "Our whole lives are going to change."

"And that's okay. I've got you." He settles his hand on my stomach, caressing me there. "I've got this little nugget too."

"Little nugget?" I rest my hand on top of his, smiling. "I don't know how I feel about that nickname."

"My nugget likes it." He kisses me, his lips light against mine. "I still can't believe it."

"Believe what?"

"That we're having a little nugget." He kisses me again, murmuring against my lips, "A baby Bennett."

"Aw, I like that. Better than nugget." The tears start again and he wipes them away with his thumbs. Kisses them away when they keep coming. We're like this for long minutes, totally into each other. So into each other, we don't even realize someone has entered the apartment until we hear voices.

"Oh my God, so I guess you two are back together."

Our heads swivel in sync toward the living room to find Caleb and Gracie standing there, hand in hand. Gracie's gaze meets mine and I lean my head against Eli's, so tempted to tell her the good news about the baby.

But I keep my mouth shut. And so does Eli.

"What are you two doing here?" Eli asks, his voice casual. Like it's no big deal that I'm sitting in his lap and we're hanging all over each other.

"I should ask you two the same thing," Gracie says as she enters the kitchen and goes straight to the fridge, grabbing a beer from inside. "Caleb didn't mention this."

"It just happened," Eli says.

"I'm assuming you knew?" She sends her boyfriend an evil glare as she hands him the beer. "And just forgot to mention it to me?"

Caleb looks slightly terrified as he takes the beer from her. "I didn't know what was happening between these two. I literally just figured it out."

Not really since he saw us together earlier, but none of us mention that.

Gracie sits in the chair Eli was in only a few minutes ago. "You two are adorable. Seriously, Ava, you're *glowing*. I can tell you're so happy to be back together."

I'm glowing for other reasons, but I'm not going to mention them to Gracie. Not yet.

I want to keep this a secret for a little while longer.

We all four chat around the table for a while, and eventually move to the living room. Caleb starts up a movie on Hulu and after only about a half hour into it, I can barely keep my eyes open, I'm so tired.

More tired than usual. Maybe it's the baby? Or the emotional letdown after such a busy and overwhelming day?

I'm not sure, but the next thing I know, Eli is gently shaking me awake and the movie is over. We say good night to Caleb and Gracie and I follow Eli into his room, going immediately to the bed the moment he shuts the door.

"You snored," he tells me as he slips off his shirt.

I pause, admiring his bare chest before I climb beneath the sheets and tug them over me. "Loud?"

"I heard you. I'm guessing Caleb and Gracie did too."

"I was tired." A yawn escapes me and I cover my mouth. "I still am."

"My poor baby." He gets rid of his sweats and joins me in bed, turning off the lamp on his nightstand. "So tired."

I let him pull me into his arms, resting my head on his bare chest. "I'm awake now. I just slept for the last two hours."

We're quiet for a few minutes, basking in each other's presence before he asks me, "Do your parents know where you are?"

I nod, skimming my fingers across his pecs. "I texted my mom earlier and told her I was with you."

"She cool with it? With us getting back together?" His voice is casual, but I can tell he's worried.

All Eli has ever wanted was my family's approval.

"Well, she didn't tell me to leave that asshole's house, stat." I laugh when he tickles my side. "You walked into that one."

"Uh huh." His fingers brush against my waist, making tingles sweep over my skin. "When are we going to tell our parents about baby Bennett?"

"Not yet," I tell him, closing my eyes when he gently rubs my belly. "I just want to savor this moment with you first."

He keeps touching me, splaying his hand across my stomach, shifting downward so he can press a kiss to my belly. "I'm going to take care of you, Ava. You and our baby. I promise."

"I know you are." I stroke his hair, loving this man who's not afraid to show all of his love for me. If I was terrified when the day first started, I'm definitely not scared now.

Eli will take care of us.

I know he will.

CHAPTER 34

AVA

I made an appointment with my doctor over the weekend for Monday, and they confirmed with me what I already knew.

I'm definitely pregnant. Only about six weeks along. My due date is July 24th. Nowhere close to a 4th of July baby. Hopefully Eli won't be disappointed.

Doubtful. He's over the moon about my pregnancy.

My doctor recommends I take prenatal vitamins and lay off the caffeine, sugar and salt. All the things I love most. I'm also supposed to get plenty of exercise and rest, and eat a healthy diet. Plenty of fruits and vegetables. She offers up a few websites and apps that are full of good information and the more she talks, the more scared I get.

"Will everything be okay?" I ask her when she goes silent. "The baby. Will it be all right?"

"As long as you take care of yourself, you should be fine." Her smile is gentle. "You're a healthy young woman. I see no problems, but I can't tell you that everything will be perfect. Sometimes—things happen."

She doesn't have to say what I'm fearing. Women lose their babies for no reason early in pregnancy. Or they take one of those tests and find out something is wrong with the baby. Or it's born with a heart defect, a lung defect, whatever.

My mind races with all the scary possibilities and I'm mad at myself for going to the doctor alone. I would've brought Autumn with me, but she's gone back home. No way can I tell Mom.

Not yet.

Ellie and Jackson came home for Thanksgiving, but I have no idea if they're still here or not. I've been a shit friend and ignored them for most of the weekend, happy in my little bubble with Eli.

I make another appointment at the front desk and leave the doctor's office, heading for my car. Once I'm inside, I pull my phone out and FaceTime Ellie.

I need my friend right now. I probably shouldn't tell her this over freaking FaceTime though. Maybe she'll meet me for lunch or something?

It's weird how my appetite came back when I got in Eli's presence again. Oh well. I'm not questioning it.

Ellie answers just when I was about to give up, and I wait for the call to connect, smiling when I see her face.

"Hey you," she says. "I haven't heard from you at all."

"I know. Sorry." I make a little face, feeling bad.

"It's okay. I heard you were sick?" Her expression is questioning. "You feeling better now?"

"Who'd you hear that from? And yeah, I'm feeling better."

"Gracie. We all got together yesterday afternoon and went to lunch."

"All who?"

"Me, Jackson, Gracie and Caleb. Tony and Hayden were coming back from San Francisco," Ellie explains. "I tried calling you, but Caleb said not to bother. You and Eli were in makeup mode."

"I still would've liked to see you guys," I say, my voice

small. I don't like feeling left out, though I know they didn't mean to do it on purpose.

"We can get together again. With Tony and Hayden too. Jackson and I are sticking around for a few more days," she says. "I miss you."

"I miss you too."

"Is it true then? You and Eli are back together?"

A sigh leaves me. "You probably think I'm stupid."

"No, I think you two are just trying to figure your crap out, and it's not easy." I love that my best friend never judges me.

I always feel like I have her support, no matter what.

Taking a deep breath, I say, "I have something to tell you."

"You and Eli are officially back together?" she asks, her tone hopeful.

"Eli and I…are having a baby."

There is dead silence for only a moment before Ellie screams.

Full-on screams, making me wince.

Making me burst into tears.

"Ava! Why are you crying? This is the best news EVER!" She is yelling, she's so excited. "Oh my God, I can't believe it! This is so exciting!"

"I know," I tell her, the tears flowing nonstop. I swear between the breakup and the pregnancy discovery, I've been an emotional, crying mess. "I just went to the OB/GYN."

"And they confirmed it?"

I nod. "I'm due late July."

"Wow. Oh my God. You're going to be a mom." Ellie can't stop smiling, but her smile slowly fades when she realizes I'm still crying. "Are you sad about this?"

"Sometimes I don't know how to feel," I admit, wiping at my face. "I'm only twenty."

"Wasn't your mom twenty when she had Autumn?"

A watery laugh escapes me. "You sound like Eli."

"What does he think?"

"He's beyond excited. Can't stop calling himself daddy." A sob escapes me and I shake my head. "I don't know why I'm so emotional."

"Where are you right now? You're breaking my heart. We need to see each other so I can hug you."

"Want to meet for lunch?"

"I'm up at the lake. Jackson rented that house again, the same one we had at Halloween." She leans in close, her voice lowering. "I think he wants to buy it. Might be my Christmas present. Can you imagine?"

I'm so happy for her, but also a little sad and envious, because what the hell? Her boyfriend is buying her a *house*? Just for fun as a Christmas present? While I'm over here knocked up and unwed? Thanks to my on-again, off-again boyfriend?

Okay fine, we're on-again and I don't think Eli is going to do anything to mess this up again, but still. I guess I'm just feeling sorry for myself.

"That's great," I say, when I realize she's waiting for me to say something. "And just come by Eli's apartment. We can hang out there."

"What about you come up to your parents' house? They know, right?" When I frown, so does she. "Or don't they?"

"I haven't told them yet."

"Why not?"

I shrug. "I'm scared," I whisper.

"Oh Ava."

"What if they're disappointed in me? They don't even know that Eli and I are back together again. I fainted at Thanksgiving, and that's when Autumn stepped in and bought me three pregnancy tests. They all came back positive."

"Who knows you're pregnant? Eli, Autumn and...me?"

"Yeah. And my doctor now."

"They won't be disappointed in you. They'll probably be thrilled. Especially if Eli goes with you when you tell them. He'll step up and say all the right things. He's good at that," Ellie reassures me.

"Yeah, you're right." I'm still scared to tell them though, which is irrational and silly, but I'm starting to realize being pregnant is making me overemotional.

About everything.

"Listen, let me jump in the shower real quick and then I'll head down there. I can bring something for us to eat. You want anything in particular?"

I think of the pineapple that was on my pizza a few days ago, and my mouth literally waters. "A fruit bowl."

"Okay…" She draws the word out.

"From the supermarket. With pineapple. Lots of it."

"I can stop at Trader Joe's and get the pack of sliced pineapple they sell," she suggests.

"Yes! That sounds amazing." My brain is literally envisioning me eating it and my stomach growls. "I think I'm craving pineapple. I can't stop thinking about it."

Ellie shakes her head. "You're going to make a really cute pregnant lady."

"You think so?" My doubt in myself is so obvious, I may as well be wearing a sign that says so.

"Yeah. And a cute mom—a good one, too."

We talk a little more and I end the call, then make my way over to Eli and Caleb's apartment.

Almost two hours later and Ellie finally shows up with my favorite salad from Panera and three packs of sliced pineapple from Trader Joe's. When I open up the bag and see what's inside, the smile on my face feels massive.

"I could kiss you right now," I tell her, just before I pull her into a bone-crushing hug.

She laughs and hugs me back. "You said you were craving it."

"I so am." I ignore the salad and take the bag of pineapple to the kitchen counter, taking out one of the containers, and grab a fork from the drawer before I pop it open and start eating. "It's so juicy, oh my God."

Ellie is shaking her head. "At least you're craving something healthy. My mom said she always wanted Dorito's when she was pregnant with me."

I laugh, my mouth full of pineapple. "My mom has told me she craved McDonald's soft serve ice cream when she was pregnant with me. She was buying those hot fudge sundaes all the time."

"At least it's dairy?" Ellie says in her defense.

"Right." I fork up a few more bites of pineapple before I snap the lid back on and slip all three containers of pineapple in the refrigerator.

We sit at the kitchen counter and eat our salads, Ellie glancing around the living room. "Where are the guys? School?"

I nod. "And they have practice after class."

"So they won't be home for a while."

"Nope."

"How is Eli? Is he excited?" Before I can even speak, Ellie sends me a look. "You can be honest with me, Ava. No one's around. Tell me what you're thinking. You seem upset."

"I did some research earlier, and this is actually normal. All the crying and worrying." I set my fork in my salad and watch her. "All those surging hormones are throwing me off."

Her eyes are full of sympathy. "Are you happy about the baby?"

"I mean, it was a total accident, but I'm not mad or upset." I frown. "But happy? I mean, I don't know. Eli seems happy. I'm just…scared."

"I think that's normal. Your whole life is going to change. Remember what Jocelyn went through?" Ellie asks.

"I know. It was a lot. I can't imagine, though I can relate

more now." I dip my head. It feels heavy. Loaded with my thoughts and worries and concerns. "Eli doesn't do well with pressure."

"You think this is going to mess with his head?"

"I don't know. My life is changing with this baby, and so is his. He has other things to consider right now, not just himself. Though he tells me not to worry. He has everything under control."

I want to believe him. I do. But I know how he is sometimes…

"Are you worried he won't step up when you need him?"

It's as if something comes over me. A wave of comfort, of knowledge in the fact that yes, no matter what I think of Eli and what I worry over, he will be there for me.

No matter what.

"He'll step up," I say, lifting my gaze to hers, my voice confident. "I'm worrying for nothing."

Absolutely nothing.

CHAPTER 35
ELI

Like an asshole, I went against Ava's wishes and blabbed about her being pregnant. I told my best friends I'm going to be a father, because how can I go around acting like everything's the same, when it's not? I can't pretend my life hasn't just changed in the absolute best way.

So I tell them. Caleb. Tony. Diego. We're chillin' just before practice on campus, eating, because when are we not, when I finally couldn't take it anymore and spilled the news.

"Ava's pregnant."

They all pause in what they're doing, their eyes wide, their expressions shocked.

Diego's the first to speak.

"Welcome to the daddy club." He holds out his hand and I slap it in return. "Congratulations. I can't believe it."

"Bro, you're crazy." Caleb shakes his head, his mouth full. He swallows, takes a drink of soda and claims, "I won't be having babies until I'm at least thirty."

"Right." Diego slaps the back of Caleb's head, earning a dirty look from him. "The minute you graduate, Gracie is going to start hinting at marriage and babies."

"Marriage *and* babies?" Caleb's eyes widen, and he swallows. "Fuck. I'm doomed."

We ignore him. He always says shit like that, yet is totally head over heels in love with his girl. I don't believe him anymore when he talks like that, as if he dreads his future with the love of his life.

We're pretty sure he doesn't.

"Does Jake know?" Tony asks in that steady, quiet way of his.

I make a face, hating how my stomach sinks at the mention of Ava's disapproving brother. "Not that I know of. Not too sure how he feels about me right now either."

"Oh, I know how he feels about you," Diego says, a smile on his face as if he's enjoying this. "He's mad at you. Says he's sick of you toying with his little sister's heart."

"Whatever. I'll win him over eventually," I say, sounding way more confident than I feel. Jake Callahan has always been tough on me. Even when I thought we were friendly, I sensed he still harbored some resentment toward me sometimes. All over some high school shit, which is petty. But I understand petty—sometimes I can be a petty ass myself. "We're gonna be actual family now."

Tony slowly shakes his head, but he's smiling, which is reassuring. "You are the last one I figured would be a father next out of all of us."

"It's crazy shit, I know, but I'm excited." I rub my hands together, glancing at each of their faces, relieved to see genuine happiness for me in their expressions. Why did I doubt they'd support me in this? "I'm going ring shopping tomorrow."

"When? *Tomorrow?*" Caleb asks, his eyes going wide all over again. He sounds traumatized. "Wait, you can't be serious. You will give all the women in our lives ring fever *and* baby fever."

"Wait a minute, you can't marry Ava before I marry Jocelyn," Diego says, seeming put out. "Then I'll think you're just showing off."

"Bro, you've had four damn years since you got your girl pregnant to make her your bride. Get on it," I remind him before I turn to Caleb. "And it's not like I did this on purpose. Ava didn't mean to get pregnant, but she is. Now I gotta step up and make everything right between us. Put a ring on her finger and get married before the baby is born so everything's legal and we have ourselves a baby Bennett."

Tony chuckles. "I think you like this."

"I love it," I say with a grin.

"Trust me, it's not all that it's cracked up to be," Diego says, and I can't help but send him a frown. "You can take your time, you know, and not rush into anything. Make sure everything's going to work out between you guys first. I only say that because you two have had—trouble recently."

"I know what I want," I say firmly. "And what she wants too. I love that girl. So fuckin' much I'm willing to give up whatever I have to in order to make her my wife."

"You won't have to give up anything," Tony says reassuringly. "You two love each other, it'll all work out."

"Just—don't get her a giant ring that's like twenty carats or whatever," Caleb adds. "You'll put us all to shame."

"Twenty carats?" Diego starts laughing. "Please. None of us can afford something like that."

"Tony might be able to." I point at him and he slaps my hand away. "He's the one who's sitting on the family fortune."

"Hayden comes from money too," he says. "A giant ring won't impress her. She probably just wants a simple gold band."

We all make *ooh* noises, giving him shit.

"You been thinking about this, huh?" Caleb asks Tony, scratching the back of his head and acting uncomfortable. "Crazy motherfucker. I need to get out of here if this shit is catching. Next thing you know my ass is in Zales at the mall and I'm buying a ring for Gracie like a chump, when I don't even plan on asking her to marry me yet."

"Ha, he said *yet*." Diego laughs.

We all laugh.

Caleb just glares.

They all talk about rings and commitment and I sit there, thinking about Ava and what she might want. She's never really said anything about the type of ring she'd prefer when we got married. And we've definitely talked about getting married before, but we were never serious about it.

At least, *I* wasn't serious about it.

I'm for sure going ring shopping tomorrow, when I have a break in the middle of the day from school. After practice tonight, I plan on going straight home and convincing Ava that she should go back to her parents' house and hang out with them for a few days while I put something together for her. Get ready to propose to her somehow. I want it to be sweet and romantic. I want to watch my girl melt and cry tears of joy when I slip that ring on her finger.

This is a time for celebration. Our lives are changing, but I'm embracing that shit wholeheartedly.

Life is good.

It can't get any better than this.

Well, that's a lie. If the NFL came knocking on my door and I got confirmation that I'm definitely going to be in the draft, then hell yeah. I'd really be on top of the world then. All of my goals reached.

We chat more about me and Ava. Babies. Diego shares horror stories about his daughter Gigi and what a little nightmare she can be, especially when she was a baby. The endless diapers full of disgusting poop, the throwing up, the crying fits, teething. You name it, he throws it out there, trying to scare the shit out of me.

The only one it works on is Caleb, who looks like he's

watching a horror show. All wide eyes and gaping mouth and endless cursing. I just smile and nod, taking it all in. Being a parent won't be fun all the time, but damn it, that'll be *my* baby, so I'm good with it.

Bring it on.

"You tell the parents yet?" Tony asks me once Diego has finally shut up.

I shake my head. "Not yet. Ava didn't even want me telling you guys."

Caleb frowns. "Why?"

"I don't know." I shrug. "She's nervous. Afraid of the unknown, I guess? She doesn't want her parents disappointed in her since she's going to quit college and stay with me."

"Is she moving into our apartment?" Caleb asks, his brows shooting up.

"Maybe…" Shit. That's one of the plans we came up with. Probably should've checked with him first, especially since one of our plans is having Caleb move out. "Would you mind if she did?"

"Nah, once football is over, I'll probably end up spending a lot of time with Gracie at her place. My class load next semester won't be too heavy," he says. "But what's your plan after school?"

"Not sure yet." My gaze slides to Diego, who's smiling. "The NFL maybe?"

"Hell yeah." Diego holds up his palm and I slap it with my own. We keep doing this. "We're on our way, Bennett."

"Hopefully," I add.

"No hope about it, we've got this." He laughs. "It's our time. We deserve this."

"Happy for you both," Tony says, sounding like a proud dad. Bet he feels like one too.

"Yeah," Caleb adds. "Maybe a little jealous too, though I'm happy for you guys."

"I love you, Caleb," I tell him, meaning every damn word I say. I love all of them. "I'm gonna miss playing with you fools."

"Me too," Tony says.

We nod in agreement, all of us quiet.

It's coming to an end, this chapter in my life. College. Classes. Football. Parties. Living with my friends. Not having to worry about work or real life. I mean, this shit is real life and sometimes, I let it get to me way too much—hello my football season junior year—but it's got nothing on what could be coming.

Again, bring it. I'm ready. I feel mentally and physically prepared.

We part ways after we eat—Tony needs to grab something from his car, Caleb has to drop something off to a class and Diego is meeting with Jocelyn—and I wander around campus, taking my time. I stop at the student store and go in to kill a few minutes, stopping short at the display of Bulldog gear near the front.

There's a red baby onesie thing that looks like one of our football jerseys. There's even one with a number one on the front with the words "Bulldog fan" beneath it. I flip the onesie over. Too bad it doesn't have Bennett on the back of it.

I grab it and take it to the girl standing behind the cash register, her eyes widening when she spots me. "Aren't you Eli Bennett?"

I nod, setting the onesie on the counter and reaching into my back pocket for my wallet. "Yep. And you are?"

"Uh, Clarissa." She says it like a question, as if she's unsure what her name is.

"Nice to meet you, Clarissa."

"Nice to meet you too." She taps away at the keypad on the register and then scans the price tag, hitting a few more keys before she rattles off the total. I slip my credit card into the reader, watching as she bags up the little onesie. "Isn't number one yours?"

"It is." I take my credit card out of the machine and put it back in my wallet.

"What a cute gift. Maybe saving it for later? When you're married and have a baby?" she asks hopefully.

"Sure." I take the bag and receipt from her, smiling at Clarissa. She smiles back, appearing a little starstruck. "I'm keeping it for when I'm married and having a baby."

Which if all goes well, will happen in the next eight months.

———

After practice Caleb and I return to the apartment to find Ava waiting for us, the kitchen counter covered in various takeout boxes from a nearby Chinese restaurant. The delicious aroma hits me the moment I walk inside and my stomach growls.

Hey, I could get used to this kind of treatment quick.

"Damn that smells good," Caleb says hopefully.

"I bought enough to feed eight, so have at it," Ava tells him.

We enter the kitchen, Caleb grabbing a plate and starts filling it. I approach Ava and sweep her into my arms, kissing her.

"You're too good to us," I murmur.

"I have selfish motives." She grins as she pulls out of my arms, going to one of the containers and opening it, pulling out a piece of…

Pineapple.

She pops it into her mouth, humming in approval. "Sweet and sour chicken with pineapple. Sooo delicious."

"You have issues," I tease her.

"More like cravings," Caleb mutters as he helps himself to

the sweet and sour chicken, kicking any pineapple he scoops out back into the container.

Ava goes still, her gaze wide when it meets mine. "You told him."

I wince. "I couldn't help it, babe. I'm excited."

Her smile softens and she exhales, like I'm a hopeless case. "I get it. I already told Ellie."

"See? It's hard to keep it in." I wanted to announce to the entire damn football team that I'm going to be a dad, but held back at the last second.

I need to tell my family first. And she needs to tell hers.

"Congrats, Mom and Dad," Caleb says with a grin as he dumps about half of the rice onto his plate. "I'm excited for you crazy kids."

"Don't act like you think we're crazy. You'll be a dad next, I bet," I tell him.

Caleb shakes his head as he heads for the table. "Hell no. I'm not ready for that."

I grab an empty plate but Ava takes it from me. "Go sit. I'll make you plate."

"Really?" I drop a kiss on her cheek. "Thanks, Princess."

I go to the table and sit across from Caleb, who's shoveling food into his mouth as fast as he can. "She's spoiling you now because you're going to have to return the favor later, you know."

"True," Ava says cheerily as she's dumping all sorts of food onto my plate. Not a pineapple in sight though. "When I'm fat and waddling around, totally uncomfortable and my belly full of his baby, he's going to have to make me dinner and rub my feet every night."

The image she describes fills me with satisfaction—mixed with an unfamiliar, primal feeling. I cannot wait to see her waddling around, her stomach round with our baby and knowing I'm the one who put her into that condition.

We eat and talk, Caleb telling funny stories and making

Ava laugh. She doesn't eat a lot—mostly sweet and sour chicken with a boatload of pineapple—while Caleb goes back for thirds and I eat two platefuls.

It's nice. Everything feels normal, yet different. I think about showing Ava the onesie I bought earlier today, but decide I won't. Not yet. I'll give it to her when I ask her to marry me.

Yeah, she'll like that. A lot.

"What are you smiling about?" she asks softly.

I glance up, realizing that Caleb has left the table. I can hear him chatting on the phone as he heads down the hall to his room. Sounds like he's talking to Gracie.

"Nothing." I shake my head, reaching out and settling my hand over Ava's. "Thank you for dinner."

"You're welcome." She squeezes my hand. "It was good, huh."

"Yeah." What's even better is having her here with me.

I haven't been this content in a long time.

Her expression changes, turning serious. "I probably need to go home."

"Tonight?" I frown.

"No, but tomorrow for sure. And eventually…we need to tell them about the baby," she whispers.

"We'll do it this weekend. Sunday," I say, thinking about how I'm going to buy her a ring tomorrow. That'll work out perfectly. We'll be engaged, ready to become a family, and her parents will totally approve of that. Me stepping up and taking care of my responsibilities.

That should satisfy them.

"Okay," she says, her smile shaky. "It'll be weird, going home and knowing what I know, yet not telling them."

"You want to tell them sooner?" Whatever she wants, I'm game.

I'll do whatever my girl wants.

"No, Sunday makes the most sense. You have practice

every afternoon and then your game. I can wait." She touches her stomach, filling me with the need to do the same, but I can't reach her. "I hope they'll be happy for us."

"Why wouldn't they? We're going to give them their first grandbaby." I start chuckling, I can't help it. "Damn, Jake's gonna be pissed. He likes being first in everything. Looks like I'm going to beat him."

Ava rolls her eyes. "It's not a competition, Eli. And I don't think Jake will be mad. Pretty sure he's not ready for babies yet."

"It'll still be fun, beating him in the grandchild race." I can't stop grinning.

Neither can Ava, even though she's shaking her head at me.

Everything's going to be all right.

I can just feel it.

CHAPTER 36

AVA

'm at my parents' house when I wake up in the middle of the night with the urge to pee. I slip into my bathroom in the dark, sitting on the toilet and peeing when I hear something heavier than urine drop into the toilet. Grabbing some toilet paper, I wipe and look at it.

Even in the dim light, from the tiny nightlight in the room, I can tell it's blood.

Panic racing through me, I waddle over to the wall and turn on the lights, glancing into the toilet before I sit back down and see…

More blood.

"Oh no, oh no," I whisper, grabbing more toilet paper so I can wipe.

Red again.

After I flush the toilet, I grab a pantyliner from the cabinet under the sink and put it in my panties, then wash my hands. I stare at my reflection, see the fear in my gaze and think to myself, what do I do now?

I never told my parents I'm pregnant. They have no clue. Mom knows I've gotten back with Eli and she supports my decision, but I never told her what else is going on.

I was too scared.

Rushing back into my bedroom, I grab my phone and send a text to Eli.

Me: **Please call me.**

I sit on the edge of my bed, chewing nervously on my fingernail. Blood could mean nothing. Or it could mean I'm having a miscarriage.

Oh God.

I rest my hand against my belly, wincing when I feel the cramp ripple through me. Maybe it wasn't the need to pee at all. Maybe I'm cramping and that's what woke me up.

"No, no, no," I murmur, hitting the call button and trying to reach Eli.

It's after two in the morning. He's for sure sleeping.

It goes to voicemail and I end the call and redial again.

Still no answer.

I text him again.

Me: **Please call me. It's an emergency.**

Me: **I need you, Eli.**

I pace my room, a wave gripping my lower belly that has me bending over. There's a gush between my legs and I run back into the bathroom, pulling down my underwear to see I've bled right through.

There's blood everywhere.

Crying, I clean myself up, grab another pair of panties and a full-blown pad this time and slip everything on.

And then I go to my parents' bedroom.

I don't even bother knocking on the door, I just walk straight in, going to my mother's side of the bed. I shake her shoulder gently, whispering, "Mom," a couple of times until she wakes up. When she spots me, she sits straight up.

"What's wrong?" she asks.

"I think—I'm having issues."

"What sort of issues?" She's frowning, confused.

"Womanly ones." I start to cry harder.

She climbs out of bed and I watch as she slips on a pair of old sweatpants and an oversized sweater. Dad doesn't even stir. The man must sleep like the dead.

"What do you want to do?" she asks me.

"I want to go to the hospital. The emergency room."

"That's so far though. How about the twenty-four-hour clinic?"

"We have one of those up here?"

"It's new," she says as she slips on a pair of old Ugg boots. "Get some shoes on. And a coat."

I rush to the hall closet and pull out an old winter coat, then slip on a pair of Autumn's old black Uggs that she left behind. I love that my mother didn't even hesitate or try to talk me out of what I want to do.

She's just doing it.

I wait for her in the kitchen, gritting my teeth when another cramp grips me and she magically appears, her purse already slung over her shoulder and her car keys clutched in her fingers. "Let's go."

I follow her into the garage and we get into the car, me checking my phone every few minutes but still no response from Eli.

He must sleep like the dead like my father.

"What's going on, Ava?" Mom says once we're on the highway that leads into town.

"I'm p-pregnant," I say, barely able to hold it together. "And I think I'm losing the baby."

"Oh, Ava." Her voice cracks and she reaches out to settle her hand on my knee. "Tell me what's going on."

I explain how I woke up and what I discovered. She nods, her gaze on the road, her hand still clutching my knee.

"I tried texting and calling Eli but he won't answer," I practically wail, banging my head against the seat.

"He's probably sleeping like your father, though I did wake him up to let him know we were leaving."

"What did you tell him?" I whip my head in her direction.

"That you aren't feeling well and I wanted to take you to urgent care."

I sit there crying for the rest of the drive, unable to speak, my mind full of all the terrible things that could be happening to me right now.

They're all just…bad. Awful.

"Are you in pain?" she asks as we pull into town and come to a stop at the light. It's dark outside, the only light from nearby businesses and there's no one else on the road.

I nod. "Cramps. It hurts."

She makes a sympathetic noise and I close my eyes, willing Eli to wake up and call me. Text me. If he knew this was happening, he'd be doing everything in his power to get to me. I know he would.

That's the only thing that reassures me as I suffer through this.

We finally arrive at the urgent care, and Mom makes me wait as she climbs out of the car and comes to the passenger side to help me out. The moment I lift out of the seat, I feel another gush between my legs and I check the seat.

I left a blood stain.

"Oh no," I say, turning to wipe at it, but Mom grabs my hand, stopping me.

"I'll take care of it later. Come on," she says, her voice gentle as she guides me through the sliding double doors.

Mom tells the nurse behind the front desk what's going on and the nurse's gaze shifts to me, her eyes going wide as she starts moving quicker. "She looks pale. Did she faint?"

"She did on Thanksgiving."

"Let's get her in a wheelchair."

Mom grips my arm and I lean against her, suddenly tired. Woozy. Someone brings a wheelchair to me and I practically fall into it, my brain blanking for an instant before I'm roused by someone saying my name.

The nurse.

"How far along are you, sweetheart?"

"Six weeks, maybe seven?" I glance up to see my mother watching me with fear on her face, her eyes glassy. I try to reach for her. "I'm sorry, Mom. I meant to tell you."

"Oh my God, Ava. It's okay. It's okay." She smiles but it's shaky and that sends me over the edge.

I start crying all over again.

"It's okay, honey. Come on, let's get you into an examination room."

The nurse wheels me in, Mom following beside me. I'm sticky between my legs and I know without a doubt that it's happening.

I'm losing the baby.

The nurse steers me into a room and asks my mother to wait outside. She then helps me change into a gown and assists me in lying down on the table that sits in the corner, my eyes closed against the bright lights overhead.

"Prop your feet on the edge of the table, honey," the nurse advises and I do as she asks, turning my head and keeping my eyes closed as she checks me beneath the gown. "She's losing a lot of blood. Let's hook her up to an IV until the doctor arrives."

"Want me to put a call into the sonographer?" another female asks.

"They won't come in until the morning. I think Dr. James can run a sonogram on her." The nurse drops the hem of my gown and comes to my side, taking my hand. "We're going to get you an IV. You're bleeding and we want to make sure you're okay. Plus, we want to get some fluids in you, so we can do a sonogram."

"To see the baby?"

Her expression grim, she nods.

I turn away from her again, keeping my eyes tightly closed, wishing I could fall asleep. But I can't. I can hear every little thing. The squeak of the nurse's shoes on the floor. The sound of her opening something. The faintly squeaking wheels of the IV stand as someone brings it in. Every single sound is amplified, and I lie there flat on my back, my arm clutching my stomach as I can feel my body literally expelling my baby.

All I can do is cry.

"I want my mom," I cry to the nurse after she takes care of the IV.

"She can come in soon, I promise," she says, her voice soft and kind.

But Mom doesn't come in. I lie there and wait and wait. I can feel myself bleeding onto the pad they put beneath me and I cry harder.

Why? I ask.

Why me?

I must drift off to sleep because the nurse walks into the room, startling me.

"The doctor is here," she says. "He'll be in to see you in a minute."

"Is my mom still here?" I ask, my throat so dry it almost hurts to speak.

She nods. "She's in the waiting room."

"I want Eli." The tears streak down my face. "Tell her to call Eli for me? Would you? That's my boyfriend. He's the father."

The nurse keeps nodding. "I'll let her know."

The doctor chooses that moment to enter the room, an older handsome man with graying temples and glasses. He smiles faintly when he sees me, glancing at the chart in his hands. "Hi, Ava. Do you mind if I call you Ava?"

I shake my head, my lower lip trembling.

"Let me explain what I'm going to do. First, I'm going to give you an examination. Then I'm going to do an ultrasound on you. Have you had one of those yet?" He checks my file again. "You're about eight weeks pregnant?"

"Close, yeah," I whisper. "And no, I've never had an ultrasound before."

"Okay. I'm concerned that if you are having a miscarriage, we have to make sure that nothing gets left behind. If that happens, it could give you an infection."

I nod, trying to understand what he's saying. "So am I losing the baby?"

"I'm not sure yet." He hands the nurse my file. "Let me wash my hands and take a look at you."

I nod, watching as he goes to the counter on the other side of the room and turns on the faucet, washing his hands thoroughly in the sink.

Be brave, Ava, I tell myself, feeling stupid but needing the pep talk. It's going to be okay. Maybe you're not losing the baby. Maybe it's just some weird, freak thing and it'll clear up fast.

But deep down, my heart knows the truth. And when he flips the bloody hem of my hospital gown back and starts to examine me, I choke back a sob, the tears blurring my vision.

I'm losing baby Bennett.

CHAPTER 37

ELI

I wake up at six a.m. to texts from Ava. A voicemail from her where I can tell she's been crying. A couple of missed calls from her.

And a text from her mother.

Fable Callahan: **Please call me when you get this message. It's an emergency.**

My heart racing, I fumble with my phone and call her, breathless as I wait for her to answer. The moment she says hello, I don't even wait for her to say anything else.

"What's wrong? Is Ava okay? What happened? Is she all right?"

"Eli, calm down. I need you to listen to me."

"Okay. Yeah. Sorry." I swallow hard, trying to control my breathing. My heart rate. When she remains silent for a few seconds longer, I can't take it anymore. "Tell me what's wrong."

"Oh, Eli." A sob leaves her and for the briefest moment I'm fucking terrified over what she's going to say. "Ava—"

No, no, no, no.

"—she lost the baby."

I say nothing. I hear her soft cries, my ragged breaths. I

rest a hand against my forehead, rocking gently back and forth, the same thing running through my head on repeat.

Ava's okay. Ava's okay. Ava's okay.

Then what her mother told me sinks in, punching me right in the face.

She lost the baby.

Oh fuck. She lost *our* baby.

"What happened? I can't believe I didn't hear my phone. I'm sorry I didn't pick up. Where are you? I'll come to you right now. I need to see Ava—"

"Eli, seriously. Listen to me right now." Fable's voice is firm, and I go still, my shoulders drooping. "Let me explain to you what happened first. She woke up cramping and bleeding. It started to get heavier, so she woke me up and I drove her to the urgent care. She was losing a lot of blood so the doctor on call came in, and he ordered a D&C. They're performing it on her now. She should be in recovery in the next thirty minutes or so."

I have no clue what she's talking about. "What's a D&C?"

"A procedure they perform when they worry that not everything—comes out during the miscarriage," she explains.

"Ava's not pregnant anymore." My voice is flat. Emotionless.

"No. I'm a-afraid she's not." She starts crying again. "I'm so sorry, Eli. Ava told me how excited you were about this. I'm sure you must be devastated."

I am. But what's weird is I'm having no emotional reaction whatsoever. I feel...numb. Like what she's saying isn't sinking in. Maybe I'm in shock. "Is Ava going to be okay?"

"Oh, she's doing really well. She's such a trooper." Her voice rasps and I can hear the pride in it.

"That's my girl," I whisper, clearing my throat. "Should I wait?" There's no way I can wait, I don't know why I said that. "Or do you need me to come help you out? I can leave right now—"

She interrupts me. "Do you have class this morning?"

I bark out a laugh. "I'm skipping class, Mrs. C. There is no way I'm not coming up there at some point this morning to be with Ava."

"I'll text you when we're on our way back to the house. You can leave then," she says.

"Okay. I can do that. I'll hop in the shower real quick." I'm already climbing out of bed.

"Eli?"

I pause. "Yeah?"

"You need to be strong right now. For Ava. For the both of you. She was so upset. Crying, asking for you earlier. You need to be here for her, and not make this about you. She's gone through something that was very traumatizing to her. She's going to need you now more than ever," Fable explains.

"I will be there for her," I tell her. "I promise."

I go through the motions of getting ready for my day, as if it's another regular day. I take a shower. Brush my hair, brush my teeth. Don't bother shaving. Get dressed. Check myself out in the mirror, reminding myself that everything's changed.

Just like when Ava told me what…a week ago? It's changed again. It's back to the way it was.

Does that mean Ava and I are going back to the way we were? Broken up and about to go our separate ways? Will she go to San Diego? Leave me behind?

No way.

I can't even stomach the thought.

Not bothering with breakfast, I wait in my room for the text from Ava's mom. I don't go out to the living room either. I don't want to see Caleb and have to explain to him what happened to Ava, and what's going on.

I'm not sure of the exact details myself. How can I explain it to someone else? And I definitely don't want to see everyone's pity. Their sadness. I can't deal.

I don't want to deal.

I need Ava—right now. I need to talk to her and make sure everything's going to be okay. I want to hold her in my arms and tell her I love her and that nothing is going to change. I still need her in my life.

She's still mine.

A sigh leaves me and I shake my head, cradling my head in my hands and closing my eyes. She told me not to tell anyone and I should've listened to her. Now we'll have to explain to our friends what happened.

And that's going to be painful.

When the text comes, I nearly jump out of my skin. I leave the apartment in a hurry, grateful I don't run into Caleb. I hop in my car and groan when I start the engine. I need to get gas.

Damn it. Of course I do.

I stop at a gas station on my way out of Fresno and fill up, impatient as shit, hating how slow it feels. How long it takes. The moment the gas pump clicks, I'm putting everything away and getting the hell out of there. I race up the highway, my lead foot in action. Every passing lane I'm zooming past cars, grumbling under my breath when I get behind a slow car. Throwing caution to the wind because I'm hellbent on getting to my girl.

By the time I'm pulling in front of her house, I'm a wreck. My insides feel as if they're twisted around each other and my palms are sweaty. My stomach cramps with nerves as I walk up the front porch and I almost want to collapse when I ring the doorbell.

Fable Callahan answers it almost immediately, and I realize in this moment she looks so much like Ava, my knees almost buckle. This is what my girl will look like when she's older. Just a little taller. Blonde and beautiful with those bottomless green eyes.

"Eli," she says, opening her arms to me.

I walk into her embrace and clutch her to me, my face in

her hair, my eyes falling closed. She rubs her hands up and down my back, offering me comfort like a mom should. I think of my own mother, how I haven't talked to her since Ava told me the news. How my mother doesn't even know she was a grandma.

Even if only for a few days.

Fable pulls away from me, her hands grabbing hold of mine. "Don't look so stressed. Ava is fine."

"Is she really?" I sound skeptical because, come on. She's probably not okay at all.

"She's doing as well as one would after losing a baby. It's hard no matter how many weeks along you are." Her faint smile turns rueful. "I lost a baby in between Ava and Beck."

"You did?" I want to see Ava, but I appreciate her mom's offer of comfort and reasoning too. It's more than I'll get from anyone else right now.

"Yes." She nods. "I was about eight weeks, just like Ava. It was tough. The experience tore Drew up, but the beautiful thing of it all, is we were blessed with Beck a few years later."

I nod, following Fable into the house. She shuts the door behind her and I notice there's a lit Christmas tree standing tall in the window, no decorations on it yet though.

"I'm telling you my little story because this isn't the end of the world, Eli. I'm not downplaying what happened to Ava. It was a lot. But she needs hope right now, not wallowing in her sadness. She will have other children. Miscarriages are very common," Fable explains.

I nod. "Okay."

"You don't need to give her stats or anything. Just—be there for her. Like she's always been for you." Fable sends me a stern look. "Don't fuck this up."

I gape at her, surprised at her choice of words. The look on my face must amuse her because she starts laughing. "Oh, you should see yourself right now. Bet you didn't expect to hear that, did you? Back in the day, I was a real tough talker. I even used to smoke." Her voice lowers. "Cigarettes."

"No way."

"Yep. I've come a long way." She approaches me, reaching up to pinch my cheek like a little old grandma would. "So have you. Go up there and show your girl some love, Eli. She needs you right now."

I'm about to head up the stairs, but I pause at the base, turning to look at Fable. "I'm sorry we didn't tell you."

"It's okay. You don't have to apologize. I understand why you kept it to yourselves. Some things are just for you." Her smile is soft.

"Yeah." I was really looking forward to telling her parents about the baby though.

Damn.

I race up the stairs, slowing my pace as I draw closer to her room. The door is partially open and I hear voices inside. Mostly a male speaking.

Her dad.

Shit.

I knock on the door before I peek my head around it, relief filling me at seeing Ava sitting up in bed, looking like her normal self. A little pale, but I was getting used to that. She's listening to whatever her dad is saying, his broad back to the door until I knocked.

He turns and when he spots me, his face falls a little.

"Eli." He nods, his expression stern.

"Mr. Callahan." I nod in return, intimidated. He might hate me. I knocked up his baby girl and put her through all this. In his eyes, this could be my fault.

My gaze cuts to Ava, whose face is crumpling.

She's crying.

Damn it.

"Eli," she whimpers.

Forgetting her dad is there, forgetting that he could blame

me for all of this, I go to her, settling on the edge of the bed, right next to her. She leans into me, her arms going around my neck and I hold her carefully, not wanting to hurt her.

But her familiar scent and soft hair have me gripping her tighter. As tight as I can get. Until we're clinging to each other, lost in each other. And I only realize her dad said, "I'll leave you two alone," after he already slipped out of the room, shutting the door behind him.

"Don't cry," I whisper when he's gone. I pull away so I can stare at her, wiping the stream of tears from her cheeks with my fingers. "Your tears absolutely destroy me, baby."

"I'm sorry. It's such—a relief to see you, Eli. I'm so glad you're here." She presses her face to my shoulder, holding onto me.

I rub her back much like her mom did to me earlier, letting her cry on me. "Are you okay?"

"Now that you're here, yes." She lifts her head, her mouth against my jaw, breathing me in. "I lost the baby."

A shuddery breath leaves me. "I know. I'm sorry I wasn't here sooner."

"You were sleeping."

"Yeah."

"I figured." She kisses my cheek, her hand reaching for one of mine. "It was awful. Just—so much blood."

I squeeze her hand. "Don't talk about it if you don't want to."

"I was scared. But my mom took care of me." A shuddery exhale leaves her and her still shiny with tears eyes meet mine. "She's a good mom."

"The best." I rest my palm against the side of her hair before I stroke it away from her face. "Just like you're going to be someday."

Her eyes fall closed and her lips tremble. "What if I can't have any more? What if that was our—one—shot?"

"Don't say that," I say fiercely. "We'll have a bunch. Six, remember? I want at least six."

She laughs, but it sounds more like a sob. "I don't know about that."

"Whatever you want, I'll do. It's all for you, Princess." I mean every fucking word.

"I'm going to be okay," she says.

"You're damn right."

"We're going to be okay?" She's asking me. Needing the confirmation that we're still going to stick together.

The relief I feel at hearing her say that nearly sends me to my knees.

"You're damn right," I repeat, leaning into her and brushing her mouth with mine. "I love you."

"I love you too," she whispers. "I'm sorry it happened."

"Oh my God, it's not your fault. Don't ever think it was." I kiss her again. "I'm sorry I wasn't there."

"That's not your fault either." Another kiss. "You should know I'm not going to San Diego."

My heart feels ready to fly right out of my chest at her words. "You staying here with me?"

She nods, her expression hesitant. "You're going to get drafted, Eli. And I want to go where you're going. If you'll have me."

"*If* I'll have you?" I can't help it. I start to chuckle. "Baby, I can't do *any* of this without you. You're coming with me, whether you like it or not."

Ava rests her hands on my chest, brushing her nose against mine. "I love it."

I crush her to me, trying to be careful. I don't want to hurt her, but she plasters herself to me anyway. "I love you."

———

I stay there all day, spending as much time with Ava as I can, before I finally head home. I skipped practice—I called Coach and explained what happened, and he was cool with me missing it. After that call, I confessed to Ava I told the guys about her being pregnant and she wasn't mad, but she did say that's why she warned me not to mention it yet.

Because of situations like ours.

I sent a group text to the boys letting them know what happened, and they were cool, of course. Full of sympathy, saying all the right things. Even Caleb. I couldn't tell them something like that to their faces. I might've broken down.

So I took the easy route.

It's early in the evening and I'm reluctantly leaving the Callahan house, exiting through the garage when I hear a familiar voice call my name. I pause and turn to find Drew standing there, watching me.

"Hey," I tell him, shoving my hands in my front pockets. We've barely talked all day. He makes me nervous. Like he might want to kick my ass for putting his baby girl through so much trauma.

Slowly he approaches me, his steps careful, his expression serious. "How are you?"

I frown, tilting my head to the side. "What?"

"I asked, how are you? How are you dealing with all of—this?" He waves a hand around, seeming at a loss of what to do.

A ragged breath leaves me and I glance down at the ground for a moment, overwhelmed by his question. I've been so focused on Ava all day, it's hitting me that no one has really asked how I'm doing.

And that's cool. I'm fine with it. Ava's the one who's been through so much.

Not me.

"I'm—I'm sad, but it's okay." I lift my head to find him watching me. "I'm just glad Ava's all right."

"She is. She will be. She's strong." Drew's smile is faint. "Like her mother."

"Yeah," I croak, hating how tore up I suddenly feel. "I was really excited about the baby."

"Ava mentioned that." Drew steps closer, settling his hand on my shoulder. "You're going to make a great dad someday, Eli."

Oh damn. My eyes are stinging and I shake my head once, trying to rid myself of the urge to cry. I need to keep it together in front of this man and not sob like a wimp.

"Thanks," I tell him, my voice rough. "I hope you're not— mad at me. For what happened."

"Why would I be mad at you? It's not your fault," Drew says, his voice low. "Just—take care of my daughter and love her as much as you possibly can, okay? That's all I want."

I nod, unable to look at him, surprise coursing through me when he tugs me into his arms and gives me a hug. I hug him back, in shock.

His words, his offer of comfort reassures me though. That he doesn't hate me.

That he loves me like I'm a member of his own family.

And it feels good, to be okay with the Callahans again.

Well, with the exception of Jake. I'll have to work extra hard to win that guy over. Autumn might want to kick my ass too.

It's all right. I'll figure it out.

I don't really remember the drive home. And when I walk into my empty apartment, I wish I could've brought Ava with me. But she needs to rest, and she needs to stay at her parents' house, in her own bed. She's going to remain there for a while, until we get our shit straight and figure out what the hell we're doing next.

And where we're going.

Even though I'm tired, I'm somehow full of restless energy and I decide to clean my room. I make the bed and gather up the clothes strewn everywhere, tossing them in the hamper that's in my closet. I throw away some old receipts then come across the box containing the ring I bought Ava yesterday and pop it open.

A two-carat round diamond in a simple platinum setting. It's beautiful, like Ava. I can't wait to give it to her.

Someday.

Soon.

I straighten up the disaster that is my desk, cramming shit in the drawers that are already full of miscellaneous crap. Gather up my notebook and textbooks and shove them in my backpack so I'm ready for school tomorrow. Come across a bag from the student store that's stashed at the bottom of my backpack and I crack the bag open, momentarily forgetting what I bought there.

Until I see the red fabric.

I pull it out, staring at the tiny onesie, checking the size. Zero to three months.

I hold it in my hands, trying to imagine a baby filling it.

Man, that's tiny.

The tears start then. Flowing down my cheeks as I crumple the onesie in my hands and tell myself to man up. Don't cry. I never cry. I have to be the strong one here. For Ava.

For myself.

But it's no use. I'm sobbing like a baby, for the baby we lost. Remembering how scared I was, thinking for one terrible moment, that I lost Ava.

I didn't lose her though. I've still got her.

I've still got my heart.

My soul.

My love.

My princess.

My Ava.

CHAPTER 38
AVA

My chest is so tight, I feel like my rapidly beating heart is going to burst through it at any minute. I can't tear my gaze off the field and my hands are clasped in front of my mouth, as if I'm praying. If I had fingernails, I'd be chewing on them right now.

We have less than two minutes left in the fourth quarter of the Mountain West championship, and the Bulldogs are playing the game of their lives versus Boise State. The score is 31-27, Bulldogs. But currently, Boise has the ball.

And it's killing me.

"They've got this." This is from my brother Jake, who's standing beside me. We're all standing in front of the glass window of our box seats. My family. My friends whose boyfriends are all out there playing the game. Jackson and Ellie are here too.

We're all here, nervous and excited. The win is so close we can touch it.

But then again, it's not. It's not close at all. One wrong move and Boise could take it. If they score right now, that'll change everything. A touchdown puts them in the lead. A field goal?

We'll be ahead by one.

One.

"You really think so?" I ask him, my voice low. I need positive reinforcement right now, and I'm surprised to get it from Jake. Granted, all of his friends are out there so of course he's going to support them.

But my boyfriend? Yeah, probably not.

It's only been a couple of weeks since I had the miscarriage, and everyone is still treating me like I'm fragile. I sort of hate it. No one wants to talk about it either. Like they're all afraid I'm going to burst into tears and fall completely apart.

"Yeah, I do."

I glance up at my big brother to find him watching the game, a USC beanie on his head because come on, this is Jake. Hannah is on the other side of Jake, chatting with our mom. They're the only ones not completely traumatized and on edge because of this game and I envy their cool.

My gaze trails Caleb as he darts across the field, ramming himself into an offensive player and taking him to the ground. I jump up and down, cheering loudly as Caleb gets up and glances around the stadium. I swear I can see his smile from here, but maybe I'm reading too much into it.

"He's played a great game," Jake says.

"He has."

"So has Eli."

I'm quiet, secretly pleased. Eli has played phenomenal tonight. For a guy who used to blame my magical vagina for ruining his game play, he sure has been doing great the last two weeks. First with the last playoff game and now tonight.

Of course, he hasn't touched my so-called magical vagina since I had the miscarriage, but we've been spending a lot of time together. Just because we lost a baby doesn't mean we lost feelings for each other.

I'd say our feelings for each other are even stronger.

"He has, huh," I finally say, my heart in my throat when

the Boise kicker walks onto the field. "Oh God, they're going to try for a field goal?"

"They held them off. They couldn't run it in," Jake says, scooting closer to me. "Even if they make it, Bulldogs will still lead."

"By only a point," I mutter.

"Yeah, and then they have the ball." He slings his arm around my shoulders and squeezes me. "Have some faith, baby sister. They could score again."

"God, I hope so." I watch, my face contorted into a wince as I wait for that ball to sail into the air.

The kicker sends it careening toward the goal posts, and at the last second it veers right.

The kick was no good.

We all start jumping up and down, cheering. The Boise offense slinks off the field, the kicker's head bent and I can feel his disappointment.

Whoops. Too bad. All I can do is scream and tackle hug my brother, who lifts me off my feet and sends me swinging as he spins me around.

"Jacob, put your sister down," Mom says.

"Haven't heard that in a while," Jake says, laughing as he sets me on my feet. He glances over at her. "Come on, Mom. We're just having fun."

"She's still recovering."

"No, I'm not," I protest. "I feel fine."

Mom sends me a skeptical look. "Really? It's only been a few weeks."

"Yeah, and I'm good, Mom. Really."

I know she's just worried about me, but the hovering is making me crazy. They're all hovering. Mom, Dad. My friends. At first my boyfriend was all over me too, but when I reassured him that I was feeling stronger, he could only whistle in admiration and tell me that I'm his hero.

Me. I'm Eli Bennett's hero. What a concept.

"As long as you're sure." I can hear the doubt in my mother's voice.

"I'm sure," I say firmly, sending everyone a look when they all seem to glance over at me at the same time. "Seriously, you guys. I appreciate your concern, but it's been a couple of weeks. I'm okay. Really."

There's a roar from the stands and we all refocus on the field. The Bulldog offense is out there, just breaking out of a huddle as they go into position. My gaze finds the number one jersey and I whisper good luck to Eli in my mind, hoping he can hear me.

Clearly, I've lost it. Now I think I can communicate with Eli through thought only.

I didn't need to wish him good luck. Every throw he makes is a good one—with the exception of the time he couldn't seem to get rid of the ball, so he threw it away before he ended up getting sacked.

But it's the last ball he throws that is true perfection. It lands in Tony's hands and he tucks it against his body, speeding toward the end zone. We've all gone completely still, watching as he dodges one defensive player. Then another. Literally spins out of the hold of yet another until he's cruising into the end zone and scoring a touchdown.

"That's my man!" Hayden screams as she jumps up and down.

We're all screaming, my gaze stuck on Eli as he runs toward Tony and they bump chests. The kicker scores the extra point and there's only a few seconds on the clock. Boise goes back onto the field and go through the motions, but the game is finished.

The Bulldogs just won the Mountain West Conference Championship.

I'm anxious as we all make our way onto the field. I don't know if we're all going to get out there, but I'm determined to find Eli and I know my friends feel the same. Hayden and

Gracie are ahead of me and they both dash out onto the field in search of their boyfriends.

I do the same, running around like a lost person, scanning the area for Eli. I've left my parents behind, and my brother, until I'm all by myself, spinning in a small circle, anxiety making my heart race as I try to spot my man.

Ah, there he is. He's talking to a female reporter, clutching his helmet in his hand, the smile on his face adorable as he speaks into her mic. Slowly I approach them, not wanting to interrupt or disturb them. But the moment Eli lifts his head and his gaze finds mine, he's done.

I smile at him.

He smiles in return, asking the reporter if she got what she needed before he leaves her, jogging over to where I'm standing. He stops in front of me, leaving some distance between us and I wonder at that.

"We won," he says, sounding proud.

"You won." I sound just as proud. "You played a great game."

"You think so?" He sounds unsure, which is so unlike my Eli. He reaches beneath his uniform, tugging a necklace out so the #1 pendant glints in the stadium lights. "I wore this for luck like you told me to."

"Looks like it worked." My gaze eats him up. I don't know why he's standing over there and I'm standing over here.

"It did." His smile fades, his gaze turning sincere. "Babe, I'm an idiot."

I'm frowning. "Why?"

"I thought I couldn't do this." He waves a hand around the stadium. "If I had you in my life. I actually thought that at one point. Like you were a giant distraction I didn't need."

I grimace at his words, hating how they make me feel.

"But it's not true. I was full of shit. I'm realizing I can't do any of this, if I don't have you in my life." His hazel gaze meets mine, so serious. So full of emotion. "I love you, Ava. So fucking much. This would mean nothing if I didn't have you in my life. I almost lost you."

The pain lessens, and I'm filled with happiness again as I go to him, resting my hands on his chest as I stare up at him. "You didn't lose me. And you didn't lose this game either. You're a winner."

"In all things." He wraps one arm around my waist, holding me to him. "In everything. Life can't get much sweeter than this."

"Oh it can," I tell him, rising up as he bends down to drop a kiss on my lips. "You have the draft coming up."

"And graduation," he says.

"And a new life to embark on." I smile as he kisses me again.

"With you by my side, right?"

Our gazes meet. Lock. "Right."

"Love you, Callahan."

"I love you too, Bennett."

"We gonna make it?" He raises his brows then bursts out laughing when he sees the expression on my face. "We are, huh."

"We most definitely are."

EPILOGUE

Ava

*S*ix months later

"Eli, what in the world?" I come to a stop at the beautiful setting spread out before me on the deck of the house that Jackson purchased for Ellie for Christmas last year. The one they rented on Halloween.

He stops just behind me, his big hands resting on my bare shoulders. He told me to dress fancy and so I'm wearing a simple black strapless dress. When I saw myself in the mirror after I slipped it on, I realized it made me feel pretty. Prettier than I have felt in a long time.

I felt even prettier because of the look on Eli's face when he first saw me.

"You like it?" he whispers close to my ear.

There are candles on every available surface, every

outdoor table on the deck, their gentle light flickering, seemingly becoming brighter as the sun slowly sets behind us. Accompanying the candles are low, sleek vases filled with perfectly blooming red roses. There's a table prepared for two in the center near the railing, with red rose petals scattered all over the white tablecloth.

"It's so romantic." I glance up at him, wondering what he's got up his sleeve. Ever since he was drafted in April, he's been on the go. Busy, busy, busy. Making plans. Meeting with his new coaches and staff. Obtaining an agent. Leaning on my father for advice, which he's given freely. They've become closer since everything happened, and…I love it.

Jake's been leaning on Dad a lot as well. He was drafted too—in the first round. Eli in the third. Diego, in the sixth.

They're all in the big leagues now. I couldn't be prouder of all three of them.

"Come with me." He moves to my side and takes my hand, leading me over to the table. I realize there's a couple of people standing close to the house on the other side of the deck, which is near the kitchen. They look ready to serve us. "I had dinner catered."

"Just for us?"

"Just for you." He drops a kiss on my cheek before pulling my chair out for me.

I settle into the chair, watching as he sits down across from me, devastatingly handsome in the black button-down shirt that fits him to perfection, emphasizing his broad chest and shoulders, and his muscular arms.

That's my man, I think as I blatantly admire him. He's all mine.

A woman dressed in black pants and a white shirt comes over, pouring us each a glass of champagne. I note the label, impressed with Eli's choice, and a little worried because that must've cost a fortune.

But then I remember the contract he was offered and I tell

myself to calm down. My man is going to be making a lot of money as long as he keeps up his end of the deal.

"Champagne already? What are we celebrating?" I'm teasing him and notice the shaky smile on his face. The way his leg bounces.

He's nervous.

Hmm.

"You. And me." He lifts his glass and I do the same, meeting in the middle of the table and clinking them together. "We did it, Princess."

"You did it," I remind him, just before I take a sip. The champagne is cool and crisp and the bubbles tickle my throat as it goes down.

"Couldn't have done it without you." His gaze is intense as he stares at me. "I love you."

"I love you, too," I murmur with a little smile.

He says it a lot. More than he ever did before. After everything that happened before Christmas, he told me he looks at me as his gift. The one thing he was given that he'll cherish above everything else.

I feel the same way about him.

These last six months, after everything we've experienced, have only brought us closer. We've been through a lot together, and we've learned so much about each other, too. It's almost as if we have a renewed purpose within our relationship—and our love. The hardships have only made us stronger, and now our life together...

It's amazing—and it's only going to get better.

I just know it.

We eat the best meal I think l I've ever had. We drink more champagne. He jokes with me, being his typical Eli self and I laugh. He says something dirty and I laugh even more.

But he's still nervous. I can sense it. And after our plates are taken away and it becomes quiet, I glance around to see that the catering staff is gone.

We're the only ones left out here.

"You look beautiful tonight." He reaches across the table to take my hand in his.

I smile at him. "So do you."

"I can't wait to take that dress off of you later." He smirks.

The promise in his deep voice makes my toes curl. "We're staying the night here, right?"

"Yeah. We've got the entire place to ourselves." His eyes twinkle. "I say we try and christen as many rooms as possible before the night is over. What do you think?"

"Don't you figure Jackson and Ellie have done the very same thing already?" I wrinkle my nose. They're not even in the country right now. Jackson is on a European spring/summer tour and, of course, Ellie went with him, documenting everything via social media and her weekly podcast.

"Nah. Jackson never had much stamina."

I laugh. "You are so full of shit."

"You think so?" He raises a brow.

I nod, bringing the champagne glass up to my lips. I might be a little tipsy. "Definitely."

"How about right now?" He suddenly gets down on one knee directly in front of me, reminding me of that day in his room when he got down on his knees and asked me to marry him.

After I lost the baby, we never brought getting married back up. I was too scared. Afraid he might've changed his mind, which is dumb.

This man is clearly going nowhere.

"Eli, what are you doing?" I ask him, my voice shaky.

"Ava Elizabeth Callahan." He takes a deep breath. "I asked you to marry me about six months ago, and then I never followed through on my promise. I suck."

I giggle. "You've been a little busy."

"I have, but that's no excuse. When a man finds the one

woman he knows he will love for the rest of his life, he needs to make a move or…"

"Lose her forever," I whisper, smiling. I might've said something similar to him a time or two.

"I love you so damn much. I want you to be my wife. To stand by my side through this new life we're forming. I'm nervous about it, not gonna lie, but I know everything will be fine if I've got you with me. What do you say?" He pops open a box I didn't even notice he had in his hand, and I gasp when I see the ring tucked inside.

It's a deep green emerald, square cut and huge, flanked by a sleek diamond on each side. I lift my gaze to Eli's to find him watching me.

"What do you think?"

"It's beautiful," I breathe.

"I had another one for you. Bought it and everything, but it was just so…I don't know. Standard? Boring? And you're not boring, Ava. Not even close. So I returned it and went in search of something else, something uniquely you. When I saw the emerald at a jewelry store a couple of months ago, it reminded me of your eyes," he says as he takes the ring out of the box. "Give me your hand."

I offer it to him, noting how my fingers tremble. His are shaky too and it takes him a second to jam the ring on my finger, both of us laughing. "It fits perfectly."

The stones sparkle, thanks to the candles, the deep green of the emerald absolutely stunning.

"Will you marry me, Ava?"

"You've had this ring for a couple of months?" I ask incredulously.

He shrugs. "I bought the other one right after Thanksgiving."

"Oh." I glance down at the beautiful gift he's given me. "You meant it when you said you wanted to marry me the first time."

"Fuck yes, I did," he says fiercely, scooting closer so he can touch my face, his fingers stroking my cheek. "You are the love of my life. My heart. My soul. We've been through some tough times. Being apart from you was one of the toughest things I've ever endured, but that means I got to fall in love with you *twice*—and that makes me a lucky man. I know this sounds like a bunch of corny shit, but I mean every word I say. Please say you'll be my wife, Princess. Let me make you my queen."

"Yes," I murmur, my mouth stretching wide with a smile that can't be contained. "Yes, yes, ye—"

He cuts off my response with his lips, kissing me hungrily, his hand sliding into my hair, his other hand touching the side of my neck, his fingers gentle as he streaks them across my skin. He kisses me until I'm moaning, my arms wrapping around his shoulders. Until I'm almost falling into his lap, right there on the deck.

Until we're both laughing and I'm straddling him, his face pressed against my chest as he nips at my skin. As he whispers that he loves me.

As he whispers that I'm his.

And that I belong to him.

Forever.

EPILOGUE PART 2

ELI

Four years later

The back yard is full of people.

People I know and love.

People who mean everything to me.

There's Jackson and Ellie, sitting with Tony and Hayden, and Caleb and Gracie. The three couples are at one of the many round tables that cover the lawn, laughing loudly, making me wish I was sitting with them. Jackson is still putting out hit songs, and Ellie is still touring with him all over the world. They aren't married. They're not even engaged, but they're enjoying their free-spirited life, so good for them.

Tony is living in San Francisco and working for the family business, and he and Hayden got married a few months ago. Just as he predicted, she wears a thin gold band on her ring finger. No flashy diamonds for rich girl Hayden.

And then there's Caleb, who works in the very town he grew up in. After graduating college, they got married right away and he got his real estate license. He's now the top agent in the mountain area. Gracie is still teaching. Rumor has it she's pregnant.

Neither of them will confirm or deny, which is just as well. We'll figure it out eventually.

Jocelyn is speaking with my wife, eight-year-old Gigi by her mom's side. Jos keeps resting her hand on her full belly, and Diego stops beside his wife at one point, pressing his lips to her cheek for a quick kiss before he grabs Gigi and sets her on his shoulders, making her laugh.

That laugh makes me smile.

Autumn and Ash are sitting under the giant oak tree, a baby in each of their arms. They had twins—a boy and a girl —a few months ago, which quietly freaked me out.

I can't imagine having twins so I wish them well. That's like twice the fuckin' work.

I spot Beck and his girlfriend, and my smile returns. I remember being young and in so much fuckin' love with Ava, I couldn't pay attention to anyone else.

I hope those two go the distance.

Diego sets Gigi on the ground and they approach Jake and Hannah, the four of them talking, Gigi keeping up conversation with Hannah before the two of them head over to the table laden with cupcakes, both of them grabbing one.

I keep seeing Gigi with a cupcake. She's going to eat too many for sure.

Jake wanted to play for the Niners, just like his dad, but the great Jordan Tuttle is still heading up that team, so Jake was drafted by the Arizona Cardinals. I wish I got drafted by the Niners too, but then again, I like where I'm at now. So does my wife.

Jake and Hannah aren't married yet, but they're engaged. She's becoming a prominent artist who shows and sells her work around the world. We have a couple of her paintings that hang in the house and while I don't normally give a shit about art, I have to admit they're cool. Like the artist herself.

I like Hannah a lot. Her fiancé? Eh.

Ha, Jake and I are fine. We're practically brothers, so we have to be. He's also an enemy—on the football field once again since our teams are in the NFC West. I play for the Seahawks, which means we live in Seattle. Here's what's crazy—Diego plays for them too. We've gotten a lot closer over the years, Diego and me. Jocelyn and Ava are good friends too. Once we came to Seattle, Ava went back to college, attending the University of Washington, where she got her bachelor's degree in international business.

Then I knocked her up. She's a stay-at-home mom now, but eventually, I know she'll take that bachelor's degree and that giant brain of hers and use it for something good.

My baby can do anything she sets her mind to.

It was hard on her at first, living in a new city. Thank God she had Jocelyn to spend time with. And while Ava misses her family and friends, we do come see them as much as we can.

Like today.

Drew and Fable Callahan are bustling around, taking care of their many guests. They offered to host this event, which I appreciate. A more central place for all of us to meet, since we're scattered all over the country.

But we're all together today, celebrating us. Me and Ava.

And our impending arrival.

Ava's belly matches Jocelyn's. They're both waddling little mamas ready to pop. My wife has been fucking radiant throughout this pregnancy. Her hair is thicker, like it gets when she's expecting, and it flows down her back in golden waves. Her cheeks are rounder and her eyes are bright. Her laugh is joyous and her spirit is addictive. Everyone wants to talk to her, be with her, love on her.

Today is her day, so she deserves it.

"Ava's going to open her gifts," her father calls. "So everyone gather around the mama-to-be."

Ava sits in a chair that looks more like a throne, and I send a questioning look in Jackson's direction, who's making his approach toward me. "Don't tell me that's yours."

He shrugs, a lopsided grin on his face. "Ellie found it stashed in one of the spare bedrooms and we thought it would be fun to bring the chair out of retirement."

I can't help but laugh. He used to sit in that chair when he'd perform at Strummers back in the day, all mysterious and shit. Making the teen girls scream in orgasmic glee.

That feels like a lifetime ago. Maybe because it is.

My mother approaches Ava, delivering a beautifully wrapped box on her lap and bending over to kiss my wife's cheek. Ava smiles up at her, grabbing her hand and murmuring thank you.

Mom's been clean and sober now for four years. Since her accident and that DUI charge that she took care of. Guess you really do have to hit rock bottom before you climb your way back up.

I'm proud of her.

My brother actually stuck around to help out Mom when he can, and he's doing well, too. We've gotten closer, and it helps, knowing that he's here for her. That I don't have to worry so much about her anymore.

Glancing to my left, I spot Ryan chatting up Ash, as he tries to juggle both of his babies in his arms. One of them starts to cry and Autumn rushes back over, taking the crying one from her husband before she returns to the circle of chairs surrounding my wife, every one of them filled with her friends and relatives. Autumn settles into the chair right next to her sister, the baby still crying and Ava watches them both with a serene smile on her face.

My heart expands and grows, which you would think is impossible considering how long I've loved this girl.

But it's true. My heart just keeps growing fuller and fuller the more this woman gives me.

"Hey."

I turn to see Fable approach, a sleepy toddler wrapped around her. I don't know when she went back into the house to get her, but she hands my daughter over to me and I take her, loving how my baby girl snuggles close to me, her warm face lodged in my neck.

"Thanks, Grandma," I say, which earns me a scowl from Fable. I'd laugh, but I don't want to disturb my sleepy little princess.

"Daddy." She grabs hold of the hair at my nape, giving it a tug. Making me wince.

My daughter is strong. Bold. Confrontational. Demanding. Arrogant.

Kenzie Elizabeth Bennett is the perfect combination of both her mother and her father. Blonde hair. Hazel eyes that lean more toward green. A sturdy little body and a huge personality.

"What's up, lovebug?"

She lifts her head and looks around, spotting Gigi sitting nearby munching on a cupcake. "I want one."

Kenzie points at the half-eaten cupcake, then wipes wispy blonde strands of hair out of her eyes.

"In a minute." I kiss her soft cheek, staring at her in awe. I still can't get over my daughter. She's so damn cute. And smart. And full of it. When she first wakes up from a nap is when she's at her calmest. I need to savor the moment while I can.

Leaning in, I breathe in her toddler sweet smell. She's two. Naps are becoming rarer and rarer, unfortunately. I'm surprised she fell asleep right at the beginning of the party. Kenzie usually stays up to all hours of the night, never wanting to miss a thing.

I walk over to where Ava's opening presents for our baby, all of the clothes neutral colors since we opted *not* to find out what we're having. Everyone thinks we're nuts. Why not find out?

Why not keep it a surprise? We found out with Kenzie, but this time, we're changing it up.

Ava receives so many presents and all the women ooh and ahh over every single thing. The guys are clustered together chatting and I plan on joining them eventually. Just need to make sure my wife opens all of her gifts first.

Fable takes Kenzie from me to get her a cupcake. Gigi falls into step beside Fable, and I'm sure she'll con another cupcake out of the woman. That girl is going to be throwing up before the afternoon is through, I can guarantee it.

There are so many gift bags and open boxes surrounding Ava by the time she's through; she looks around helplessly, a giant smile on her face. "Thank you so much, you guys," she calls out to everyone. "This baby is so loved."

Among the murmurs of approval and the 'you're welcomes,' I notice the one little bag sitting by the side of Ava's throne, right by her foot.

"You missed one," I call out.

Frowning, she glances around, but doesn't spot it.

"Right there, baby." I point at it and she looks down, snagging the tiny white gift bag by the handle and settling it into her lap.

"There's no card." Her gaze meets mine. "I don't know who it's from."

"Open it," I tell her, my heart starting to race when she peeks inside.

She pulls out a small lump wrapped in pale blue tissue, and slowly unfurls it to reveal...

A red baby onesie with the number one on the front, 'Bulldog Fan' written in script beneath the number.

"Aw, this is so cute." Her gaze scans the crowd and there are people nodding in agreement, but no one claims the gift, which makes her frown once more. Her gaze finds mine again.

I stare back at her, filled with so much love for this woman, I can feel my eyes start to grow damp.

Aw, fuck. I'm gonna cry.

Ava rises to her feet and waddles through the sea of open boxes and gift bags, gently kicking them aside. She squeezes through two chairs, walks right past her daughter, who's currently sitting in Fable's lap with her face covered in white frosting, and only stops when she's standing directly in front of me.

"When did you get this?" she whispers, holding the onesie up in her hand.

My wife is so smart. Always on to me, I swear.

"A really long time ago," I whisper back, one tear tracking its way down my face.

Her eyes fill with tears too and she reaches for my face, wiping the single tear away with her thumb. "Oh Eli. I love it."

"I think we're having a boy."

"I do too," she murmurs, dipping her head so she can gaze at the onesie, the number one on the front of it. The sun glints off of her blonde hair and she's never looked more beautiful. She traces her finger over the number one before lifting her head to meet my gaze once more. "You bought this after I told you that first time, huh?"

"Yeah. Never got a chance to give it to you. And then I didn't want to make you sad. Eventually it got packed away during one of our moves. I found it about a year ago, but Kenz was too big to wear it. So I stashed it away in my closet, ready to bring it back out when the time was right."

Ava shifts closer, leaning her head against my chest. I wrap my arm around her shoulders, pulling her even closer. "This is my favorite present by far."

"You're my favorite," I whisper against her temple, kissing her there. "Don't ever forget it."

"How could I?" She smiles up at me. "You'll never let me."

"You're damn right," I say firmly, glancing down when I feel a little someone wrapping her arms around my leg. Without hesitation, I scoop up a frosting-covered Kenzie and hold her to me. "I got both my girls. Another baby on the way. What more do I need?"

"Nothing," Ava says, reaching out to swipe at some frosting in Kenzie's hair with a laugh. She cradles our daughter's cheek with her hand, her shining eyes meeting mine once more. "Absolutely nothing."

ACKNOWLEDGEMENTS

Ooooh, this book. I worked so hard on it. Endless editing, removing, adding, etc. I worried over it so much, wanting to get the conclusion to Eli and Ava's story just right. I hope I succeeded and that you're happy. That's all I want. And if I made you cry, then that's a bonus because let me tell you, I cried a lot writing the end of this book. These two...you might think I'm ridiculous for writing so many books about them, but I love them! I hope you do too.

Thank you readers, reviewers, bloggers, etc. who read the **College Years** series and cheered me on, asked for more, and let me know which book was your favorite. I have a hard time choosing which one is my fave, but I'll go with Eli because come on...it's Eli.

It feels like this is it, the end of the era, but guess what? We still have Beck Callahan's book to look forward to! I adore him and Addie. Really hope you get my newsletter so you can read those **When Bae...**installments featuring the two of them.

p.s. - If you enjoyed **The Senior**, I would greatly appreciate it if you left a review on the retailer site you bought it from, or on Goodreads. Thank you so much!

ALSO BY MONICA MURPHY

LANCASTER PREP

Things I Wanted To Say (but never did)

A Million Kisses in Your Lifetime

Promises We Meant to Keep

WEDDED BLISS

The Reluctant Bride

The Ruthless Groom

The Reckless Union

COLLEGE YEARS

The Freshman

The Sophomore

The Junior

The Senior

DATING SERIES

Save The Date

Fake Date

Holidate

Hate to Date You

Rate A Date

Wedding Date

Blind Date

THE CALLAHANS

Close to Me

Falling For Her

Addicted To Him

Meant To Be

Fighting For You

Making Her Mine

A Callahan Wedding

FOREVER YOURS SERIES

You Promised Me Forever

Thinking About You

Nothing Without You

DAMAGED HEARTS SERIES

Her Defiant Heart

His Wasted Heart

Damaged Hearts

FRIENDS SERIES

Just Friends

More Than Friends

Forever

ONE WEEK GIRLFRIEND SERIES

One Week Girlfriend

Second Chance Boyfriend

Three Broken Promises

Drew + Fable Forever

Four Years Later

Five Days Until You

A Drew + Fable Christmas

STANDALONE YA TITLES

Daring The Bad Boy

Saving It

Pretty Dead Girls

ABOUT THE AUTHOR

Monica Murphy is a New York Times, USA Today and international bestselling author. Her books have been translated in almost a dozen languages and has sold over two million copies worldwide. Both a traditionally published and independently published author, she writes young adult and new adult romance, as well as contemporary romance and women's fiction. She's also known as USA Today bestselling author Karen Erickson.

facebook.com/MonicaMurphyAuthor

instagram.com/monicamurphyauthor

bookbub.com/profile/monica-murphy

goodreads.com/monicamurphyauthor

amazon.com/Monica-Murphy/e/B00AVPYIGG

pinterest.com/msmonicamurphy